THE
UNDERLING

This is where the power is, you see.
Always. The underneath.

—Michael Ondaatje, *The Cat's Table*

THE
UNDERLING

Ian McKercher

GSPH

GENERAL STORE PUBLISHING HOUSE
499 O'Brien Road, Renfrew, Ontario, Canada K7V 3Z3
Telephone 1.613.432.7697 or 1.800.465.6072
www.gsph.com

ISBN 978-1-926962-41-2

Cover art, design, formatting: Magdalene Carson
Printed by Custom Printers of Renfrew Ltd., Renfrew, Ontario
Printed and bound in Canada

Library and Archives Canada Cataloguing in Publication
McKercher, Ian, 1946-
The underling / Ian McKercher.
ISBN 978-1-926962-41-2
I. Title.
PS8625.K467U53 2011   C813'.6   C2011-907570-9

First printing April 2012
Second printing June 2013

For Frances Leona Sumner McKercher
and
all secretaries past and present

PART
ONE

—— PRELUDE ——

OTTAWA, 1934

The man was sitting up in bed dipping toast fingers into a soft-boiled egg, when the butler ushered in Wilbur Grace.

"Wilbur! Pardon my pyjamas. I am unwell, but this central bank issue will not wait upon my health."

"Isn't the legislation moving forward through the Banking and Commerce Committee, sir?"

"At a glacial pace, Wilbur." The man sighed as he set the bed tray aside. "Time is our enemy. We need to open another front."

"Sir?"

"Suppose we set up a kind of research bureau, a detailed archive of Canadian banking and business information. Then the new governor would not lose a second on appointment."

"Excellent idea, sir."

"Glad you agree. Get started."

"Me? Sir? The Department of Finance owns my soul. I barely have time to wash my socks."

"Wilbur, I have many tasks. My health has abandoned me. Who if not you?"

"The Minister of Finance?"

"Mr. Rhodes wishes to be re-elected, Wilbur, and probably wants to be prime minister. He wouldn't risk driving such a controversial issue."

"He would if you insisted."

"He might go through the motions, but that's all."

"Perhaps the deputy minister?"

"Clark? Clark is such a conscientious civil servant! He will want legislation for direction. No, it must be someone outside the chain of command."

"Please remember, sir, that, although low on the totem pole, I am indeed in the chain of command. My section chief, Mr. Dowd, reports through Mr. Clark to Mr. Rhodes."

"Tsk, Wilbur. Do not play the humble card with me! You know all the arguments. You must do this, or we will lose it."

"Lose the bank, or lose the election?"

"The next election is likely already lost. But a firmly established central bank would be a fine legacy. I feel the clock ticking, Wilbur."

In the long silence, the man cleared his throat again. "How about carte blanche? And a generous budget?"

"How much?"

"How much carte or how much budget?" The man laughed, which set off a coughing fit. "You will report directly to me."

"No interference?"

"None."

Wilbur Grace felt the queasy seduction of his better judgment. "I'd need at least ten thousand dollars cash," he ventured.

The pyjama-clad man's eyes widened.

"Well, I'd need three or four good staff people. And offices close to the Department of Finance. And furniture and phones and filing cabinets . . ."

"All right, all right!" A hand lifted in surrender. "Ten thousand," the man said, collapsing back onto his pillows. "But cash?"

"With 'the clock ticking,' I can't be submitting requests in triplicate for every paper clip. I will, of course, keep meticulous records. It's the people's money, after all."

"Fine. I'll have Crossman draw a certified cheque on the Privy Council account payable to Wilbur Grace."

"Messieurs Rhodes and Clark will need an explanation, or they will believe me insubordinate."

"I'll summon them first thing tomorrow. They will be relieved to duck responsibility."

"Finally, if I'm racing around the country after twelve-hour days, I'm not staying in government-rate hotels eating beans on toast."

"Wilbur, I thought you were a socialist!" The man chuckled. "It's your ten thousand. No interference." The man paused for a moment. "Do you hear anything from the Court of King's Bench these days?"

"Justice is being well served, I'm told," Dr. Grace replied.

"Good!" the man exclaimed with a shallow smile. "Now, when can you start?"

MISS GILHOOLY'S TYPING CLASS

Frances McFadden's ordinary life fell into the clutches of the Bank of Canada at 3:20 p.m. on a warm Monday in May 1934.

Afternoon typing class was winding down beneath the serene portrait of King George V that hung above the front blackboard. Below her sovereign, Miss Gilhooly stood with a similar regal bearing, hands clasped tightly under her modest bosom, head held so high that she appeared to arc backwards like a tautly drawn bow.

Into this orderly scene burst the ruddy-faced principal, Mr. Forestall. Miss Gilhooly's eyes flickered over to acknowledge him, while the rest of her physique remained relentlessly on duty. He approached obliquely, and lips moved, but voices could not be heard above the staccato tapping of twenty-nine Underwood typewriters.

Frances noted that the forced whispers between Mr. Forestall and Miss Gilhooly did not appear congenial. Pursed lips betrayed discord beneath their otherwise professional stances. The eyes of the two educators darted first toward Jenny Townsend, an above-average typist but a terrible speller. Next, they drifted in tandem to Claudia Pucci, a vain Italian girl who got the highest marks in the class because her father bought her a typewriter to practise on at home.

Then their searchlight gazes swept left to Frances, and she made two mistakes at five marks off a piece—*damn! damn!*—before her nimble fingers regained their rhythm. At the shrill ring of the pre-dismissal bell, Mr. Forestall gave Miss Gilhooly a final glower and marched out the door.

The class quickly put away their typing paper and shrouded their hulking Underwoods with grey dust covers; they sat silently, eyes front and backs rigid. There was no slouching in Miss Gilhooly's class. Slovenly posture led directly to loose morals, which led to unmentionable diseases and an early death. At the final bell, there was not a flinch from the superbly disciplined students until the tremulous voice of a strangely crestfallen Miss Gilhooly murmured, "Class dismissed."

As Frances approached the door, Miss Gilhooly said, "Frances, may I have a word?"

"Yes, Miss Gilhooly," Frances replied. Vera McFadden, whatever her failings, had taught her daughters excellent manners. Miss Gilhooly closed the classroom door and sagged down at her desk.

"Frances, Mr. Forestall wishes to speak with you in his office."

Frances's eyes widened. A trip to the principal's office usually meant a detention or at least a bawling-out for misdemeanours real or imagined. Frances was not generally what her friends, the Crazy Deavys, referred to as "the misdemeanour type."

Miss Gilhooly gazed abjectly down at her red spiral-bound lesson plan book and said, with a tiny tremor in her voice, "Mr. Forestall is going to offer you a job."

Frances slid down into the front desk seat. "For the summer?" she asked in surprise. In 1934, summer jobs for girls were impossible to find.

"No," said Miss Gilhooly. "Full time. Starting immediately."

"But we still have six weeks of school left, and I have a whole year to go before I graduate."

"Yes," Miss Gilhooly sighed, "Mr. Forestall already knows. Apparently, a man from some new bank needs help immediately. The senior class is quite small this year, and the Placement Office has found them positions already."

Miss Gilhooly drank in a deep breath. "I do not think it educationally sound to take a young girl — how old are you, Frances?"

"Seventeen, Miss Gilhooly."

" — out of school . . . seventeen! Before she has graduated and has a diploma to insure her future." An angry sheen deepened the colour of Miss Gilhooly's heavily rouged cheeks. "What if this bank man finds an experienced secretary later and lets you go? Where is your security then?"

Frances was dazed. The job offer was amazing enough. But a public display of emotion from a schoolteacher?

"You'd better get to his office," she said with resignation. "Don't be badgered. Only accept this offer if it suits you." Miss Gilhooly nodded her head curtly for emphasis, as though making the best of a bad case.

Frances recognized the goodwill behind this counsel, a compassion that contrasted with Miss Gilhooly's stern, narrow face. "It's very kind of you . . . to warn me." Miss Gilhooly smiled widely, displaying pretty pearly teeth. In three years of typing class, Frances had never before seen this dazzling smile.

"On your way."

Frances's steps echoed down the empty hall. She pushed open the door of the main office and walked into the beady glare of the head secretary.

"You are late, young lady," declared Miss Dawkes, with castigating civility. "Mr. Forestall is waiting!" Frances met her glare without fear or insolence, and wondered if Miss Dawkes was a graduate of the High School of Commerce. She hoped not.

Frances knocked on the door of honey oak and pebbled glass. "G.K. Forestall, Principal" was printed on it in gold leaf letters outlined in black. "Come in," sang out a resonant baritone voice, honed from years of cross-examining students and solos in the Anglican Church choir.

"Sit down, Miss McFadden," said Mr. Forestall, in a formal but congenial tone. Frances's official student record lay open on his desk. She caught a glimpse of her pigtailed Grade 9 photograph stapled to the bottom corner, a picture only slightly less embarrassing than her mother's company in public.

"How is your family?" queried Mr. Forestall casually, as though he might actually be interested.

"Fine, sir," responded Frances. In truth, her mother was daily becoming more neurotic, her sister Alsa had died two months earlier of tuberculosis, and her father—well, Mother and Alsa were the good news. Frances felt intuitively that none of this would be of interest to Mr. Forestall. "And your family, sir?" responded Frances politely. Frances did not like to be the focus of attention, and had developed defensive conversational skills to get the ball out of her own court.

"My family?" flustered Mr. Forestall. "They're fine," he said, raising his voice to signal the end of that topic. "Now, Miss McFadden, I was wondering—" he waited for a dramatic two beats, "—I was wondering if your family might need some financial help?"

No one with Frances's mother's pretenses at middle-class respectability ever discussed money—how much they made, or how much they needed to pay the bills. Her mother worked as a shift nurse at the Civic Hospital. Her father was gone. Their home was simply furnished, but not uncomfortable. Frances would never have dreamed of discussing her family's financial situation with someone as remote to her life as a school principal.

"I honestly don't know, Mr. Forestall," Frances replied. "My family lives as well as others these days. I don't believe we need charity, but thank you for asking."

"May I speak frankly, Miss McFadden?" Mr. Forestall's tone suggested that frankness wasn't his normal mode of discourse, but he was prepared to make an exception for expediency. "A man phoned this afternoon desperate to find an assistant immediately. He wants someone young, because the position is unique and he doesn't want to waste time 'unlearning,' as he put it, an experienced clerk from a traditional office." He picked up a pipe from his desk and absently began to clean out the bowl. "Are you interested?"

Frances thought for a moment. "My training here at school has been fairly traditional, Mr. Forestall. I'm not sure that I would be any different from—"

"No," Mr. Forestall cut in, "I mean, this Mr. Grace, the man who phoned, values flexibility and initiative over, ah, a narrower set of skills. Miss Gilhooly says that you are the most mature student in her class. Your Official Student Record says—" he glanced down, "—that you were seventeen in January. You look older than that to me."

Mr. Forestall stared at her for several moments—long enough to make her blush and look down. To shift the focus, Frances asked, "What kind of a job is it, sir?"

"Well, it's a new situation. Apparently the Canadian government is about to set up a central bank, a kind of bankers' bank." He leaned forward to check some notes on his desk. "It will regulate all banking activity in Canada and deal with international exchange issues. They think this new bank will help the government direct the economy out of these hard times."

"Math is not my strongest subject, Mr. Forestall. I don't think I'd make a good bank teller."

Mr. Forestall glanced down at her student record again. "Your math marks are quite adequate. Besides, Mr. Grace said this bank has no tellers. It is really a central office to help other banks. It's like a wholesale bank. Understand?" he asked hopefully.

Frances understood that Mr. Forestall barely understood, and she did not ask further questions.

"Mr. Grace is with the Department of Finance. This new bank—I believe they're going to call it The Bank of Canada—just recently received Cabinet approval, and Mr. Grace says they are a year behind already. He wants a girl who can start at once."

Silence. It made no sense to her.

"Miss McFadden, I realize this is quite sudden, and you'll want to think it over. But there isn't much time. I believe that a job with the government is a plum, especially in these times. It pays a fair wage, and is secure. You'll be eligible for a government pension."

Pension? The furthest Frances had ever planned ahead was to huddle with Mary and the Crazy Deavys about whether to go to the Rialto or the Roxy to catch the Saturday matinee. Her eyes slowly looked around the office, stunned, like an accident victim.

"Miss Gilhooly says you're the best student in her Grade 11 class," added Mr. Forestall, like a salesman trying to close a deal. "The other two Grade 11 classes are not strong, and the Grade 12's are all placed. If we're to help Mr. Grace, it has to be you."

"But Mr. Forestall, I haven't finished high school yet."

"True. You'll miss these last six weeks as well as your final year. And frankly, we provide an excellent education at the High School of Commerce; but experience is a better school. It would count triple with any future employer."

Frances was floored to hear an adult opinion that was identical to her own. She sank into silence once more. She did not understand Mr. Forestall's enthusiasm for her to take this job, until he broke the third period of silence with a confession.

"Actually, Frances, the High School of Commerce has recently had some difficulty placing graduates within federal government offices. There were a few untoward experiences that, well, soured some government personnel departments on our students. This was unfair and unfortunate, and we'd like to reconnect. This Bank of Canada is a brand-new department. They are bound to need more secretaries, typists, and stenographers.

"You could pave the way for other Commerce students to follow." He paused and picked up his pipe. "However, truth to tell, Miss Gilhooly doesn't believe the school should throw you to the wolves just to open the door for others. I don't see the government as wolves, do you?" he asked rhetorically, sucking a match flame down into the burled walnut bowl of his pipe.

Truth to tell. The truth ebbed her strength, and yellow spots of light popped in front of her like phantom balloons that could not be blinked away.

"I don't know what to say, Mr. Forestall. I must discuss this with my mother." *My mother!* She couldn't believe that she'd ever say such a thing.

Mr. Forestall beamed. "Certainly. Quite responsible!" he said with satisfaction. "Just drop in before school tomorrow and let me know your decision."

Miss Dawkes was murmuring confidentially into the telephone as Frances drifted across the outer office to the hall door. Her locker opened with a panicked metallic cry that screeched down the empty hall. *Mother, Mother, Mother. Mother hates surprises.* Homework tucked under her arm, she stepped from the dark hallway out into the brilliant May sunshine.

2

HOME TO MOTHER

Home was in the working-class suburb of Rochesterville. The McFaddens lived in a red brick farmhouse dating from the 1860s that had subsequently been boxed in by narrow dwellings to house the employees of the nearby lumber mills. Frances crossed Bronson Avenue and at Cambridge Street turned north to mount the rickety wooden bridge that arched over the Canadian National Railway tracks.

She had walked this route a thousand times, usually in the company of Mary O'Brien and the Crazy Deavy sisters, Katie and Dorothy. Her friends had likely lingered for her by the west door of the school until the late-afternoon radio soap operas drew them home.

Frances unlocked the front door of 180 Rochester Street and put her schoolbooks on the hallstand. Her mother's winter coat hung in the front closet, fragrant with lavender perfume. Familiar, if not exactly welcoming. She walked back to the kitchen and picked up an apple and a paring knife before returning to the front porch, which was bathed in tender sunshine. Frances cut crisp crescent wedges out of the apple and pondered.

Did she want this mystery job? Many people quit school the day they turned sixteen to go to work. Frances found the routine of secretarial classes boring, but otherwise painless. Question two: What would her mother think? Vera McFadden's behaviour was becoming more erratic daily. Mother and daughter had never shared the close bond evidenced at the Deavys'. Dorothy and Katie giggled and shared confidences easily with Mrs. Deavy, like three sisters. They would flirt outrageously with the shy milkman, or conspire to trick their father to treat them to ice cream cones. Frances could not imagine this rollicking camaraderie with her own mother.

There was no hostility in the McFadden home, but a tautness was almost always present. Alsa's tuberculosis had briefly drawn Frances closer to her mother. Her sudden death had jarred them apart again. Vera steeled herself through the mechanics of Alsa's funeral, but then deteriorated. Father didn't have the time—*didn't take the time?*—to return from St. Louis for his elder daughter's funeral. His condolence card had been brief.

When Lionel McFadden had first experienced spells of unemployment, Vera took on shift work at the Civic Hospital to pay the bills, but her nervous nature suffered. Her training as a nurse had undermined her faith in God, which ironically led her to the occult for guidance. She would pore over the horoscope column in the *Ottawa Journal*, scavenging for hope. She became a furtive client of Madame Zarina, an ancient gypsy who read tea leaves above the Wong Lee Laundry on Somerset Street.

Although Vera McFadden was of teetotalling Presbyterian stock, she took to keeping a small flask of "medicinal" brandy in the house for "emergencies." The brandy bottle was stored in the second floor linen closet between the off-season sheets. It nestled in cotton through the winter and sweltered in flannel from April till October. Vera took her medicine unobtrusively, in a teacup. The brandy never appeared in the big farm kitchen; the teacup rendezvoused with the linen closet. Vera was slight of build, and taut. A generous teacup of brandy anaesthetized her nicely for the evening.

Mother's Day had been a nightmare. Reverend Grisham's sermon at Erskine Presbyterian Church paid tribute to mothers everywhere. He lauded their sacrifice and nurturing natures, but it rubbed the scab off Vera's fresh loss. Frances's every attempt to lift the gloom failed.

She was caught off guard by the complications of getting a hot meal on the table all by herself. The chicken was dried out and the vegetables limp. In an attempt to make the meal special, Frances had laid the dark walnut dining room table with her mother's silver. But the large room echoed emptily each time a sterling fork touched a plate, mocking their small party. With the pie inedible, and the tea too strong, Vera McFadden had wordlessly risen from the table and walked out the front door, leaving Frances alone with her inadequacies and a sink filled with dishes.

Well, that was yesterday, and this was today. If Mother didn't like the job offer, which was what Frances expected, should she argue with her? The McFadden household did not have the tradition of arguing that Frances observed at the O'Brien or the Deavy houses. Recreational squabbling embarrassed her until she realized that the combativeness was not personal, but just another parlour game, like charades or Monopoly.

At the McFaddens', parents decreed what should be done, and children did it. Alsa used to ignore her parents as long as possible, then sulkily give in. Frances found compliance easier, and sullenness a self-punishment.

"Can you help me with these?" Vera arrived on the porch suddenly, with three freshly laundered nurses' uniforms over her arm and a bakery box from Fenton's. Her face glistened with the humidity, and her anxious eyelids drooped. Frances took the uniforms and carried them into the cool hallway. Vera took a teacup upstairs, and Frances heard the hinges of the linen closet door squeal.

The good china hadn't salvaged Mother's Day, but it might generate the right tone at the less formal kitchen table. Out came the dinner plates, the crystal water glasses, and the good Delft salt and pepper shakers. Upstairs, the water gushed into the big claw-footed tub.

Frances took the leftover roast chicken from Mother's Day dinner out of the icebox. She cleaned the meat from the carcass onto pieces of crusty Italian bread. Carrots and peas went into a saucepan on the stove, and the gravy boat was emptied on the lot.

When Vera came down for dinner, her face was ruddy from the bath, or perhaps from the teacup. Her eyes swept the beautifully laid kitchen table, before returning to Frances. Frances smiled. "I thought a little step up would be a nice change on a weeknight," she said. "And I need to talk to you about something."

Vera's empty teacup clattered down on the counter. She stared open-mouthed at Frances for a brief moment. "Are . . . you . . . are you in trouble?" she asked, sinking into a chair.

Frances blushed. It was not unknown for Rochester Street girls to get themselves into trouble. It had happened to Little Ella Schroeder, who hung out with the gum-chewing, bright-lipsticked crowd that loitered away the evenings outside Drury's Grocery Store. Frances did not wear makeup, by parental decree, and was forbidden to leave the house after supper without a purpose or a destination. She had an embarrassing dearth of experience in the arena of "trouble."

"No, no, Mother. Mr. Forestall spoke to me today after typing class. He offered me a job."

Vera looked up sharply. "What? After school? That's not a good idea. It will interfere with your homework."

"It's for a permanent job starting immediately. Some new bank is opening in Ottawa. Needs an office assistant right away."

"What kind of an educator wants you to drop out of school?" demanded Vera. "Before you graduate? What a ridiculous idea!"

Frances strangely did not feel defensive. She felt she was explaining some complex task to a child. "Dinner's ready. Why don't we eat?" She loaded plates and set them down. "I was surprised, too. I don't have to take this job. Mr. Forestall just asked if I was interested. He told me to let him know by tomorrow morning. They may not want me anyway."

"They? Who are they?"

"All I know is that a new government bank is about to open in Ottawa. I didn't quite understand it, but it's not like the Bank of Nova Scotia."

"Why would any employer want a student? There must be all sorts of experienced people available these days." In Vera's voice derision and suspicion competed evenly.

Frances laughed. "Mother! You sound like Charlie Chan! I don't think this is a front for an opium ring. Who knows why this man phoned the school instead of putting an ad in the paper? All the Form Four girls are already committed to jobs when school ends. Remember? Mary O'Brien is set to start at Goudy Manufacturing."

Vera began to eat quietly.

"What have I got to lose by telling Mr. Forestall that I'm interested?" said Frances. "If the position has been filled in the meantime, I stay at school. If the job is still available . . . well . . . we consider the offer and make a decision."

"Do you want to quit school? You're so young!" Sudden events unsettled Vera.

"You sound just like Miss Gilhooly. Why am I at school in the first place? To become a secretary. This is a chance to skip a year."

"But you haven't finished your training!"

"It doesn't seem to matter. I'm not misrepresenting myself. Mr. Forestall had my school record wide open on his desk. I'd have to learn on the job. The only difference is that I'll be paid as I learn. It sounds to me like opportunity knocking."

This scored a point. Vera McFadden loved aphorisms, and often used them with the girls. "An ounce of prevention . . . the early bird . . ." She liked "opportunity knocking" in particular. They ate in silence as the wall clock ticked off the day.

"Wouldn't the extra money be helpful?"

Vera glared over her eyeglasses. "We are not needy, Frances. Between my job, and what your father is sending us, we're doing fine."

Father is sending us money?

"All right. We don't *need* the money, but it wouldn't hurt to have me employed. Who knows how long Father's current job will last?"

"Don't speak ill of your father. He means well."

"I'm not speaking ill of him. The world is in a Depression. It isn't anybody's fault, but jobs disappear. And poor Alsa . . . to get tuberculosis at eighteen! Life is so unpredictable."

Vera's fork clattered down on her plate. She stared at her daughter. Absorbed by her dissolving roles of wife and mother, she hadn't noticed Frances growing up.

Vera rose slowly. "Let's put the teakettle on and see if we can make sense of this." When the kettle screamed, Vera "hotted" the pot, while Frances cleared the dishes. This slow ritual of performing simple tasks calmed them both. After two sips of tea, Vera asked in a quiet, non-judgmental voice, "What do you think about this, Frances?"

Frances had rarely had her opinion sought, and hesitated. Finally she said, "Well, before I got this offer today, everything was fine. I can ignore this offer, and life will continue to be fine. What do you think?"

An epiphany. The mutual retreat drained the tension completely.

Vera opened the drawer in the harvest table and took out a worn deck of cards. "Let's see what the cards say. You check our horoscopes in tonight's newspaper." She tapped the end of the deck on the table, then expertly split it in two and shuffled several times. Vera laid a cross of thirteen cards face down between them: seven in a horizontal line, bisected evenly by a vertical line of six more cards. The Maltese Cross spread. She flipped one card face up in the centre of each quadrant of the cross.

Frances read her mother's horoscope aloud: "Virgo: A good day for making plans. Don't be reluctant to listen to others. Boats that don't leave the harbour don't sink, but they don't travel anywhere, either." And then her own: "Capricorn: Someone unexpected can help you out. Don't let emotions overtake reason. There will be rewards for being careful, but curiosity can be an advantage."

"This sounds . . . ambiguous," said Frances.

Vera harrumphed at her daughter's naiveté. "Those both support your trying for the silly job. '. . . make plans . . . leave the harbour . . . unexpected help . . . satisfy your curiosity . . .' They all line up," she added reluctantly. She looked at the upturned cards. "Hmmph!" she exclaimed again. "All clubs! Who'd have guessed it?" She began turning over the other cards, one at a time, working in from the corners of the cross toward the centre, until only the centre card was still down. There were four face cards in the vertical column: jack of spades, queen of diamonds, king of hearts, jack of hearts. All six of the cards in the horizontal column were lower than a ten.

Vera's mouth twisted in thought, while she tapped the deck absently against the tabletop.

"What? What?" asked Frances.

"Well, it's mixed. The four black sentinels," she said, pointing to the clubs in the quadrants, "are auspicious. No blood-red hearts or diamonds—which can distract, like vanity or jealousy. Very stable. The rising face cards also suggest power in the future, although the jacks can be fickle tricksters." She pointed to the horizontal row. "The ground line is so-so. Rising strength without balance sounds wobbly to me, and there are no aces at all. That's weak."

"What about the last card?" asked Frances.

"There is a choice here. You can bring it into play or not, because it's the fulcrum, and can turn everything for you or against you. I usually don't chance the final card. The horoscopes are positive, I'd say, but the cards are neutral. The fulcrum card could cancel everything."

Frances did not believe in fortune-telling, but her inquiring nature begged for resolution. She could feel her heart racing. "I want to see the final card."

"Risk it all?"

" 'Curiosity can be an advantage,' Mother."

"Then *you* do it."

Frances reached out and flipped the card over. The ace of clubs.

"Dear God!" exclaimed Vera.

She quietly gathered the cards up into the deck and raised her eyebrows at Frances. A tight smile of resignation creased her lips. "That settles it," she said, reaching for her teacup.

3

FRIENDS

Frances dreamt all night long. Calico kittens playing beneath the basement stairs in some apparent danger. A smiling Geordie Hilton from her Presbyterian Youth Group standing in the dining room, wet and naked. Well, naked from the waist up, anyway. Frances dared not look lower, even in her dreams. Had it been Buddy Drury, the grocery boy, however . . .

Were they omens? Dreams meant nothing to her, and she didn't want to ask her mother. Frances pretended to eat breakfast, moving cornflakes and milk around in a bowl before furtively washing the evidence down the sink. Her mother smiled wanly. They chatted about the weather. Frances grabbed her books from the hall table and left for school.

Her school friends were waiting for her at the corner of Gladstone Avenue. Mary O'Brien and Dorothy Deavy were a year older than Frances. They would graduate in June to enter the workforce. Mary had a sometimes charming childlike literalness and was a much younger eighteen than Dorothy.

Rochesterville males were interested in Dorothy Deavy, but her wit was intimidating. She could imitate any voice she had ever heard, call up any radio or movie personality, parent, or teacher at will. She allowed herself to be squired to a movie or a Saturday night church hall dance when asked. She radiated self-confidence and would not be rushed into attachments.

Katie Deavy was sixteen and had a precocious wit. She could not sit still in school and was constantly in trouble for talking, or passing notes, or absently drumming her fingers on the oak desktop.

The standard school punishment was "the writing of lines," either a page of the Concise Oxford Dictionary or a chapter from the King James Version of the Holy Bible (revised 1901). Both books could be found on every schoolteacher's desk in Ontario. Katie often had detentions before school, during lunch hour, and after school to complete her penance. Mr. Pulfer, the math teacher, assigned her pages of words between aardvark and dysentery, and chapters from Genesis to Judges.

Miss Aldwinckle, the shorthand teacher, allotted lexicon from E to H as well as moral edification from the Book of Ruth through Second Chronicles. And so on.

Katie made a variety of interesting discoveries in the Oxford Concise that she was happy to share with her friends. Words like lesbian, fornicate, erotic, and sodomite coyly slipped into her daily discourse, and sent her friends scurrying for dictionaries of their own.

The Bible was full of other surprises for a sixteen-year-old, particularly quotes that might make Mary blush: "He whose testicles are crushed or whose male member is cut off shall not enter the assembly of the Lord," Katie would whisper when a good-looking boy passed. Mary would stammer, "Katie Deavy! It's blasphemy to pretend that's from *The Bible!*"

"Deuteronomy 23, Verse 1. Check it out, Mar," countered Katie. "That is, if a good Catholic girl is interested in reading about male genitalia." Mary flushed vermilion. The sisters shared the gift of being effortlessly entertaining, and this tarred them into the collective compound noun "thecrazydeavies."

"Well, if it isn't the Houdini of Rochesterville. Quite the disappearing act yesterday after school," observed Katie.

"Sorry I missed you," said Frances. "I had to see Mr. Forestall."

"Gosh, Frannie! Are you in trouble?" asked Mary.

Frances laughed. "No. No, Mar. My mother asked me the same thing last night, meaning, well, you know . . . a girl just can't do one thing different without people thinking the worst!"

At Mary O'Brien's sleepover three weeks earlier, the foursome had played "Truth or Consequences" in hushed whispers under the eaves in Mary's attic bedroom. There was no rule about "Truth or Consequences" topics, but the game invariably drifted toward sex. The dare to tell the truth was a liberating opportunity. There never were any "consequences" for not telling the truth, and who would know, anyway? They teased Frances for "the truth" about Geordie Hilton, who always walked her home from church and Youth Group.

"He's so good-looking!" exclaimed Dorothy. "That wavy blond hair and those blue eyes!"

"He's so virile," added Katie. "Why do you lead him on so?"

"I don't! He follows me home like a puppy. What am I supposed to do? Tell him he can't use the sidewalk?"

Frances did not know why she wasn't attracted to Geordie but was magnetized by Buddy Drury. Buddy had turned sixteen halfway through his third try at Grade 8 and quit school to work in his parents' grocery store. He wore tight jeans and a T-shirt with a pack of Export A cigarettes tucked in an upturned sleeve. He had strong cheekbones and sensuous lips. His undisciplined hands had taken quick liberties a few times with Frances, and she was forced to feign annoyance. She knew he flirted with every female between six and sixty in the neighbour-hood. His carnal nature was transparent. At the time, Frances did not understand the shallowness of lust. Buddy Drury's name was a secret mouthed silently on her pillow.

Despite Katie's relative youth, she had the most actual experience with boys. That went little beyond tongue-kissing in the back row of the Roxy Theatre with a boy wearing a Glebe Collegiate cardigan. "Then he got fresh," said Katie, "so I dumped my popcorn into his lap and left."

"You let him tongue-kiss you!" squealed Mary. "Ugh!!"

"And *then* he got fresh?" queried Dorothy.

"You wasted popcorn?" reflected Frances. "Was he *that* offensive?"

Nuggets from Katie's dictionary transcriptions spiced her chatter. "I felt some demonstrative act was called for in response to the breach of protocol."

"Protocol?" queried Mary.

Katie cracked her bubble gum. "It means, 'Don't snap my bra strap, Buster—without an invitation.' Roughly."

"What was the Glebe guy's name?" asked Dorothy.

"I don't know his name, for heaven's sakes! We weren't that intimate!"

Dorothy was intrigued by the Forestall summons. "What did his Lordship want, then? He doesn't pay much attention to anybody he can't bawl out for something."

"You didn't kill the French teacher, did you?" Katie asked. "She's mine! Her death must be slow and painful, like her classes."

"He offered me a job. Starting immediately, with some bank."

"Christmas!" said Katie. "You're going to get out of school right now? With ol' man Forestall's blessing? This is better than winning the Irish Sweepstakes!"

"What does your mother think?" Mary asked.

"Mother . . . well, it could have been worse. We talked it over, and she didn't say no."

"Really?" exclaimed the Deavy girls together. There was much left unsaid in their surprise.

Frances went straight to the office. Miss Dawkes pointedly ignored her for a full minute before cocking an eye in her direction and queried, "Yes?"

"Mr. Forestall asked to see me before school today."

"Again?" Miss Dawkes threw the word back like a dagger.

Frances glared at her. Mr. Forestall opened his office door into this field of tension. He was, however, professionally incurious about the emotions of females and wished only to get on with his day.

"Ah, Frances. Please come in." Frances darted past the corner of Miss Dawkes's desk and into the office.

"Have you and your mother reached a decision?"

"Yes. My mother—" *My mother believes in signs and omens and drinks brandy every night . . .* "—agrees that this is an interesting opportunity."

"Good!" said Mr. Forestall, his own opinion confirmed. He reached for the phone. "I'll call Mr. Grace and set up an interview."

"An interview?"

"It's standard procedure in hiring. You would have studied interviewing in the Grade 12 Office Management course. Hello, Mr. Grace? It's Forestall at the High School of Commerce. I've got someone for you. Can I send her down to your office for an interview? Oh, it isn't? Well, where, then? The Château Laurier? I'll check."

He looked up, covering the phone receiver with his hand. "Can you make it down to the Château Laurier for twelve noon today?"

"No, sir. I have accounting until 11:40, and—"

"Never mind accounting. Hello, Mr. Grace? Miss McFadden will meet you at twelve sharp. Right. I'll tell her. Not at all. Good day." He set the receiver triumphantly back on the cradle of the telephone.

"Well," he said, pulling a notepad forward, "this is your lucky day. I have never been to the Château Laurier for lunch myself. You're to ask for Mr. Grace in the Canadian Grill Room." He scrawled a note to Mr. Benning, the accounting teacher, and handed it to her.

"What if I'm late getting back for afternoon class?"

Mr. Forestall walked over to the door. "Miss McFadden, you are on the brink of a new life, making your own decisions and living with the consequences." He smiled briefly. "Good day."

Frances drifted out the doorway in a trance. She floated to her locker and to Home Form. Through business practice, French, and shorthand, her eyes could barely focus. The word "interview" blinked in front of her like a theatre marquee. She had never been interviewed. She did not know the rules.

Suddenly it was 11:00 a.m. Heading down the hall to accounting, she noticed Miss Gilhooly coming toward her.

"Miss Gilhooly!" she gasped. "Help! I've got to go to an interview with the people from the bank, and I don't know what to say."

Streams of chatting students broke around them in the hall.

"When is your interview?"

"I have to leave in twenty minutes to meet a Mr. Grace at the Château Laurier."

Miss Gilhooly brightened. "A good sign! No one would waste a Château lunch on a marginal candidate." She looked right into Frances's eyes. "There are just two things you need to remember, Frances. First, just tell him the truth. If he doesn't like the truth, it is his job, not yours, to find someone whose truth suits him. A man who doesn't like the truth would be a very hard man to work for. Secondly, he has a problem and you are the solution. He wants to say 'yes' to you. Your only task is to make it easy for him to say 'yes.'"

Miss Gilhooly gently squeezed Frances's hand. "You'll be fine." She smiled again, with her perfect pearl teeth. "Better get to class."

"Oh, Miss Gilhooly! One more thing. I've never eaten in a fancy restaurant before. I don't know the etiquette."

"Just watch your host. He chose the venue. He'll know the rules."

"Thank you!" Frances sang over her shoulder, as she ran to accounting. Mr. Benning had closed the classroom door. He pointedly looked at the clock and back at her when she entered, feigning annoyance, although she knew he liked her.

"I apologize for being late, Mr. Benning. Mr. Forestall asked me to give you this." He read the note then nodded her to her seat. Frances liked accounting. She loved the precision and black-and-white certainty. Next to English, it was her favourite class. She loved the ambiguity and delicate shading in English literature. This appeal of opposites, she knew, was ironic. She loved irony most of all.

At 11:20, she packed up her books. While eight students were chalking out the accounting homework problems on the blackboard, she quietly let herself out the classroom door. Even though it was a warm day, her teeth began chattering uncontrollably as she left the school.

4

INTERVIEW

A full thirty-minute walk at a brisk pace took her past the Parliament Buildings to the fairy-tale castle façade of the Château Laurier Hotel. The exercise took the edge off Frances's anxiety. A smiling doorman in green livery opened the large brass-framed glass door.

"Oui, mademoiselle?" inquired a short, smiling bellhop. A gold badge on his livery said "Marcel."

"I have an appointment to meet Mr. Grace in the—" In the maelstrom of the day, she had forgotten where.

"In the Algonquin Lounge? In the Canadian Grill? In—"

"Yes! In the Canadian Grill."

"Of course! You must be Mademoiselle McFadden. Please follow me."

Frances was not accustomed to the ways of first-class hotels, and there was a wonder in it. Marcel glided ahead of her with the fluidity and enthusiasm of a ballet dancer. He wheeled into an elegant dining room. A fleet of linen-covered tables stretched to the horizon. Bejewelled ladies and serious, suited men murmured over the sound of cutlery. Marcel passed Frances on like a baton to Raymond, the tuxedoed maître d', who set sail across the room, leading her to a man reading by the window.

Raymond smiled. "Monsieur Grace, Mademoiselle McFadden has arrived." He swung her chair back from the table. Frances started to sit down just as Mr. Grace rose to shake her hand. She struggled to rise again, but her legs buckled as Raymond tucked her into the table. Tumbling backward, her wayward hand struck a glancing blow off a fluted crystal vase that held half a dozen daffodils and fern greens. The vase tipped precariously to the right. Horrified, Frances shut her eyes tight.

Mr. Grace easily arrested the vase and reset it to the side. When no crash came, Frances peeked to see a belt buckle across the table. Her eyes scaled the buttons on a starched white shirt, over a paisley bow tie, to a good-natured face smiling down on her.

"Miss McFadden, pleased to make your acquaintance."

"Henri will be with you momentarily," Raymond said before floating away.

Mr. Grace piled his papers into a battered leather briefcase beside his chair. Although an adult, he did not look old like Mr. Forestall or Miss Gilhooly. His blue eyes sparkled behind wire-rimmed glasses, and a hank of recalcitrant hair hung down onto a playful face. He looked like a child dressed up as a man and extracting great pleasure from the charade.

"Now," he said pleasantly, "should we stand on ceremony? Shall I call you Miss McFadden?"

"My name is Frances."

"Fine, then, Frances," he continued with a smile. "Shall we dine first? I find business too early in the day can cloy the palate." He opened the huge menu. "Do you tend to eat a large lunch, like the Europeans?"

"I tend to have a sandwich," Frances said. She opened her own menu to see an assortment of confusing descriptions.

"May I recommend the poached salmon from *la table d'hôte*? It's quite special."

"Fine," said Frances, with relief. Her only experience with salmon was out of a can with creamed peas on toast. She liked that. She warily eyed the phalanx of flatware at her place setting. There were three forks of varying sizes to the left beside her linen napkin, and three knives and two spoons to the right.

Henri arrived, and Mr. Grace ordered in French for both of them. Henri and Mr. Grace joked back and forth, brimming with conviviality.

"You speak French really well," remarked Frances after Henri left. "But you don't have a French-Canadian accent."

"I'm from Toronto, actually, but I studied in Paris for two years, where my French improved greatly."

"What did you study?"

Mr. Grace gave her a mock scowl. "I thought this was *my* interview." Then he smiled. "I did post-doctoral work in international finance."

"You're a doctor?"

"Well, not a 'useful' doctor, as my mother would say. Not a medical doctor. A Doctor of Philosophy in Economics."

"That sounds useful to me."

"I agree. But my mother always hoped that I would be a medical missionary in China, and I have been a profound disappointment." Mr. Grace's self-deprecating smile suggested some liberties with the truth.

"Should I call you Dr. Grace, then?"

"I only use 'Doctor' when I'm writing reports. I've discovered that

Canadians are reluctant to challenge a document signed by a doctor."

Henri was back with a bottle of white wine. He showed the label to Dr. Grace and gave him the cork, which he sniffed. A splash of yellow liquid shot into his glass. Dr. Grace held the stemmed glass up to the window light. He held it under his nose and breathed deeply. Then he sucked the liquid into his mouth with a slurping noise that would have earned a stern rebuke from Frances's mother, but only made Henri smile.

Dr. Grace nodded, and said with a mock British accent: "Yes. It has travelled rawtha well with little injury, and will greatly assist the salmon."

Henri filled both wineglasses then placed the bottle in an ice bucket beside the table. Frances had never seen either an open wine bottle or an ice bucket. She had never tasted an alcoholic drink in her life. The medicinal brandy in the second floor linen closet had never been prescribed for any of her ills.

Dr. Grace raised his glass. "To things unsung, like spring in Ottawa, and other new beginnings." Glasses clinked. Frances watched him drink, then took a small sip. It tasted cool and fruity and a little tart. "What does one study at the High School of Commerce these days?"

"English and history, and commercial courses like shorthand and business practice."

"And how are your marks?"

"Mostly in the eighties."

Henri returned with two beautiful salad plates. Each plate was covered with a bed of leaf lettuce, topped with a pinwheel arrangement of alternating peeled grapefruit fingers and avocado slices in an oil and nut dressing. Frances had never seen a real avocado, but recognized it from a colour cover story in the *Ladies' Home Journal*. Dr. Grace picked up the small, outside fork and began on his salad. Frances followed suit.

"Any work experience?"

"No," Frances confessed.

"No one's ever paid you to do anything?"

"No. Just babysitting."

"*Just* babysitting? People entrust you with their most precious treasure—their link with posterity—and you don't value it as work experience?"

"It's only the Dubrofskis down the street. When they're short-staffed on a busy Saturday, Mrs. Dubrofski helps out at their store. I watch their kids. She doesn't pay me much."

"Do you like looking after children?"

"Well, Sollie is a handful, but the two girls are fine. I get them to help me entertain Sollie. They like playing 'grown-up.'"

"You must have the patience of Job! I tried working at the YMCA camp one summer, but the little tykes drove me to distraction. My admiration for teachers increased tremendously. Anything else?"

"I teach in the junior Sunday school at Erskine Presbyterian Church, and I help run the refreshment booth at their Christmas bazaar. But I don't get paid."

"It still counts! It proves that you're reliable, and can work with both children and adults. Do you handle money at the bazaar?"

"Yes. Mrs. Thomas gives us a cash float to start. We have to prepare a bank deposit at the end of the day. Sort the bills and roll the coins."

Henri arrived with the salmon, poached pink and steaming, flanked by tiny potatoes, green beans, and carrots. In his gloved hand, he held what turned out to be a slice of lemon wrapped in cheesecloth, and when Dr. Grace nodded, Henri squeezed the juice up and down the length of his salmon. Henri turned to Frances, who had figured out the charade and nodded, receiving the same baptism for her own salmon. Henri topped up their wine glasses. Frances was feeling the warmth from her throat spread throughout her body.

"And what do you do for fun?"

"I read or go to the movies with my friends." She took a longer draught of the soothing wine.

"What do you like to read?"

"Oh, novels, mostly. I love Jane Austen. I tried the Brontës — well, *Wuthering Heights*, anyway, but found it a little depressing."

"Do you read the newspaper?"

"Just the funnies. The news seems so gloomy."

"Like the Brontës?" asked Dr. Grace with a smile.

Dr. Grace chose the large fork and a flat scimitar-shaped knife from his cutlery arsenal to begin an attack on his salmon. Frances followed his lead. The salmon was delicious.

"How would your friends describe you, if I were to ask them about you?"

Frances reflected. "I think my friends would say that I'm loyal and laugh easily."

"I admire loyalty and a good sense of humour above all things."

The conversation carried on pleasantly between mouthfuls of the salmon and delightfully crisp vegetables. Eventually, Henri cleared away the plates with another murmur of French. He drained the bottle into their glasses and carried the ice bucket away.

"Now, to work. Frances, I need an administrator who can run an office pretty well single-handedly. Essentially, this person needs to be organized and have two basic skills. Can you take shorthand?"

"Yes. Pitman."

"Here's a pad and a pen; I'm going to read you a letter and I want you to take it down word for word. Okay?"

Frances nodded.

Dr. Grace read to her in a quiet quick staccato. "To Justice Lorne Cameron, Supreme Court of Canada, 111 Wellington Street, Ottawa. Sir: The House of Commons Committee on Banking and Finance is currently considering legislation to create the Bank of Canada. There are many political and economic issues to be resolved, but I am writing to ask your opinion on two areas that some feel might be *ultra vires*. Section 24, subsection vi, paragraph 4 (see attached) might contravene the British North America Act. In particular—"

When he finished, Frances read it back to him. She had written "ultravirus" and stumbled over the pronunciation.

"It's u-l-t-r-a new word v-i-r-e-s. It's Latin. It means 'outside the law.' But the rest is excellent! The administrator will have to take notes at meetings, and details such as 'subsection 7 of article 8 on page 9' must be absolutely accurate.

"Next. Here's an article from the *Toronto Globe* that I was asked to comment on in regard to the pending legislation. It's about four hundred words long," he said, handing it over. "Can you write a summary in fifty words?"

Frances read carefully, underlining as she went. She read it twice more, then wrote, then scratched out, then wrote some more. When she looked up, Dr. Grace said, "Read it to me."

Frances took a deep breath. "Gordon St. James, of the Canadian Bankers' Association, believes that a central bank in Canada would be a waste of taxpayers' money. It would needlessly duplicate areas that are now well managed by the banking industry. A level of bureaucracy would be added that would hinder the current financial system."

"Fifty words spot-on! Very good! I have thousands of pages of reports and articles that I should read, but simply cannot get to. I'll need them summarized."

Dr. Grace put down his pen. "Now, about the job. Are you interested?" He might have been offering her a choice of candies from a box of Laura Secords.

Frances drew in another long swallow of mellowness. She thought for a few seconds. "Perhaps you should tell me more about it," she replied.

Dr. Grace laughed. "Perhaps I should. Canada is just about to open a new national bank. What they describe as a 'bankers' bank.' It will be called The Bank of Canada."

"Why do bankers need banks?"

"Most other countries have central banks, so this isn't a new idea. Bankers run their banks to make a profit for their shareholders. The fate of the nation is not at the forefront of their concern. The banks really control the money in circulation, because they set the rates at which they will lend it, and judge who is worthy of a loan. The government can't direct the Canadian economy unless it can manage its relations with the banks.

"Part of the reason for the current depression in Canada is that there is no central monetary authority. That has led to instability, and businesses won't invest in new machinery and create new jobs when they are unsure of the future. The Bank of Canada will govern all banking activities in Canada, issue a common currency, and deal with other central banks."

Never having experienced intoxication before, Frances couldn't put a name to her extremely pleasant state. She gazed earnestly at Mr. Grace. "That sounds," she said, enunciating every syllable slowly, "like a very good idea."

"I'm glad you think so! I feel the same, although many Canadians disagree. And this is where you come in. I do not work for this bank. I work full time for the Department of Finance— more than full time, actually—helping to shepherd the legislation along on a bill that will create the Bank of Canada. A draft of the bill is currently before the House of Commons Committee on Banking and Commerce. It's a slow process, but hopefully in another eight to ten weeks, the legislation will be passed, and the Bank of Canada will legally come into existence."

"Why do you need an administrator if the bank doesn't exist?"

"Good question. Certain parties are very impatient with the legislative process. Every day lost sets us back a month helping Canada climb out of this depression. The legislation will eventually pass. The Conservative government has a majority in the House of Commons. It's just a question of time. But certain parties—"

"Certain parties?"

"Pardon me. I report to a section chief who reports to the deputy Minister of Finance, who reports to the Minister of Finance, who reports to the prime minister. In theory, I should get all my orders from my section chief. In fact, this does not always happen. They don't all agree on procedure, nor do they want the blame if anything fails. 'Certain parties' means 'persons in positions of authority who do not wish to have any traceable profile.' Can you live with the ambiguity?"

Frances thought for a moment about her undefined emotional relationship with her mother. "I like to understand what's going on around me." She drained the last mouthful of gold from her wine glass.

"Don't we all? I will give you clear instructions, and always stand behind you when you carry them out."

"I still don't understand. The Bank of Canada doesn't exist. Why does it need an administrator?"

"Certain parties have instructed me to get a research office set up so that not a second is lost when the legislation inevitably passes. I'm working full time on the legislation, so I can't really run this office myself. I need a clever, well-organized manager. When can you start?"

There was a delay as Frances processed the words in her mellowed brain, making her appear thoughtful and reflective.

"What would suit you?" she said at last.

Dr. Grace beamed. He liked the consideration. He liked the willingness to serve. "Today is pretty far gone. How about tomorrow?"

"Tomorrow?" Frances sounded out the word tentatively.

Dr. Grace fished a small leather booklet out of his briefcase. "No, can't do it tomorrow. Have to be in Montreal. May have to stay over. By the way, are you free to do some travelling outside Ottawa for the bank? Toronto? Montreal?"

Leave my mother alone with a deck of cards? "Certainly," she said.

"Wonderful! All right, then. Thursday. I'll see you at 8:30 a.m. Thursday at the new—" he laughed, "—office. It's at 51 Queen Street, on the fourth floor."

He scribbled on the back of a card and handed it across to her.

"That's it? That's the interview?"

"That's it, Frances McFadden. I need a sharp cookie who can operate on her own most of the time. You're just the ticket." He signed the chit that Henri had left beside him and closed his briefcase. He smiled his genial smile. "Oh. Do you have any questions?"

"My mother was curious as to why you don't want someone more experienced. There must be many out there these days."

Mr. Grace rolled his eyes. "Well, tell your mother that I tried 'experience' when I was on the Macmillan Royal Commission last year. I had three disasters in as many weeks. One was a specialist, which meant she only did shorthand and refused to answer the phone or maintain the files. The second one wouldn't get off the phone, and was constantly getting calls and office visits from various men and irate loan agencies. The third one insisted that her previous employer's office procedures were much superior to mine. They didn't seem to mind if she showed up late every day, or stretched her lunch hour out to ninety minutes. I want a fresh start, and you're it."

He looked at his watch and stood up. "I must run. Henri will get you dessert and coffee if you like. Till Thursday," he said with a mock salute. He picked up his battered briefcase and was gone.

Frances dreamily looked out the window at the green spring and the Ottawa River carrying the meltwater of a long winter down to the sea. She felt very light-headed. She didn't know if she could stand up without falling down. Dessert and coffee sounded like a very good idea.

5

TRANSITIONS

The giddy glow from the interview and the Chardonnay percolated in the spring sunshine until Frances arrived home. Vera McFadden was furious. "What do you mean, you got the job? I thought Mr. Forestall was just going to give you more information."

"Well, it all happened very quickly. Mr. Forestall called Dr. Grace, who wanted to interview me at noon, so I met him, and he hired me. I start Thursday morning."

"You took his offer? Just like that?" Vera attacked, as if she had caught Frances stealing from the cookie jar. "Do you have a contract? What are your wages? Is this a permanent position?"

Frances wilted under the barrage. She wondered if her mother's initial support had been tactical, convinced that she had no chance of being hired.

"Mother, I was just following your advice. This Bank of Canada is brand-new. Many details still need to be worked out. This Dr. Grace is a nice man. I'm sure he is not trying to trick me."

Mostly, Frances wanted to say, "Aren't you proud of me?" but she knew her mother's favourite quote of all, "Pride goeth before a fall," would fly back, an arrow to her heart. Close to tears, she went upstairs to change and wash her face in cold water. Her solace that evening was that she wouldn't ever have to do another lick of homework. On the way to an early bed with Conan Doyle's *The White Company*, she could hear the cards being shuffled and re-shuffled on the kitchen table.

The Crazy Deavys and Mary O'Brien were another thing. "Not fair! Not fair!" complained Katie after her initial backslap of congratulations. "I'll be the only one left in jail next year!" Dorothy's and Mary's joy at her success was mitigated by this sudden change to their daily rituals. The foursome had walked to school together every day since Frances and Katie started Grade 1 together. The eleven-year regime was over.

"Hey! I'm not abandoning you! You're still my best friends," Frances exclaimed.

Miss Dawkes was far too cheerful as she handed over the withdrawal form that needed to be initialled by all of Frances's teachers. A long line of recalcitrants slouched against the wall outside Mr. Forestall's office, awaiting his attention, so Frances was unable to thank him, or get a little cat rub of appreciation for a success that seemed lost on others.

Frances did the rounds of her teachers, dropping off textbooks and sharing the news of her job with those who asked. Miss Gilhooly was away at a cousin's funeral, according to the young supply teacher who was handling the typing class. The loneliness of the uncelebrated achievement set the tone of her last day at school.

By eleven a.m., Frances had all of her sign-offs. She cleaned out her locker and handed her paperwork in to Miss Dawkes. It was a little like handing her own head to Jezebel. With far too much enthusiasm, the secretary drew a thick red line through the name "Frances Elizabeth McFadden" on the High School of Commerce register.

Frances took the streetcar downtown. When Vera had finally capitulated the night before, she immediately pronounced Frances's school wardrobe "too threadbare for the real world." Appearances remained paramount to Vera, no matter how leery she might be of this phantom bank. "I've read nothing about it in the newspapers," she sniffed.

Still, she had advanced Frances fifteen dollars against her first paycheque to flesh out a working girl's wardrobe. Frances purchased three pairs of knee socks that picked up the colours in her only two skirts. She bought two good-quality cotton blouses. She would have to wash one each evening, so it could dry to be ironed the next night, until she could afford more. Her underwear drawer was impoverished. The newest additions were her sister's hand-me-downs. She found it very unsettling wearing a dead person's underwear, especially with the elastic shot. Safety pins would have to hold things together until she got paid.

A cloudburst caught Frances in front of the Roxborough Hotel, and she darted into the lobby to wait it out. The barbershop door off the lobby was open, and the fragrance of Old Spice aftershave, her father's favourite, engulfed her. The image of his clean-cut face and shy smile instantly materialized. She liked her father. The gentle failure.

Lionel McFadden had left second-year Arts at Queen's University to take officer training when the war broke out in 1914. Nothing about his demeanour suggested the slightest suitability for a military career. He was deferential to authority, but was self-deprecating without the humour that made this trait charmingly Canadian. However, his quiet competence and his love of detail were noted, and he was quickly dealt into the Quartermaster General's Office as a supply procurer. Lionel had a latent gift for logistics and felt at home right away.

He travelled frequently to Toronto and Montreal by train on army procurement business, and it was on one of his return trips to Kingston that he met Vera Fields. Frances knew this story from family folklore. It was the next steps in the courtship dance, the nuances and subtleties of availability, love, invitation, and proposal that she could not imagine either of her parents taking part in.

They married in February of 1915. Just after Alsa was born in 1916, Lionel was promoted and posted to headquarters in Ottawa. On January 7, 1917, the *Ottawa Journal* reported the birth of Frances Elizabeth McFadden, second child of Captain and Mrs. Lionel McFadden.

Captain McFadden proved remarkably successful at assembling great piles of supplies that warriors needed and relaying them forward by train and ship to the front lines in France. The war ended, and he unwound the mountain of now surplus supplies so efficiently that one day in August 1920, after twenty-two months of unravelling as much as can be unravelled from a war, he was done. A grateful government gave him two little ribbons for his ribbon bar and three months' pay with his discharge papers.

He quickly discovered two disadvantages of civilian life. Men demobilized immediately after the end of hostilities had secured the pick of the jobs available. Also, the procuring of millions of pieces of military equipment, usually untendered, with unlimited government funds, was not replicated in private industry. Lionel McFadden worked, sequentially, with the large department stores: Ogilvy's and Eaton's and Murphy–Gamble's. Sometimes it took a year to prove he had no command for the cut and thrust of commercial enterprise, sometimes less.

Because of the need to dress the wounds of war, Vera had kept on with her nursing career until she was into her second trimester with Alsa, when she retired to parent. Lionel's inability to draw a steady income eventually forced them into the rundown farmhouse on Rochester Street. In January 1929, Arthur Fields passed away, leaving his daughter Vera a $3,000 inheritance. She purchased the old farmhouse and paid all the bills. There was enough left over to re-shingle the roof, paint everything once, and buy a few pieces of furniture. The money was not spent joyously; it was more like the laying in of supplies for a siege.

The market crash in 1929 took them under. With Frances now almost thirteen, Vera began to seek out shifts at the local hospitals. She began by filling in for nurses on holidays. She eventually found regular work doing the less popular evening and night shifts on the more demanding wards.

Lionel McFadden bore the wounds of this failure with some confusion and embarrassment, but without complaint. Ever a quiet man, he withdrew even more. He did the laundry and cooking and kept house while Vera became the breadwinner.

Frances liked books, and often would join her father reading in the living room when her homework was done. Occasionally, Alsa would spread out on the floor with a movie magazine. Vera McFadden rarely entered the living room. She preferred the big farm kitchen, from which the slap of cards on the pine table was often the only sound in the house.

Frances favoured the novels of Jane Austen, Sir Walter Scott, and Sir Arthur Conan Doyle. Lionel McFadden enjoyed history and biography. Sometimes a historical novel provided a bridge between their separate worlds. Frances relished this warm, collegial intimacy with her father. She would have preferred laughter and physical contact, but knew of parents who were domineering and sometimes violent, so she appreciated what she had.

When Lionel McFadden left to hunt for employment in Toronto, the house seemed surprisingly empty. Mother always ruled the roost, and her father had not filled a large role in family life. Still, he left a silent void, like a chair's footprints on the carpet when furniture is moved. He wrote weekly when he began working at the YMCA, and Vera would pass along the letters to be read by the girls. Within a year, he got a promotion to the St. Louis Y, and, overwhelmed by work, wrote less frequently. Vera would read excerpts from his letters at dinner. Then fewer letters. Then silence, like a disease in the family that could not be spoken of. Alsa's death had drawn only the briefest of notes.

The sun came out again quickly, and Frances walked up to Wellington to catch the streetcar home. She was looking out the window at the Parliament Buildings when a body plunked down beside her.

"Oh! Hi, Frances. How come you're not in school?"

"Hi, Geordie. How come *you're* not in school?"

"Dentist." He held up the appointment card like it was a hall pass. "And you?"

"I quit. I'm out of school for life. Or," she added reflectively, "perhaps I'm into the school *of* life."

Geordie's jaw dropped. If Frances had told him she'd just been arrested for shoplifting, he wouldn't have been more surprised. "What! Weren't you doing fine?"

"I was, but I got offered a job starting tomorrow, so I took it."

Geordie Hilton was in his senior year at Lisgar Collegiate. In three weeks, he was writing his departmentals, hoping to get into the University of Toronto in the fall. Both his parents were university graduates. His older brother was at McGill. He did not number a single high school dropout amongst his acquaintances. Until now.

"But won't you . . . didn't you . . .?" He blushed and sat silently for a minute. Finally he said, "Is this what you wanted all along?"

"It'll do."

"But you're so smart!"

"University was never in the cards."

"It just, you know, it sounds so final," Geordie continued. "To start working. I probably won't begin a career for another four years. I guess you've reached adulthood before me, and me a year older!" he laughed. "Who hired you?"

"I'm going to work in a research office for the new central bank."

"Golly! For the Bank of Canada? That'll be so exciting!"

"Well, you're the first person I know who has even heard of it."

"Dad teaches economics at the University of Ottawa. He's been attending all the public meetings on Parliament Hill. He thinks the Bank of Canada is long overdue."

"Glad to hear it." Frances picked up her packages and stood up. "This is my stop."

"Can I help you carry those home?"

"Your dentist appointment?"

"Oh, right. Well, see you at church."

"See you."

Nice boy, that Geordie Hilton. This should cool his puppy dog fever.

6

BEGINNINGS

Licari's Italian Bakery shared the back fence with the McFadden house. Frances drew the happy aroma of freshly baked bread into her dreams before she awoke. She laughed. She wasn't going to school anymore! She bounced twice on the edge of the bed, and leapt into the day.

In front of the bathroom mirror, Frances paused to take stock. She had an inkling of what office workers looked like from the clusters of permed and lipsticked women who gathered each morning at the streetcar stops along Bronson Avenue. They had always seemed much older and so intentional, with brown paper lunch bags and large, mysterious purses clasped purposefully in nail-polished fingers.

Dorothy Deavy's mature lexicon described Frances as "distinctive." Mary O'Brien was "gorgeous"; however, her body embarrassed her, and she hid beneath careless hair and loose-fitting clothes. Katie Deavy's small features were "cute and perky," and she played this to the hilt. Frances was in between, with one of those precociously adult faces that would change little in forty years. Inquisitive hazel eyes and a broad forehead gave her an air of intelligence and curiosity. She had chestnut hair that bracketed lightly freckled cheeks that she felt were a trifle fat.

Vera McFadden sat in the kitchen smoking a Player's Mild and drinking orange pekoe tea. She looked up nervously when Frances came downstairs. Nervous for herself? Nervous for Frances? Probably just nervous about anything that changed. The stage on which Vera's life was playing out was being swept clean of actors. She had lost Lionel to distance and Alsa to death. Now, suddenly, Frances was exiting into the wings.

"Do you have streetcar fare?"

"I'll walk," Frances said. "It can't be a mile to Queen Street and Elgin."

"What if it rains?" Vera asked, watching smoke from her cigarette drift through the brilliant May sunlight that fell on the kitchen table. Vera saw the climate as malevolently whimsical, and carried an umbrella everywhere, "in case."

"I'll wear a sweater, and take change for the bus if I need it."

"When will you be home? When should I get dinner ready?" These questions were not about supper, but a final scrabble for some scrap of control. Ennui flavoured Vera's recipes for the two of them. She "heated something up," things that were mushy and indistinguishable, served over boiled potatoes or stale bread.

Freedom beckoned, but Frances kept her voice expressionless. "I imagine they will dismiss me at five-thirty or six. I'll find out the hours so you won't have to worry." Vexed, but unworried, Vera glanced up quickly, but Frances did not meet her eye.

Frances walked through the front doorway of the Blackburn Building at 8:22 a.m. according to the wall clock in the lobby. The elevator girl—a woman, really—in a navy uniform and white gloves sized her up when Frances asked for the fourth floor.

"There's only construction workmen up there," she declared, with that "Gotcha, sister!" look in her eye.

Frances looked directly at her for several seconds before stepping to the back of the elevator. "That's right," she said.

White Gloves slammed the sliding cage gate shut and the elevator shot up. They lurched to a stop after the short ascent, and she slammed the gate open again. "Fourth floor," she sang out, eyes front.

Frances followed the sound of hammering down the hall. She turned through an open doorway into a scene of dust and ladders and hanging wires. Two men on a scaffold were installing new glass in a large skylight that ran the length of an outer office. Another was trowelling plaster on the long wall to the right. She could see Dr. Grace through an open doorway to the left with a squat man in paint-spattered overalls. Frances approached them obliquely through the din.

"I can't promise nothin', Dr. Grace. I got two men off bad sick."

"Curious," said Dr. Grace, without sarcasm, "that in the Depression, help is hard to find."

The small man looked up over his glasses. "Good help, Mr. Grace, is always hard to find."

"Not for me," said Dr. Grace. "Frances, my agent of deliverance, my Joan of Arc, meet Mr. Boyle. He is in charge of dust and disruption."

Frances nodded to the skeptical Mr. Boyle, who nodded briefly before returning to his workmen. Dr. Grace directed Frances through a connecting doorway into a smaller office, where two wooden boxes lay on either side of a card table. A telephone sat on the windowsill.

"Step into my office, Frances, and we'll plan the financial security of the country, while young Boyle builds our headquarters."

Frances regarded everyone over twenty in the general category of "adult," but "young Boyle" was old enough to be Dr. Grace's father. Dr. Grace looked around proudly, through the construction debris and dirt, and said: "Well, what do you think?"

Frances liked Dr. Grace. He brimmed with optimism, embracing the challenge of chaos like a resolute captain on the bridge of a storm-tossed frigate. She had never experienced the like either at home or at school.

"Well," said Frances, "if our country needs us, we should get to work."

"Bravo!" said Dr. Grace. "I knew you were a fighter the second you attacked the daffodils at the Château Laurier!"

He sat down on one of the crates, directing Frances to the other one. "I'll be travelling quite a bit, so it is going to be up to you to put things in order here. Do you have a notepad?" Frances had not thought to bring one, and suddenly realized that she had forgotten to pack a lunch as well.

Dr. Grace handed her pen and paper from his briefcase. "Your first job is to get the steam up in young Boyle's pipes, or get rid of him. He and his merry band have been loitering here for two weeks, with next to nothing to show for it."

"You want me to fire Mr. Boyle?"

"Well, all my wailing and gnashing of teeth has had no visible effect on his progress. You have to work here full time, so you have to decide how long you want him as an office mate. Let's have a quick reconnoitre of the place."

The lengthy outer office was surprisingly bright thanks to the long skylight. Four smaller offices opened along the outside wall. The corner office had windows facing west and south. The rest of the offices were not as wide, but the same depth, and each had a large double window. At the far end of the outer office was an archway into a narrow hall. Through it to the right were shelves above a counter, and cupboards underneath. At the end was a vault big enough to walk into. To the left across the archway, the hallway opened into a square space with a sink, lit by a smaller skylight. Off this were two washrooms, side by side, marked "Ladies" and "Men." A plumber was working in the Ladies'.

When the plumber saw Frances and Dr. Grace, he shook his head. "What a mess. Filthy, water damage, rotten wood. And stink!"

Dr. Grace grimaced, and they retreated back to his office card table. "The previous tenants must have kept wild buffalo up here. No wonder we got it so cheap."

"Do we need all this space?"

"Well," replied Dr. Grace, "I need an office, mostly to hide from the soul-sucking vampires in the Finance Department, so I can actually get some work done. They keep press-ganging me into endless meetings. We need a meeting room. You need an office. We must have someone fluent in French who can do translation with fairly complicated material. How's your French?"

"Well, I was passing Grade 11 French, but no one would mistake me for bilingual."

"A third of Canadians use French as their mother tongue, so we absolutely need a first-class translator. You'll need an assistant to help with typing and filing."

Frances stopped writing. "And what will this file clerk be filing? What are we actually going to be doing here?"

Dr. Grace smacked himself on the forehead. "How thoughtless! What we have to do, Frances, is set up an archive of information so that the new Central Bank governor has background resources at hand immediately on his appointment."

"Won't the new governor be a banker? Why does he need a resource library?"

"The new governor will certainly have banking experience, but he will be some British Lord Fauntleroy who will know little about the Canadian economy or who the major players are."

"Why would they appoint a British lord to head a central bank in Canada?"

"It is certainly not my idea, Frances, but Canadians seem to have a sense of inferiority when it comes to the world stage. There is a tragic assumption that no native is capable of real first-rate work. It drives me to distraction."

The phone rang. Dr. Grace looked over at Frances, who took a deep breath and answered on the third ring.

"Good morning," she said, apprehensively. "Bank of Canada. May I help you?"

Dr. Grace leaned back and beamed.

"One moment, please. I'll see if he's in." The conspirators smiled and she passed the phone over.

"Grace here," he said confidently. His face fell immediately.

"Yes, sir! Absolutely, sir. It was a delivery girl, sir. Poor thing was just trying to be helpful. Shall I have her fired, sir? As you wish, sir. It won't happen again, sir. Yes. I'm leaving for Toronto on the noon train. I know you did, sir, but it was the first train I could get. I will call immediately when I return Monday. Thank you, sir. And you too, sir." He hung up the phone and burst out laughing.

"That was the aptly named Mr. Crossman, the assistant deputy Minister of Finance. He called to bawl me out for not being in Toronto yet." He slapped his knee as if being dressed down by a mandarin was the most humorous possible way to start the day. "Oh, and we are *not* the Bank of Canada, he forcefully reminded me. The Bank of Canada doesn't exist until the charter legislation passes the House of Commons."

"So who are we, then?"

"Frances, Frances, Frances. If you are going to be successful in the nation's capital, you need to thrive on ambiguity. However, even if we're only in business for eight to ten months, we still need a name for our little organization here for the bank account, letterhead, et cetera." Dr. Grace pursed his lips reflectively. "It has to sound official, to impress those who aren't official, but it can't sound as though it has anything to do with the government of Canada."

"How about the Canadian National Banking Archives?"

"CNBA? Not bad, but CN might get confused with the CNR — Canadian National Railways. Also, I'd prefer to avoid using the word 'banking.' Far too accurate. It would make Canadian bankers very apprehensive. We need something a little vaguer."

Frances was scribbling word combinations. "How about Canadian . . . Financial . . . Resources . . . Archives?"

"CFRA? I like it, Miss McFadden! But 'archives' sounds too dead and dusty. No one will return phone messages to an archive. How about 'Agency'? Canadian Financial Resources Agency? CFRA? Sounds impressive, yet delightfully vague and mysterious. Good enough?"

"Good enough. Why wouldn't the Department of Finance look after these details?"

"The Department of Finance favours the concept of the Bank of Canada, but they are very nervous about Dr. Wilbur Grace's little fly-by-night emporium here."

"Then who . . .?"

"Certain parties, of course," smiled Dr. Grace. "The Department of Finance is filled with wonderful, hard-working people, but they do everything by the book. To their credit, this is generally a good idea in government. They are horrified that I'm setting up this office to get a jump on things."

"Are we illegal, then?"

"We are within the law, but not part of the law. Think of it this way, Frances. Canada wouldn't need a police force or a court system if there were no criminals. However, knowing the weakness of mankind in general, the government hires policemen and judges. It is prudent to be ready for crime, even if you don't desire that it take place. We, too, are part of the prudence team.

"It's a tangled web, indeed. I'd rather not get into the sordid details. It's not that I don't trust you. Trust can be a burden, however, and I don't wish to add that to your load on the first day. Let's just say that I don't get *all* of my instructions from the Department of Finance, even though technically that is the body I report to."

"Don't they mind your taking orders from someone else?"

"Frances, Frances, Frances! You are a veritable bloodhound! All will out in time. The startling truth is that the Department of Finance needs me more than I need the Department of Finance. This dramatically changes the normally dynamic governing employer-employee relationships."

"I don't understand. Why did they hire you, if not to follow their directions?"

"Truthfully? They hired me out of fear. They did not have any PhDs in Economics working for them, and the economy is in ruins. I think Finance Department officials feel higher education is a waste of time, but with disasters on every economic front, they hired me as a sort of insurance policy. They had no confidence that I could help the situation, but at least they could say 'See, we hired an expert, and even *he* couldn't solve the problem.'

"I persuaded them to set up a Royal Commission on Banking and Currency last year to look into the country's economic problems. It meant they could put off making any decision for a while. So they appointed me secretary to Lord Macmillan's Royal Commission, and since then I have been meeting with bankers, businessmen, and politicians to draft the legislation."

The phone rang, and again Frances picked it up. "Canadian Financial Resources Agency," she said, winking at Dr. Grace. "May I help you? One moment please, I'll see if he's in." She handed the receiver over. "It's a Mr. Birchall."

"Hello? Ah, Mr. Birchall! We were just talking about our account with you. My . . . my chief administrative officer will be right over to sign all the papers. She and I will share the heavy paperwork until the Central Bank legislation is passed and the governor appointed. Her name's McFadden. She's my '2-IC' as they used to say in the army. We can come over now if you can get everything ready. I'm leaving for Toronto on the noon train, but McFadden can handle details. See you shortly. Goodbye."

Frances looked stunned. "I'm the second in command at the Bank of Canada? I don't even have a bank account."

7

BIRCHALL AT
THE BANK OF MONTREAL

D r. Grace started packing up his briefcase. "You'll like young Birchall . . ."

"As much as young Boyle?"

"Ho ho! You're quick, McFadden. Birchall's the manager at the main branch of the Bank of Montreal on Wellington Street. We've worked on some committees together. He is cut of the sturdy blue gabardine of generations of bankers. A little fussy, but fussy isn't a bad characteristic for someone who is handling your money.

"Speaking of which, I have a cashier's cheque here from the Privy Council office for ten thousand dollars. That should get us started. Here, you look after it. I lose everything. I just have to check the plumbing and we can go."

Frances clutched the cheque. Ten thousand dollars! The Deavys rented their home for forty dollars a month. This could pay their rent for twenty years. Her change purse seemed suddenly vulnerable. She had no pockets. Then she remembered Mae West in *Shanghai Train*. When Clark Gable gave her his last hundred dollars for safekeeping, she had tucked it into her cleavage. Mae West had considerably more to work with, thought Frances, as she slid the cheque inside her brassiere.

Dr. Grace returned and put on his suit jacket. "Let's use the big corner office as a meeting room. It should seat eight to ten around a conference table. I'll take the connecting office. What about you? You're the boss. Where's your space?"

"I should be right out here near the hall door. I can direct traffic and keep an eye on things. We could put the translator in the third office and the file clerk in the fourth."

"How about storage? We'll need at least twenty four-drawer filing cabinets to keep track of all the paper."

"Twenty?"

"At least. Probably closer to thirty. Yeah, get thirty. All of the material from Lord Macmillan's commission is piled up in boxes over at the

Finance Ministry. They want it out of there. And all of the committee files related to the current legislation need a home. We'll need a filing cabinet for each of the ten Canadian chartered banks. And we need to build files on the central banks of at least a dozen countries."

"Does each need a four-drawer filing cabinet?"

"Sure. We'll want background on how they were set up, annual reports dating back twenty years, organizational structure, government fiscal policy, information on major private charter banks, exchange rate history, et cetera. A filing cabinet fills up quickly."

"We could put a row of filing cabinets right there against the inner wall. Close but out of the way."

"Fine. Then order the furniture to outfit the offices. Oh, and get a small icebox. We can keep it in that alcove back by the bathroom. I need fresh milk for my morning coffee, and ice is essential for afternoon meetings. Get a hot plate, some dishes and cutlery. Good, but not fancy. Young Crossman up in Finance will want detailed accounts of every nickel we spend. Doesn't trust a soul, which I suppose is good for the Canadian taxpayer. Oh! You need a contract. What are you getting paid?"

Frances laughed. "You hired me! What were you planning to pay me?"

Dr. Grace smiled sheepishly. "Do you see why I needed a—what did I call you—a chief administrative officer so badly? I don't do details well. What do you think you should get paid?"

"I don't know! I've never had a job before, other than babysitting for Mrs. Dubrofski. She paid me fifteen cents an hour."

Dr. Grace laughed. "I think we can do better than that. Tell you what. Phone a bank and a couple of offices and ask them what they pay their administrative staff. Then write me a five-sentence report on what you should be paid. We'll make an informed decision. Crossman will be delighted."

"Why would a company tell me what their employees are paid? Isn't that confidential?"

"Normally, but, remember! You're conducting a survey on behalf of the Bank-of-Canada-to-be. It will be kept confidential if they co-operate. If they don't co-operate, they can be called before the Finance Committee of the House of Commons to see what they're hiding. They're probably hiding a lot more than the salary of their head secretary. And they don't want to waste their time testifying before parliamentary committees.

"Now, on to young Birchall."

They rang for the elevator. When White Gloves opened the elevator cage door for them, Dr. Grace extended his hand in greeting. "Good morning, Miss—"

"Stanton," said White Gloves, a little startled by the proffered hand. "Stella Stanton." She shook his hand limply.

"My name is Wilbur Grace, and I'm pleased to make your acquaintance, Miss Stanton. I've only been to the new office a few times. I come in the rear door and take the back stairs to help keep fit. This is my colleague, Miss McFadden. Have you met? We'll all be seeing quite a lot of each other."

This was all news to White Gloves. Frances hesitated. "We met this morning, Dr. Grace, but were not formally introduced." She extended her hand. "How do you do, Miss Stanton. I'm Frances McFadden."

Stella Stanton seemed unaccustomed to polite society or formal introductions. She thought that maybe she was being put on, but wasn't exactly sure, so she limply shook hands again. On the ground floor, the elevator cage door did not crash open quite so insolently.

Dr. Grace had long legs and marched like a man with a mission. Frances had to scurry to keep up with him. "Now, Frances, did I notice a certain coolness there during the introductions with Miss Stanton?"

"Miss Stanton was needlessly rude to me this morning when I arrived, and I suppose I responded in kind," she confessed.

"What happened?"

Frances explained. "So she slammed the elevator gate closed, and slammed it open on the fourth floor to get the last kick in." Frances giggled. "Kind of silly, isn't it?"

"Silly indeed, Frances, but we need to patch this up immediately. The Bank of Canada is unborn and friendless in this wide world. We need every ally we can get.

"Here's my read on Stella Stanton. School dropout from a poor Irish Lowertown family. Probably making more money as an elevator operator than anyone in her family has ever made. Wants to marry someone with a steady job and raise a family. She could be very helpful to us, don't you think?"

Frances thought. "Well, she'll meet everybody who comes looking for us. She'd know the scuttlebutt on all the tradesmen. That could be helpful."

"Precisely! Also, if we're away, she can take messages and deliveries for us—if she is so disposed. Or, she can direct thirty filing cabinets halfway across town, if she is not. So, as soon as I get young Birchall on the team, you go right back there and win Miss Stanton over. A deal?"

"A deal," Frances conceded uneasily.

"The very best way to win someone to your side," Dr. Grace continued, "is to throw yourself on their mercy and ask for help. Then they don't need to fight you for the catbird seat. It works every time. Watch."

The new art deco Bank of Montreal on Wellington Street had lofty ceilings and elegant stands of windows. Dr. Grace led Frances to a corner office at the rear. The door was open and the bank manager waved them in. Mr. Birchall was quite handsome for a bank manager, thought Frances, who had never met a single bank manager in her life. He had a robust, outdoorsy look to him behind a trim moustache. "Grace! Good to see you again."

" 'Morning, Mr. Birchall. This is Miss McFadden, my associate at the new office."

"Pleased to meet you, Miss McFadden.

"So, Grace, how are the committee meetings going?"

"We are making haste slowly, but the momentum is unstoppable. Legislation should be before the House for a final vote by early July, and then we're up and running. Which brings me to our business here. I've been instructed to set up a research office in advance of the Bank of Canada's charter being issued. We don't want to be a year behind on the day we open for business."

"Capital idea! How can I help?" He offered Dr. Grace a cigar from a humidor on his desk. They both lit up, and collegial clouds of smoke billowed in the May sun.

"We need an operating account. We cannot of course call our new outfit The Bank of Canada yet, because it doesn't exist. So we plan to call ourselves the Canadian Financial Resources Agency, or CFRA. We would like to set up a double signature account here under that name. We'll need some office cheques printed immediately."

"Certainly. Where will your start-up funding come from?"

"You know Richard Crossman in the Finance Department? He set it up with a government cashier's cheque payable to me for ten thousand dollars."

Mr. Birchall whistled. "A personal cheque from Crossman?"

"Yes, well, Mr. Crossman was under orders from a higher authority, or he would never have been so cavalier. I suggest you phone him to show you're checking up on me, and to reassure him that I haven't skipped down to Rio with the swag."

Mr. Birchall laughed so hard that he choked on the cigar smoke. When he recovered, he pressed a buzzer on his desk, and a clerk in a gartered shirt and a green eyeshade came in. "Mr. Nutley, we need to set up a double signature account for the Canadian Financial Resources Agency—the CFRA. Can you get the paperwork going, and the authorization forms?"

Nutley nodded.

"Immediately?"

Nutley vanished.

"Now who will sign for the CFRA?" asked Mr. Birchall, clearing the ash from his cigar.

"Why, McFadden and I, of course," replied Mr. Grace.

Mr. Birchall eyed Frances carefully, in her finest schoolgirl clothes. Properly dressed with her hair done up, Frances might have passed for nineteen. In her kilt skirt and knee socks, she looked exactly like a seventeen-year-old. He puffed quietly for a moment. "Of course, a signing officer legally has to be of the age of majority," he said obliquely, addressing the cigar smoke.

"Mr. Birchall," replied Dr. Grace with a reassuring smile, "the highest government authorities have entrusted me with getting the wheels moving on the Bank of Canada. They do not wish to waste another second. McFadden and I are the entire staff of the CFRA. Double signature is a government requirement on all accounts. Quite prudent, I'm sure you'll agree. The Bank of Montreal holds the Canadian government account, and it seems appropriate that this additional honour should be yours."

There was a long pause. Mr. Birchall bit his lip and frowned at the floral pattern in the carpet.

"If, however, you would prefer that we take this ten thousand to another banking house, we will," added Mr. Grace, playing with the bait. "We need to start work today. Can you accommodate us?"

Mr. Birchall looked at Frances. Ten thousand dollars represented three times his annual salary. He took a long draw on his cigar.

"Mr. Birchall," coaxed Dr. Grace, "I admire your work. You are a credit to the Bank of Montreal. We want you as our banker. Do you want us?"

Mr. Birchall blew out three perfect smoke rings. He re-crossed his legs and leaned back away from them both. Dr. Grace looked anxious for the first time. Charm wasn't working, threats weren't working. He needed something concrete for a closer. Then, he smiled.

"Miss McFadden, can you show Mr. Birchall the cheque?"

The cheque? The cheque hidden in my brassiere?

"Certainly, sir," said Frances. As she put her notes down on a side table, she pointed to a large oil painting of a lake in fall foliage on the office wall.

"That is such a beautiful painting, Mr. Birchall! Is it your own work?"

Dr. Grace turned to appraise the artwork behind him, and Mr. Birchall jumped up and went over to it. "Do you like it? It's my wife's canvas. Painted at our cabin up in the Gatineau Hills. She studied art at the Royal Academy in England for two years. She's had a few shows in Toronto and Montreal, but hasn't sold much. She thinks her style is too bold for Canadian tastes."

"The colours are so uplifting!" said Frances. "What do you think, Dr. Grace? Could we acquire a few pieces of Mrs. Birchall's work for our new offices?"

Dr. Grace turned to stare at Frances, eyes blinking. "An excellent idea, Miss McFadden! Mr. Birchall, can you ask your wife to show us more of her work?"

Mr. Birchall was beside himself. "Be delighted!" he beamed, returning to his seat. Frances handed him the government cheque. He looked at the signatures and shook his head in wonder. Then, holding his cigar at a jaunty angle, said, "Grace, I'll need something on file. Would you mind giving me a statement of intent and direction concerning the CFRA signing officers?"

"Certainly!" exclaimed Dr. Grace with a broad smile. "Could you draft it up quickly? The noon train waits for no man, and McFadden needs operating capital in my absence."

Again the buzzer sounded, twice this time, and both Nutley and a woman in wire-rimmed glasses appeared at the door.

This time, Mr. Birchall performed introductions.

"Mr. Nutley, our chief accountant, and Miss Hicks, my personal secretary, let me introduce Dr. Grace from the newly minted Canadian Financial Resources Agency, and his chief administrative officer, Miss McFadden. They are setting up a rather large business account, with this cheque as an initial deposit." He handed it to Nutley, whose eyes widened. "They need a dozen blank cheques ready today. Have you got the paperwork, Nutley?"

A neat file was presented to the manager.

"Thank you, Nutley. Can you get those cheques prepared? Dr. Grace has a train to catch. Oh, and petty cash—do you need any?"

"A hundred dollars should do us for the time being," said Dr. Grace.

"One hundred it is, then, Nutley. Miss Hicks, can you draft a memo in duplicate for us? It should say: 'The signing officers for the Canadian Financial Resources Agency are Dr. Wilbur Grace and Miss Frances McFadden. Due diligence has been observed in the appointment of these officials.' And leave space for the two signatures. Thank you, Miss Hicks. Can we have that right away?"

By the time the official papers had been signed, Mr. Nutley was back with a starter set of cheques and a promise to order two hundred more from the printer. He handed one hundred dollars to Frances, who decided her change purse would do for such a paltry sum.

Miss Hicks returned with the memorandum. Having duly signed, Dr. Grace rose. "Mr. Birchall, always a pleasure working with you. McFadden, here, will deal with Nutley or Miss Hicks from now on and keep out of your way. Have your wife contact McFadden about a viewing of her art. I must go. I'll keep you apprised of progress on the Hill."

"Thank you, Grace. Good day, Miss McFadden."

When they were safely on the street, Frances asked, "What is the age of majority?"

"The age at which you can legally do business."

"What age is that?"

"In Canada, it's twenty-one years."

"But—"

"Frances," Dr. Grace cut in, "I always want you to tell me the truth. I will always tell you the truth, in return. There will be some things about which I may be curious, but I will not ask, because I need to *not* know the answer. Understand?"

Frances was silent.

"We have been ordered to get the archives up and running at once. It is our duty not to delay an instant. We will be as pleasant as possible, but it may occasionally be necessary to overlook some niceties of process. Clear?"

"Absolutely, sir." Frances paused for a few seconds. "Is this what they call fraud? Will we go to jail?"

Dr. Grace burst out laughing. "Frances, we are going to have such fun working together! You look after the office, and I'll look after keeping us out of jail."

"Yes, sir."

"I will phone you every morning at 8:30 a.m. to check in. I expect to return to Ottawa Monday afternoon. Carry on! Oh—that pitch for Mrs. Birchall's artwork was a stroke of genius! He was slipping away and you hooked him. Next, go get Stella Stanton."

He waved a merry farewell as he marched down Wellington Street to the train station.

8

LUNCH WITH STELLA

When Frances came through the back door of the lobby, Stella Stanton was standing in a small alcove between the back stairs and the elevator, out of sight of the front door, reading a magazine and smoking.

Frances took a deep breath. "Miss Stanton, can you help me? This is my first day on the job here, and I forgot my sandwich. Could you recommend an inexpensive lunch spot?"

Stella Stanton took a long drag on her cigarette and looked Frances over.

"Miss Stanton," she stammered, "I apologize if I appeared rude this morning. This is my first day on my first job, and I'm quite nervous. I'm sorry if I offended you."

The elevator operator squished her cigarette into the sand ashtray. Finally, she said, "Okay, kid. Call me Stella. I eat lunch either at the Honey Dew on Sparks Street, or at Cairncross's Drug Store around the corner. My lunch break is in twenty minutes. Ya wanna come along?"

"Oh Miss Sta . . . Stella, thank you! I'll be back in twenty minutes." She turned to walk up the stairs.

"Kid! You trying to put me out of a job? Hop in." She jerked her head toward the empty elevator. Frances followed her into the cage, and the elevator door closed with a gentle flick of her hand. "Where to, ma'am?" she asked.

The Honey Dew was crowded, and they had to circle twice before they found a booth. "What are you and the professor doing up in the old Alliance office? Those guys were a wild bunch, let me tell ya."

"I know practically nothing. This Dr. Grace hired me on Tuesday right out of Grade 11 at the High School of Commerce. I'm going to be a secretary for some kind of a bank office."

"You gonna run a bank up there?"

"No. As I understand it, some new bank is going to be created by Parliament, and we have to begin getting background files ready so it can start up quickly. It's going to regulate the economy or something. So it's more like an office than a bank. We're not going to have tellers and wickets. By the way, who was in that office before us? They sure left it a mess."

"Alliance Business Forms was up there for years. They used to have parties on payday — every second Friday. The ball usually got rolling at lunchtime. I went to a couple, but it was too wild for me."

Stella sipped spoonfuls of soup. She had a pretty face, but there were dark circles under her eyes, and an inch-long red scar low on her left cheek. When she laughed you could see she was missing a left upper molar. Frances wondered how wild "too wild for Stella Stanton" would have to be.

"Anyhow, one day they're there, the next day, poof, they're gone. Heard they were six months behind on the rent. I guess with companies going broke left and right, there isn't much call for business forms."

"Who's in the other office on the fourth floor?"

"Harmer Property Management. Three guys and two secretaries. They're all at some convention in Montreal for a couple of days, or you'da seen 'em. They look after a bunch of buildings in Ottawa, including ours. They like to joke around, but they're not wild like that Alliance crowd." She shook her head. "I could tell you stories that you would not believe, kid."

"And the rest of the building?"

"This and that. An insurance company, some accountants, a travel agency, little cigar store off the lobby. That's it."

"How long have you worked at the Blackburn Building?"

"Coming up two years in September. Longest I've ever been in one place. Before that, I worked a buncha sales jobs around town, but I'm no good with snotty people. If they didn't like the merchandise, they'd start givin' me lip, and I've got the Irish temper, so I'd give it right back. Then boom, I'm fired.

"Oh, and my cash never balanced." She snorted. "I wasn't stealin' money, I swear to God, but I could not get it to balance for love or money." She grinned and lowered her voice. "And I tried both!

"So, the elevator business suits me. No books to balance, and not much chance to get snotty, just 'third floor, fourth floor, lobby.' Although you came pretty close this morning, kid." Stella smirked and lit a cigarette. She offered the pack to Frances, who shook her head. "Funny to think that I'm thin-skinned about some things. Most things, I'm tough as nails. It can be boring sometimes, but I got my mags and my smokes, and I make it through." She changed the topic. "You got a boyfriend?"

"Me? Oh no. My mother thinks I'm too young. She thinks boys only want one thing."

Stella blew a narrow jet of smoke out the side of her mouth. "Your mother's right about that. How old are you, kid?"

"Seventeen."

"I'd been pregnant twice by the time I was seventeen. Lost 'em both before I was even showing. Damn lucky. The ol' man would have killed me for bringin' disgrace on the family." Stella snorted again. "He's one to talk. Drinks up every nickel that comes into the house, then gets into a stinking black rage. Smashes dishes and anybody who ain't quick enough to duck. If my mother had any choice, she'da left him long ago."

"Do you have any brothers and sisters?"

"My older brother Frankie is in the Kingston Pen. Armed robbery. He was always nice to me. Hid me when the old man got pissed up. I visited Frankie in the Nicholas Street jail, where they held him before the trial. He claimed he didn't do it, but he hung with a tough bunch—ya heard of the Brewster Gang?—and I wouldn't put it past that crowd. He would never rat on a buddy, though, even if it meant doin' time in the slammer.

"Three younger kids at home. Bridget and Colleen and Danny. That's why I work, really, to keep bread on the table for them." Stella checked her wristwatch. "Jeez! Gotta scram."

They walked quickly back to the Blackburn Building. "This guy who's fixing up our office, this Mr. Boyle, you know him?" asked Frances.

"Seen him around the last two weeks. Never seen him before that. How's he doing?"

"Well, he's not getting much done. Dr. Grace is concerned with the delay. Do you know any other tradesmen?"

"Sure. What do you need? Carpenters? Plumbers?"

"I think that stuff is almost finished. The place has to be cleaned top to bottom and then painted. Mr. Boyle was supposed to do that, too, but he's slower than molasses."

Stella thought for a minute. "You mind hiring Chinks?"

"Who?"

"Chinks. Chinese. Only guy I know in that line of work is Huey Foo. Runs a restaurant down on Dalhousie. He's got a crew that moonlights doing cleaning and painting evenings and weekends. But they're all Chinks. Every last one of them."

"Are they good?"

"Good? Listen. Chinks know clean! They run every laundry in town."

"How can I get in touch?"

"Bluebird Café on Dalhousie. It's in the phone book. Ask for Huey."

Frances left Stella at the door to the Blackburn Building and walked down to Hay Stationary to stock up on office supplies. An attentive clerk directed her to their selection of the latest typewriters. She tried out several, but liked the quiet Remington Select the best. It was, however, the most expensive, and she couldn't decide.

Back in the office, Frances called the Bluebird Café and left a message for Huey Foo to call back. She checked the Yellow Pages for printers and called Ottawa Printing Supplies, which had a big ad.

"Yeah?" asked the gruff voice that answered the phone.

"Hello. I'd like to order some office supplies," said Frances.

"Whaddaya need?" demanded the voice.

"Well, I'm not sure. It's a new office and I don't exactly know what we need."

"Well, I ain't no fortune teller, lady. Don't waste my time till ya gotta list." The line went dead.

A little shaken, Frances made a list and tried Premium Printers, whose ad stated that they "served government offices and the professional trade." The lady that answered was polite until she heard the size of the printing order. "Oh, no," she laughed. "We don't even set a press up for less than five thousand items. Small orders are just not worth our time. We cater to the trade. Good-day." Click.

Frances felt the rejections like a sledgehammer. She looked out the dirty window for a few minutes, then took a deep breath and tried Imperial Printing in LeBreton Flats.

"Hello," she said tentatively. "I'd like to get a quote on a small printing order."

"Sure. What do you need and when do you need it?"

"I need two sets of business cards, some letterhead typing paper, and business envelopes. I need it all as soon as possible."

"Yeah, yeah, everybody does. You want it this afternoon?"

"Well, no; how about late next week?"

"Probably can do that. How big a run do you want? How many

cards? How many envelopes? How many colours? What bond card stock and paper?"

"I need to run your questions past my boss tomorrow morning. I'll get back to you by ten a.m."

Frances spent the afternoon on the phone. It wasn't exactly like the exercises in her old Business Practice course. She got cut off several times and put on hold once for almost ten minutes before she hung up and tried another number. It was very confusing. Office furniture could be bought new or used, but could not be rented. Typewriters and adding machines could be bought new or used or rented. If you bought, the seller paid for transportation. If you rented, you paid. There were too many choices.

About four o'clock, she remembered that Mr. Deavy was the sales manager at Yeoman's Used Furniture. He always talked to her like an adult, especially about politics. He was a staunch socialist and belonged to the CCF. Dorothy and Katie rolled their eyes when their father got political, but Frances listened attentively.

"Mr. Deavy? It's Frances McFadden. Fine, and yourself, sir? Yes. I started work today. We're just moving into a new office, and it's completely empty. I need to furnish the place—chairs and desks and filing cabinets.

"Well, that's part of the problem—this is a temporary office. We'll only be here ten months or so. Should I buy furniture or rent it? It's for the government. I need to account for every cent.

"Okay. I'll sketch out a floor plan and bring it over. I'll be there by five-fifteen."

Frances had a headache. She suffered occasionally from migraines when under pressure. The dust and construction noise in the office didn't help. She drew a layout of the place and made a list.

Yeoman's Used Furniture was in the Byward Market on Cumberland Street. Frances poked chair seats and tried desk drawers as she worked her way down toward Mr. Deavy's office at the back of the narrow store. She handed him the list.

"Okay, Frances, you said you wanted 'good,' but not 'best.' Solid and functional, but short-term. My advice? Buy good-quality used. It's often as good as new. Most stores will buy the whole kaboodle back when you're done with it. At a discount, of course.

"Have a look around. The price is marked on everything. Half of our second floor is filled with filing cabinets. We have all kinds of tables and desks and chairs. You don't have to buy from us, of course, but you'll get a sense of the cost.

"Larry!" he called to a young red-headed clerk just passing his door. "This is Miss McFadden, and she has a shopping list. Can you show her some good deals in the mid-price range? And no flirting on company time, Larry." Larry blushed to the roots, and cracked his shin on an open drawer as he fumbled his clipboard.

Much of the used furniture looked brand-new. There were some twenty filing cabinets that were still wrapped in heavy shipping paper from the factory. Where she expressed interest, Larry would put a dot on the price tag, and record the inventory number and price.

In half an hour, they were done. "Okay, Larry, what's the damage?" Larry disappeared into an office and she could hear the cha-ching of a mechanical adding machine. When he emerged, he said, "Seven hundred and thirty-six dollars, delivered."

It sounded like a lot of money. Frances wondered if the price was open to negotiation, but she did not wish Mr. Deavy to think her ungrateful.

"Any luck?" he asked.

"Larry was most helpful," Frances said with a smile.

"He didn't misbehave?"

"A perfect gentleman and a credit to Yeoman's Furniture."

Larry squirmed and stepped into a wastepaper basket attempting to escape.

"I'll have to put the list to Dr. Grace tomorrow morning. We have a tight budget."

Mr. Deavy looked at Larry's price list and whistled. "I'll talk to the boss. We might be able to do a little better for such a big order."

"Thanks! I'll get back to you by ten a.m. How does your delivery system work?"

"We can usually get an order out to you on twenty-four hour's notice. It would come C.O.D. You pay the driver."

"Fine. We don't need it yet. The office is still being renovated. Oh, I forgot. Do you have typewriters?"

"We have some, but they're pretty scruffy. Treat yourself and buy something new. Any store will give you a one-year guarantee on a new machine, and free service."

"This is swell of you, Mr. Deavy!" said Frances, shaking his hand. "Say hi to the girls for me."

9

FRIDAY

Frances was wide awake by five-thirty Friday morning. She break-fasted quietly so as not to wake her mother and was at the Blackburn Building by six-thirty. The front door was locked. She walked down the lane off Elgin Street and found the back door locked as well. She noticed what looked like a doorbell near the top left-hand corner of the door frame and pushed it. A faint static buzzing eminated from within the building. She was turning to leave when she heard a bolt being pulled back and the door creak open. Two bloodshot eyes in an unshaven face stared out at her.

"Whaddaya want?" barked a hoarse voice.

"Oh, hello. I'm Frances McFadden, and I just started work here yesterday. On the fourth floor. Can I get into my office, Mr. . . . .?"

Dark, hooded eyes looked her over. The door inched further open, to reveal a gaunt man in dirty coveralls. "Helluva mess up there. I'm not wasting my time cleaning that hall till those workmen are out of there."

Frances squeezed in between the man and the doorframe, past the stench of sweat. "Thank you, sir. Are you the custodian?"

"Stationary Engineer. Night shift. These bastards make me swab down the halls, too. Told Kinkade it was dangerous leaving that boiler unattended. He don't give a shit if the building blows up."

"Well, I hope it doesn't blow up today," said Frances with a brief smile before heading up the back stairs.

The phone rang at 8:31.

"Good morning. Canadian Financial Resources Agency. May I help you?"

"Well, good morning from Toronto. How's business in the nation's capital?"

"I've been here since six-thirty, but I almost had to break in. For some reason they lock the building at night."

"How thoughtless. Did you jimmy the door, or scale the side of the building?"

"Some very strange man crawled out of the basement hoping to shoo me away. He claimed to be the stationary engineer."

"You doubted him?"

"Well, the 'stationary' part threw me. I thought engines normally moved, and that was why they required engineers to drive them."

"You've been watching too many movies. Train engines move. Other engines, like power stations, or steel mills or building furnaces, have moving parts, but they don't travel anywhere. Hence stationary engineers."

"Anyhow, peculiar guy, but he let me in."

"Have you seen anybody in the Harmer office?"

"No. Stella said they were all at a conference in Montreal until Monday."

"Well, on Monday, look up Ken Kinkade. I set up the lease through him. Ask for a key to the outside door and a couple more office keys. How did things go with Miss Stanton?"

"We lunched at the Honey Dew and have arrived at a much better understanding."

"Good! She will be most helpful as undercover agent number one for the CFRA. Anything else?"

Frances ran through the office furniture options and the price list.

"Sounds good. Close the deal. How about delivery?"

"We need to get Mr. Boyle out of here and have the place cleaned up first."

"How long will that take?"

"Not much happened yesterday afternoon. The skylight, plastering, and bathrooms are finished. The place is still disgustingly dirty. I'm getting an outside quote on cleanup and painting. If I get a good price and they can start right away, it's so long Mr. Boyle."

"Excellent plan."

"What would be a good price for cleaning and painting?"

"It's a big office. I'd say one hundred and fifty dollars would be fair."

"Okay. Now, Mr. Deavy at Yeoman's Used Furniture told me we'd be safer buying new typewriters with a service warranty than the old clunkers he had for resale. I checked out several models."

"And?"

"The top-line Remington Select is just a dream but it's more expensive."

"How much more?"

"They were thirty dollars, and the Underwoods and the Smith Coronas were closer to twenty."

"Get three Remingtons."

"Three?"

"Might as well have everyone working on the same machines. You're going to be working your tails off. Should have good equipment. What's next?"

"Telephones. We have one line right now."

"Get four separate lines put in. Have them come in through a switchboard at your desk, so you can screen calls."

"Do they make a four-line switchboard?"

"You pay them enough money, they'll make anything."

"You want me to screen your calls?"

"Absolutely. If I'm hiding there to get some work done."

"Now, stationery. After several misadventures, I finally spoke with a very nice lady at Imperial Printing. She asked me a bunch of questions about types of paper and ink colours before she could quote me a price."

"Get something that stands out a bit, so a guy getting twenty letters in the morning mail will open ours first."

"What do you want on your business card? Just Doctor Grace with phone number and address?"

"No. Wilbur K. Grace, Ph.D. Most people think that doctor means real doctor. I don't want people calling me up for a ruptured appendix."

"What title do you want under your name? President? Chairman?"

"Far too pompous. This is Canada. But I suppose I need some title. People in Ottawa respond well to titles."

"How about director?"

"I like it! Authoritative, yet delightfully ambiguous. What title are you going to put on your cards? Didn't we tell young Birchall that you were the chief administrative officer? How's that?"

"Very cumbersome. I don't think I need a title. You're the big cheese."

"*De jure. De facto*, you are the big cheese, or at least the co-big cheese. How about deputy director? Managing director?"

"No. And no. People would look at me and just laugh."

"How about secretary-treasurer? You're doing administrative work, and you're looking after the books."

"What's wrong with just secretary?"

"Not important enough. It needs some jazz."

"You were secretary to Lord Macmillan's Royal Commission."

"That was different. He was a lord. When they make me a lord, I'll make you my secretary."

"Okay. Secretary-treasurer."

"How is the salary research going?"

"I got a little gruffness, but when I asked them if they wanted to give me information in the strictest confidence, or go on record at the hearings of the Commons Committee on Banking and Finance, they obliged."

"So what is the salary package looking like?"

"Starting secretaries in Ottawa earn in the twelve- to fifteen-dollar range for a forty-four-hour week, including Saturday mornings. More senior office administrators were getting sixteen to twenty dollars for the same work week."

"So what do you think you're worth to the Canadian Financial Resources Agency, Miss McFadden?"

"I'd say somewhere in the fifteen to sixteen dollar range."

"Without prejudice, how did you arrive at that number?"

"Without prejudice?"

"Legal term, but my father used it all the time around the house. It means, 'I'd like to know the answer, but I don't wish to influence the answer.'"

"I don't get it."

"Father would come into the kitchen and say to my mother, 'Without prejudice, Leona, when will dinner be ready?' He was not being judgmental on the speed of her dinner preparation. He had a five-minute task and a fifty-minute task, and just wanted to know which one he had time for."

"You should have been a teacher. You have a marvellous way of explaining things. Okay. While it is true that I am a starting secretary, sorry, secretary-treasurer, I also have administrative responsibility for organizing and running this office. So I'm in the high-beginner-low-administrator range."

"Very reasonable. What if we split the difference? Fifteen-fifty?"

"Fine."

"Good. That's your salary until we add the new staff. Then you're up to seventeen dollars a week to reflect your added responsibilities."

"Very generous. Mother will be pleased."

"Add this conversation to your notes on how we arrived at this salary schedule, and keep it on file. Otherwise I'll forget. Did you buy a ledger to track our expenses?"

"I did. I've already got some bills, so I'll set up accounts received and accounts paid files, exactly the way I was taught at the High School of Commerce."

"Isn't education wonderful? Pay accounts the day we receive the invoice. Prompt payment guarantees continued quality. Include a line of thanks for services rendered. Politeness is a lost art, and it really stands out. Oh. All those people in your salary survey? Draft them all a personal thank-you note for my signature. We're building an empire here on courtesy and inoffensiveness, which is about all we have to offer."

"Right. Oh. My mother asked—I hate prefacing a question that way, but I wouldn't ask you if she hadn't asked me—my mother asked me if this was a permanent job."

"Your position as secretary-treasurer of the Canadian Financial Resources Agency lasts until the Bank of Canada is fully functional. My guess is that will be about ten months. We have enough money to operate for a year, if the Bank set-up is slow. Tell Mombo that you have a guaranteed job until May 15th, 1935. That is the best I can do. You will learn so much about the Canadian banking business in the next twelve months that the new Bank of Canada governor will likely hire you immediately. Unless he's an idiot. In which case, you wouldn't want to work for him anyway.

"As you expand your network in the banking-business-government community, be on the lookout for interesting places to work. Do your darnedest to leave a good impression, so a dozen people would want to hire you if the B. of C. doesn't work out. Fair enough?"

"Fair enough."

"Okay, Miss McFadden. You've done a month's work already, and I'm proud as punch of you! I'll call in tomorrow for an update."

At ten-thirty, Mr. Boyle shuffled in and tapped tentatively on the door to Dr. Grace's office, where Frances was wielding the phone.

"The men been in yet?" he asked.

"An electrician was here rewiring light switches and electrical outlets. That's it."

"How about cleaners and painters?"

"Not yet."

Mr. Boyle sighed and sat down on the empty crate opposite Frances. He shook his head. "I don't know what I'm going to do."

"Mr. Boyle, Dr. Grace is concerned with getting this office up and running. They're ready to deliver our office furniture as soon as the place is cleaned and painted. When will that be?"

Another sigh. "Listen, Miss, I just can't give you an honest answer."

"Dr. Grace appreciates your workmanship; it's just—well, the clock is ticking."

"I know. Look, I have two other crews working on larger projects. I'll see if I can free anybody up to finish your office."

"We need to know today, Mr. Boyle."

"Okay. I'll get back to you by three this afternoon."

Frances was on the phone confirming the stationery order to Imperial Printing when she heard footsteps in the outer office. "I'll set up some proofs, but I'd like you to see them before I run them," said the lady at Imperial. "Can you come over tomorrow about noon and have a look?"

"Sure. One-nineteen LeBreton Street?"

"Right. See you then."

Frances hung up to see a brown moon face in a porkpie hat looking at her through the doorway. "Can I help you?" she asked.

The man entered, followed by a thinner brown face in an expensive leather jacket. "Miss McFadden?"

"Yes."

"Huey Foo," said the porkpie hat. "You got cleaning, painting job?"

Frances jumped up. "Yes. How did you find me? I just left a phone number."

"Easy, miss. Only one place in Ottawa with this phone number. Phone talk no good. Need to see what you want. What you want?"

"Pardon the mess. I need to have this suite of offices cleaned and painted."

As they did the tour, Huey Foo spoke softly in Chinese to the black leather jacket, who silently scribbled notes on a small pad.

Huey Foo grimaced. "Very, very dirty. Must be cleany-clean, or paint no sticking. When you want?"

"As soon as possible. What would you charge to clean and paint the whole place?"

An animated discussion followed in Chinese. Leather Jacket was younger and thinner than Huey Foo, and much more stylishly dressed. He spoke quickly and seemed angry in a quiet Chinese way. Huey Foo's tone never changed, but Leather Jacket barked, and sucked air in loudly through his teeth.

"Take many people do this work. Is possible. Soon, not so possible."

"How much?"

More Chinese chatter, with Leather Jacket shaking his head, and making a demonstrative cutting action with his notebook hand. Finally, Huey Foo said, "Middle of June. Four nights' work. One hundred dollar cash. Fair price."

"That is a very fair price, Mr. Foo, but we need it done next week. How much for next week?"

Several clipped comments in Chinese were batted back and forth between Leather Jacket and Porkpie Hat, before a stalemate. After a silence, Mr. Foo said, "Please? Use phone?"

Frances nodded and she listened to one end of a Chinese conversation during which there were long pauses. Finally, Mr. Foo said, "*Hao, hao,*" and hung up. He said three syllables to Leather Jacket, who shrugged and turned away.

"Next week, one hundred fifty dollar, cash."

"When next week?"

"Thursday night clean big dirt. Friday night clean small dirt. Paint one coat Saturday, one coat Sunday. Finish six o'clock Sunday night. One hundred fifty dollar cash."

"Okay!" said Frances.

Mr. Foo gave a long look at Leather Jacket, but said nothing. Leather Jacket's eyes sought the ground. "Fine deal, miss. Need office key."

"I'll have keys for you by Thursday night."

"Good do business with you, miss. See you Thursday."

10

SATURDAY

Frances slept in Saturday morning, and didn't arrive at the office until seven-thirty. Stella peeked out at her from the alcove behind the elevators.

" 'Morning, Sunshine. You're sure here early."

"Hi, Stella. I just wake up and want to be here."

Stella snorted. "My home's a lot like that, too."

Frances blushed. It was too close to the truth. "Say, I arrived early yesterday morning, and had to ring the bell at the back door to get in. Who's the guy who opened the door?"

"Old man Sloan. He's trouble. He's on nights, eight till seven in the morning. I usually get here just as he's leaving."

"Eleven hours a night?"

"Sounds like long hours, but he don't do dick. He's supposed to look after the furnace and clean the hallways. The furnace don't need much attention in the summer. He just slouches down there in his cave and plays with himself, far as I can tell. Gives me the creeps."

"He told me the boiler is dangerous and has to be monitored."

"He's lazy. Always smells of booze in the morning. I can tell if he's been using the elevator. There's a liquor cloud in the cage. When Mr. Kinkade gets on his back, Sloan'll throw a quick mop down the halls for a while, but you can hardly tell."

"Don't the tenants complain?"

"The offices are cleaned by private contractors. Sloan just does the halls. As long as the dust bunnies aren't big enough to mug ya, most people don't notice. But that's not the real problem." Stella took a long draw on her cigarette. "He's a jerk. He put his arm around me a couple of times, copping a feel. 'Just being playful,' he claimed.

"Teased me about Frankie being in prison, like I'm a jailhouse whore. 'Frankie's away,' I says, 'but Frankie'll be back. In the meantime, the Brewster Gang are just a phone call away.' That backed him off. The Brewster Gang may be outlaws, but they look after their own. Keep clear of Sloan. He's a coward and a bully—a bad combination."

At eight twenty-nine, the phone rang.

"Well, hello, sweet bird of youth. How's the CFRA today?"

"All's well, Dr. Grace. Phone lines will be installed Wednesday, with the requested switchboard. We parted company with Mr. Boyle yesterday afternoon, and I've hired a cleaning and painting contractor to get us all tidied up next weekend."

"You fired young Boyle? How did he take it?"

"He was whistling while he packed up his tools yesterday afternoon. I think I made his day."

"And the new contractor? Did he have references?"

"Not exactly."

"Frances! How do we know the new guy won't be as slow as young Boyle? You have to check references, or the office will be under construction for ten years."

"I'm sorry," said Frances, biting her lip.

"Hey! Don't feel bad. You've been on the job for two days, for heaven's sake! Just make a note for the future—check references, okay? Where'd you find the new guy?"

"Stella gave me his name. A Mr. Foo. He's Chinese. Surprise, surprise. His crew works nights and weekends. They're starting here Thursday night. And I'm going in to the printers this afternoon to check some mock-ups of our business cards and office stationery."

"Good. Next item. You need a very good translator and an excellent file clerk. Pronto. Run ads in both city papers. For three days. Have respondents reply to a box number at the newspapers."

"What should we say in the ad?"

"You'll want résumés, samples of work, and references, to make the first cut."

"The first cut?"

"Yes. There'll be a lot of interest. It's the Depression. You don't have time to interview them all."

"Um, why am I saying 'we,' and I'm only hearing 'you'?"

"You will have to do the interviews. I don't have time."

"I don't know how to do interviews! I just dropped out of high school, remember? I can't be hiring translators!"

"You did a great interview with me on Tuesday. You're a seasoned veteran."

"I can't—"

"Hey. You have to work with these people. You should pick them."

"I don't even know how to describe their jobs! How can I interview—"

"Job descriptions are overrated. You want a filing clerk and a translator. Period. Mostly, you want people you'd like to work with. My guess is that you'll get twenty-five to thirty applications for each job. Cut two-thirds of them on the strengths, or should I say, weaknesses, of their applications. Interview six to eight for each job. Choose the best."

"You won't help me at all?"

"Miss McFadden, I hired an office administrator—sorry, secretary-treasurer—to run this office. Run it. I have every confidence in you."

"But I forgot to check references—"

"And you won't forget again, will you? Besides, I hate doing interviews."

"You hated interviewing me? You hid it pretty well."

"Well, the Canadian Grill at the Château Laurier has such a pleasant ambience. The salmon and the Chardonnay were particularly well matched."

"What if I did a second cut by interviewing and reducing the candidates to, say, three for each job. Could you spare two hours to help with the final choice?"

"Maybe. One hour."

"Six interviews! Ninety minutes?"

"Okay. You're a tough negotiator, McFadden."

"How about wages?"

"Don't advertise the wages, but they will ask in the interview, I suppose. What say we pay them both 75 percent of your salary. What would that be?"

"Well, research showed that I'd be getting sixty-two dollars a month. That would give them forty-six-fifty each."

"Too nickel-and-dime. Offer a respectable fifty dollars a month for each position. We've got to spend that ten thousand somehow. Draft up the ads. And start getting the *Ottawa Citizen* and the *Ottawa Journal* delivered to the office. Better get the French paper, *Le Devoir*, as well. We've got to start building our files."

"And how exactly do we do that, Dr. Grace? I'm new to the archives business."

"An archivist has essentially two tasks. First, know what you need on file. That'll be my homework. I'll have an outline for you by Monday. Second, know how to find what you've filed. As you know, organization is not my long suit." He paused. "Do you know what a 'long suit' is?"

"Sure. I used to play bridge."

"Used to? Like, when you were younger and didn't know any better?"

"It was the only fun thing our family did together. We played bridge marathons while my father and my sister were still around. I think my parents had a second child because they needed a fourth for bridge."

"Anyway, call the records manager at the Public Archives Office on Sussex Street. Her name is Norma Sutherland. Ask her for the quick-and-dirty on how to set up an archives and a cross-indexing system."

"And she'll just drop everything to teach me?"

"She'll be happy to talk to you. Just mention my name. She has a crush on me. Tell her what we're trying to do, and ask her how to start up from scratch. Throw yourself on her mercy! Remember?"

"Right. We're building an empire."

"And call Dan Macron in the Finance Department for his advice."

"Does he have a crush on you too?"

"Ho, ho. He's the records manager at Finance. He'll be ecstatic to get all my Macmillan Commission boxes out of his hallway. He'll do anything to help. Dan is kind of like a golden retriever—always happy to bring you things. Drools a bit, but very helpful.

"Oh, and you should probably meet Rose Malone. She's secretary to the deputy Minister of Finance. Nice lady! Apple cheeks and perpetual smile. I call her 'Momsie.' She's the mother hen up in Finance. An extremely reliable resource. Bakes wonderful shortbread cookies, which she doles out sparingly to the favoured."

"Like you?"

"Of course. It's kind of a litmus test of how well I'm doing in the office."

"Why would the deputy minister's secretary want to talk to me?"

"Come, come. Not all civil servants are cold and officious like me. She's unmarried. A brood hen without a brood. Fix those helpless hazel eyes on her, and she'll drop everything to nurse you."

Helpless hazel eyes?

"I'll phone in Monday for an update."

"Are you staying in Toronto all weekend?"

"Yes. Meetings all day today and Monday morning. Dinner with the Judge and Leona tonight."

"The Judge and Leona? Is that a singing group, or are these new secret agents for the bank?"

"Parents. Father is the taciturn Judge Harold Dempster Grace of the Court of King's Bench, and Leona is my dear mother."

"The one who wants you to be a medical missionary?"

"The very one. 'Bye. Keep the home fires burning."

The rest of the morning was taken up with phone calls, and it was noon in no time. Frances took the streetcar down Somerset to LeBreton Street. Imperial Printing and Engraving was in a shabby garage-type building at the back of a weed-filled yard. When she opened the door, a bell and a flashing light both were tripped in a clattering backroom. The office was small, and every horizontal surface was piled high with paper and sample books. The hypnotizing thumpa-thumpa-thumpa of a printing press wheezed to a halt, and a heavy woman with her hair in a red kerchief walked into the office. A cigarette dangled from the left side of her mouth.

"Help you?" she asked. Ash splashed down the front of an ink-stained work shirt.

"Yes. I'm Frances McFadden, from the Canadian Financial Resources Agency? I phoned about having some business cards and stationery printed up."

The woman squinted through cigarette smoke as she wiped her black hands on an even blacker cloth. "Pleased ta meetcha. I'm Lolly O'Byrne. I'm the chief cook and bottle-washer around here. Just a sec." She disappeared into the backroom momentarily, and re-emerged with a file folder that she laid on the counter in front of Frances.

"I was kinda expectin' someone older, Miss — "

"Frances, Mrs. . . . ."

"Call me Lolly."

"Well, Lolly, I was kind of expecting a man to be a printer. Don't know why. I've never met a printer before," said Frances.

"There was a Mr. O'Byrne, but the cancer got 'im, so I'm Imperial Printing and Engraving now. I used to do the books for him, and help out on big jobs, in the days when we had big jobs. When he took sick, he taught me how to run our three presses. Scary at first. Noisy and dirty. But not much to it once ya know how.

"Have a look. You said you wanted something a little different." She flipped open the file folder. Sample business cards were printed in embossed blue ink on different grades of card stock in various type fonts. The letterhead was printed up on paper of different grades and colours.

"Now, truth is, most folks want black ink on white stock. Classic and traditional. Cheaper, too. But this dark blue can be easily read, and looks just a touch special." She pulled one sheet of cream rag out of the pile. "Looks real striking, don'tcha think? I just finished a run of some invitations to the Governor General's garden party. Had the press inked up, and some paper left over."

"Very impressive." said Frances. "But isn't it more expensive?"

"Fran, mostly you're paying for press set-up and time. My best rag paper doesn't raise the price much."

"I like the look of the blue ink on the cream-coloured paper. My boss might think it's too flashy."

"Okay, well, I have this hundred-and-fifty-pound stock in double white. It would look distinctive with a Times Roman bold font." Lolly pulled a sample book off of the nearby filing cabinet and showed Frances the difference. "Or you could go for the blue and cream and the boss be damned," cackled Lolly.

"I'm thinking that if it's good enough for the Governor General, my boss would like it. Could you tone the cream down a little?"

"Certainly. The G-G uses Bristol Cream. Here's English Ivory, a shade lighter."

"Can you show me what the Blue Umber embossed looks like on English Ivory?"

"Still got that ink on the press. Take just a minute to run."

The finished product was stylish but not gaudy. "Okay. Let's go with it. Anyone else in Ottawa using that combination?"

"The G-G is the closest. Most people stick with boring old black and white. Of course, most of my orders come from men. You're too young to know, Sweetie, but men like boring."

Frances ordered three hundred business cards for herself and for Dr. Grace. She ordered three thousand sheets of letterhead, and a thousand envelopes. Lolly suggested note cards and matching envelopes in the same paper stock, and Frances agreed. "That will be fourteen-fifty, and an extra dollar for delivery. I'll have that out to you by next Thursday."

Frances walked up Nanny Goat Hill toward home, then cut over to Mary O'Brien's house.

"Frances!" cried Mary, giving her a big hug in the doorway. "Come on in. We're baking cookies. You wanna see *It Happened One Night*?

The Deavys are both mad about Clark Gable and want to catch the seven o'clock show."

After the movie, they got the front booth at the Mirror Grill and ate ice cream sundaes.

"So what's the working world really like?" asked Katie.

"As much fun as school?" asked Dorothy, with an eye roll.

"Well, remember how we complained about those boring assignments we did in Office Practice and Accounting? They're saving my bacon!" She sighed. "It's a lot of work, but I love it!"

"What's to love?" asked Mary.

"Everything is brand-new and exciting. My desk is a borrowed card table, and the only seats are old crates. I love doing things on my own. No teachers or parents telling me what to do."

"Doesn't your boss order you around?" asked Mary.

"Is he a dreamboat?" demanded Katie, with a much-practised sidelong leer.

"Dr. Grace gives me lots of freedom, and is very forgiving with my mistakes. It's fun! He's not bad-looking, but he's no Clark Gable. Probably not your type, Katie. He must be in his thirties, but he acts kind of like a big goofy boy. He teases me, but not in a mean way. Says I've got 'helpless hazel eyes.' We laugh a lot. He's often away, but phones me every morning to check in. I've never been in charge before, and I'm having a ball!"

— 11 —

HUEY FOO'S ARMY

The Monday morning phone call from Toronto approved the hiring ads for the newspapers. The three Remington Select typewriters arrived from Hay Stationery with a large order of office supplies. Norma Sutherland at the Public Archives invited Frances right over.

Mrs. Sutherland's purple-framed glasses hung from a lilac cord around her neck. When Frances explained her situation, she waved a dismissive hand. "Simplicity itself, my dear. A simple cross-indexing system will give you a logical filing format. Take a copy of the booklet we use to train staff. It has explicit directions. Call if you get stuck." She paused. "Oh, and how is that darling man, Dr. Grace?"

Next, Frances stopped at the Finance Department to see Rose Malone.

"Oh!" Miss Malone cried. "You're Dr. Grace's new girl! He told me you might call." She leaned in close and whispered, "He thinks you're wonderful! Now, Harriet Westington in our secretarial pool is assigned to Dr. Grace. A dear woman, and Dr. Grace would never hurt her feelings, but I know he was looking for someone more — well, entrepreneurial — for the bank archives office. He told me, 'Momsie' (he calls me Momsie, the silly boy!), 'I need a privateer for the bounding main down at the new office.' Harriet is very conscientious, and won the civil service spelling bee two years in a row, but no one would mistake her for a privateer. She much prefers to work here in the pool. So, she's happy not to be you, and . . ." she paused, "are you happy?"

"Oh, yes!" exclaimed Frances.

"Wonderful!" cried Rose, clapping her hands, as though she had just won a prize. "Well, have a word with Harriet, because you'll both be needing to track down Dr. Grace, who has a habit of disappearing." She leaned in again for another conspiratorial whisper. "Ask her advice on how he likes his letters done. She'll be so pleased."

Frances did this, and the prim Miss Westington was delighted. Rose Malone handed Frances a file as they walked out into the wide East Block hallway. "Here's a list of all the deputy ministers' secretaries, if you have any questions whatsoever. A small group of us meets every Tuesday at 4:00 p.m. sharp to harmonize the formats of filing and minute-taking and memo-sending between departments." She paused reflectively. "You know, Frances, it would be a good idea for you to meet this group to hear how things are set up on the Hill. I host next week, so I'll just put you on the agenda."

The week blurred past. Mr. Kinkade from Harmer Property Management gave her keys to the office and the main door. The locksmith arrived Thursday morning and reset the tumblers for the vault. She arranged with Dan Macron from Finance to deliver all the Macmillan Royal Commission files.

She drafted letters for Dr. Grace's signature to the managers of the ten Canadian chartered banks introducing the CFRA and asking for organizational charts, biographies of officers, and annual reports for the past twenty years. Similar letters were drafted to the Bank of England, the United States Federal Reserve, and a dozen other national banks. She ordered a copy of *Who's Who* and the city directories for Ottawa and every provincial capital.

Dr. Grace either phoned in the morning or dropped in late in the afternoon. He liked her crisp but friendly writing style and approved her drafts with only minor revisions. He was very impressed with the new stationery.

Frances went out to lunch with Stella on Thursday and saved the lunch she had packed to eat over the supper hour while she waited for Huey Foo's cleaners to arrive. Just after seven, she heard a commotion in the hall.

"Miss Fran?" asked the familiar porkpie hat. "Please meet head cleaner Lao Lee." Lao Lee was an ancient man with several teeth missing in his smile. Long random hairs sprouted from his chin. His trousers were cinched by a black belt that circled his narrow waist almost twice. He bowed to Frances and said, "Thank you. Thank you. Water? Stove?"

Frances pointed to the alcove, and a pigtailed girl headed off with a canvas bag and kettle. "Cleaner, painter," smiled Lao Lee, gesturing toward a crowd of round-faced, brown-eyed people who flowed shyly in from the hall. All were short and wore baggy clothes. They carried mops, pails, and bundles of bamboo poles of various lengths tied up with cord. They looked like refugees, or a circus troupe.

Lao Lee's singsong voice directed the cleaners in groups of three into different rooms. Each cleaner unrolled a narrow cloth apron that had stitched compartments holding screwdrivers, knives, and brushes of various sizes.

The bundles of thick bamboo came apart magically like pick-up-sticks, to produce a pair of stilts and an adjustable platform. The stilts were almost eight feet long. One cleaner set the stilts against the wall and eyed the distance to the ceiling before inserting a pegged bracket two-thirds of the way up. What looked like a wooden shoe was pegged tightly into place into the bottom of each stilt. A cleaner sat on the floor and strapped the stilts securely to his legs with broad bands of cloth. On a signal, he lay down flat, and his two workmates tilted him up to a vertical position, where he caught his balance against the wall. The ceiling and wall tops were now in easy reach.

A bamboo platform some four feet high was quickly constructed in the corner opposite the stilted man. A cleaner limberly swung up onto the platform. The third cleaner disassembled a set of eight nesting pails and filled each with either soapy water or clear rinse water. Small pails were handed up to the stilted cleaner, who hung them on hooks on the outside of his stilts. Medium-sized pails went up on the platform. Larger pails were placed under the window. The largest reservoir pails by the door were constantly refilled by the pigtailed girl, who also removed the dirty water.

Like the hands on a clock, the three cleaners followed each other around the room. The stilt man cleaned the ceiling and the top three feet of the wall. The platform man cleaned the mid-wall. The floor man cleaned the bottom four feet and all around the large cast-iron radiator under the window. Each scrub brush pass instantly revealed a lighter swath on the filthy surfaces.

In ninety minutes, the walls and ceiling of all four offices were done. Then, the stilt men were helped to dismount, and everyone took a tea break in the outer office. The girl passed out small handleless cups of steaming Chinese tea to the cleaners, who squatted on their haunches while they sipped. Slices of apple and almond cookies were handed around.

After fifteen minutes, a shallow bark from Lao Lee brought everyone to their feet. Teacups were drained and returned to the girl. Platforms were moved to the outer office. Stilt men were helped aloft and work began again. One cleaner was left in each of the offices to scrape and scrub floors stained by waxed-over dirt and gum, dust, and construction grit.

Frances marvelled at the quiet, relentless process, like ants cleaning the carcass of a dead animal. By ten-thirty p.m., every surface was transformed. Huey Foo reappeared, as the Chinese workers cleaned their tools and washed out their pails in the kitchen sink.

"It looks amazing!" exclaimed Frances.

Huey Foo's face registered neither joy nor sorrow. "Big dirt go today. Small dirt go tomorrow. Then get walls ready for paint. Okay leave bamboo stilt and platform here? Save carry."

"Certainly," said Frances. "The furniture doesn't come until next week."

"Have office key? Building key?" Frances handed them over. "Tomorrow. Same time." Huey Foo gave Frances a nod that wasn't quite a bow, and Lao Lee herded his flock out the door. On Friday night, the scene was repeated to lift the final layer of grit. Then the cleaners lightly sanded all surfaces. "Paint team here Saturday, 1:00 p.m. Like to paint in sunlight."

On Saturday morning, Frances dropped into the Shanghai Grocery Store on Somerset Street on her way to work. An oriental girl about her own age was behind the counter.

"Some Chinese people are working at my office. Can you suggest a treat?"

The girl brought down a large, clear glass jar with a white lid. "This is Jade Morning Tea, my grandmother's favourite for special occasions."

"I need enough to serve fourteen people twice. And a light snack?"

"These bean paste moon cakes are fresh this morning." Frances bought three dozen.

"A small token of my thanks for your good work," she said to Lao Lee. "The office is so much brighter!" He smiled his gap-toothed smile, and bowed deeply. "Thank you! Thank you!" he said. He gave an enthusiastic translation to his crew and a ripple of shy smiles and nods ran through them.

Blank newsprint was spread over all the floors, and the stilt-mounted painters coated all the ceilings in a flat eggshell white. The walls and woodwork were painted a rich cream, making the offices seem bigger and brighter. The ghost of the old green wall paint was subdued but not defeated by the first coat of paint. In two hours, the small offices were done, and tea was served.

The painters had just returned to work when a large gum-chewing man with a clipboard walked in, skirting the painters.

"Can I help you?" Frances asked.

"This the Canadian Financial Resources Agency?" he asked, looking at his clipboard.

"Yes."

"I'm from Yeoman's Used Furniture. We got your furniture order on the truck down in the back alley. Very narrow. Helluva time backing in."

"There must be some mistake," said Frances. "That furniture order was supposed to come on Monday. We're not ready for it."

"Well, it's on the truck, and I have to get it off the truck 'cause I got two more deliveries this afternoon. So, where do you want it?"

"Mister," said Frances, "I'm sorry, but we can't take delivery today. There is no place to put it until they finish painting the office tomorrow."

The man from Yeoman's scrutinized the invoice. "Funny," he said. "This did say 'Monday, May 28,' but somebody scratched that out and wrote in 'Saturday, the twenty-sixth, afternoon.' So that's why the truck got loaded today. Want to call the store and see what gives?"

Frances got through to Mr. Deavy, and he tracked down the dispatcher. "Hi, Frances. Jake Wallace phoned the Blackburn Building to set up the Monday delivery, because we'd be tying the elevator up for over an hour. The building superintendent told him that we absolutely could not deliver on Monday and disrupt the tenants. He said to send the furniture over on Saturday afternoon, after everybody closed for the day."

"It's the first I've heard about it. And I've got a dozen painters here with scaffolding all over the place. I just can't take this delivery now."

There was a long pause on the line, and muffled voices at Mr. Deavy's end. "Listen, Frances, it takes an hour to load that truck. If we have to unload it back here, reload it sometime that's convenient for your building super, then unload it again at your end, that's twice the work at twice the cost. I gave you a good price. Is there anywhere they could store the furniture at your end?"

"Mr. Deavy, there is nowhere to put it. The office is full of painters. There's just the hall down to the elevator."

"How big is the hall?"

"It's long, but not very wide."

"Put Gord on the line."

Frances handed the phone to the delivery man. He said "nope" four times, and "yep" once. Then he rolled his eyes and said, "All right Mr. Deavy. You're the boss. We'll give it a try." He turned to Frances. "He says to stack the load in the hall. It's going to be a rabbit warren out there. Better hope there ain't a fire."

In an hour, the furniture was packed along the hallway, leaving a very narrow passage from the office to the elevator or to the back stairs.

"There you are, lady," said Gord, damp with sweat, as he handed her his clipboard for the sign-off.

Frances signed and wrote out a cheque. She looked at the jungle outside her office doorway. "How am I going to get all that furniture into the office when the painters are done?"

"That's a problem, lady," he said with a mock salute of his clipboard. "But not my problem. Good luck!"

The painters left at seven. They giggled at the furniture, and shuffled sideways past as though it were a child's game. Frances took the inventory list, and squeezed down the hall. Everything was there. She was down by the Harmer office door when the elevator whirred into motion. The door opened, and Mr. Sloan poked his grizzled chin out at her, like a chicken pecking for grain.

"What's this mess? You can't leave all this in the hall. I've got to clean."

"Well, Mr. Sloan, the furniture was supposed to arrive on Monday, after the office had been painted. Someone changed the delivery date, and the office isn't ready for it. I tried to send it back, but the people from Yeoman's Furniture wouldn't take no for an answer."

"Oh, yeah, I remember. Kinkade never wants the elevator tied up during working hours. Gave me very specific instructions. So I told Yeoman's to deliver Saturday afternoon. Didn't know you were painting. Nobody tells me nothing. But you can't leave it here. The fire marshal would close the building in a second."

Frances took a deep breath. "What if we don't tell the fire marshal, Mr. Sloan? The painters will be done Sunday night. No one else is going to be up here. I'll get it moved as soon as I have a place to put it."

"Can't wait."

"Well, then it is your responsibility, Mr. Sloan, because you told Yeoman's to deliver it today. Do you want to move it somewhere?"

"I don't move furniture."

They glared at each other.

"Tell you what, Mr. Sloan. I'll take responsibility for the furniture's being here. I'll explain to Mr. Kinkade that I needed some temporary storage."

"Yeah, but how about cleaning the hall? I don't work Sundays. It has to be cleaned by Monday morning."

Frances wondered if anyone would notice. "If you can leave me with a bucket and mop, I'll get it cleaned as soon as the furniture is moved."

"By Monday morning?"

"By Monday morning," she said, without a clue as to how she would manage it. "Do you have any moving equipment?"

"There's a couple of dollies in the basement storage room. Put 'em back when you're done."

The painters were hard at it when Frances arrived Sunday afternoon. The rooms were luminous in their new clothes. The green ghosts that had lurked under the primer coat were locked there, invisible forever. The four offices were finished by tea break at three o'clock. Frances was ecstatic. At four o'clock, Huey Foo and Leather Jacket arrived. Lao Lee gave them a quick tour, and they returned to Frances at her card table. She had brought two chairs in from the hall, and was busy clipping the Saturday papers and building new files.

"Your team has done a wonderful job, Mr. Foo. Dr. Grace will be very pleased."

"Glad you happy, Miss Fran. Lao Lee say painters finish at six. Right on time. I must go to other business. Is possible to get one hundred fifty dollar now?"

"Oh, certainly," said Frances. "Just let me get a cheque out of the vault."

"No cheque, Miss Fran. One hundred fifty dollar cash," said Huey Foo.

"But I don't have one hundred and fifty dollars cash," said Frances. "You can cash this cheque at any bank tomorrow morning."

"Have business tonight, miss. Must have cash money now. We agree one hundred fifty dollar clean and paint, cash on delivery. I keep bargain. Now you keep bargain. Both party keep bargain, good business."

"Mr. Foo, I'm sorry. I misunderstood. I thought a cheque on our account was the same as cash. I don't have a hundred fifty dollars cash."

Huey Foo looked at Frances for a long minute, then shook his head slowly. "Huey Foo never break agreement. That bad business. Business depend on trust. You trust. I trust. That good business. Painters finish at six o'clock. I wait six o'clock for one hundred fifty dollar cash money." Huey Foo sat down on the empty crate and absently put a toothpick in his mouth.

"Mr. Foo, it's Sunday night. Everything is closed. I can give you a cheque now, or the cash tomorrow morning when the bank opens. That's all I can do," Frances pleaded.

Mr. Foo gave Frances another long look, then said one sentence to Leather Jacket in Chinese. Leather Jacket moved to the chair across the card table from Frances. He looked her straight in the eye, and said in perfect English, "You have a contract with Mr. Foo. He has provided you with a service in return for one hundred and fifty dollars cash on delivery. Mr. Foo always delivers. That's why he is a successful businessman. All he wants is the contract fulfilled. That means cash by six o'clock tonight. Is that clear?"

"Yes," said Frances. "It's clear. I am happy to pay. His service is excellent. I just can't get my hands on that kind of cash by six o'clock on a Sunday night. Surely you understand that."

Leather Jacket made an attempt at patience. "Mr. Foo found people to work here at night and on the weekend, so as not to disturb your business. This was hard to do, but part of his contract. Your part of the contract is to get him one hundred and fifty dollars cash by six o'clock. You have two hours. That's seventy-five dollars an hour," said Leather Jacket with a slight smile. "That shouldn't be hard for the secretary-treasurer of the Canadian Financial Resources Agency."

How did he know that? My business cards aren't even out of the box. "I don't have the cash!" she repeated.

Leather Jacket's tone sharpened. "Mr. Foo does not break agreements, and no one breaks agreements with Mr. Foo." He smiled. "I should say, no one breaks agreements with Mr. Foo more than once. You do not want to join that group, Miss McFadden."

"But I can't help it!" exclaimed Frances.

Now it was Leather Jacket's turn to take the long pause before he spoke again. "Your mother is Vera McFadden? She works the evening and night shifts in the emergency ward at the Civic Hospital?"

"Yes."

"She often comes home to 180 Rochester Street late, and alone."

"Yes."

"Mary O'Brien is your good friend? She lives at 145 Bell Street with her parents and a younger brother, Robert?"

"Yes."

"Robert likes to fish down by the Ottawa River during the spring runoff. Wading in fast-flowing water can be very dangerous."

"Yes."

"Charlie Deavy is the father of your friends Katherine and Dorothy. He works at Yeoman's Used Furniture. He sold you the furniture in the hall?"

"Yes."

"Yeoman's warehouse is very old. A fire trap. Many people would be out of work if anything should happen to that building."

"Yes," said Frances.

"Mr. Foo wants one hundred and fifty dollars cash delivered to him here, by six o'clock. We will wait."

"Yes," said Frances.

— 12 —

MORTY DUBROFSKI

Frances went down the stairs two at a time. It was 4:10. She ran up to Sparks Street and caught the Bronson streetcar. Her right hand was trembling involuntarily. The streetcar was almost empty as it rumbled past rows of closed stores.

The cookie jar at home had less than five dollars in it. Her mother's assistance would be painful to seek and punishing to receive. No more than a few dollars were likely available at either the Deavys' or the O'Briens' even if she could bring herself to impose on friends.

Where to look? Nothing was open on Sunday except hotels and hospitals. Neither was in the short-term loan business. Who would have a hundred and fifty dollars cash on a Sunday afternoon? And who would loan it to her if they had it?

Frances had run the office cash down to three dollars buying tea and moon cakes for the painters. She had planned to top the float up at the bank on Monday. She wondered if she would still be alive on Monday. She could walk right to the train station and leave town, but that left her mother and Robbie O'Brien and Mr. Deavy's warehouse very exposed.

How about Erskine Presbyterian Church? They filled the pews for three services every Sunday, and took a collection each time. How much? Would Reverend Grisham give her a loan? He was a quiet, rotund man. More distant than unfriendly. He was worth a try.

Frances got off the streetcar in front of the limestone church. The front door was open, ready for the evening vespers service. The cavernous sanctuary was empty, as were the offices behind the chancel. Next door was the church manse. Frances walked quickly up the stairs, and rang the bell. A chair scraped on linoleum at the back of the house. Mrs. Grisham shuffled toward her down the hall.

"Hello, dear."

"Good afternoon, Mrs. Grisham. Is the Reverend home?"

"No, dear. He's taking a service for a sick minister up at Arnprior. He took the train right after lunch. The student minister, Reverend

Combs, will take the vespers service. If you have a spiritual concern, I'm sure he can help you."

A spiritual concern? I may need a funeral service tomorrow. Frances liked the young intern with the dark curly hair, but she doubted he had two nickels to rub together.

She turned the corner onto Rochester Street and checked her watch. It was 4:35. Mother would be a bear. Five doors from home, a bone-chilling scream sliced into her thoughts. She turned toward the sound to see Mrs. Dubrofski stumble onto the porch, cradling her sobbing blood-soaked son, Sollie, and dragging her crying daughter in tow.

"Frances! Help!" she yelled, as she sank down on the top step. Mrs. Dubrofski was much younger than Frances's mother, and much younger than Mr. Dubrofski, for that matter. She had a sensuous mouth and striking eyes. The eyes were frantic.

"Can you take Leah? Morty just left with Rachel to get ice cream, like he knew trouble was brewing. Can you believe? Ice cream just before dinner? There is no telling Morty nothing some days." Frances picked up the four-year-old girl, and rubbed her back to soothe her sobbing. They followed Mrs. Dubrofski into the house, back to the kitchen.

"So, a minute ago, I'm cooking dinner, listening to *The Shadow* on the radio. The kids are playing on the stairs, and suddenly, bam, bam, scream, yell, all hell breaks loose. 'Scuse my French. I come running and there is Sollie crying in this gusher of blood, and Leah blubbering, 'Sollie fall down! Sollie fall down.' Can you get me a damp cloth to see what the damage is?"

Frances dampened a tea towel at the tap. She began dabbing gently at Sollie's face, whispering, "How's my cowboy? How's my brave boy, Sollie, Sollie?" Mrs. Dubrofski cradled Sollie on her ample bosom, and his blood flowed freely over them both. Leah, face filthy with tears and snot, reached for a sugar cookie on the table.

The flow of blood was quickly traced to Sollie's left nostril, and was dammed with a corner of the tea towel. He had a scraped cheek, and a bruise was beginning to purple his upper left arm. One cookie calmed his wail to a whimper.

"Sollie fall downa stairs," explained Leah helpfully, holding her hand out for another cookie. "Boom, boom. Lotsa blood. He scare me!" she said, desirous of attention but none of the blame.

"Frances, you're so calm!" Mrs. Dubrofski brushed her blouse ineffectively with the tea towel. "No wonder the kids love you to babysit!

Here," she said, standing up, "take Solomon while I change and get him some clean clothes. Looks like there's been an axe murder in here!" She laughed and headed up the back stairs. "Put the kettle on," she called. "We deserve a cup of tea."

Frances was filling the kettle when she saw the kitchen clock. It was 4:55. "Mrs. Dubrofski!" she called up the stairs. "The kettle's on. The kids are fine. I'm sorry, but I have to go."

She could hear water running in the bathroom. "Give me a sec. Does this boy not have one clean shirt?"

A succession of drawers slammed open and closed like an off-stage drum before Mrs. Dubrofski came downstairs again, looking fresh in a clean dress, carrying Sollie's pyjamas. She shrugged. "All I could find that was clean or dry. Wash is out on the line with everything else. Here—you change him, and I'll make tea." She pulled the tea towel corner out of Sollie's nostril, and stuffed in a floret of toilet tissue.

Frances sat Sollie on the kitchen table beside the cookies and stripped him. He yawned when he saw his pyjamas and let her clothe him in their softness. "Mrs. Dubrofski, I'd love to join you for a cup, but . . ."

"What's your hurry, Frances? I saw your mother an hour ago. She was heading to the hospital to cover an evening shift for someone sick. Your mother and I, Frances, we don't always see eye to eye, but I respect her work ethic."

"Mrs. Dub—"

"So you don't need to rush home for dinner. Stay and join us. We owe you."

"Mrs. Dubrofski, I have to go. I've got a big problem. I haven't even told my mother."

"Problem? Maybe I can help."

"I doubt it. I need a hundred and fifty dollars cash by six o'clock."

"A hundred and fifty dollars!" she exclaimed. Her eyes narrowed and her voice dropped. "You in trouble, Frances? You can tell me. My lips are sealed. My cousin Miriam was in trouble and nobody lifted a finger. I swore I'd never let that happen again. You need an abortion? I know a woman in Hintonburg who'll look after you for twenty bucks. What sort of shyster is charging you a hundred and fifty?"

Frances blushed, but pressed on. "No, no. It's not that kind of trouble. I owe somebody—"

"Gambling debts? You play the numbers? Or the horses? You, Frances? Presbyterian and all?" She shook her head in disbelief.

"No, no. I hired some people to clean and paint the office I work in—"

"You working? You quit school? When did all this happen?" Mrs. Dubrofski threw her hands up in exasperation. "The neighbour ladies keepin' secrets from me now, are they?"

"No. Sorry. I just got the job last week," Frances hastily explained.

The screen door slammed, and Morty Dubrofski walked in with Rachel, who had the ruins of a chocolate ice cream cone all over her face. Mr. Dubrofski was the sole owner of Dubrofski Brothers' Dry Goods on Somerset Street. His older brother, Lenny, had moved to Florida with his family to run a kosher delicatessen. Morty gave Mrs. Dubrofski a kiss on the cheek, nodded to Frances and walked to the icebox for a cold beer. "Hot day," he said.

"Morty," said Mrs. Dubrofski, "we gotta help Frances. She needs a hundred and fifty dollars cash until tomorrow morning."

Mr. Dubrofski, his head tilted back to draw the cold beer down, almost choked.

"What?"

"Frances needs a hundred and fifty by tonight at six o'clock. Short-term loan until the banks open. We gotta help her." Mrs. Dubrofski looked steadfastly at her husband.

"What are you talking about, Ethel! That's a lot of money to give to a kid! If we had a hundred and fifty dollars," he added.

Mrs. Dubrofski crossed her arms and glared at her husband. She said something to him in a foreign language.

Polish? Yiddish? Frances didn't know. It wasn't French. Short volleys shot back and forth between them. Mr. Dubrofski waved his beer to stress his points. Mrs. Dubrofski folded her arms tighter and tighter for emphasis, enhancing her cleavage tremendously.

It was 5:15 by the kitchen clock.

"Mrs. Dubrofski," pleaded Frances, breaking into a lull in the hostilities, "thank you for trying to help. I have to go."

Ethel Dubrofski held up her hand at Frances, and narrowed her stare at her husband.

"Whaddaya talking about, Morty! We trust her with our children all the time. The fruit of our loins count less with you than a measly hundred and fifty bucks? What kind of a father are you?"

Morty Dubrofski moved to escort Frances to the door. "Like to help you, Frances. You're a gem with our kids, and we'll hire you any day. Times are tough, and I can't afford to take a flyer on a hundred and fifty smackers with five mouths to feed. Sorry," he said as they walked to the front door. "Your father was a good man. I liked him. He had no business sense at all. He flogged me a couple of crates of war surplus underwear that are still gathering dust in the store attic. I'll be lucky to get a nickel on the dollar for them as rags. No hard feelings, but one McFadden financial disaster is all I can take."

He opened the screen door for her. "Thanks, Mr. Dubrofski. I didn't mean to impose. Mrs. Dubrofski kind of drew me out." She turned to go.

"Who, ah, who do you owe the money to, if you don't mind me asking?"

"A contractor named Huey Foo."

Morty Dubrofski's right hand darted out like a shortstop and caught Frances's upper arm. "Not Hong Kong Huey Foo?" he demanded.

"I don't know where he's from. He has an accent. He's the cook at the Bluebird Café on Dalhousie Street."

"*Jesus*, Frances!"

Morty spun her around and they marched back to the kitchen where Ethel Dubrofski was wiping her eyes with the bloody tea towel. Morty opened the icebox and pulled out a package wrapped in butcher paper marked "VEAL" in black block letters. He sat down at the kitchen table and undid the tape to reveal two thick piles of banknotes.

"Frances, Let me give you a little business advice," Morty said, as he started to count. "Don't ever fool with Hong Kong Huey Foo. He plays for keeps. How much do you need?"

Ethel broke in. "You know this guy?"

"Know *of* him. Abe Sayer had a run-in with him over some invoices. Didn't pay up. Then his next fur shipment to Montreal—his *uninsured* fur shipment to Montreal—disappeared on the highway. Without a trace. That's why the Sayers are in the rag business now. And my brother Lenny didn't sell out to me at bargain basement prices and move to Miami just because he loves palm trees. How much do you need, Frances?"

"One hundred and fifty dollars cash by six o'clock."

They all looked up at the kitchen clock. It was 5:40.

"Ethel, call Murray at Red Line taxi and get a car over here on the double. Here you go, kid. One hundred and fifty and fifteen dollars for insult. Count it yourself."

"Insult?" said Frances, thumbing through the bills.

"Yeah. These Chinks take offence when a deal goes haywire like this. I think 10 percent will cover it."

"And a taxi?" said Frances. " I've never ridden in a taxi in my life."

"You're running out of daylight, sweetheart, and I don't want you walking through this neighbourhood with my hundred and fifty bucks hanging out of your pocket. Here's an extra buck for cab fare. Tip Murray big if he gets you there on time."

A car honked at the front of the house and Frances jumped up, her eyes filling. "Oh, Mr. Dubrofski! Thank you! You'll get every cent back as soon as the bank opens tomorrow."

"I'd appreciate that, kid," Morty said, pulling another beer from the icebox.

13

DEBTS

The Red Line cab raced through the empty Sunday streets and reached the Blackburn Building in eight minutes flat. "That'll be thirty cents," said Murray Schultz.

"Thanks," Frances said, handing him the dollar. "Keep the change."

"Whoa, big spender! Call me any time, young lady!"

Frances took the elevator to the fourth floor. She edged along the piled furniture to her office. Huey Foo and Leather Jacket were sitting on the crates by the card table, smoking.

She dropped the package in butcher paper on the table. "Here you are," she said. It was three minutes to six.

They both gave her a long, silent look, then looked at each other, then Leather Jacket opened the bundle, and counted. He counted again. He uttered a quick sentence in Chinese.

Huey Foo said, "Too much money. Contract for one hundred fifty dollar."

"Please accept the extra for the inconvenience I have caused you. I'm sorry that I misunderstood," said Frances.

There was a brief staccato of Chinese, then Huey Foo replied, "No need extra money. Agreement one hundred fifty dollar cash for painting and cleaning by six o'clock Sunday. Now six o'clock. Work done. Money here. All square." He stood up. "Happy do business with you, Miss Fran. Go now do other business."

Huey Foo passed a wad of bills over to Lao Lee. Leather Jacket stood up. "Mr. Foo knew you would honour the bargain." He bowed, and paused before adding, "Are you all right?"

Frances followed his gaze to her blouse, splotched all over with Sollie Dubrofski's blood. Her hand instinctively tried to cover her shame, like a nakedness. "I'm fine," she stammered.

Leather Jacket dipped his head with the briefest of smiles, then left.

Frances sank down on the nearest crate.

They think I killed somebody and don't even care!

The painters were tying their bundles of bamboo and rolling up their aprons. Frances looked around the office. The rooms glowed.

"Very beautiful! Thank you for your work," she said to Lao Lee.

He gaped at the red blooms on her blouse and nodded with a nervous smile. The face of the young girl who had served the tea clouded with concern. "Are you hurt, miss?" she said, eyeing the bloodstains.

"I'm fine. Please thank everyone for their hard work."

The girl translated. There were nods and appreciative murmurs.

"We will go now. Will you go home, too?" asked the girl, politely.

"No," said Frances. "I need to move the furniture in."

"Move now?"

"Yes. It's a fire hazard. It has to be out of the hall before the building opens tomorrow."

"By yourself?"

"Yes. The custodian left me two dollies to use."

The girl quickly translated to Lao Lee. There were murmurings of "*Hao, hao,*" from the listening painters.

The girl turned back to Frances. "Miss, you have been kind to us. We will help you move the furniture."

"Oh no," said Frances. "You've all worked extra hours for four days. You must be exhausted!"

The girl translated, and listened to several comments. Then she said, "Many hands make quick work. We will help you."

Frances glanced at the fifteen dollars left on the card table. "I would be happy to pay you fifteen dollars to move the furniture."

Again the girl translated. There was a wide-ranging discussion, which Lao Lee finally closed with a definite comment. The girl said, "Miss, we work only for Shao Foo. We cannot take other pay."

"I appreciate your offer, but I cannot ask you to do this for free," Frances replied.

Again the girl translated, and there was a flurry of Chinese. Finally a broad-shouldered painter spoke gruffly in a woman's voice, and there was a wide exchange of glances. Lao Lee said something to the girl, and she translated.

"Miss, you have money that we cannot take. You have work that we could do. Chen Luang has a suggestion. The Chinese Benevolent Society in Ottawa helps many Chinese orphans and widows and immigrants. It has helped us all. We are happy to move the furniture for free. If you wish you could make a donation to the Chinese Benevolent Society."

"I'd be delighted!" said Frances.

The painters swarmed on the furniture like locusts, Frances directing traffic. In thirty minutes, everything was moved in and the hall was mopped.

On the way to work Monday morning, Frances walked along Sparks Street and stopped at the newspaper offices to pick up the want-ad replies. There were many of them, as Dr. Grace had predicted. She made a quick sort before leaving for the Bank of Montreal. She was at the front door at ten o'clock sharp. The friendly smile of a mousy teller in a brown smock evaporated when she saw the size of the cheque Frances wished to cash.

"Do you have any identification?" she asked.

"I do not," said Frances. "But Mr. Nutley or Miss Hicks could vouch for me."

"Mr. Nutley is at a meeting at our Rideau Street branch, and Miss Hicks is ill today. Perhaps you could come back tomorrow?"

"Miss," said Frances, "I need this cheque cashed immediately. Speak to Mr. Birchall if you must."

Worry clouded the brown mouse's face. She excused herself to show the cheque to a thin woman in a red dress at a desk near the vault. Heads bobbed over hushed whispers. The thin woman came over to speak to Frances, trailing the teller like a puppy.

"You are . . .?" She looked down at the signature on the cheque.

"Frances McFadden. Of the Canadian Financial Resources Agency. We have an account here, and I need to draw on it."

"This is a rather large cheque."

"It's a rather large account."

The thin woman pursed her lips. The brown mouse peered curiously out from behind her.

Frances could feel her heat rise, but was trying desperately to stay calm. "Miss . . .?"

"Struthers," said the thin woman.

"Miss Struthers. I have an important appointment at ten-thirty. I need this cheque cashed now. If there is a problem, I suggest that you speak with Mr. Birchall."

The long pause told Frances that Mr. Birchall was not normally imposed upon by the likes of brown tellers and thin women in red.

"Would you like me to speak to Mr. Birchall?" asked Frances.

"Miss Hicks handles Mr. Birchall's appointments and she isn't in today."

"Is Mr. Birchall in?"

"Yes, but he's with clients and can't be disturbed," said Miss Struthers.

Frances reached over the counter, plucked the cheque from the hand of Miss Struthers, then marched directly to Mr. Birchall's corner office. When Miss Struthers deduced her intent, she scurried after her on her own side of the counter. Frances beat her to Mr. Birchall's door, knocked twice, and marched in on the smiling bank manager and two laughing men in dark suits. Mr. Birchall looked as though he had been caught telling an off-colour joke, and jumped to his feet.

"What. . .?" he exclaimed before he recognized her. "Why, Miss Mc-Fadden!"

Frances heard the footsteps of Miss Struthers and the brown mouse as they rounded the counter and appeared in the doorway behind her.

"So sorry, sir!" exclaimed Miss Struthers, over Frances's shoulder. "We had no idea she'd burst in on you!"

Mr. Birchall disarmed them with a look. He smiled at Frances. "How can I help you?"

"I have to cash a cheque," said Frances a little snappishly. "I understood that it was the business of banks to cash cheques, but I've been having some difficulty accomplishing this task."

"She has no identification," explained the brown mouse.

"She wants to withdraw a large amount of money," added Miss Struthers.

Wordlessly, Mr. Birchall held out his hand. Wordlessly, Frances handed over the cheque. He read it, picked up a pen, and initialled it.

"Miss Struthers," he said emphatically to the thin woman. "And Miss Dawson," he added to the brown mouse. "This is Miss McFadden. She is a valued client of the Bank of Montreal. And a connoisseur of art," he said with a smile. "Please honour any request from her, and don't bother me on her account again." He gave a perfunctory smile to his staff, a much more genial smile to Frances, and sat down.

Frances nodded a curt "thank you" to the manager, gave the same nod to the open-mouthed seated men, and, turning, handed the cheque back to the brown mouse, who retreated in rapid, shuffling backward steps out the door, like a courtier leaving the presence of the king.

Frances hailed a taxi on Wellington and was at Dubrofski Brothers' Dry Goods on Somerset by 10:35. She was directed up the stairs to Morty

Dubrofski's office on the mezzanine at the back.

"Sorry to get here so late, Mr. Dubrofski," she said, laying the crisp pile of bills on his cluttered desk. "Banks will be the death of me!"

Morty Dubrofski put his cigar in the ashtray while he counted the money. He smiled. "One hundred and eighty-two?" he asked.

"Yes," said Frances. "The insult money and the taxi fare bring it up to one hundred and sixty-six. You were right. I needed them both. I don't know the going rate for short-term loans, but you saved my life last night, so I added 10 percent. Will that do?"

Morty's face split with a wide grin. "Frances! I'm not a loan shark. Here's your sixteen bucks back. Between a stuffy bank and a Chinese mobster, you've had quite an introduction to the world of business."

Frances nodded.

Morty continued. "I stay away from those bloodsuckers at the banks if I can help it. I have no truck with the Chinese tongs. And I never give personal loans. But you made this all work, kid. Congratulations."

"Well, Mr. Dubrofski, I'll never forget you helped me. Government regulations demand this double signage bank account, so I must learn to live with the Bank of Montreal. However, I've seen enough Chinese contractors to last me a lifetime."

By five o'clock, when Frances had sorted the job applications on the conference table, she heard footsteps in the outer office, then "Holy Smoke!" Dr. Grace waved to her through the open doorway. He carried his battered briefcase in one hand and a shopping bag in the other.

"This office looks just like . . . like an office!" he exclaimed. He darted in and out of all the rooms before returning to her. "Was it only last Wednesday that it looked like a war zone here? This calls for a cel-ebration!" He withdrew two liquor bottles and a quart of soda water from the shopping bag and set them on the oak credenza. He handed Frances a square blue Birks box, which she opened to find six Waterford crystal old-fashioned glasses.

"I forgot whether we had glasses and ice yet, so I brought both just in case." He filled two tumblers with ice cubes and poured a liberal liba-tion of amber liquid into each. He put a wisp of soda in one glass, and topped the second glass right up before handing it to Frances.

"Cheers," he said, raising his glass to her. He drained half his glass, while Frances sniffed, then sipped delicately. It smelled like autumn and tickled her throat as she swallowed.

"This is Macallan single malt Scotch. Like silk smoke, isn't it? Should really drink it neat, but the soda opens the molecules and aids digestion, as my father used to say. It is only for important occasions like the birth of kings. That," he said, pointing to the other bottle "is the common house Scotch, for ordinary events." He drained his glass, and filling it again, eyeing the neat piles of papers spread across the table.

"Well, how do they look?"

"Dozens of file clerks," responded Frances. "But there aren't that many translators out there. We only have ten applications."

"We only need one. Any good prospects?"

"One claims he speaks eight languages, but English doesn't seem to be one of them. Another says she is fluent in six languages, including Russian and Ukrainian. One man says he knows English, French, Spanish, and German, and can translate from any one to any other. The rest stuck to English and French. Two didn't type their résumés."

"Cut the non-typers. Either can't read, or can't follow directions. Or can't type. And take a pass on the non-English speaker. Can you interview seven?"

"Sure. How do we know if the applications were actually typed by the applicants?"

"You can test them. Give them a passage to type and translate right here."

"But I can't judge the translations."

"I can help, if they're brief. Why don't you give them something short but challenging to translate, like . . ."

"Like the *Gettysburg Address*?"

"Perfect!" exclaimed Dr. Grace. "That'll test their mettle. How about the file clerk?"

"Lots of interest. Twenty-four applications. But six weren't typed. Four were filled with spelling mistakes. A couple actually sounded over-qualified for the job."

"Someone over-qualified is either lying or will not be happy just filing. Cut them all. Can you weed out half a dozen more?"

"Probably."

"How will you run the interviews?"

Frances reflected. "I'll tell them that candidate selection is a three-step process, and that interviewees had made it to the second step. I'd be checking their paperwork, and administering the practical tests and preparing their documents for your consideration, if they make it to step three."

"There's something more, Miss McFadden. I can see the wheels turning behind those hazel eyes."

Frances smiled. "I want to see how they react just to little old me. I want to feel genuine respect and courtesy, or I don't want to work with them."

"Clever girl. Oh, and those who don't make the cut?"

"I'll draft the thanks-but-no-thanks letters for your signature."

"You're a born manager, McFadden. You'll be prime minister someday. Put the booze in the vault for safekeeping."

—— 14 ——

EVENING WITH SLOAN

Frances set up the translator interviews for late Wednesday. Two applicants bowed out when they heard the wages. Two just didn't show up. Frances liked this natural selection process. It left her with less to decide. One candidate was irked at having to deal with a mere secretary and sighed herself out of the job.

This left the effervescent Miss Romanovitch, "of the St. Petersburg Romanovitches," and the reticent Mr. Mueller. Polar opposites. Miss Romanovitch was an expansive woman of indeterminate age. It was she who commanded six languages, including Russian. She spoke in a cultured voice glazed with a faint Eastern European accent.

"Every language we acquire is another window for our soul," she trilled, her voice running up and down the scale like a mountain goat. "There is such a richness in reading both Tolstoy and Shakespeare in the original! Don't you agree? It's a shame that they have been so poorly translated! Perhaps, when I have the time, I will lend my attention to the task." Miss Romanovitch's eyes flitted around the office like a hummingbird. She wore elaborate costume jewellery and a low-cut dress that barely contained her ample bosom.

It was impossible to tell if Mr. Mueller's eyes darted anywhere. His gazed fixedly at the floor, eyes flicking up occasionally, like a frog tonguing an insect, and then returning to the linoleum. The right pant leg from a threadbare brown suit disappeared inside a blue argyle sock. Frances had never seen such a lack of pretension. She liked him immediately.

When Dr. Grace phoned she laughed as she described the two finalists. "They both typed fast and accurately. You'll have to check the translations.

"Miss Romanovitch looked like an opera singer. I expected to hear her break into *Aida* at any moment. At first, I thought Mr. Mueller was having trouble with the typewriter in your office. I'd hear a clatter of typing, then he'd rip a page out and insert another. Turns out he was translating into German and Spanish as well as French. I thought I was shy! Mr. Mueller clings to the wall like a mouse. And he could not look me in the eye."

"Quite the choice. The Czarina or Caspar Milquetoast. Who do you like for the team?"

"I want you to meet them. I've set up final interviews at 4:00 and 4:20 p.m. on Friday."

"But you've got a preference."

"I want a second opinion."

"Your opinion is good enough for me."

"I appreciate that. I still want a second opinion."

"Okay. It sounds like vaudeville, anyway. I need a little light entertainment after all this committee work up here. You doing the clerks tomorrow?"

"Yes. Seven candidates. It won't sift out quite so easily."

"The Bible says, 'Judge not lest ye be judged.' But your job is to sort them out by using your best judgment. Don't be afraid to do it. I'm in Montreal all day tomorrow. Keep up the good work, kiddo."

Five of the seven file clerk applicants showed up for their interviews on Thursday. A disparate bunch. A heavy smoker with slow eyes. A tall man with massive hands that somehow didn't jam up the keyboard. A man in a filthy sweater with his arm in a sling, apologetic about not being able to do the typing test. A blonde, anxious nail-biter. A needy woman in a fox fur wrap.

Broken Arm either a fraud or incapacitated for the near future. Cut.

Smoker's Breath stank and the reek of her clothes was asphyxiating. Cut.

No Nails put the carbon paper in backwards. Cut.

So that left Huge Hands and Needy Nelly for Dr. Grace's consideration.

"What do you mean, 'Needy Nelly'?" he asked.

"Well, she wrung her hands constantly. Said she needed the job desperately to support her family. Still, her typing and shorthand were quite strong."

"Do needy women wear fox wraps?" asked Dr. Grace.

"As it wasn't a fashion contest, I didn't ask. Still, we need somebody, and if she needs a job, maybe both our needs could be met at the same time."

"In economics, they call that 'a double coincidence of wants.'"

"A what?"

"When she has something we want, and we have something she wants, that's called a double coincidence of wants. Before they invented money, that was how all commerce took place. If you had a horse and wanted six sheep, and I had six sheep and wanted a horse, we just exchanged, and everybody was happy."

"But what if I didn't want your six sheep? I wanted a trip to Niagara Falls instead."

"Excellent point! That is exactly why money was invented as a neutral exchange agent. You part with your horse for money and buy a ticket to Niagara Falls. I exchange my sheep for money and buy a cottage in the Gatineau Hills. Isn't money handy?"

"It'd be handy to have some. See you Friday afternoon for the interviews."

Frances worked past eight p.m. to finish typing all of the rejection letters for Dr. Grace's signature and to complete her filing. She was building up two sets of index cards. The green box contained working contact information of anyone she dealt with officially, the advertising offices at the city newspapers, Mr. Dubrofski, Lolly O'Byrne.

The black index box had the names of anyone she had set up a file on as she clipped the newspapers. This collection was growing by twenty to thirty files a day. Although not exactly confidential, Frances felt uneasy leaving the index boxes on her desk, so locked them in the vault with the Scotch each night before she left.

The new combination lock on the safe was very precise. She had to stand in her own shadow when working the dial, and squint to hit the setting bang-on. It was the smell that broke her concentration before she was aware of any sound. It was a bitter-sweet odour, like the aroma of her mother's brandy. Then she heard a raspy breathing behind her and froze.

"Well, well, well. What we got here? A safe-cracker?"

Frances whirled around to find Mr. Sloan glaring down at her with bloodshot eyes. The vapour of liquor knocked her backward.

"We . . . we had the lock reset, and it's a little tricky," explained Frances.

"You're quite a little trick yourself," said Mr. Sloan, hemming her in the narrow passage as he moved forward. "You been staying late just so you'd bump into ol' Sloan?"

"Oh, no. I was just trying to get my work caught up. I forgot all about you."

"Forgot about me? That's not a very nice thing to say about your ol' friend Sloan." His right hand reached out and touched her neck. His stink of sweat and alcohol sucked the air out of the cramped passageway.

"No one here now, girlie. No one in the whole building 'cept you and Sloan. We could have us a party." His fingers tangled in her hair.

"No, please," Frances struggled against him. "No, please, Mr. Sloan! I have to go home."

"I can make you at home, right here, sweetheart." His left arm reached around behind her, and he forced her up toward him.

"No, please! No, please!" Frances's words were cut short as his lips closed down hard on hers. She struggled fruitlessly. She held her breath against his stench and shut her eyes to block him out.

Suddenly, his head snapped back, and his arms released Frances to stumble back against the vault door. She peeked and saw Sloan walk backward in short, stuttery steps, like a film being shown in reverse. Sloan's head crashed against the cupboard to his left, then his whole body rebounded into the air, before his lank form smashed down onto the counter beside her. He lay on his back, bewildered. An arm drew Sloan's head up by the hair. A short stick materialized in front of Sloan's face. Before his frightened eyes, the stick flashed open into a knife, then the knife point lowered beneath Sloan's field of vision to prick into his neck below his chin.

A slow, quiet voice broke the silence. "When Miss Fran say 'no,' she mean 'no.' Undastand, Missa Sloan?"

Under the porkpie hat of Huey Foo, dark eyes searched Sloan's face. Leather Jacket lifted the knife point into Sloan's throat, so that a drop of blood appeared on the blade.

"Undastand English, Missa Sloan?" Huey Foo repeated.

"Yes," whispered Sloan.

"Good," said Huey Foo. "Miss Fran is honoured business associate. You dishonour Miss Fran, you dishonour Huey Foo. Undastand, Missa Sloan?"

Sloan nodded his head right into the stiletto blade at his throat and winced back. Huey Foo said something in Chinese, and Leather Jacket lifted Sloan by the hair to a seating position, smashing his head against the cupboard over the counter again.

"Know Willie Berton, Missa Sloan? Night watchman at Earle Street Apartment?"

Sloan's eyes widened into saucers. He was silent until he felt the knife again. "Yes. Yes!"

Huey Foo sucked air through his teeth. "Too bad, Willie Berton. Got good advice. Not follow good advice. Too bad." Huey Foo sucked more air, making a tsking noise. "Know Larry Walton? Your neighbour, Missa Sloan?"

Sloan was pale, and the rivulet of blood on his neck stood out in bold contrast. "Yes . . . I knew him . . . before . . ." His voice trailed as he tried to swallow.

"Very sad, Missa Walton. Missa Walton also get good advice. Not follow. Very sad his family." Huey Foo gave another tsk, and shook his head. "Now, Missa Sloan, I have good advice for you. Never touch Miss Fran again. Never speak Miss Fran again. Anything happen to Miss Fran, I come find you. Miss Fran catch cold, Miss Fran scrape knee, I come find you. Undastand, Missa Sloan?"

"Yes." Sloan's forehead glistened with sweat.

"Good. Undastanding make good business. You go now."

Leather Jacket effortlessly lifted Sloan off the counter by the hair and shoved him through the archway. Sloan stumbled out the door slamming it behind him. Frances was shaking, and biting her lip, leaning against the door of the vault. Her eyes were moist, and her breath came in little snatches. She looked helplessly at Huey Foo and Leather Jacket.

Huey Foo smiled. "So sorry disturb you, Miss Fran. Forgot return office key on Sunday. Very thoughtless. Here." He took a pair of keys from his coat pocket and handed them over.

"Thank you! Thank you!" Frances said, between jagged gulps of air.

"Respect make good business, Miss Fran. Disrespect not good business. We have Ford car downstairs. You look tired. Want drive home?"

— 15 —

CATHARSIS

Frances barely slept all night. She'd taken a hot bath, but the stench of Sloan lingered. Vera McFadden came in around midnight, after her evening shift. It might have helped to talk to her. It might have made things worse.

Next morning, there was no heat in her walk to work. She got to the Blackburn Building at 8:40 a.m. Stella whistled. "Hey, Fran! You're late! What's up?"

"Didn't sleep well," was all Frances said.

The phone was ringing as she unlocked the office door. She wouldn't have answered it, but craved the silence.

"Miss McFadden?" demanded an icy male voice.

"Yes." She dropped listlessly into her desk chair. "May I help you?"

"This is Lionel Helmsley at the Department of Finance. I must speak with Dr. Grace."

"I expected him in last night from Montreal, but haven't heard from him. Is there a message?"

Exasperation seethed at the other end of the line. "This is most unsatisfactory. The joint Commons-Senate Committee reviewing the Bank Act met until the wee hours last night, and they have concerns about the impact of the new legislation on agriculture and manufacturing. These are impatient men, Miss McFadden," he said impatiently. "You have no idea where Dr. Grace is?"

"He had meetings yesterday afternoon in Montreal. He hoped to get out on the seven o'clock train, but I haven't heard from him."

"Then you'll have to come over and take their questions."

"Mr. Helmsley, I cannot leave the office unattended. I'm sorry, but . . ."

"I beg your pardon, Miss McFadden! I insist that you be in Committee Room C in the East Block by ten this morning to meet with these men."

"Mr. Helmsley, I do not know anything about those files that you have mentioned."

"It is your duty! Are you refusing me, Miss McFadden?"

"Dr. Grace has ordered me to get this office shipshape immediately. I cannot do that if I leave it unattended."

"I find you most uncooperative, Miss McFadden. Dr. Grace will hear about this." The phone line went dead.

Frances contemplated. Yeoman's misdirected furniture. Huey Foo. Morty Dubrofski. The Bank of Montreal. Sloan. And now the imperious Mr. Helmsley. It was too much. The phone rang again. She took several deep breaths and answered on the fifth ring.

"Frances! I'm at Union Station. Freight train derailment in front of the night-liner out of Montreal last night. No one hurt, but I had to spend ten hours in the Rigaud station with one light bulb and a million mosquitoes. I'm tired and filthy and am racing up to a meeting on the Hill. Just wanted to touch base. What's up?"

Silence.

"Frances? You there?"

Another pause. "Dr. Grace, I can't work here anymore. I'm sorry."

"What are you talking about?"

"I've tried my best, Dr. Grace. I just can't do it. I'm sorry to let you down."

"Can't do what? You've never let me down!"

A short sob escaped from her throat. "I came in to type my resignation. I'll leave it on your desk."

"Frances, can you hold on until noon? We need to talk, but I have twenty things to do up on Parliament Hill."

Silence.

"Promise me you'll wait for me until lunch?"

Silence.

"For old time's sake?"

Frances had to laugh. "Dr. Grace, we just met two weeks ago at the Château Laurier. Does two weeks make for 'old times'?"

"Two weeks! It seems like we've been working together for a lifetime. Please wait until noon?"

"All right."

"Thanks! See you soon."

Frances walked back to the washroom. She locked the door and sat down on the toilet seat. Gigantic sobs convulsed her.

She had slowly washed her face in the kitchen sink before she noticed

Dr. Grace was sitting at her desk, looking over the office log. "No wonder you're exhausted! Look at the hours you're keeping. Thursday and Friday seven a.m. until ten p.m. Sunday: noon until nine o'clock. You're logging eighty-hour weeks, for goodness sake!

"Come on into the conference room. I've got coffee and blueberry muffins from the Elgin Street Deli."

"I thought you were busy until noon on the Hill."

"The people in Committee Room C can wait. They think they need me. They don't. I don't need them. I need you."

The coffee had double cream and single sugar, just the way she liked it. They ate the muffins and then he said, "What's the trouble?"

Frances sighed. She did not like to complain. She gave him the short list of disasters, including Helmsley, but omitting Sloan.

"First of all, I've let you down by not being here to support you. I call every day, but that is clearly not enough, considering what you're dealing with. I promise to do more.

"That said, you have met every challenge. Furniture arrived at the wrong time. You found temporary storage, and got it all moved in. A little misunderstanding about cash or a cheque. Most people use these terms interchangeably. Mr. Foo wanted cash, so you got it. Very resourceful. Two clerks try to stonewall you at the Bank of Montreal, you go right to the top dog. I would have done the same thing. Paid Dubrofski back promptly. Good credit rating!

"Refused to be bullied by Helmsley. Bully for you. My mother used to say, 'The measure of a man's greatness is the size of a thing that it takes to get him annoyed.' You're not going to be measured by a jellybean like Helmsley.

"How can you feel anything but elation? Remember what this office looked like two weeks ago? Prime ministers have done less for Canada in their careers than you've done in two weeks. They got statues on Parliament Hill. Make a note, will you? 'Commission bronze statue of Frances for front of the Blackburn Building.' "

Frances smiled but bit her lip. "I can't . . . I can't work here anymore."

"What?" he asked softly, waiting. "Frances, I can't help if I don't know what's wrong."

She looked down, then looked into his listening eyes. He leaned forward. She told him about Sloan.

"Oh God, Frances!" Dr. Grace came over and knelt down beside her chair. "I want to hug you, but I'm afraid to touch you, because I'm a goddamn man."

Frances dropped her head on his shoulder. Three sobs escaped from her before she regained control. He gave her hand a comforting squeeze.

"It's an outrage, and it's never going to happen again." Dr. Grace walked out to Frances's phone. "Hi, Jake. It's Wilbur Grace. Yes. We're almost in business. Could you drop down to our office right now? We need to chat. Thanks." He hung up.

"You'll like Jake Kinkade. Have you met him yet?"

"I've said hi in the hall a couple of times. Look, Dr. Grace, I don't . . . I can't . . . This is a tough story to tell to strangers."

"I understand. I'll do the talking. I want Sloan out of here today."

There was a "Hello?" from the outer office.

"Hi, Jake," said Dr. Grace, shaking his hand. "Come on in. You've met the brains of our outfit, Frances McFadden?"

"Wow! Look what you've done here in two weeks!" Jake Kinkade said with a wide smile. "If I'd known this place would clean up so well, I would have charged you more!"

"Jake, we're delighted to be here, except for one thing. This guy Sloan."

"Yeah, he's not much of a cleaner. Are the dust bunnies getting too big for you?" Jake laughed.

Wilbur Grace did not smile. In a few circumspect sentences he outlined the previous evening's events. "If the painting contractor hadn't dropped in to return the keys, I hate to think what might have happened."

Jake Kinkade was ashen. He had two young daughters.

"This is criminal," he said. "We should call the police right now."

Frances shuddered.

"We could do that," said Dr. Grace. "We probably *should* do that. I hate the thought of Frances, the innocent victim, here, paying the price of all the publicity, and the anxiety of a court trial. And sad to say, judges are loath to convict when it is just one person's word against another."

"But there were witnesses!" said Jake.

"My guess is that Mr. Foo runs a cleaning service full of illegal immigrants, and would disappear if subpoenaed."

Now Jake Kinkade looked glum. "I can just fire him."

"Maybe not right away," suggested Dr. Grace. "How many buildings does Harmer Property Management look after?"

"Twenty-six in Ottawa. Why?"

"I want Sloan out of here today for good," said Dr. Grace, "but I don't want him taking anything out on Frances. Is there room for some lateral movement among your building superintendents? What if you told Sloan that you need him in another building immediately. A building a long way from here. Added responsibility. A raise, even. No hostility. Move him today. In six months, fire him if you want, once the scent is off."

"Sure. We've got an apartment building in Eastview. I think Sloan actually lives down that way. The custodian has been laid up. We have one female custodian, Edna Atkins, who does swing shift when others are off sick. She's covering in Eastview. I could move her here and shuffle Sloan over there. How's that sound?"

"Good by me. Good by you, Miss McFadden?"

Frances nodded.

"If he comes by here to pick up his things, I want you with him at all times. I don't want him to set foot on the fourth floor."

"Agreed. I'll look after it right now." Jake Kinkade turned back to Frances. "I'm terribly sorry this happened, Miss McFadden. I hope it doesn't poison you on your new office. You've made it look so comfortable."

Frances stood up to shake his hand. "Thanks for listening, Mr. Kinkade. And thanks for taking action."

On Friday, Dr. Grace showed up early to check over the translations before the interviews.

"The Contessa and Caspar both have good French. My German is rusty, but at least I can see Caspar isn't faking this. Bring them on."

The Contessa was wearing the same garish dress from the previous interview, but had changed her costume jewellery. She was effervescent and gracious. Dr. Grace had a conversation with her in French, then turned to Frances.

"Do we need anything further, Miss McFadden?"

"I don't believe so, Dr. Grace."

"Then thank you, Miss Romanovitch. We have several more interviews before we make our final decision. Miss McFadden will call you before noon tomorrow."

"*Merci, Monsieur le Docteur*," said the Contessa and curtseyed as she withdrew.

"Where's the next candidate?"

Frances checked her watch and went to the office door. No one. She walked down the hall and around the corner to the elevator. No one. As she returned, a shadow caught her eye through the window in the stairway door. She opened it to see Mr. Mueller sitting on the stairs.

"Mr. Mueller, we're ready for you. Won't you please come in?" she said, holding the door open for him. Sweating profusely, he wobbled to his feet. He looked everywhere to avoid meeting Frances's eyes, until she said, "Do you find me offensive to look at, Mr. Mueller?"

"Oh, no, Miss McFadden. I didn't mean to give offence. I'm just . . . I'm terribly nervous. I'm too shy for this job. I'm sorry to have wasted your time."

"Mr. Mueller, it's not your fault that you are shy, so you need not apologize. I'm shy myself. Being interviewed can be stressful for anyone, shy or not. Ten people applied for this translation job. Only two candidates are still in contention, and you're one of them. That's quite an accomplishment. Dr. Grace is conducting the final interviews. He's kind and fair. You can relax."

Frances took his arm and led him in. Dr. Grace smiled as he shook Mr. Mueller's hand.

"Tell me, Mr. Mueller, do you like music?"

Mr. Mueller looked up, surprised. "I love music, Dr. Grace. It is all that I live for."

"What do you play?"

"The piano and violin, but my passion is the viola da gamba."

"Who is your favourite composer?"

"Of the Russians, I like Mussorgsky best. Of the Germans, Handel."

"There can't be many job opportunities in Ottawa for viola da gamba players these days."

"True. So I find myself here with you, Dr. Grace."

They conversed for several minutes in French. Mr. Mueller's eyes never left Dr. Grace's face for the whole conversation.

"Do we need anything further, Miss McFadden?"

"I don't believe so, Dr. Grace."

"Then thank you, Mr. Mueller. A pleasure to meet you. Miss McFadden will call you before noon tomorrow with our decision."

Mr. Mueller rose and smiled for the first time. He bowed. "The pleasure was mine," he said and took his leave.

Frances looked quizzically at Dr. Grace. "Well, I thought he was going to faint, and you brought him back from the dead. Lazarus Milquetoast. How did you know he liked music?"

"A hunch. He sits rigid on the edge of his seat, like a string player. He had a row of calluses on the fingers of his left hand that might have come from fretting the strings. His translations were, well, musical, rather than the literal ones produced by the Contessa." He looked at Frances and laughed. "I like him. But I defer to you."

Frances smiled. "I liked him too."

"He will need clear direction and emotional support, but his writing looks exceptionally good."

"Let's take him," said Frances, moving the translator files off the desk. "Now for the file clerk."

When Big Hands and Needy Nellie left, Dr. Grace said: "Not really much difference, although I didn't get the same vitality that I felt from Mr. Mueller. What do you think?"

Frances sighed. "I don't dislike either of them. I'm sure they both would be quite competent."

"But . . . ?"

"Well, I think of someone like my friend, Mary O'Brien. She has so much energy . . . and an amazing photographic memory! And yesterday the company that was to hire her on graduation went bankrupt."

"Is this Mary O'Brien still available? Call her up right now and we'll interview her."

"But she's my friend!"

"So?"

"Mary will think I'm just taking pity on her."

"You looked through—was it thirty applications? Were any of them as good as Mary O'Brien?"

"Frankly, no. But she didn't take part in the process! She can't . . . it's not fair if—"

"Frances, life isn't fair. There's really only one consideration. Would she take liberties because she's your friend?"

"Never! She'd work twice as hard to prove herself worthy."

"Well, I don't know anything about her, but you say she's got the talent we need. Can you get her down here, pronto?"

A quick phone call brought Mary away from cooking dinner and downtown in fifteen minutes. She was hot and out of breath and had flour on her blue blouse. Frances introduced Dr. Grace, who asked half a dozen polite questions. Then he said, "Miss O'Brien, would you have any trouble working under the direction of Miss McFadden? She's the boss here."

"I have known Frances McFadden since she was in Grade 1. There is no one I hold in higher respect."

"Do we need anything further, Miss McFadden?"

"I don't believe so, Dr. Grace."

"Then thank you, Miss O'Brien. Miss McFadden will call you before noon tomorrow with our decision."

PART
TWO

16

NETWORK

Frances McFadden was falling in love with her job. The electric surge of being at the controls woke her before six a.m., and she exulted in escaping her mother's home for the liberty of the Blackburn Building. She beat Stella Stanton to her station, and bounded up the stairs to get a pot of coffee percolating. The hopeful bubbling of freshly ground Pride of Arabia was as infatuating as freedom.

After the Sloan incident, Dr. Grace insisted on lunch at the Château Laurier every Friday. He guaranteed daily contact through either a morning phone call or a late-afternoon visit.

"What if there's an emergency, and I need you immediately?"

"Emergency? Like a swarm of locusts?" Dr. Grace asked.

"I don't know!" exclaimed Frances. "Shouldn't we have some plan? My mother leaves an extra house key under the back stoop 'in case.' What if we had a code word that said emergency without saying 'emergency'?"

He thought for a moment. "The greatest disaster to befall the Scottish nation was the Battle of Culloden in 1746. 'Culloden File' could be the code for 'drop everything and come running.'"

"Sounds important, yet innocuous," agreed Frances.

"Let's hope we never have to use it."

Frances was nervous about her first Inter-Departmental Support Coordinating Committee meeting on Parliament Hill. The three maidens and three widows who made up the "Tuesday Tea Group" had collectively logged over two hundred years on the government payroll serving senior deputy ministers.

Rose Malone called the meeting to order at exactly 4:00 p.m. She introduced Frances as the new secretary-treasurer of the equally new Canadian Financial Resources Agency. Rose asked for a volunteer to take minutes. After twenty seconds of explosive silence, Frances succumbed. "If it would help, Miss Malone, I'd be happy to take minutes."

"God bless you, dear," responded Rose with an icy glare around the circle.

Frances kept silent unless addressed. The agenda boasted a lengthy list of items, but the women showed no haste. Twice she was told by the maker of an acerbic comment to "strike that from the minutes, dear." Frances boiled a second kettle for tea and refilled the cookie tray. As five o'clock approached, Rose noted that it was Lily's turn to host the following Tuesday and adjourned the meeting. Frances typed up the minutes and dropped copies in the mail when she left for home.

Late Thursday afternoon the phone rang. "Hello, Frances, dear," said Rose. "Thank you so much! Your minutes were prompt and error-free. Would you be interested in being the permanent secretary of the Inter-Department Support Coordinating Committee?"

"It would certainly help me understand how government departments function, Miss Malone, but I'll need to run it by Dr. Grace."

Dr. Grace greeted the news like an Olympic victory. "Egad, Frances! You have won the collective hearts of the Momsies in one meeting! They practically run the government of Canada. You could learn more cutting up fruitcake for them than you could at a Cabinet meeting. By all means, go!"

In the middle of the second week of June, Dr. Grace had Frances order in lunch for the CFRA staff. "Future leaders of the Bank of Canada will depend on the resources you're compiling here," he said. "Unfortunately, my duties at the Department of Finance don't permit me to provide the direction that you deserve. However, I have every confidence in Frances.

"I need your help for a special project," he added with his disarming boyish smile. "The Bank of Canada's administration will be catering meetings in their offices until their own dining room is set up. Every Wednesday, I'd like you to order in lunch from different caterers. Then rate the quality of the food and the service. By Christmas, we should have excellent research on food purveyors in Ottawa—invaluable to the new governor. Will you help?"

Mary giggled and Mr. Mueller relaxed enough to smile. "No task is too daunting in the service of our country, sir," said Frances.

"Thank you, team!" Dr Grace replied. "Sadly, I will not likely be able to join you regularly. In my place, invite people that make your life here easier. I'd start with Stella Stanton. And Jake Kinkade's secretary, Maeve. Lolly what's-her-name from Imperial Printing. Mr. Birchall's wife might like to see how well her art looks. Invite them over one at a time for an informal lunch. You'll build bridges, and they'll remember the CFRA in a positive light."

"Too bad that so many can't come for lunch," said Frances.

"Oh? Who?" asked Dr. Grace.

"Well, there's the staff at the Château Laurier, and all the delivery men."

"Good point. How could we include them?"

Mary brightened. "My mother makes the best cookies east of Calabogie, or so my father claims. If we covered supplies, I bet she'd bake batches of cookies for us to spread around."

"Yes, Mary! We'll hire your mother to bake three dozen cookies twice a week and send them in with you. When delivery people come in, hand them a couple of cookies and a coffee. When you're down at the telegraph office, drop off half a dozen cookies for the operator. Mary, can I put you in charge of the cookie file?"

Mary beamed.

At their first regular Château Laurier lunch, Dr. Grace was careful to reintroduce Frances to key staff members. "All of these people can be secret agents for the CFRA, Frances. Signed up with a little courtesy and consideration. They get paid very little, so always give them a generous tip."

Dr. Grace leaned back and took a long swallow of the Chardonnay. "Another thing. I'm going to start leaving you with some reading material. Books and articles on banking, business, and international finance. I want you to read half an hour a day to get a better background in the banking business."

Frances stifled a laugh. Reading material! That was the code the Deavy sisters used when discussing boys in front of their parents. "Mrs. McFadden, I'm just going over to the library to check out some reading material and wondered if Frances could join me?" It was very difficult for a parent to deny an anxious scholar access to reading material.

"Dr. Grace, I just don't have the time. I'm in here before seven a.m. and never leave before seven p.m."

"You are Joan of Arc! But you must read to broaden your focus, to see how things interrelate. Otherwise you'll get bored or terribly confused. So, let's see . . . how do you currently prioritize your daily work?"

"Prioritize?" Frances felt weak. "I'm not that organized. I deal with the phone calls and the mail and the interruptions, and just keep working until seven. If something isn't finished, I take it home."

"You're going to drive yourself into the loony bin working that hard! Today, at six p.m., stop everything. Focus only on what you plan to do the next day. Make your must-do, should-do, and would-like-to-do lists to greet you next morning. You'll find it very therapeutic to draw a line through the things you've finished. Then leave and forget the office. The reading goes on the A list. It's like training for the Olympics — it has to be done every day.

"Next item. I want you to start keeping track of your overtime. You were hired to work a forty-four hour week for . . . what are we paying you now?"

"Well, you said that once the office was staffed, I'd be getting seventeen dollars a week."

"Let's make that eighteen dollars. So that's about — " he doodled in the margin of his notebook, " — forty cents an hour. For everything over forty-four hours a week, you should get time and a half, which is . . . a penny a minute! Aren't we generous! The government doesn't pay overtime, but we are not exactly the government, and I know that you're working full-out every second. So keep an account, and we'll reimburse you, one way or another."

Frances smiled. "Any interest on overdue accounts?"

"Absolutely! Outstanding overtime after thirty days should earn you the same 3 percent interest as government bonds. Compounded semi-annually, if they're that tardy."

"At least it should be a good bookkeeping exercise," replied Frances.

"Another thing. Ever since the famed age-of-majority issue with young Birchall at the Bank of Montreal, I've been thinking. What if you expanded your wardrobe to include a few outfits that made you look a little older?

"Hey, no need to glare at me! I hired you for who you are, and you don't need to disguise yourself for my benefit. Here's the thing, though. Looking older invests you with authority without your actually being older. Do you think I like wearing this three-piece suit every day? It's hot and itchy, but it lends an air of maturity to my boyish good looks. I wear the uniform that helps me do my job. So I want you to get two or three 'older office woman' uniforms. My father used to say that if you buy good quality, it lasts much longer."

"Dr. Grace, I can't afford to buy underwear on my salary," she blurted, then blushed. "I'm sorry, but I had to borrow money from my mother to buy what I wear now. I have to pay her back, and turn over a dollar-fifty a day for room and board. I can't afford 'good quality,' even on eighteen dollars a week."

"Well, then, I authorize you to spend seventy-five dollars from the office account to bolster your work wardrobe. Appearance is important in this business."

"Seventy-five dollars!" Frances exclaimed. "How do you think we're going to slip that past Mr. Crossman? Two dresses and three business ensembles from Holt Renfrew?"

"Take the money out of petty cash. Bring in all the receipts. Write it in the ledger as office equipment."

"Office equipment! What if we get audited?"

"Item one: these are materials that you need to work effectively in this office. Like your typewriter or the filing cabinets. Office equipment. Item two: there is more chance of Mr. Crossman's travelling to the moon than auditing our piddling little account. The annual government budget is over two billion dollars. He has to check it all, looking for million-dollar errors. He doesn't have time for small potatoes."

"Why is it, Dr. Grace, that you take such great delight in being an outlaw? Can I charge overtime for the length of my jail sentence?"

"You Presbyterians are obsessed with punishment. Relax. You get the clothes, I'll take the responsibility.

"Next item. How much of the office could Mary or Herbert run right now, if you were kidnapped by aliens?"

Frances reflected. "Not much. Twenty-five percent?"

"Not good enough. We have to keep the blood pumping at the CFRA at all costs. I know they're both shy, but I want you to get them comfortable making decisions. I want you to train Mary to take over if you're out of the office."

"Like, jailed for long periods?"

"Stop that. Mary needs clear directions. Write up a list of all the informal rules and procedures. Take all the guesswork out of it for her.

"And Plan C, Herbert needs to be trained to fill in for *her* in an emergency—say you're in Toronto, and Mary is sick—so the office keeps running." Dr. Grace drained his coffee.

Frances felt a strange reluctance. "Don't you trust me to do it all?"

"You can't do it all. Anyway, this is not about you, or even me, for that matter. The truest test of how good we are is that the CFRA can run without us.

"I gave Mary the cookie portfolio so you wouldn't have to worry about it. Give her more portfolios. She should start a file on counterfeit money. Young Birchall told me on the q.t. that some 'funny money' was showing up in Ottawa. Give some managerial tasks to Mr. Mueller, too. We want them both to feel like partners at the CFRA."

It sounded logical. It sounded practical. But Frances could feel an unwelcome itch gnawing on her bones.

— 17 —

LUNCH AT MURPHY–GAMBLE'S

When the dust settled in the third week of June, Frances took out the new CFRA stationery to pen a note of appreciation to Miss Gilhooly. She enclosed her business card for a lark.

Miss Gilhooly called on Wednesday afternoon. "Frances, I am so proud of you! Six weeks ago, you were typing those ridiculous high school exercises, and now you're secretary-treasurer of the Canadian Financial Resources Agency!"

"Thanks, Miss Gilhooly. I owe it all to your recommending me to Mr. Forestall."

"Nonsense! You deserve the credit. You deserve a celebration. Can I treat you to lunch Saturday at Murphy–Gamble's?"

Lunch? With a teacher? Teachers eat lunch?

"I know it's short notice," continued Miss Gilhooly into the pause, "but I'm leaving Ottawa for the summer the minute school finishes. It would be a delight to see you first."

A delight? To have lunch with a seventeen-year-old?

"That's very kind, Miss Gilhooly, but I have to work until twelve-thirty on Saturdays."

"Fine. Twelve-forty-five it is. I'll get us a table."

What would they possibly talk about over lunch? Miss Gilhooly must be over fifty. Frances knew nothing about her personal life. Their teacher-student relationship had been one-dimensional.

The dining room on the fourth floor of Murphy–Gamble's Department Store was renowned for quality at a reasonable price. At 12:45 exactly, Frances stepped out of the elevator into the foyer crowded with shoppers waiting for tables to clear. Frances edged up to the maître d'. He was shorter than Raymond at the Château Laurier and looked harried.

"Does Mademoiselle have a reservation?"

"I don't—" began Frances.

"Then Mademoiselle will need to wait forty minutes to an hour for a table."

"Is a Miss Gilhooly here by chance?" Frances asked.

"Gladys Gilhooly?" The maître d's attitude changed instantly. "Right this way." He guided her across the crowded room to a window table overlooking Sparks Street.

Miss Gilhooly rose. "Thank you, Reggie!" she exclaimed as she extended a gloved hand to Frances. Reggie placed another menu on the table and pulled a chair back to receive Frances. Frances managed to seat herself without knocking anything over.

"Goodness, Miss Gilhooly! Do you own shares of Murphy–Gamble's? You have the best table in the room, and Reggie treats you like the Queen."

Miss Gilhooly flashed the pearl teeth. "I have known Reggie Armstrong since he was in breeks and knee socks. I've helped him out a few times," she added mysteriously. She gave Frances a commending look. "My dear, look at you—the image of the young professional!"

"Thanks, Miss Gilhooly, I—"

"Stop with this 'Miss Gilhooly' business. We are equals now, both professional women. Please call me Gladys."

Frances grabbed for her water glass to calm her nerves. "Certainly, Miss . . . Gladys."

Lunch was surprisingly pleasant. Gladys Gilhooly was animated and full of humour—the complete antithesis of her classroom persona. "Examinations are all over at the school, and we are just mopping up. Mr. Forestall hosts a staff luncheon on June twenty-ninth, and then, like a benevolent zookeeper, frees us for the summer. My train leaves that afternoon, and I'm bound for Nova Scotia, as the song goes."

"That sounds exciting. I've never even been as far as Montreal."

"I grew up on a farm in the Annapolis Valley, and I adore the summers down there. My bachelor brothers, James and John, run the family farm, and they put up with my eccentricities if I cook and clean. I sleep in my old childhood bed under the eaves with the windows wide to the wash of the fresh salt breeze. Do you have summer holiday plans?"

"No," said Frances. "The legislation to establish the Bank of Canada is expected to pass the House of Commons any day now. I don't really mind. I'm learning new things all the time."

"And your boss?"

"Dr. Grace? His real job is with the Department of Finance, so he's rarely around. I have a lot of freedom to take initiative. I guess that's another reason I enjoy it."

"It will be a working holiday for me on the farm. Farmers eat their big meal at noon, so I'm busy in the kitchen all morning, but then I'm free to paint or read or walk for miles along the salt marsh trails. It's an Eden!"

"You paint?"

"Landscapes, mostly. The Annapolis sky is absolute magic, with clouds shifting every minute."

"And what do you read?"

"Usually mysteries. Especially Agatha Christie. I so enjoy Hercule Poirot and Miss Marple. I can never figure out who done it! I read some of the modern Americans—Hemingway and Fitzgerald. I find most nineteenth-century writers too pompous and wordy."

Frances, who read few twentieth-century writers, was surprised to be outflanked on modernity by an aging typing teacher, and changed the subject. "Do you leave your home empty while you're away in the Maritimes?"

Gladys snorted. "Pooh! I've squatted in a bed-sitting room on Flora Street for the past three years, and thank the Lord I'm finally out of it." She did not elaborate. "I've had the most amazing luck! I'm taking a tiny, truly minuscule apartment at the Balmoral Arms in September."

Frances gasped. "I thought the Balmoral was built for the carriage trade." Then she bit her tongue.

"And you don't count high school teachers in that category?" Gladys burst out laughing. "You are absolutely right, my dear!" She leaned closer. "There's a little scandal attached to apartment 1H that took it out of the regular market."

Frances leaned forward. "Scandal? But the building's not two years old. I thought there was a waiting list for apartments."

"So how does a high school teacher, of very modest means, jump the queue?" asked Miss Gilhooly, with eyebrows raised impishly. "*Un problème pour Monsieur Poirot, peut-être?*

"A woman from my church, Betsy Knowles, lives at the Balmoral. Her husband is one of the Knowles Furniture Knowleses, and they have oodles of money. Well, Betsy has taken me on as a charity case, like some women take up eradicating malaria in darkest Africa." Miss Gilhooly rocked with merriment. "This particular apartment—I think they call it a bachelorette—is barely more than a closet. And," she added as she sipped her tea, "until last month, it was the home of the mistress of the second secretary at the British High Commission, and her Pekinese dog, Ming."

While Katie Deavy had added the word "mistress" to the vocabulary of her friends, Frances had never heard it used in conversation before. She tried to appear calm. "What happened to her?"

"Second secretary posted to Cairo. Mistress and Pekinese followed a discreet two weeks later. It was one of those 'hush-hush-but-everybody-knows' things at the Balmoral. Some were horrified at this iniquity. Some were impressed that a second secretary could afford to keep a mistress. One wag started referring to the place as 'The Immoral Arms'!

"Anyhow, the room stinks from the dog, who obviously wasn't walked as often as she should have been. And the decor! The apartment was painted over in dark mauve, and heavy damask drapes covered the only window. It looks like a bordello, although I confess to not being an authority on such places.

"The only people interested in such a small *pied-à-terre* were old maids like me, but those on the waiting list turned it down on the grounds of gloom or stink or notoriety. The building manager, Mr. Carlyle, mentioned this quandary last week to Betsy in the elevator, and she phoned me right up. Presto! I have the lease from the first of September. Mr. Carlyle assured me they would fumigate the apartment completely, and sand the floors if necessary to get rid of the stench. He'll even repaint the entire apartment a neutral white."

"There can't be many schoolteachers at the Balmoral."

"None, I assure you. I owe my good fortune to Betsy's reference and my membership at St. George's Anglican Church. Betsy is the doyenne of the Metcalfe Street Bridge Club. They play every second Tuesday night year-round. When she's absolutely desperate for players, she has me fill out her third table. I'm not very good. My brothers would be mortified if they knew I played cards. None of that toying with the devil's pasteboards in a Nova Scotia farmhouse! However, I manage to live with my conscience." She smiled. "Do you play bridge, Frances?"

"I used to play with my family. It's cheap entertainment in hard times, but I haven't played much lately."

"Coincidentally," added Gladys, "I filled in this week with Betsy's bridge club, and the conversation was right in your bailiwick. That crowd is well connected and their competitive spirit extends to gossip. Anyway, it's all this brouhaha about the new money the Bank of Canada will be printing up.

"What a tempest! Most of the bridge club favoured bilingual bills, but Margaret Cleary insisted that the new Canadian money should be printed only in 'the King's English.' She does have a portrait of George V over her living room mantel. But this idea of completely different sets of bills in English and in French seems ridiculous. Why *are* they doing it?"

Frances had not heard one word about the new currency, but she thought it would sound evasive to say so. "Gladys," she said, summoning up a world-weary look on her young face, "I merely do the typing and the filing over on Queen Street. I do not run the Bank of Canada." She paused for a moment before adding, "Yet."

They both burst out laughing.

─── 18 ───

SOURCES OF INFORMATION

Late the following Monday afternoon, Dr. Grace slumped through the office doorway. "Frances, be a dear and fetch the fixin's," as they had taken to calling the single malt Macallan and support materials. "Please hurry, or you may have to administer it intravenously."

He picked up the files from his in-basket and circled into the conference room. He had signed a dozen letters by the time Frances returned with the tray of glasses, soda water, ice, and the half-empty bottle of Macallan.

"Good God! Is this all that's left?" he said, filling a tumbler with ice, and splashing in a cascade of amber. "Have the mice been into it?"

"Just the usual mouse. The Macallan only comes out of the vault under doctor's orders."

"Will you join me in a small libation?"

"I might, if there are no more accusations about pilfering."

"Good!" he said. "It's a slippery slope when a man begins to drink alone."

Glasses lifted in salutation. He drained half the glass.

"Rough day?" she asked.

"The only thing that keeps me from flinging myself off the Peace Tower is the promise of refreshment in this sanctuary." He sank back in his chair.

Frances crossed her arms. "Make sure you leave me with at least a dozen signed cheques if you do yourself in."

"Do I get no pity from my only solace?"

"My mother used to say, 'There's no profit in pitying the pitiful.' " She sipped her drink. "You do mix a smooth Scotch and soda. Have you considered bartending as a career?"

He threw her a baleful look. "Is it my imagination," he asked, "or is your tone of detached irony beginning to sound very much like my own?"

"Funny you should say that. Mary O'Brien commented yesterday that I was beginning to sound just like you. I took it as a compliment.

Don't you? Isn't imitation supposed to be the greatest form of flattery?"

"My mother and your mother would not approve of your picking up my bad habits."

Frances laughed. "I quite fancy irony in a Jane Austenish sort of way. Now what's the trouble?"

"The trouble," he said, pouring a second double over the melting ice, "is adults behaving like children. They have all the attributes of men—moustaches, body odour, poor taste in clothes—but they persist in being whiny and petulant. Everyone in Ottawa is hot and tired and would love to flee the city for summer fun with friends and family. However, the prime minister, with no family and few friends to flee to, holds us here, shotgun to head. He will not adjourn the House of Commons until the Bank Act is passed into law, and Honourable Members cannot, or will not agree on the final details. A hopeless log-jam."

"Really? I thought things were going well."

"We're 97 percent there, but agreement still eludes us on two vital issues."

"Which are?"

He sighed and shook his head. "It's all confidential. I shouldn't be talking about this. Even to my most trusted confidante."

"One item must be the ownership question. Confidentially, Saturday's *Ottawa Citizen*, quoting unnamed sources, said that the Liberals and the CCF favour public ownership of the Bank of Canada, but the banking community wants it to be privately held. Come to think of it, the article did not mention a government position. Doesn't the government have a position?"

"What you did not read in the *Citizen* is that the government is of two minds on the matter. They're waiting to see which way the wind blows hardest." He sighed again. "It would be unprofessional for me to say more."

"About the bilingual currency issue?"

Dr. Grace sat bolt upright. "You didn't read *that* in the *Citizen*. There aren't a dozen people who know about it, and we've all sworn oaths under the Official Secrets Act." He looked deeply troubled. "I didn't let that slip in a weak moment, did I?"

"You did not."

"The Momsies! You smelt that in the air at Tuesday Tea."

"I did not."

Dr. Grace frowned. "Well, then?"

"It's all the neighbours on Rochester Street talk about these days over the back fence. The best detergent for a whiter wash, and the bilingual currency issue."

The image appealed to Dr. Grace, and his easy pealing laughter relaxed him. "Come now, Frances, share your sources."

"Please, Dr. Grace! You never reveal your sources. Surely you extend the same courtesy to me?"

"Hoist with my own petard. Nothing is so aggravating. You're right, of course, although I have difficulty imagining the washerwomen of Rochester Street handing you a confidentiality oath to sign while they pin up the sheets." He sighed again. "It is hardly my concern if the government can't keep the lid on their own secret meetings, but people would assume that I told you."

"Have no fear, Doctor. I'm too tired to think when I leave the office, and I'm sorry to tell you, nobody I know cares a fig about the Bank of Canada."

"Are you worn out working here?" asked Dr. Grace.

"Oh, no! I love the work. I just don't need to talk about it. I'd get bored with the sound of my own voice."

Dr. Grace smiled. "You *are* Saint Frances! The perfect office administrator. Knows all. Doesn't mouth the family secrets. Won't even tell me her sources!" He reflected for a minute. "We should make a deal. We need to be better informed than anyone else in Canada on banking and fiscal issues. A lot of things are public knowledge, but are not common knowledge. I have held off sharing information with you because I didn't wish to betray confidences, or burden you with confidences, either.

"We now have to move beyond that position. You keep your ears open. I'll keep my ears open. We'll share what we learn, but we will keep our sources private. And, shared information never leaves this office. A deal?" he asked, holding out his drink.

"A deal," said Frances, reaching over to clink glasses.

"By 'a deal,' Miss McFadden, I mean that you would deny under oath hearing something I had told you in confidence."

"A deal," repeated Frances, taking a deep sip of the Scotch.

"You don't fear for your immortal soul and eternal damnation for perjury?"

"Why would perjury bother me?" asked Frances. "We've already committed bank fraud and are embezzling government funds through fictitious expense accounts."

Dr. Grace drained his second glass. "I need to be in Montreal on Wednesday and Toronto on Thursday for critical meetings. All concerning the 'confidential' issues we've just so brazenly discussed. Since you know all about them, you might as well come along. Wednesday night in Montreal. Thursday night in Toronto. Be back here on the express train in the early afternoon on Friday. Can Mary move beyond the cookie 'n' counterfeit files to handle the traffic here with young Herbert?"

Frances grimaced.

"Oh, give them a chance! This would be good for them. Biking without the training wheels. You can check in twice a day."

Frances put on a modest scowl. "I just got our phone bill. Long distance calls are expensive!"

"True, but taxpayers' money is not being wasted if we are saving them the far more expensive consequences." He paused for a moment. "Do you have enough information on our office operating expenses to project a budget through the middle of May next year?"

"Probably."

"Good. That can be your homework for the train. We need to know if we have enough cash in the bank to meet all obligations. I fear there won't be any new revenue from 'certain parties' if we run out of loot."

Frances reflected. "I've only been on the train twice, for Sunday School picnics. Both trips were quite boisterous and not very conducive to homework."

Dr. Grace grinned. "Well, well. 'Boisterous'? 'Conducive'? You've picked up more than irony from Jane Austen. You probably travelled coach. There is nothing for it then but to book us a first-class compartment to Montreal, then to Toronto and back. Get us good rooms at the Mont Royal in Montreal and the Royal York in Toronto. By the way, how is the personnel file on the Bank of England senior management coming along?"

"Pretty well. They clearly have a sense of destiny over there, and have complete biographical sketches of all their top executives."

"Better bring the file along for my homework. It's time to start hypothesizing about the new governor. That will be the first agenda item once the legislation passes. You'll need two changes of clothes from your new 'adult' wardrobe. We're going to the big cities, and have to show the flag. Also, pack lots of letterhead and envelopes and carbon paper so we can keep up with correspondence."

"But I won't have a typewriter."

"First-class hotels have a wide variety of services available to valued customers. I'll meet you in the first-class lounge at Union Station Wednesday morning at seven."

Mary and Mr. Mueller were skittish at the thought of the office without Frances. She reassured them and promised to phone twice a day. Frances hesitated about entrusting them with the "Culloden File" emergency code, but felt it a necessary precaution "in case."

Her mother was another issue.

"You're going to be out of Ottawa for two days with this man?" snorted Vera. She was imagining the worst, and was annoyed that Frances hadn't consulted her. So quickly had Vera dissolved as a factor in her life that it never occurred to Frances that she should ask permission. Because of Vera's evening shifts at the Civic Hospital, they rarely saw each other, except on weekends.

"Mother, it's just Montreal and Toronto, with Dr. Grace, a senior economist with the Department of Finance. The legislation must go to the House of Commons next week. The business communities in Toronto and Montreal wish to be consulted one last time."

"And this man can't function on his own?" Vera continued. "Why does he suddenly need your invaluable assistance?" Her sarcasm was a fountain of disbelief.

"Mother, Dr. Grace is my boss. I follow his orders. Most of the time I do that at the office. There are difficulties with the final details of the legislation. He wants me to take notes and do follow-up correspondence. It's the travelling office. We leave Wednesday morning and will be back Friday afternoon. He asked if I could accompany him, and I agreed. Do you want me to back out?"

Vera did not like it, but she did not wish Frances to go back on her word to Dr. Grace. She came from a day when one did not go back on one's word. "A promise made is a debt unpaid" was one of her favourite homilies. The medicinal brandy paid for its keep that night.

19

MONTREAL

A friendly redcap directed Frances to the First Class Lounge at Union Station on Wednesday morning. Overstuffed armchairs surrounded small pools of light from shaded table lamps. Dr. Grace kept up an animated conversation on baseball with a black porter, who carried their luggage. They settled in to their compartment, then walked back to the dining car. A thick linen tablecloth underlay elaborate metal serving-dishes as the window's panorama poured by. The coffee was hot and rich. "Wow!" she said.

Their taxi waited at the Mont Royal Hotel while they registered. Dr. Grace knew the doorman, the bellman, and the front desk clerk by name and introduced Frances. When he saw the room numbers on the keys, he asked that Frances's room be changed to one on the north side of the hotel on the second floor. He apologized to the desk clerk. "Vertigo and the morning sun both bother my colleague," he said, and the change was quickly accommodated.

Back in the cab, Frances said, "Vertigo? Morning sun? Is there something about my health that I don't know?"

"My fault," Dr. Grace said, leaning back. "They had given us adjoining rooms by mistake."

"No mistake. I asked for adjoining rooms," replied Frances.

He gave her a hesitant sidelong glance.

"Well, Doctor?"

"It's a delicate topic," he said, uncomfortably.

"My vertigo? Or my aversion to sunlight?"

Looking straight ahead, he said, "Adjoining rooms on the sixth floor of the Mont Royal Hotel have connecting doorways. If we have adjoining rooms, they will assume that we are having a romantic liaison." He actually blushed.

"They?"

"The hotel staff."

"Well, that's quite a presumption. Anyway, what do they care, as long as we pay the bill?"

"Well, they don't care, in any moral sense. But they know. Hotel staff are poorly paid, and their knowledge can be purchased."

"Whose good name are you trying to protect? Yours or mine?"

"Better just to take suspicion out of play."

A confusion of emotions silenced Frances until she said, "Dr. Grace, I have never stayed in a hotel. I have rarely slept away from my mother's house in my life. The Mont Royal Hotel is huge and a little scary to a girl from Rochester Street. I reserved adjoining rooms as I was hoping for some security from the good doctor next door. Anyway, wouldn't a man travelling with his mistress and wanting to allay suspicions get rooms on different floors?"

"Well, they would have no private time together, without the bell-hops, the chambermaids, and the room service attendant knowing. It's like having servants. They know everything."

"Really? My mother would hate that. That must be why we don't have servants."

On the twelfth floor of the head office of the Bank of Montreal, a dozen men representing eight different banks awaited them. Frances already had index files on over half of those present. Dr. Grace introduced her and asked if they minded if she took notes. They did not.

In 1934, for the first time in history, the Toronto Stock Exchange had done more business than the Montreal Exchange. An aura of defeat permeated the elegant boardroom, and the discussion was tentative and defensive. "Where will the new Bank of Canada head offices be located?" asked a man with a British accent.

"Do you have any suggestions I could take back to Ottawa?" said Dr. Grace.

"Montreal, of course. The history of Canadian banking was made here," he replied.

"And do you have a second choice?"

"Just not Toronto," replied a bald, large-jowled man, with a pained laugh.

"And where will the new governor come from?" asked another.

"It's not part of the legislation, so is outside my mandate," said Dr. Grace.

"No city in Canada has the banking expertise Montreal has," stated a white-haired man.

"True," replied Dr. Grace, "yet curiously, every banker in Montreal who testified before Lord Macmillan's Royal Commission on Banking and Currency opposed the idea of a central bank. You have collectively removed yourselves from contention. And if not from Montreal—"

A moustachioed man said, "Perhaps someone from outside Canada? Someone without prejudices or jealousies?"

Dr. Grace looked over at Frances to make sure she was noting all this down. "One final question: Which consideration do you value the highest? The provenance of the governor, the ownership of the Bank, or whether to have French on the new currency?"

"I don't see a need for going to a common currency at all," said a cigar smoker. "The various banks serve this need quite well printing their own currencies."

"Gentlemen, the draft legislation assigns this authority to the new Bank of Canada. What language should be used on the new bills?"

Eight favoured a bilingual currency. One man said that there should be two sets of currency, one in each of English and French.

"What a nightmare that would be to sort out," said a broad-shouldered man.

Frances and Dr. Grace returned to the Mont Royal for a late lunch. A meeting room in the hotel had been booked for 3:00 p.m., and ten men showed up. Again Dr. Grace introduced them to Frances, and again she collected business cards for her files. There were three politicians, six from business and industry, and a Monsignor Gervais, from the Bishop of Montreal's Chancery. About half spoke with French accents, although the conversation was all in English. The discussion tended in the same direction as the morning session. When the meeting broke up at five, Dr. Grace begged an hour for a bath, giving Frances a chance to get in touch with the Ottawa office before dinner.

"How are they doing?" Dr. Grace asked when he rejoined her.

"Mary's confidence has grown in just one day. I could hear her beaming on the phone."

"A credit to your coaching, Miss McFadden. Never disparage the amateur. You just need to unleash their energy."

The meal was as good as anything Frances had ever eaten in her life. "You must be happy," she said over coffee. "Everybody agrees on private ownership and bilingual bills. Why did you ask them for their second choices?"

"I can't guarantee anything, but politics dictates that they will get some crumb. They know Montreal is not the business fulcrum it once was, but they're still important, and the Bank needs their co-operation. If they think they have had an influence on the final decisions, they'll feel obliged to support the new Bank.

"Can you do some letters tonight to today's participants?" He took a fountain pen and a small notepad from his suit coat pocket and handed them to Frances. "Here's the bones of the note. You can flesh it out.

" 'Dear' — use first names —

" 'Thank you for your input on Wednesday concerning the new Bank of Canada. I will convey the wishes expressed today to the Standing Committee on Banking and Commerce. The legislation will be before the House of Commons early in July. When the act is passed, please recognize how you have served our Dominion through your participation. Yours sincerely, Wilbur K. Grace, et cetera.'

"And cc them all to E.N. Rhodes, Minister of Finance, and to R.B. Bennett, Prime Minister of Canada."

"The prime minister wants to know about this?"

"I want the participants to know that they're being drawn to his attention. It's a little thing, but it's about all we've got. You can get a typewriter and stamps from room service."

"I should have these done before ten o'clock. Shall I bring them up to your room for signatures?"

Dr. Grace looked at her over his glasses. "Have we not been listening, then, Miss McFadden? When they're done, send them up with a bellhop. Said bellhop will wait while I sign them, and will return them to you for envelope stuffing. We both tip the bellhop on receipt. Put them in the mail tonight to impress all with the lightning speed at which we work."

In their compartment to Toronto, Dr. Grace went over the Bank of England biographies, making notes in the margins, and spent some time on the organizational chart. At eleven o'clock, he rang for ice and soda and took a silver flask from his suit coat pocket.

"The sun is past the yardarm." He held the flask out to Frances, but she shook her head. "On paper there are three good candidates for governor, and another three that would do in a pinch. It will probably come down to whom they can do without. A five-year secondment to the colonies could earn a fellow a knighthood, if he were willing to put up with the mosquitoes and the muskeg.

"Prime Minister Bennett will want their deputy governor, but I doubt he can be spared. There's an assistant to the governor, and a chief cashier named Holmes. I'll get a note off to Charles Fanshaw in their public debt department. Good chap. Met him in graduate school at the Sorbonne. He might have an inkling who our man will be."

"Does it make any difference?"

"It makes all the difference. Next to the prime minister, this will be the most important man in Canada. And for us, forewarned is forearmed. The better we know the new man, the better we can accommodate him."

"I still think it would make most sense to choose a Canadian to govern a Bank of Canada," Frances said.

"Frances! The fact that it makes sense essentially rules it out of consideration. Have you learned nothing of politics, and the hypnotizing effect of the Canadian inferiority complex, in your tenure with the CFRA? Meanwhile, we have other fish to fry. Toronto will be going for the jugular. There will be none of that deferential hooey that we got in Montreal."

20

TORONTO

In the boardroom of the Toronto Stock Exchange, brimming ashtrays and empty glasses indicated that a meeting had been in session for some time. Men were standing and stretching. A man with a cane and a forced smile left the head of the table and limped over to greet Dr. Grace. A sombre man in a blue pin-striped suit accompanied him.

"Ah, Grace! So good to see you again."

"Mr. Hollinger, may I introduce Frances McFadden, the secretary-treasurer of the Canadian Financial Resources Agency? Miss McFadden, this is Lloyd Hollinger, president of the Toronto Stock Exchange. He's chairing today's meeting. And this is Jackson Dodds, president of the Canadian Bankers Association." Both smiled and nodded but hands were not offered. "You don't mind if Miss McFadden takes notes?"

The smiles drained. "I understood this meeting was to be off the record," wheezed Mr. Dodds. "How can we get down to brass tacks if anything a man says can be bandied about?"

Dr. Grace smiled disarmingly. "The Committee on Banking and Commerce is in the final stages of drafting the Bank Act legislation. I want to ensure that all of your concerns are captured."

"Grace," said Mr. Hollinger, "there are some very delicate and private issues, here. Maybe Miss McFadden could go shopping for a couple of hours." He smiled obliquely at her.

Dr. Grace looked calmly at each man in turn. "I need Miss McFadden's assistance in recording the exact tenor of your thoughts."

"I just don't think we'll get the honesty the topic deserves if we're not *in camera*," said Mr. Dodds, shaking his head.

"Besides, frank talk may be rough on a woman's ears," added Mr. Hollinger.

Dr. Grace could feel Frances heating up. "The Montreal business community was delighted to make Miss McFadden's acquaintance yesterday."

Mr. Hollinger looked up sharply. "You gave Montreal an audience ahead of us?"

"They initiated the request. As a result of their asking, a similar courtesy was extended to you."

"What did they say in Montreal?" asked Mr. Hollinger.

"Gentlemen! Surely if Toronto expects confidences to be respected, you wouldn't want me tattling on your colleagues in Montreal?" replied Dr. Grace.

"Bolton and his crowd don't wear the pale patina of past glory very well," concluded Mr. Dodds.

"Can you guarantee complete discretion?" asked Hollinger. "There are contentious issues here. We don't want to see them in tomorrow's *Globe*."

"Addressing the newspapers on policy issues is neither our job nor our inclination. The press is unlikely to know we exist, unless someone here informs them."

Mr. Hollinger looked at his watch. "All right. Let's get started. But don't blame me if the conversation gets raw."

Dr. Grace took the only empty seat midway down the long conference table. Frances sat against the wall behind him, beside the coffee table. A wide-shouldered man named Fitzpatrick started off. "Now, Dr. Grace," he said in a patronizing way, "we are concerned with government interference in our free market economy. A central bank will have a deleterious effect on market decisions and the laws of supply and demand. I say this as a concerned Canadian, not merely as a businessman."

Dr. Grace returned the volley. "I'm sure the government, especially a Conservative government, through the Bank of Canada, has no desire to interfere in a market economy that is working well. Mr. Fitzpatrick, as a businessman and a concerned Canadian, are you happy with your company's current performance?"

Mr. Fitzpatrick sputtered. "Well, God knows times have been tough since the crash, but things are starting to turn around. I think this central bank idea is going to destabilize a delicate situation."

Dr. Grace looked around the table. "Is there a man here that is happy with the way the market is functioning now? Is that the message you wish Ottawa to hear? The newspapers are screaming for government action. Where are they getting that message from, if not from you?"

George Steadman, president of Massey–Ferguson, spoke up. "What we need, Dr. Grace, is tax write-offs to retool our factories for new products. That would stimulate the economy, by God!"

"That might stimulate production, but would it stimulate consumption? Who would buy your new products? A central bank that regulates credit to the ten Canadian banks could loosen credit and increase the flow of money into the pockets of consumers. A farmer who wanted to buy one of your tractors could get a loan from his local bank. He'd hire a man to help harvest the crop and need more boxcars to ship his grain. That would stimulate the economy."

Next came Gerald Ross of the Canadian Manufacturers' Association. "What you can tell Ottawa, Dr. Grace, is that we need higher tariffs to protect the Canadian market from foreign interference. That would create jobs and put money in the pockets of the newly employed."

"It is a curious thing to hear a businessman in an exporting country support the idea of tariffs, Mr. Ross," replied Dr. Grace. "The Canadian market is minuscule compared to those in the United Kingdom and the United States. Any duties that Canada imposes would be met by reciprocal tariffs. Don't you want to sell your factory's products in those larger markets, un-handicapped by tariffs? And, if you need to import machinery for your factory, do you really want to pay high tariffs to get it? Can't Canadian-made products compete in the marketplace without protection? Foreign manufacturers would need to produce a better product more cheaply than we do and bear the transportation costs."

"Gentlemen," interrupted Mr. Hollinger, "this is not a forum on world economy. What we need is a strategy to stave off creation of this central bank."

"Gentlemen," parried Dr. Grace, as if replying to a toast in his honour, "neither you, nor I, can stop the creation of the Bank of Canada at this point. I return tomorrow to Ottawa with a report from you and your colleagues in Montreal. The Committee on Banking and Commerce meets on Monday for final considerations. Their report will go to the Cabinet on Wednesday, and the printer on Friday, and the legislation will be before the House of Commons in the first week of July for a vote."

"So the buggers just plan to ram it through," exclaimed a red-faced man with a large moustache, "regardless of what people think!"

"No," corrected Dr. Grace patiently. "You have had lots of opportunity to let your feelings be known, and you're getting a final chance now. According to the papers, both the Liberal Party and the CCF agree with the need for a central bank, and will vote with the government on this legislation. However, there are some details that are still up for discussion."

This brought a broadside of invective.

"If we're going to have this bank foisted upon us," complained one, "it better be located in Toronto. We want to keep an eye on it."

"And," added another, "a man from Toronto should be appointed to run the damn thing."

"And another thing," complained Mr. Fitzpatrick, "forget this foolishness about bilingual currency. Two miles west of the Quebec border no one speaks French, reads French, or does business in French. The bills need to be in the King's English."

The bombast faded into silence. Several men shifted uneasily in their chairs, but no one came to Dr. Grace's defence. Frances kept her head down. There was a shuffling of papers and clearing of cigar ash in the large black glass ashtrays.

Suddenly, the door at the end of the room opened, and a messenger in an uneven haircut and a baggy suit strode up to Mr. Hollinger and handed him a note. The distraction brought all eyes to the chairman as he read: " 'Urgent phone call for Dr. Grace.' "

It sounded like a death knell, but Dr. Grace turned it aside adroitly. "Gentlemen," he said, calmly looking around the table, "nothing is more urgent to me than a satisfactory conclusion to this meeting." He paused, reflectively. "That said, I don't wish to appear rude to the prime minister. Miss McFadden, could I call on your usual diplomatic tact to deal with the call?"

Frances rose with her notebook to follow the messenger out. He closed the meeting room door, and jerked his thumb at a phone receiver lying on a small table to the left. "Good luck, sister," he said. "They wanted the doctor and nobody else."

Frances picked up the phone.

"Hello?"

"Willie?" queried an elderly female voice. "Pookie? Is that you?"

Pookie? "No, ma'am," replied Frances. "Dr. Grace is . . ." *being eaten by wolves. . .* "is unable to get to the phone right now. He's terribly sorry. This is Frances McFadden. May I help you?"

"Frank Marsden?" puzzled a genteel voice that sounded like lavender. "I don't believe I know a Frank Marsden—"

"If you can give me your name and phone number, ma'am, I'll have Dr. Grace call you as soon as possible."

There was a sigh on the line. "It's about dinner," the voice replied with a tone of urgency.

"Give me the message and I promise to pass it directly to him."

"Well, then," she said reluctantly. "Tell Pookie: Seven for seven-thirty. The Nobles were otherwise engaged, but the Carscallans and Underhills will be here. Tell him not to be late this time, and to bring his poor woman to round out the table. Read that back please, Frank."

Frances read slowly and clearly.

"That's very good, Frank."

"Whom should I say is calling?"

" 'Who,' Frank. You need the nominative case. 'Who should you say is calling.' Pookie has only one dinner engagement for tonight. He'll know." There was a pause. "But for your edification, Frank, it's Goo-Goo. Don't forget your promise. Good day." The phone went dead.

Frances quickly transcribed her shorthand and folded the message twice before returning to the conference room. The siege had lifted. A ripple of laughter and toothy smiles danced around the room. She placed the note on the table in front of Dr. Grace, where it lay untouched while he gave close attention to a bald man at the far end of the table.

"All right, then, gentlemen, let me see if I have this down correctly," Dr. Grace said. "The group feels strongly that the Bank of Canada should be privately owned, but it should be structured in such a way that no one person or business has undue influence over its direction. Is that correct?" Heads bobbed in agreement where there had been clenched jaws and scowls only minutes earlier. "Banknotes should be printed in English, but there is no objection to banknotes printed in French for use in French-speaking areas. Correct?"

Twenty heads nodded up and down, as though a breeze were blowing through poppies. "If you can direct Miss McFadden to a typewriter, she will type a copy for Mr. Hollinger and a copy for me to present to Ottawa."

Mr. Hollinger led her to an empty office, and she was back in ten minutes.

"Thank you, then, gentlemen, for your considerations. This," Dr. Grace said, holding up the memo, "will be the sole and complete report of the meeting. Concerns not directly related to the legislation were aired today. I leave it to you to present those concerns as forcefully as you wish to your members of Parliament. I'm a civil servant with prescribed responsibilities, and it would be pointless for me to advance items outside my mandate. Good day." He stood up.

Every eye in the room watched Dr. Grace reach out for Frances's note. He scanned it briefly it before putting it in his battered briefcase. Mr. Hollinger and Mr. Dodds escorted them to the elevator. "Well done, Grace," said Mr. Hollinger, shaking his hand. "A bit stormy for a while there, but we seem to have coalesced under your guidance."

Mr. Dodds also held out his hand. "No hard feelings, eh, Grace? Business is business."

"Of course not, Mr. Dodds. Brass tacks are brass tacks."

When they were safely in the elevator heading down, however, Dr. Grace exclaimed, "Bastards!" to the thin air.

21

LEONA AND THE JUDGE

As they swept into the lobby of the Royal York, Dr. Grace said, "I need to make a phone call. Can you get us a quiet table in the bar and order me two doubles of their best Scotch with the fixin's?"

He was back in ten minutes. Frances had ordered a ginger ale. He iced and sodaed, and downed the first drink in a single draught, before the properties had time to meld. As he set up the second drink, Frances said: "You are very good, Dr. Grace, at wringing consensus from disharmonious parties. Congratulations."

He looked across at her and smiled. " 'Wringing consensus from disharmonious parties' sounds vaguely familiar. Who writes your material, Miss McFadden?"

"A Jane Austen paraphrase," she confessed. "But the borrowing doesn't make it any less fitting."

He exhaled deeply. "That meeting was exhausting. But we salvaged what was possible here under heavy fire." He sipped deeply and raised his eyes looking for the waiter. "You know what saved us?"

Frances shook her head.

"The phone call from the prime minister."

"But it wasn't the prime minister."

"No, but they all *thought* it was! They very much liked having the prime minister cool his heels while they instructed me on how the legislation should read. If that very conservative crowd is past caring for him, his days are numbered. They were so self-satisfied that they became almost amiable after you left." He laughed. "A little theatrical I suppose, but it worked! And I didn't have to lie, Miss Presbyterian Ethics."

Frances smiled. "Technically, perhaps, but you let them believe a falsehood. Or did you know for a fact that it wasn't the prime minister?"

"Well, I didn't tell him where I was today. Did you?"

"No. So, who did know you were in that meeting? Pookie?"

Dr. Grace laughed loudly enough to get the waiter's attention, and two more doubles were ordered. "That was my mother."

"Goo-Goo is your mother?"

"Yes. My first words, apparently, immortalized forever. We usually dine together when I'm in Toronto. I asked her to invite some people whose opinions I need to hear on the Bank legislation."

"Won't your 'poor woman' want your undivided attention over dinner?" asked Frances with eyebrows raised. "She must not get to see much of you these days." Frances purloined one of the double Scotches, feeling that three should be the limit for a doctor on an empty stomach.

Dr. Grace reddened. "I just got off the phone with Mother, trying to dissuade her about this invitation, but she's very superstitious about uneven numbers at the dinner table. So you'll have to come along."

Frances choked on her drink and a spray of Scotch misted the table. "Me? You refer to *me* as your 'poor woman'? How humiliating!" She stood up.

Dr. Grace jumped up and gently touched her shoulder. "No, no, no," he said. "Please give me thirty seconds to explain."

Frances sat down, flinching her body sharply away from him and emptying the double Scotch to chase the bad taste.

"I have the highest regard for you and your work. I only speak of you in the most flattering of terms. Terms that really would embarrass you. My mother hears the accolades, and your patience in dealing with a son whose faults she knows only too well, and she thinks, 'Ah, poor over-worked, under-appreciated soul, who single-handedly carries the Bank of Canada, and Wilbur Grace's shortcomings, on her back.' Mother is not easily moved to empathy. A 'poor woman' from her, let alone an invitation to dinner, is like winning the Victoria Cross twice over.

"She is losing her hearing, and, I'm sad to say, her mind is starting to unwind. She's a little scattered, and fills in a lot of blanks with the wrong words." He looked contrite. "But she's a man's only mother, and a dear heart. I'm sure you'll like her."

Frances's flare of anger passed like a summer storm. "So, I'm your date for dinner? I don't have anything to wear!"

"There's a Holt Renfrew in the hotel lobby. I got you into this mess. Just order what you want and charge it to my room."

"I have never shopped for evening clothes. Won't you help me?"

"Men hate to shop."

"Women hate to be called 'poor.' "

They picked out a simple but elegant black dress. With black pumps, silk stockings, and costume jewellery, the bill came to seventy dollars.

Frances was horrified. "That's a month's pay! You can't afford to pay for this. Can't we cover it under 'office supplies'?"

"No. Dinner with Goo-Goo is a command performance, but an office function it is not. Don't worry. I'm a big shot in the Finance Department. Money means nothing."

In the taxi, Dr. Grace explained the rules. "The men will gather in Father's study for a pre-dinner drink. Boyd Carscallan is a corporate lawyer in Father's old firm, and Gordon Underhill is the Industry Minister in the Ontario Conservative cabinet. I need to hear if they've noted any holes in the Bank Act legislation. So that is going to leave you alone with the ladies. They will ask you polite questions. Ask the same question right back. People love to hold forth on their own opinions. They'll think you're a marvellous conversationalist."

"It's kind of scary," said Frances.

"You'll be fine. You look like a million dollars. Just try not to knock over the daffodils."

The taxi drew to a halt in front of a flagstone path that meandered back through open wrought iron gates up to a grey stone mansion.

"You didn't tell me you grew up in a castle!" Frances whispered forcefully to him as they went up the walk. She felt a long way from Rochester Street.

"It's just a place to sleep and eat." He pressed the doorbell, setting off a peal of receding chimes like a grandfather clock.

A grey-haired black woman in a white uniform opened the door. She broke into a wide smile. "Master Will!"

"My, my, Emma!" said Dr. Grace, sweeping her into his arms. "Why is it that as I grow old and frail, you get younger every day? Miss Emma, may I present my colleague from Ottawa, Frances McFadden?"

Emma took Frances's hand in an approving way. Frances warmed to her instantly.

"How do you do," said Frances, never having touched a black person before.

"Jus' fine," Emma drawled.

"How's Mr. Curtis?" asked Dr. Grace.

"Jus' fine, Master Will. You'll be tastin' his lamb and greens soon."

Through a wide archway to the right, three men were conversing. An erect, greyer model of Wilbur Grace introduced himself as Theo Grace. His eyes sparkled. "Welcome, Miss McFadden. May I introduce my good friends Boyd Carscallan and Gordon Underhill?"

When hands were shaken all around, Judge Grace said to Frances, "And how are things in the East Block these days?"

The East Block? The East Block?

Dr. Grace took Frances by the elbow. "Gentlemen, excuse me for a moment. I need to hand Miss McFadden over to the matriarch."

He led her to French doors that opened onto a patio where three women sat in wicker chairs. They rose, and Dr. Grace performed introductions, kissing each woman on the cheek. "Now, Mother," he cautioned, "Miss McFadden has had a trying day. All morning on the train from Montreal. All afternoon in a smoke-filled room of nattering, uncivil men. Be gentle."

"Not to mention all day with you, you bad boy," said Mrs. Grace with a charming smile.

The ladies admired Frances's dress and inquired politely about the Ottawa weather. Mrs. Grace's face in repose carried a disarming smile. If she recognized the voice of Frank Marsden, she did not let on. When Emma summoned them in to dinner, the men were more pointed in their inquiries.

"Now, Miss McFadden," said Judge Grace, dipping a piece of lamb into the mint sauce, "what sort of an employer is Will? You can speak frankly here. You're among friends."

"He's the best employer I've ever had," replied Frances, realizing that everyone was listening.

"Do tell!" exclaimed the judge.

"I benefit by being the only employer that Frances has ever had," said Dr. Grace to broad laughter.

"That said, Judge Grace," continued Frances, "your son anticipates problems, and always offers a range of possible solutions. He never gets angry when I make mistakes. He provides general guidelines, then trusts me to use my own judgment."

"Goodness!" exclaimed Mr. Underhill from across the table. "A paragon. No faults at all?"

Frances thought. "Well, sir, when I first met Dr. Grace, he warned me that he was a little disorganized."

"A little!" exclaimed Mrs. Grace. "Willie has trouble getting his foot into the correct pant leg!" Hearty laughter all around.

"His frankness has meant that I anticipate it, so it's never a problem."

"Speaking of personal faults, Miss McFadden, how do you find the prime minister?" asked Mr. Underhill.

Frances thought this an unusual question from a Conservative cabinet minister. "You are likely a better judge of that than I," she responded.

"But you were talking to him this very afternoon!" put in Mr. Carscallan.

Frances shot a glance to Dr. Grace, who cleared the puck.

"Now, Mr. Carscallan, what little bird has had your ear today?" he said.

"Arthur Radcliffe called me late this afternoon. He was all aglow about how Will stood up the prime minister to sort through the new Bank of Canada legislation at the stock exchange. Bennett was trying to butt in, and Will sent his secretary to deal with the old man. That would have been you, right, Miss McFadden?"

"By the way, Mr. Underhill, will the bank legislation affect the coming Ontario election?" asked Dr. Grace.

Mr. Underhill leaned in conspiratorially. "*Entre nous*," he said, "I think it's clear sailing. Premier Henry is confident that the voters won't be bamboozled by Mitch Hepburn."

"He's only thirty-seven," put in Mr. Carscallan. "Barely older than Will, for goodness sakes!'

Again, much laughter at Dr. Grace's expense, but he didn't seem to mind.

"Mother, Father, distinguished guests: It has been a pleasure to tuck into Curtis's roast lamb in such good company. Please excuse us. Miss McFadden and I have promises to keep and miles to go before we sleep. I'm sure this group can keep the candles burning for a good while yet on the back of Father's excellent Cabernet Sauvignon."

"Well, you certainly knocked their socks off," said Dr. Grace in the taxi. "You've come a long way since that standoff with Stella Stanton."

"I've had a pretty good role model, Pookie. How come you're such a lawbreaker if your father is a judge?"

"Every family needs a black sheep," he replied.

A sudden thought occurred to Frances. " 'How *are* things in the East Block these days?' "

Dr. Grace laughed. "It's too long a story after too long a day. I'll fill you in later. We both need to get a good night's sleep. We can finish everything on the train back to Ottawa."

"Why did you want to get out of there so fast, then? Your parents are delightful," said Frances.

"Wilbur Grace's formula for success in the poker game of life: 'Quit while you're ahead.' We were sailing in the shoals, there. The Carscallans and Underhills are loyal and loving, but tongues wag, especially after a night of drinking. We grabbed what we needed and got out."

"Which was?"

"Boyd Carscallan is one of the brightest constitutional lawyers in Canada. I needed an opinion on a few 'hypothetical' considerations regarding federal-provincial powers in the new bank legislation."

"Did we pass?"

"We passed. And Frank Underhill is in the provincial cabinet, and I wanted to know if Ontario would fight us."

"And?"

"I don't think it really matters. The Conservatives won't survive the provincial election in July. Conservatives, by nature, conserve, maintain, keep intact. After five years of unemployment and hard times, people want something new—anything new. Even Mitch Hepburn."

—— 22 ——

SUMMER SPECULATION

On July 3, 1934, the Bank of Canada Act passed final reading in the House of Commons. To celebrate, Dr. Grace brought a cake to the Wednesday CFRA staff meeting.

"That's it?" asked Mr. Mueller, dabbing unsuccessfully at the icing in his moustache.

"Actually," clarified Dr. Grace, "the legislation was introduced back in February, then, after a second reading, it went to the House Standing Committee on Banking and Commerce. They bashed it—and me, as their step-'n'-fetch-it lapdog—around for four months. There were many changes, some to make things more clear, some to make things less clear. The bill returned to the House of Commons yesterday for the final vote. The great Canadian compromise is now the law of the land."

"Congratulations!" said Mary.

"Thank you. It's good to have that finished so I can get back to the pile mildewing on my desk at the Department of Finance. A thousand details need addressing before The Bank of Canada is up and running, but the good Mr. Clark, deputy Minister of Finance, can look after those."

"What could possibly still need to be done?" asked Mr. Mueller.

"The Bank of Canada is a private entity brought into existence by public legislation. An interim board of directors needs to be appointed while they issue stock. Once there are stockholders, they can elect the real board of directors. That sounds simple, but it will take several months. The big next step is to name the governor."

"And will Mr. Clark do that, too?" asked Mary.

"No. Prime Minister Bennett will do that. He'll likely pick a senior executive from the Bank of England."

"Do you think so?" asked Frances, with a rising inflection of voice that suggested she did not think so. "Why wouldn't a Canadian banker be chosen?"

"Out of the question," replied Dr. Grace.

"Why?"

"Many reasons. As you've observed at our Toronto and Montreal meetings, no Canadian banker believes we need a central bank and no Canadian banker wants the job."

"Wouldn't there be great prestige in being the first governor?" inquired Mr. Mueller.

"Bankers are businessmen. They get stock options. If their bank is successful, they make oodles of money. Even though the Bank of Canada will operate at arm's length from the federal government, the governor will still be a public servant and be paid much less than a bank president.

"Also, a British lord lends a certain cachet to any new entity, both within Canada and abroad. We colonials are quite enamoured by a British lord. Hats come off and knees are bowed deferentially. Point of fact, the Earl of Bessborough is the Canadian Governor General. Lord Macmillan was asked to lead the Canadian Royal Commission on Banking and Currency last year."

"But we're not a colony anymore," said Mary.

"The United Kingdom is still the 'Mother Country,' and the apron strings are long. Most Canadians do not really feel independent from Great Britain, in business, in culture, or in government."

"Won't a British lord be viewed as a foreign meddler?" asked Mr. Mueller.

"On the contrary, a British lord, being external to Canadian financial institutions, will be deemed above the fray of local warring interests."

"Like Toronto and Montreal," observed Frances.

"Exactly."

"I still can't agree, Dr. Grace," continued Frances. "You said that the new governor will be the second most important person in Canada. Prime Minister Bennett needs to appoint a Canadian who understands why our economy doesn't work and how to relieve unemployment."

"Do you think so?" smiled Dr. Grace. "Perhaps we should have a friendly wager, Miss McFadden."

"I'd be happy to bet, Dr. Grace, but it would be unchristian of me to take your money."

"I wouldn't want to lead you into the morally shaky grounds of gambling," mused Dr. Grace. "What about a non-monetary bet?"

Frances thought for a moment. "How about this," she said. "A two-month exchange of your office chair against my office chair, when I win."

"I do enjoy that big high-backed swiveller. Is that all you want?"

"You wish to suffer more? All right, let's add in two months of your fetching the Macallan and fixin's for afternoon vesper services."

"Is it so burdensome then to serve a distraught man a wee dram after a long day?"

"I didn't say that. I've been doing it for nearly two months now. You've bragged about your experience as step-and-fetch-it for the Banking Committee. Why should *they* get all your good services?"

"Excellent point," he agreed. "And as I'll win anyway, it's inconsequential."

"And what prize would tickle your fancy, in the unlikely event that some bureaucratic mix-up directs the appointment to a non-Canadian?"

"Hmm," murmured Dr. Grace. "How about you pay for a personal ad in the *Ottawa Citizen* that says, 'W.G. knows all; I bow to his omniscience. F.M.' Deal?"

"Whoever would have thought you'd turn out so wicked," Frances replied, "when your parents are so nice?" She reached across the table to shake his hand.

In mid-July, Dr. Grace prepared to leave for Brussels to represent the Canadian Department of Finance at a forum on international payments. "Here is my cabin number on the *Alora* and my hotel in Brussels. You can reach me by telegraph any time. The conference ends on the 27th, and I may spend a few days in England before heading home. Do you foresee any problems?"

"No. We have our hands full cataloguing the thirty boxes of files that Finance sent over on the House Committee's deliberations on the Bank of Canada Act, on top of the daily grind."

"Would it be cheating if I snooped around the Bank of England sizing up the candidates for governor?"

"Exhaust yourself needlessly if you wish."

"I'm betting on a Bank of England man because the prime minister is such an anglophile. But it could be an American as well. Clifford Clark likes the idea of someone from the U.S. Federal Reserve. Would an American appointment count for you or me?"

"You have the foreign field all to yourself. I have the domestic field."

"I hope to be back in Ottawa about August tenth. I'll have a tremendous pileup of work to catch up on, but I did promise Mama that I'd get up to the cottage on Lake Muskoka before the end of the summer. Filial obligations run deep in the Grace family."

"It doesn't sound like such an imposition. Lounging on the dock while Emma brings you countless Scotch and sodas."

"Actually, Mama usually gives Emma and Curtis holidays when she's at the cottage, so I'm often forced to fend for myself."

"Good! Get practised up and I won't have to train you."

The summer heat dragged down the leaves of the dusty Ottawa elm trees while wavy mirages danced above the pavement. Frances sent Mr. Mueller out to purchase three desktop fans. In the weak breeze, they drained cartons of papers and rendered them indexed and retrievable in the long row of bulging filing cabinets.

Attendance at the Momsie meetings was irregular because the city, like the House of Commons, was in recess, and holidays were taken while bosses were away. On July 31, they met in the Trade and Commerce offices, and the topic of the new governor came up in an offhand way.

"Any news over at the CFRA, Frances?" asked Lily Dupuis.

"No. Dr. Grace is in Brussels, and the phone barely rings. He's of the opinion that there might be a candidate at the Bank of England."

"There has been some informal sniffing around the back door over there," said Glenora Whittiker from the Privy Council Office. "The prime minister desperately wants a big name for the post."

"Well, Montagu Norman would never let his deputy governor out of his sight. They are so tight, I think they have matching pyjamas," said Rose Malone.

"Mr. Clark talked about a couple of senior men at the U.S. Federal Reserve, but they are going through a major reorganization in Washington, and it seems all hands are needed on deck."

"Henri Bourassa did write a very passionate article in *Le Devoir* about why the Bank of Canada must have a Canadian governor. Do you suppose he meant French-Canadian?" put in Violet Walker.

"It is too bad that no Canadians have any central bank experience. That seems to be the stumbling block for a local man."

Frances rarely spoke at these meetings, but her curiosity was aroused. "Experience is a wonderful attribute, but doesn't enthusiasm for the job count for anything?" she asked. "The prime minister didn't have any experience being a prime minister when he was elected to the position, did he?"

Knowing looks were shared around the room. Finally, Frances

asked, "What?"

"Well, dear," said Rose in a consoling voice, "politicians are indeed amateurs. They come and go at the whim of the people. The civil service is professional. We are here before they arrive with their suitcases, and we are here to clean up after they leave. I know that democracy is all about 'the will of the people,' but the people sometimes send us a motley crew, and the country must be kept running in spite of them."

Lily looked up from her knitting. "Many elected officials are well-meaning. Still, I don't think you want an amateur running the Bank of Canada."

Frances, who was very much the amateur herself, wasn't convinced.

Dr. Grace returned on August 10 looking tanned and relaxed. "The sea air has done you good," said Frances. She set the refreshment tray down on the conference table.

He poured them both modest drinks with lots of ice. "It was delightful. They feed you very well on board. I think I've put on ten pounds."

"Learn anything interesting?"

"In Brussels, no. Bankers still tend to dine well even in hard times, and the fate of the working world is rather remote from their lives. The German bankers were saying that things were finally starting to turn around there, with manufacturing growing." He took a long slow sip, and smacked his lips.

"In London, I raised a few glasses with my friend Fanshaw at the Bank of England. He reported that the Canadian High Commissioner has been to visit Montagu Norman at least twice. So they're fishing, but it seems vague. I've narrowed my favourites down to three candidates. Ernest Harvey is the deputy governor—a good man, but can they spare him? Then there's Henry Skinner, an assistant to the governor, with considerable experience advising the set-up of new central banks. Very strong credentials. The only other senior executive of stature is Sir Nigel Holmes, the head cashier, but we don't have a similar position here."

A week later, with the morning mail, Frances received a large package from Rolland Forsythe, of the Secretary's Office at the Bank of England. It contained several files that Frances had requested and a brief note.

> *Thank you for the materials you sent along on the Canadian economy. It will do splendidly. We are all at*

sixes and sevens as our Deputy Governor has formally gone on convalescent leave for "health considerations," and the Assistant to the Governor left on Thursday to serve as the first Governor of the Reserve Bank of New Zealand. This leaves our front bench quite light, and there is much scrambling to pick up the slack.

At the Tuesday Tea, on August 28, Violet Walker asked the others about how they handled long-distance telephone bills. "Our bill was getting so out of hand that the deputy minister now must approve anything outside of Montreal or Toronto."

Rose Malone stirred her tea. "I just got off the line twenty minutes ago to Murray Bay, Quebec, of all places. Had a devil of a time getting through. And the operator barely spoke English."

"What in God's name drew you to Murray Bay?" asked Violet.

"Oh, the Finance Minister wants some fellow from the Royal Bank up here on the double. He works in Montreal, but is away on holidays. Had a deuce of a time tracking him down."

When Frances returned to her office, she thoughtfully got out the big *Oxford Atlas of Canada* and looked up Murray Bay.

Just before noon on August 31, Dr. Grace raced in. "I'm stealing out of this cauldron early for the long weekend. Clark will be mad as a hatter if he discovers me gone, but Mother will disinherit me if I do not make a showing at the cottage. Anything I need to deal with here?"

"A dozen signatures and you can go. Any news on the governor's appointment?" Frances asked casually.

"Nothing," said Dr. Grace. "And the prime minister is leaving for England tomorrow, so nothing's going to happen for a while."

"Care to double the bet if one of us can name the successful candidate?"

"Have you heard something?"

"Nothing definite, but the tea leaves are saying 'Canadian.'"

"Double it is. I'm happy to bet against the tea leaves."

23

THE BALMORAL CROWD

In mid-August, Frances received a short note from Gladys Gilhooly. It was written on thick art paper with a quick watercolour sketch of a lighthouse in the upper right corner.

> *Dear Frances:*
> *It is wonderful down here with a sea breeze ruf-fling the orchard fruit. Preserves are neatly racked in the root cellar. My brothers are sick of being bossed around, so I decamp next week for Ottawa.*
> *Can get into my apartment at the Balmoral early, and would like to render it liveable before school starts.*
> *Reggie has reserved my table at Murphy–Gamble's for Saturday, September 1st. Can you join me for lunch?*
> *Sincerely,*
> *Gladys*

Gladys Gilhooly looked radiant. She was tanned, and her eyes sparkled like a child's with a secret. "So good to see you again, Frances! But you're looking a little pale, dear girl."

"I have been putting in long hours. I don't seem to be organized enough to get my work done in an eight-hour day."

"Nonsense! You need to look after yourself or you'll ruin your health."

"How's your apartment coming along?"

"Well, it doesn't smell of dog urine anymore, and it doesn't look like a brothel." Gladys laughed. "There is an odour of fresh-cut wood—not unpleasant—I guess from sanding the floors down. And Mr. Carlyle had the room painted, as promised. However, it's quite a bright white—like a hospital—clean, but not particularly restful, so I've been repainting at my own expense. The walls are a light yellow and the woodwork is an ivory cream. I'd like to repaint the ceiling in an eggshell, but I have a touch of vertigo, and am not good on ladders."

"I could paint the ceiling for you," offered Frances.

"That would be so helpful! But you're already working too hard! You need your holiday."

"The Deavys are at their cottage for the Labour Day weekend, and I spend too much time with Mary O'Brien as it is. I had no plans, other than doing my laundry."

"Why don't we go straight back to the apartment, then? *Carpe diem?* I have several of my brother's old shirts that you could wear to paint in."

A fifteen-minute walk south on Metcalfe brought them to the Balmoral Arms. Apartment 1H was on the main floor, down the hall to the right. It was an L-shaped room with a nook at the far end. A tiny kitchenette shared a common wall with the bathroom. Drop sheets covered everything but the smell of fresh paint.

Frances undressed in the bathroom and hung her work clothes over the shower curtain rod. She tied the long sleeves of one shirt around her waist like a skirt, with the tails reaching her ankles. She put on another shirt that hung below her knees. "Your brothers," she said, "must be tall men."

"Indeed," answered Gladys, who had changed into almost a matching outfit. They both looked like circus clowns.

Frances had never painted a ceiling before, but caught on quickly. Gladys would chat for a while, then work away quietly in the kitchenette. In the late afternoon, heavy footsteps approached down the hall, and cigar smoke drifted in through the open door.

"Who're you?" demanded a male voice of the figure garbed in rags on the stepladder.

Frances turned to look down at a thick-necked man in a brown fedora.

"I'm Frances Elizabeth McFadden," she replied as she carefully edged the corner of the ceiling. "Who are you?"

"Carlyle," he said, as if that should explain everything. "You don't do that for a living, do ya?"

"I do not. What do you do for a living?"

"I'm the building manager and I'm looking for Miz Gilhooly."

"Gladys," piped Frances, "you have a gentleman caller. A Mr. Carlyle."

Gladys had been painting in the cupboard under the sink, and scrambled out. She looked like a giraffe draped in a tent.

"Oh! Mr. Carlyle! How good of you to drop by. This is the electrical outlet that doesn't appear to work," she said sweetly, as if offering him a gift.

Mr. Carlyle unplugged the floor lamp from the back corner and moved it over to the indicated outlet. It didn't work. He grunted. "George is up on the fourth floor fixin' some fuses. He's got a long list, but I'll try to get him down here later. You here all afternoon?"

"Yes," answered Gladys, who suddenly realized her social obligations. "Mr. Carlyle, may I present my good friend Frances McFadden? Frances, this is Mr. Carlyle, the superintendent here at the Balmoral Arms. He has been most helpful in restoring my new apartment to respectability." Gladys Gilhooly, who ruled typing class with an iron hand and wrapped her brothers around her little finger, was a marshmallow before Mr. Carlyle. "Frances works for the Canadian Financial Resources Agency on Queen Street," she explained, as if introducing people who she hoped would become friends.

Mr. Carlyle snorted again. "People are complaining about the smell of paint, so keep the door closed."

"Oh, certainly," said Gladys, far too eager to please. "I'll leave the windows open all night to air the room. I'm so looking forward to moving in tomorrow!"

"Actually," put in Frances, "the air from the hall moves through the apartment, drying the paint, and carrying the odour out the window."

"Air moves both ways," said Mr. Carlyle. He pulled the door shut as he left.

"Bit of a burr under his blanket, as my mother would say," said Frances, continuing with her painting. "I wonder if residents complain about cigar smoke?"

Gladys gave a self-deprecating laugh. "I think he's used to dealing with a better class of tenant than high school typing teachers."

"Or office clerks," added Frances.

There was an abrupt knock at the door, and Gladys opened it. "Betsy! Do come in and see my little *pied-à-terre*." she exclaimed. A well-dressed woman holding a cigarette elegantly in her nail-polished fingers, strolled in.

Betsy did a quick look around, and smiled. "How quaint and compact!" It was unclear from her tone whether this was a compliment or a criticism. Betsy's eyes wandered up the stepladder to the paint-spattered worker. Gladys performed introductions again.

"Gladys," Betsy said, "I need you to play bridge on Tuesday. All my other spares have shingles, or hives, or still haven't returned from summer holidays. I'm two players short."

"Betsy, I can't! I'm in the middle of moving, and September is crazy for a teacher."

Betsy Knowles gave no weight to either excuse. "Gladys, I have never failed to fill three tables in fifteen years. It's your duty now that we are housemates."

"Betsy, I'm not even that good a player. Surely . . ."

"That's wonderful!" Betsy concluded pre-emptively. She started for the door and caught Frances out of the corner of her eye. "You don't play bridge, by any chance?" she asked.

Frances carried on painting. "I do," she said. "I mean, I have. But not recently."

Betsy surveyed Frances like a cat eyeing a wounded bird. She blew a stream of smoke ceiling-ward. "What do you need to open a one-heart bid?" she tested.

"Thirteen points, and at least five hearts to an honour," replied Frances, without looking away from her paintbrush.

"You'll do. I'm in six South West. The first hand is dealt at seven-thirty sharp. Don't be late." She marched out of the room without waiting for a response.

Gladys shut the door, then came to the base of the ladder. "You'll have to pardon Betsy. She's a little abrupt."

"Rude, I'd say," said Frances as she moved the ladder for the final assault on the ceiling.

"Could you please come on Tuesday?" Gladys pleaded. "I'm not much of a card player myself, but I owe Betsy my toehold here. She has no children, so the bridge club is her life."

"Only for you, Gladys, would I do this. I probably haven't played a hand of bridge in two years."

That night, Frances got out a contract bridge scoring pad and reviewed it. Her mother was feeling bored enough to deal out several hands so Frances could brush up her bidding skills. On Tuesday, she went straight to the Balmoral Arms from work. She knocked on Gladys's door shortly after seven. Furniture had transformed the room into a home. There were still boxes in the corners, but the promise was there.

As they rode up on the elevator, Gladys briefed her on the crowd.

"Betsy Knowles has built the Metcalfe Street Bridge Club into one of the most prestigious tables in the city. It's her pride and joy."

"Why does she need to draft a ragamuffin like me, if it's so prestigious?"

"Betsy has very high standards. I think she frightens people. These are serious card players. They play for money."

"Money?" echoed Frances in shock.

"Well, a piece of silver from Birks. But don't worry. We are 'irregulars' and don't pay no matter how poorly we play."

A maid opened the door and escorted them down a panelled corridor to the living room. Betsy Knowles stood up to introduce them. "You all remember Gladys?" she said. "The dear girl has just moved into the Balmoral this week, so we'll be seeing a good deal more of her." Frances was introduced to the seven seated women as "Gladys's good friend." The apartment was vast compared to the Gilhooly nest on the first floor.

Gladys and Frances sank down together on the sofa, and the maid immediately reappeared with dainty crystal glasses on a silver tray. "Port or sherry?" she asked with a French accent.

Frances took the darker liquid to calm her nerves and listened to the chatter. Betsy looked at her wristwatch several times, and jumped up when the doorbell rang. "The Semples are finally here," she said. "Marie, I'll get the door, you set up the tables."

The Semple sisters, Clarissa and Debra, were introduced to Frances. They were middle-aged twins and wore expensive identical outfits, which would have been cute on six-year-olds. Betsy handed around a silver dish holding twelve bridge tallies and they all drew. Frances played the first round with Mrs. Beauchamp, the only woman with a French accent besides the maid.

The rules became apparent immediately. Once the deal was completed, all chatter stopped. Bidding was quick and clear. The elderly Nora Ray, seated at Frances's right, often asked for a review of the bidding, which her partner, a Miss Dawes, patiently supplied. Once the last trick in a hand was played, conversations that had been cut in mid-sentence at the deal picked up again. After four hands were completed, players entered their scores on their tallies and moved to a new partner for the second round.

Frances got into trouble only twice. Nora Ray pushed her up to three no-trump, hoping to make a quick game bonus, but they were overbid and went down one. Another time, when she was playing with Clarissa Semple, a disastrous trump split put them down three. If one table finished a round more quickly than the others, there was banter while they waited. Nicknames were bandied about that everyone except Frances appeared to recognize.

"Bunny will be joining us at Montebello this weekend, with his new interest."

"One diamond."

"Is it that willowy blonde thing from The Hunt Club?"

"One spade."

"Yes. Wouldn't Gloria be rolling in her grave."

"Two hearts."

"Have they appointed a new DM at Treasury Board?"

"Gordon said it will be a shuffle—likely Harold Pitts from the Solicitor General's office. Apparently Macky Watson is desperate to get him out of there."

"Three clubs."

"Is the man no good?"

"On the contrary, he's twice as good as Macky, who doesn't stand for that sort of thing."

"Pass."

"Oh, Clarissa, guess who I bumped into today at the Château Laurier? Graham Towers."

"Four spades."

"What's Graham doing in Ottawa? I thought he and Molly were up at Murray Bay until mid-September?"

"Pass."

"I asked him the same thing."

"Pass."

"And?"

"Well, come to think of it, he never actually answered. He admired my mauve silk scarf, and wanted to know where he could pick up one for Molly. I should have asked him if he'd heard anything about the Bank of Canada appointment. He'd know most of the candidates. "

"Pass."

"I thought the prime minister was desperate for someone from the Bank of England?"

"He is, but he refuses to take the bootblack, and apparently no one else could be spared at the heart of Empire."

When the clock on the mantel chimed ten, Betsy Knowles announced, "Last hand, ladies."

The tallies all went to Debra Semple, who seemed to be the club accountant. In the dining room, assorted baked goods and crust-less sandwiches cut into the shapes of hearts, spades, clubs, and diamonds awaited them.

"The damage?" asked Betsy.

Debra read off the scores, with "oohs" and "aahs" from the crowd. Frances had placed a respectable sixth. Gladys was second to last. The French woman, Giselle Beauchamp, placed first and took a silver fork home for her efforts.

The Semple sisters, last to arrive, were first to leave. "Working girls, must be off," said Clarissa. "The cock crows early!"

Gladys and Frances were next to leave. Betsy showed them to the door. "I do hope you'll join us again, Frances. Do you have far to go?"

"No," said Frances, "just down on Rochester Street."

"Rochester Street?" queried Betsy, as though she had misheard. "That's miles!"

"Two streetcar rides, and I'm there."

Betsy opened a drawer in the hall table and took out a dollar bill. "Here, dear, take a cab. Can she call from your apartment, Gladys? Goodnight!"

Frances was too stunned to reply until they got to the elevator.

"Well," declared Gladys. "Betsy never offered me cab fare when I lived way over on Flora Street."

24

THE NEW GOVERNOR

Next morning, Frances dug out their file on Graham Towers. It was thin. He had started with the Royal Bank in 1920 as an economist, had held several foreign postings, and in 1933 became assistant general manager of the Royal Bank. She phoned the True Search Clipping Agency in Montreal.

"Good morning," she said. "I'm doing a report on senior bank executives, and our files are incomplete on Morris Wilson, the general manager of the Royal Bank, and his assistant, Graham Towers. Could you do a quick search, and send the findings up special delivery to Ottawa today? Wonderful!"

On Thursday, Frances slipped out for lunch with Stella at the Honey Dew, where she bumped into one of the Momsies, Glenora Whittiker, who was in a tizzy.

"Keep this under your hat, Frances," Glenora whispered, eyes as wide as saucers, "but there was a great row in the Privy Council Office this morning! Sir George was red as a beet. I thought he was going to have a heart attack!" She leaned in and confided, "Sir George is acting prime minister while Mr. Bennett is in Europe. He met with a man about the Bank governor job. Well, the fellow will take it, he said, for thirty thousand dollars! Can you imagine the nerve! The prime minister doesn't earn that much! Sir George refused to approve it, and wired Mr. Bennett for instructions." Glenora's double chins shivered in seismic convulsions.

Dr. Grace was preoccupied with a magazine article when he wheeled into the office shortly after six. He picked up his wire in-basket, carrying it through the connecting door into the conference room. He came out to direct Frances to the vault for the fixin's when he woke to his new surroundings. Frances was perched high behind her desk in his large leather executive chair.

"A trifle presumptuous, aren't we?" he asked.

"I'll have my Macallan over crushed ice," Frances said, without looking up. "Better make it long on soda. I'm behind and have to work late."

"What?" he said. "Don't tell me!"

"Graham Towers was just appointed governor of the Bank of Canada," Frances said.

"Towers? From Montreal? When?"

"Cabinet. This afternoon."

"But the prime minister is out of the country!"

"Order-in-Council."

"How did you find out?"

Frances smiled the "now-now" look. "We haven't forgotten our little protocol on revealing sources, have we?"

"But are you sure of your sources?"

Frances looked up at the wall clock, which said 6:20. "It was likely on the six o'clock news. You can read all about it in the paper tomorrow."

Dr. Grace sank into one of the waiting room chairs. Frances threw him a bone. "Glenora Whittiker in the Privy Council Office phoned at four. She was flustered and wanted to borrow our file on Graham Towers. I took a chance and asked if this was concerning his appointment as governor. She would never have volunteered the information, but she was in despair. 'Yes,' she said, 'and they can't find his biography on file for the press release! The prime minister must have taken it with him to England.'

"I said, 'It's quite a large file. Why don't I write something for you?' She only needed the bare bones—knowing that the press would flesh out all the details. Glenora was very appreciative."

"So, you wrote the Privy Council Office press release on the appointment of Graham Towers?"

"I did. Mary ran it over to them at four-thirty. Here's a copy."

Dr. Grace read it quickly. "Well, I'll be damned!" he said. "Where's the Towers file?"

"Check your in-basket, Doctor. You just carried it into the conference room. A lot of soda," Frances reminded him. "I need to keep a clear head."

Dr. Grace was halfway to the vault for the Scotch when he stopped and turned. "If you are so far behind, why didn't you send the file over and let PCO look after it?"

"Apparently, PCO loses files. They lost their Graham Towers file, anyway. I didn't want them to lose ours. They were very grateful for the bio. It's nice having the PCO in your debt. Also, I thought it might interest you."

"You saved it for me?"

"Privy Council Office are friends. You're family. Crushed ice, now, not cubes."

The Canadian Press, Ottawa, September 6, 1934

Towers Appointed Governor

An announcement of the government's selection of Graham Ford Towers as the first governor of the Bank of Canada was made late this afternoon by the Honourable E.N. Rhodes, Minister of Finance.

Mr. Towers is appointed for a period of seven years. A central banking expert will be hired to act as deputy governor.

The head office of the Central Bank will be in Ottawa and branches will be established in various cities.

The Toronto Telegram, September 6, 1934

Bankers Approve Choice

Members of Toronto banking institutions today stamped their approval on the appointment of Graham Ford Towers, 37-year-old bank official, as governor of Canada's new Central Bank.

"An excellent appointment," said H.F. Patterson, general manager of the Bank of Toronto. "He has a keen mind and is very competent."

Beaudry Leman, general manager of La Banque Canadienne Nationale, said, "I feel that both Canada and Mr. Towers are to be congratulated. He is briefed not only on the domestic factors of Canada's problems, but also on her trade with foreign countries."

The Montreal Star, September 7, 1934

Graham Towers to Europe

Mr. Graham Towers, newly appointed governor of the Bank of Canada, will sail for Europe on Saturday week, accompanied by his wife. He will make a study of the mechanisms of European central banks.

Dr. Grace hoped to get Graham Towers over to visit the CFRA offices early in the next week. Mary and Mr. Mueller tidied. Frances re-hung the art to advantage and picked fresh flowers for the waiting-room table. All for naught.

Dr. Grace dropped in Thursday afternoon to say Governor Towers had left for Montreal and would sail on Saturday for Europe. "Don't be disappointed. He had a whirlwind of meetings and was beyond absorbing anything new. I saw him briefly this morning at the Finance Department. I had time for one sentence, and explained that the Canadian Financial Resources Agency was busy gathering material that I hoped he would find useful."

"What did he say?" asked Frances.

"He was very polite, but I'm not sure he even knew what I was talking about. A school of piranhas had surrounded him, all trying to tear off a little piece of the man for themselves. He was wise to get out of the country."

Frances pondered. "Since he's a Canadian banker, how much does he need the Canadian Financial Resources Agency?"

Dr. Grace shook his finger at her. "Don't talk like that. Your team has built an invaluable resource that only an idiot would ignore. Graham Towers is not an idiot."

"Do you know much about him?"

"Not a lot. If you read the papers, he sounds like God's gift to banking."

"The funny thing is," put in Frances, "that if Mr. Graham Ford Towers is such an obvious choice for governor this week, how come no one was mentioning him as a candidate last week?"

Dr. Grace laughed. "No one but you! How did you figure it out?"

"Now, Dr. Grace, a girl can't give up all her secrets, or she's defenceless," she smiled.

"I think it is a good time for you all to take a break. What is your overtime up to?"

Frances opened the ledger. "Three hundred and fifty-four hours," she said.

"Good Lord! You started here—"

"May seventeenth. Seventeen weeks ago today."

"And you've logged eight extra weeks of time since?"

"I'm not very efficient."

"I guess you are! So what are you owed in overtime?"

Frances did a quick calculation. "Straight time, it would be $141.60."

"And time and a half?"

"$212.40."

"And at 3 percent on accounts more than thirty days overdue?"

"$221.10."

"You'll be able to retire by the time you're thirty. Anyway, we'd better track news reports of any European central banking officials that Governor Towers visits," said Dr. Grace. "Who does our clipping service in England?"

"Burroughs & Burroughs, Purveyors of News Services to His Royal Majesty, George V," replied Frances.

"And are you and the King happy with the service?"

"The King and I are content. They clip *The Times*, The *Daily Mail*, and the *Manchester Guardian*, so we get the Liberal, Conservative, and Labour response to most items."

"And in Europe?"

"We get two papers done in each of Paris, Berlin, and Madrid. Mr. Mueller translates anything that looks pertinent."

"What if the governor goes to Sweden or Portugal?"

"Either the British papers or Reuters will sell any interesting tidbits back to the Canadian papers. I don't think we need any more clippings. We're running ten days behind filing as it is."

"I thought I was in for a bit of a holiday, but they're letting contracts to design the new currency issue, and now that we're selling shares in the new Bank of Canada, the actual share certificates have to be designed. They've appointed an acting board of directors until the shareholders can elect their own board. Oh, these directors may call up looking for background material on the legislation or the new governor. Can you pull something together?"

"I can do something on Governor Towers, but I don't understand the Bank of Canada Act well enough to summarize it."

"You don't?"

"I don't. I'm a high school dropout, remember? You'll have to do it."

"Me?"

"You, and I don't want to release information packages to every Tom, Dick, and Harry that phones up. Can you get me a list of directors?"

"Frances, lest we forget, the basic principle behind the CFRA is that

I have too many things on my desk, and I need you to look after the paper flow."

"Dr. Grace," Frances replied, "lest we forget, you have a PhD in economics. I dropped out of Grade 11, for some reason, to come down here as a clerk. I do not understand monetary policy. I would *like* to understand it. I have a copy of The Bank of Canada Act beside my bed, and when I'm too exhausted to fall asleep, I pick it up. It's a wonderful narcotic."

"Most economists don't understand the Bank Act, either. Clark up in Finance wrote most of it. He'll be disappointed to hear that you don't find it entertaining."

"Well, don't tell him, if it will ruin his day. You still need to do the summary."

The *Paris Tribune*, September 22, 1934
Canadian Bank Governor
Tours European Central Banks
Graham Towers, governor of the newly created Bank of Canada, arrived in Paris yesterday to begin a fact-finding mission on how central banks are run. Over the next three weeks, he has plans to meet with central bankers in Paris, Stockholm, Basel, Brussels, Amsterdam, and London before heading home.

The Times, London, October 29, 1934
Secondment to Canada
Sir Nigel Holmes, cashier of the Bank of England, yesterday was appointed deputy governor of the Central Bank of Canada for a five-year term.

The 53-year-old baronet is a career banker, having served in the employ of the Bank of England since 1902. He has visited Canada once to see Niagara Falls.

25

KINGSMERE

Dorothy Deavy called Frances after supper. "Hi, slug, how's the working world treating you?"

"No complaints. How are things at Glebe Collegiate?"

Dorothy had quit her job after eight short weeks and returned to high school to get her senior matriculation. "The math and science are hard, and I need a break. How does this sound? Father is willing to lend out the Kingsmere cottage this weekend to his wild daughters." Mr. Deavy must have been within earshot to catch this. "Katie and Mary and I are catching the bus up on Saturday. You want to come along?"

Frances felt guilty that she had seen her friends so little over the summer. Then she felt hurt that Mary O'Brien had been invited first. Mostly she felt exhausted, and could barely make a decision.

"I'll have to ask my mother." She remembered her mother's irritation when she left town with Dr. Grace without asking permission. Vera was out in the backyard reading the paper.

"Oh, certainly, dear," said Vera without looking up.

Frances got back on the phone to Dorothy. "I can go."

"Great!" said Dorothy. Frances could hear a "yahoo!" from Katie in the background. "Just take a change of clothes and your toothbrush in to work on Saturday morning. You and Mary can grab the streetcar down to the Gatineau Bus Terminal. Katie and I will meet you there in time for the one o'clock bus."

Saturday dawned warm and blue-skied. Frances's excitement for the excursion rose. She had been working so hard that she had not allowed herself much time for fun, or even the anticipation of fun.

Frances let Mr. Mueller go at 12:15. She and Mary changed in the office washrooms. The Gatineau bus station was small and dated. The Deavys were laden with two shopping bags each.

"We bought enough food for a week!" exclaimed Katie. "In case we get snowed in!"

The old bus chugged across the Chaudière Bridge right beside the

Eddy Pulp Mill. The girls competed for the most hideous facial reaction to the stench. They headed up the Low Highway, dropping off passengers every few miles. The bus turned west into Old Chelsea and dropped them in front of L'Épicier Laframboise.

"Wait here," said Dorothy. "I just have a couple more things to pick up." They sat down on a wooden bench beside cases of empty Coca-Cola bottles and soaked up the sun. Dorothy was out quickly with two young men in tow.

"The Laframboise boys are doing a delivery down the north road. They'll drop us at the cottage if some of us don't mind riding in the back." Dorothy rode inside, between the brothers.

"The tall one, Luc, is kinda sweet on Dorothy," Katie confided to the others as they bounced along in the back of the pickup. "He's shy, but sure gives her great service in the store."

"Does Dorothy like him?" asked Mary, twisting her head for a better look at the suitor.

"I think she likes the good service," laughed Katie. "And a truck ride sure beats a long walk on a hot day."

The Deavy cottage had been built by Mr. Deavy's father, known as Grampa Walt, to distinguish him from Uncle Walter, Mr. Deavy's older brother, who still ran the family farm. The back end of the Deavy farm abutted the north side of Kingsmere Lake at an angle, giving them ownership of several hundred feet of shoreline. Grampa Walt had built the cottage over several winters, when the farm was mostly dormant, and his restless energy needed an outlet. When he died in 1922, Uncle Walter took over the farm, and Dorothy's father got the cottage as his share of the inheritance.

The truck turned off the gravel road into the trees. It took the narrow trail slowly, to ease the jolting over tree roots, or maybe just to stretch out the pleasure of female company. The Deavys' modest cottage stood in a little glade. The back door faced up the hill, while the front door opened onto a wide screened porch overlooking the lake. A hand pump stood to the right of the kitchen sink. A battered couch and chairs faced a cobblestone fireplace. There were two small bedrooms. There was no icebox, so milk, bacon, eggs, and meat were packed into a galvanized pail and lowered into the dug well beside the cottage. The well had a wooden cover that lifted easily to reveal a water mirror eight feet down.

It was like a day at the fair. All fun and carefree, and parent-free, and away. In the heat of the day, they went out on the water in the Deavy armada. Mary rowed the old red rowboat, and Katie sat in the back pointing out local sights. "That's where Mr. Carson fell down drunk in the woods, and was thought to be drowned. The green cottage on the point is owned by moonshiners. A buck a bottle for their high octane. See that willow hanging into the water up there? Susie Stapleton fell outta the tree and woulda drowned, but a branch caught in her underwear and kept her afloat long enough to scream for help. The underwear was a complete write-off."

Dorothy had taken the stern paddle in the cedar strip canoe with Frances in the bow. They paddled along the north shore, then through the reeds at the end where Whipple Creek flowed in, then back along the south shore.

"Those two cottages belong to Mr. King, the former prime minister," said Dorothy. "Sometimes you see him out fishing in the twilight. He waves when you wave, but mostly keeps to himself. Father is a stalwart CCF supporter, and doesn't fraternize on principle."

From the King cottages, they swung directly across the lake to their own dock. It was unusually hot for September, and they all went for a swim in the late afternoon. Frances fit easily into an extra bathing suit of Dorothy's. Mary had brought along her old red woollen bathing suit that barely covered her mature body, and she grimaced as she tussled into it. They splashed each other and played tag and climbed out on the dock to fling themselves in again and again before lying down to dry in the sun.

At six, they headed up for dinner. It was much cooler in the shaded cottage. Katie started kindling burning in the big fireplace, while Dorothy fired up the Findlay kitchen range. They toasted thick slices of buttered French bread in the popcorn basket over the fire. Dorothy pulled two bottles of wine out of the groceries she had picked up in Old Chelsea.

Mary's eyes went wide. "Dorothy! How did you get this?" she exclaimed.

"I turned eighteen in August, so I'm legal in Quebec."

"Mr. Laframboise would probably sell wine to any six-year-old with a dollar bill," chimed in Katie. She dug a corkscrew out of the utensil drawer and eyed it suspiciously. None of them had ever opened a bottle of wine before, and they shredded the cork to crumbs in the process. Katie poured generous portions into coffee mugs, fishing out most of the cork flotsam with a tea strainer.

"Here's mud in your eye," said Katie.

"To eternal youth," said Frances.

"Friends forever," said Dorothy.

"Jeez, I hope my parents don't find out!" said Mary.

Dorothy and Katie had been given watered-down wine occasionally when their parents drank it with dinner. Mary had never had an alcoholic drink in her life. Frances did not want to discuss her own tippling with Dr. Grace.

Katie read the label: "Cabernet Sauvignon, dry, with a fruity nose. The first swallow teases the taste buds for the joy to come." She took another drink. "They're right! I've been successfully teased." The others sipped and nodded.

Dinner was spaghetti with tomato sauce, a large market salad, and more toasted French bread. A bowl of fresh fruit served as dessert. By this time it was dark, the fire was stoked, and the second bottle of wine was almost gone. They were all flushed with the wine and the delight in each other's company.

"Let's play strip poker, then go for a skinny-dip!" said Katie.

"I've never played strip poker in my life!" giggled Mary.

"I've never played poker in my life," added Frances. "Can we play strip bridge?"

"Aren't we too old for skinny-dipping?" asked Dorothy.

"You're never too old for skinny-dipping," replied Katie. She dug a deck of tattered cards out of a drawer, and put a coal oil lamp on the floor beside the fire. "Let's go," she said.

"But we're hardly wearing anything!" exclaimed Frances.

"Quick game!" said Katie, dealing out the cards.

"How do you even bet?" asked Mary.

"Everybody has to ante. Peel off something," she said, pulling her blouse over her head without undoing the buttons. "If you think your cards are better than everybody else's, you bet a lot, or you can fold."

"What wins?" asked Frances.

"Four of a kind beats three of a kind, beats two beats one."

"Is that all there is? In *Trouble at Cripple Creek*, didn't Clark Gable draw a straight or something? What's a straight?"

"Who cares. They weren't playing strip poker," said Katie.

"Okay," said Dorothy, "I bet my shorts!"

"I see your shorts, and raise you my bra," replied Katie, casually doffing clothes into a pile in the centre.

"Now what?" asked Frances.

"Shorts and bra to call. 'Call' means I have to show my cards," replied Katie.

"You're showing just about everything else," said Dorothy, taking off her own bra.

Frances and Mary, a little tipsy, and completely confused by the game, the laughter, and the freedom, were swept along and clothes flew in the autumnal glow of the firelight.

"I have an ace!" exclaimed Katie proudly, slapping her high card down on the pine floorboards.

"I have two eights," said Mary. "Is that better or worse?"

"I have two queens," said Dorothy. "Gotcha both beat!"

"All I have is a bunch of hearts," said Frances, placing her cards on the floor.

"That's a flush!" said Katie. "You win!"

"I do? But there are no of-a-kinds."

"Don't matter. A flush is way up there. Better than four-of-a-kind."

"So what do I do with all these clothes? Put them on?"

Hysteria.

"Deal another hand," said Katie. "I wanna go swimming. While I'm still sober," she added, collapsing into laughter. Dorothy shuffled the cards, then passed them along to Mary, who dealt awkwardly, trying to cover herself up with her arms.

"Ante!" shouted Dorothy.

"But all we have left is our underwear!"

"Not anymore," said Katie, rolling onto her back to get her underwear off. A flurry of contortions followed and panties flew.

"Nobody but Frances can bet," said Mary. "We're all broke."

"We're all buck!" said Dorothy. "Buck naked!"

Mary won with three jacks. The excitement helped her forget her starkness.

"To-the-lake, to-the-lake, to-the-lake-lake-lake," sang Dorothy, and they all danced naked out the screen door and across the dewy lawn to the dock, which glowed palely in the moonlight. Like a train untracked, they followed each other in single file off the dock and into the water.

"I feel so free!" exclaimed Mary, rowing backward with her arms.

"Yes!" replied Dorothy. "I may never wear underwear again."

There was splashing and duck dives to expose crescent moons descending. They brought their feet together, and lay back on the water's surface to form a cross. They did back rolls and came up snorting and coughing. Their laughter drowned out the sound of a truck prowling up the lane. When it swung in beside the Deavy cottage, the lights shot down and lit their faces like targets in a shooting gallery.

"Omigod," said Dorothy. "Who's this?"

"We're naked!" stage-whispered Mary, in case anyone had forgotten.

The lights went out when the engine died, and two doors slammed in the autumn air. In the sudden darkness, they realized the moon had gone in as well.

"Dad? Mom? Uncle Walter?" inquired Katie.

Two male voices muttered in French, then laughed as they stumbled down to the dock.

"Hey! Dor-o-tee, dat you?" called one.

"Kay-tee, you dere?" asked the other.

"Luc?" asked Dorothy. "Gaetan?"

"*Oui, oui*. Big dance up at Hotel Sur Lac. You girls wanna come? Dance? Hey?"

"Yeah! Come on!" echoed the younger voice.

The Laframboise brothers had also been drinking.

Frances felt a curious detachment, as though she were watching a play in which she was an actor.

"Gaetan Laframboise! You get right back in that truck and get out of here!" yelled Katie.

"Kay-tee! Please! A kiss!" Gaetan knelt down at the end of the dock, staggered, and nearly fell in. The brothers laughed uproariously.

"Luc," said Dorothy, "It's great to see you, but you'd better go. Dad gave us specific instructions that no boys were allowed at the cottage this weekend."

"But we are men," said Luc, "and such a lovely night for a swim."

"Yeah," said Katie, "too bad you didn't bring your swimsuits. Anyhow, we've got company and can't go to the hotel. Sor-ree! Now scram!"

Mary was beginning to panic. "Dorothy," she whispered, "I can't stay afloat much longer!"

"Luc, Gaetan. You're lovely boys. Please go. Father would be very angry if he knew you were here. He'd certainly take this up with your father."

This was a sobering thought. René Laframboise was a foot shorter than his sons, but strong as an ox. The awkward silence was broken by a man's voice behind the girls. "Boys, you heard the ladies. Time to go."

The girls swung around to see the dim silhouette of a man in a boater hat sitting in the stern of a canoe twenty feet away. The Laframboise brothers quickly shuffled backward on the dock.

"Yes sir," said Luc, the ebullience out of his voice. He looked down, then slapped the seat of his pants in a defining way. "*Allons*, Gaetan." He grabbed his reluctant brother by the arm, and they crossed under the trees to the truck without looking back. The motor coughed then roared into life. When the tail lights disappeared over a crest in the lane, the girls looked around for the canoe, but nothing moved against the shadow of trees on the far shore.

"Mister?" called Dorothy, but there was no response until a loon warbled from down the lake.

"Hey, Mister?" echoed Katie, a little louder, but there was only the sound of water softly lapping against the shore.

They scrambled up the ladder at the end of the dock, and stood luminously in the diffused moonlight, intently searching the lake surface for several moments. Frances's teeth started to chatter and she said, "How about hot chocolate by the fire?"

26

BENNETT

Returning from a Momsie meeting in late October, Frances found Mary O'Brien crying in the front lobby of the Blackburn Building. "Mary! What's wrong?"

"Oh, Frances," gasped Mary, her bosom heaving, "there is an awful man in the office looking for Dr. Grace. When I said he wasn't in, he insisted that I go right out and fetch him. Mr. Mueller is handling the phones from your desk. I ran up to the Department of Finance but neither Harriett Weston nor Rose Malone knew where Dr. Grace was. I didn't know what to do next!" She teared up and wrung her hands. "I felt terrible leaving Mr. Mueller with that man, but I couldn't go back empty-handed."

Stella whisked them to the fourth floor. As they came down the corridor, Frances glimpsed the back of a tall man in a dark blue suit. Random filing cabinet drawers hung open, and he was scrutinizing something intently. He did not hear them approach, or did not care if he did.

"Good afternoon," said Frances. "May I help you?" she asked in a tone of insulted civility.

The man turned, dismissed them both with a glance, and returned to foraging in the files. "Looking for Wilbur," he said.

"He is not in the filing cabinet," Frances snapped, plucking the file from the man's hand, and slamming the drawer shut under his nose.

The man peered down at her. "Your files are completely disorganized," he said, shamelessly.

"I'm glad you found them so," Frances replied. "They are coded to protect them from unauthorized scrutiny."

The man sighed. "Where is Wilbur? I sent the girl to find him, and I see she hasn't done it."

"Dr. Grace was in this morning, and said he was busy at the Finance Department for the rest of the day. That's up on Parliament Hill in the West—"

"I know where the Finance Department is!" countered the man. "I have just come from Finance, and Wilbur was not there."

"Would you care to leave a message?"

"No, no!" He looked down at a gold pocket watch he had taken out of his vest. "Fetch this McFadden creature for me then."

Mr. Mueller, who had been watching the drama from the comfort of Frances's big desk chair, now scurried for the sanctuary of his office. Mary sidled surreptitiously into her own office, from where she could call the police or an ambulance.

Frances was taking deep breaths, trying to control her immodest rage. At last she said, "I am Frances McFadden."

"You?" scoffed the blue-suited man as though he had caught her out perpetrating a fraud. "I mean the McFadden that runs the office when Wilbur is away."

"That is I," responded Frances, glaring up at him.

"You can't be serious!"

Frances walked over to her desk and picked up a business card. She marched back and handed it to him.

"Frances McFadden, secretary-treasurer of the Canadian Financial Resources Agency, at your service," she stated, without the least hint of servility.

The man held it out at arm's length and tilted his head back to read it. He put the card in his vest pocket and headed for the door without looking back. "Tell Wilbur that Bennett was around," he said.

Shortly after six, Dr. Grace showed up. He went straight to the vault for the single malt and then to the icebox, then back to the conference room. "Join me?" he inquired of Frances, as he fetched his in-basket. She quietly poured herself three fingers of Scotch, and dropped two ice cubes in on top. Dr. Grace looked up to confirm the size of the libation.

"Rough day?"

Frances took a deep drink, then sat down. "The vilest man on earth was here this afternoon looking for you."

"I trust you told him I had left on a world cruise and would not be back until the new year?"

"He was the most brazen person I have ever met. Had Mary in tears. I'd come back from the Momsie meeting, to find her hiding down in the foyer, with Mr. Mueller up here watching shop. This man was rude and impudent. He did not believe me when I identified myself, and failed to introduce himself at all, then stomped out. He continuously referred to you as 'Wilbur,' which I found quite ill-mannered."

"Oh-oh," said Dr. Grace. "Only two people on earth call me Wilbur. One is my great-aunt Gertrude. What did he look like?"

"He was tall and bald."

"Did he have enormous eyebrows and dark eyes?"

"Yes! Beady little eyes. Oh, when he marched out he said, 'Tell Wilbur that Bennett was around,' but he didn't say Bennett who. Bennett Smith? Bennett Jones? Altogether a very nasty person. Know any Bennetts?"

"Just one."

"Is he pompous and arrogant?"

"Some might say that," said Dr. Grace as he finished signing the last of his correspondence.

"So, who is he?"

"Richard Bedford Bennett."

"The prime minister! That was R.B. Bennett?"

"Yes. He doesn't seem to have made a very favourable impression."

"Oh, good Lord! What have I done?" Frances said, holding her head in her hands. "He wasn't very civil, and I wasn't very civil. Oh, no!"

"Well, never mind. He can be a little headstrong. I'm surprised you didn't recognize him with all your news clippings. You do have a file on him?"

"Oh, certainly, but those newspaper pictures are so grainy. And I never expected the prime minister to drop in. He was pawing through the filing cabinet, and I was incensed, and . . . oh, my Lord!" Frances took a deep double swallow of single malt. "He said, 'Where is this McFadden creature?'—creature!—and then he would not believe that I was McFadden! Will I be fired?"

"Don't worry. I'm doing him a favour, so I can bargain for your future with the government. Your future is a lot more secure than his—I'm sure the Conservatives will never get re-elected. Mind you, the prime minister is very hard-working. He puts us to shame. Did you know that he's his own Minister of External Affairs, and House Leader? Doesn't delegate very well. Usually. But he's had some health problems, so he's slowing down a bit."

"You're 'doing him a favour'? How do you even know him?"

"Funny story. In brief, he knew my father. Thirty years ago, they were articling students together at a small law firm in Chatham, New Brunswick."

"I thought you said your father was a Liberal."

"He is. In those days, the bread and butter legal work in small towns came from the government. Governments can change at each election, therefore a Liberal lawyer and a Conservative lawyer would set up a pragmatic partnership. Father articled to the firm's Liberal, Mr. Mickleham, and R.B. Bennett articled to the firm's Conservative, Mr. Tweedie. When they were called to the bar, there wasn't enough local business to take either man into the partnership, but both were given excellent references. R.B. went out to Calgary to work in James Lougheed's office, and my father got a position with Ray, Young & Wake in Toronto."

"Were they close?"

"Not really, although they respected each other's intelligence and work ethic. Mr. Bennett sometimes has difficulty seeing the merit of any idea opposed to his own view. They clashed on politics, of course."

"I'm missing something, here," said Frances. "If they weren't particularly friendly, and they held different political views, and they practised law two thousand miles apart, how did this lead Wilbur Grace to the prime minister?"

"Well, there was a woman."

"A woman brought them together?"

"No, a woman tore them apart. Her name was Martha McKeague. She was a schoolteacher in Chatham, and a wonderful baker of blueberry muffins, I'm told. She was a Methodist, as was Mr. Bennett. They met at church. He squired her about to strawberry socials and such. Apparently, she was more interested in deepening the relationship than he was, so he backed off. My father, an Anglican, noticed her at a skating party, and found her quite charming. It was a small town, and there weren't that many unattached young women around. Father knew that Mr. Bennett had socialized with her at one time. Being a gentleman of the old school, father asked R.B. if Miss McKeague was free of any commitment to him.

"Mr. Bennett claimed that Miss McKeague was free to make blueberry muffins for whomever she wished. So my father began courting her, and they got on famously, which put Mr. Bennett into a high rage. He expected Miss McKeague to rebuff my father because she was pining for him. Anyway, there were angry words and unkind remarks about character directed at my father, who is normally mild-mannered."

"Except when his integrity is questioned?"

"Exactly. Just before seconds were to be named for the duel, the job offer came in from Calgary, and Mr. Bennett decamped for the Northwest Territories."

"Martha McKeague isn't your mother?"

"Oh, no. While Grace and Bennett were posturing, she accepted an offer of marriage from the Anglican priest, a great fan of blueberry muffins.

"I think after some time and distance, Mr. Bennett calmed down and regretted his comments to my father, but he was far too proud to apologize. Shortly after I arrived in Ottawa, I received an invitation from the prime minister's office for dinner at the Rideau Club. I expected that there would be a whole table of newly hired civil servants, but there were just the two of us. He inquired about my thesis work and my thoughts on the Canadian economy. Eventually he asked if I was related to Theo Grace of the Court of King's Bench. When I acknowledged my relationship, he didn't act surprised.

"The prime minister didn't get any more personal than that, but he continued to ask me cryptically about how things were on the Court of King's Bench. When I mentioned this bizarre query to my father, I got the background story. Father laughed, thinking back on it all, so obviously no grudge was held. Then Father began to ask me how things were in the East Block, where the prime minister's office is. I became the go-between for their enquiries into each other's well-being.

"I get along surprisingly well with Mr. Bennett. He does have a deep interest in improving the Canadian economy. He was genuinely appreciative of my point of view. Possibly he was deferential to me to make up for the insult to my father. He has no family of his own. We began having lunch or dinner together about once a month."

"But if you dine out once a month with the prime minister, people must know."

"The prime minister is quite discreet. We always eat in a private dining room upstairs at the Rideau Club, which already is a very private place. I have never mentioned these dinners to a soul, not even my father. I haven't noticed that I'm treated any differently from my peers at the Finance Department."

"So what favour does he owe you? It can't be just that he feels guilty for insulting your father thirty years ago."

"Take a guess," smiled Dr. Grace. "If you can scoop me on Governor Tower's appointment, this one should be a cinch."

Frances mulled for a minute, then a thought struck her. "Mr. Bennett wouldn't by any chance be familiar with 'certain parties' in Ottawa?"

"Well done, McFadden!" said Dr. Grace. "Mr. Bennett *is* certain parties."

"Oh, my God," said Frances. "He not only runs the country, he is personally responsible for creating the Canadian Financial Resources Agency?"

"Yes. See? He can't be all bad."

"So these files are really his files?"

"In a manner of speaking."

"But why did he refer to me as 'this McFadden creature'? That boiled me."

"Probably my fault," Dr. Grace confessed. "You remember that little misunderstanding with my mother referring to you as 'my poor woman' having to work with her inept son? Well, in much the same way, I perhaps exaggerated what a gruelling taskmaster you were here."

"Why?"

Dr. Grace sighed. "The prime minister is highly principled and highly political, but not always highly practical. So when he bore down on me to take some action that wasn't very feasible, I would sometimes say, 'Good idea, sir, but McFadden would never stand for it.' I got tired of fighting him on every issue. R.B. liked the idea that there was a hard-driving taskmaster in the office who kept me on my toes. He kind of embellished the image of you as being not unlike himself — hard-working, dedicated, brooking-no-fools. He likely expected someone different in appearance."

"So Frances McFadden became the Creature from the Black Lagoon."

"Yes, and it worked when rational arguments did not."

"For instance?"

"Well, Mr. Bennett is a Methodist Maritimer who abstains from alcohol and cigarettes. To him, these characteristics exemplify perfection in humanity. He suggested that all staff for this office be sifted through the abstemious-Methodist-Maritimer sieve. So I told him that McFadden would never agree. He always backed off at the fear of offending 'The McFadden' — his term."

"Well, that game's blown now that he's met me."

"On the contrary! Weren't you domineering and imperious? You completely validated my description. He might actually be easier to handle now that he's seen the tough nut I'm forced to deal with every day."

27

SCOTTY MELDRUM

Graham Towers returned from his European tour of central banks on November 8. On November 20, he announced that Duncan (Scotty) Meldrum, of the Bank of Nova Scotia, had accepted the appointment as the first secretary of the Bank of Canada.

"The secretary is the nuts-and-bolts man, responsible for organizing the internal structure of the Bank, including all hiring," said Dr. Grace. "Meldrum has a sterling reputation in Toronto banking circles. A bit of a ladies' man, with an eye for the finely turned ankle. Likely he doesn't even know that our little organization exists. He's coming to Ottawa on Monday, and I'll bring him around. It's up to you to convince him that the Bank of Canada needs the three of you."

Frances had private chats with her team before they left work on Friday.

"Mary, you have a photographic memory—a priceless asset in keeping a command of these thirty filing cabinets. I want you to become a permanent Bank of Canada employee, and I need your help. On Monday, tie your gorgeous hair back with a pink bow. Wear your cream blouse."

"But it's too small! I'm bursting out of it!"

"Wear it with your tartan skirt."

"I got that skirt when I was thirteen. It's too short!"

"Wear it. You would be invaluable to this Bank. We just need to make sure that Mr. Meldrum notices and accepts the truth."

She walked down and knocked on Mr. Mueller's door. "Mr. Mueller, the Bank of Canada needs your services badly, although they may not know it just yet. On Monday, we have a test. I want all of us to pass."

Mr. Mueller sat bleakly before Frances. His hands clasped and unclasped nervously. Finally, he uttered, "Miss McFadden, I can't come in Monday and face this . . . this inquisition. I'll write out my resignation, and you can hand it in."

They were both silent. Finally, Mr. Mueller's eyes fluttered up behind his huge glasses to see Frances staring right at him.

"Mr. Mueller, your command of four languages is a rare gift. I want you to offer your gift to Mr. Meldrum on Monday morning. Given half a chance, Mr. Meldrum will recognize your strengths. But I need your support."

Another long silence followed, but slowly the hands stopped fidgeting. Mr. Mueller took a huge breath and looked up, holding Frances's gaze for almost five seconds, a personal record. "How can I help?"

"That's the spirit! I need two or three samples of work you've translated recently. Then I need you to stand up straight, eyes front, and even if you cannot continuously look Mr. Meldrum in the eye, at least look in his direction, not at the floor."

"That's all?"

"That's all. Mary and I will be right here beside you. We are all in this together, Mr. Mueller."

A slight smile played at the corner of Mr. Mueller's lips. "Like the Three Musketeers?"

Frances clapped her hands. "Exactly! One for all and all for one! Are you with us?"

Mr. Mueller smiled modestly. "I am," he said.

The booming voice of Scotty Meldrum announced itself as soon as Stella Stanton opened the elevator door on the fourth floor. It echoed down the long corridor and through the closed door of the CFRA. Frances jumped up to survey the troops. Mary's bosom was barely contained by her cream chemise blouse, and she had a sweater draped modestly over her shoulders.

"Sweater off, Mary O'Brien. Please stand up. Straight. Head back, shoulders out. Good. Posture is important, even when you're a genius."

"If I'm a genius, why do I have to dress like a tramp?"

"You look quite fetching. If we can't win at the front door, we'll win at the back."

Frances moved on to the next office doorway. "Mr. Mueller, can I see your best side?"

Mr. Mueller stood up beside his desk for inspection. His pants were freshly pressed and his tie was perfectly knotted. Frances waited until his eyes left the floor and he looked at her right ear. "Good, Mr. Mueller. And the voice?"

Mr. Mueller took a deep breath, and then said in a clear voice, "The Three Musketeers, Miss McFadden!"

Frances curbed an impulse to hug him. "Wonderful! I'll come and get you after I've softened Mr. Meldrum up a bit. We'll be fine!"

Frances could now hear a Scottish brogue carrying clearly through the door to the hall.

"Now, Grace, exactly what kind of a bootleg operation is this 'Canadian Financial Resources Agency,' for the love o' God?"

"We knew the Bank of Canada would need reference resources when it sprang into being, so we've set up an advance office."

"What have ya here?"

"I spend a twelve-hour day up at the Department of Finance, dancing the deputy minister's jig, so McFadden actually runs the place. She has an archivist to handle the files and a translator to bring the annual reports on the French, German, and Spanish national banks into English for easy reference."

"Term positions?"

"Yes, but I feel some obligation to—"

"Grace," cut in the Scot, "we canna staff the Bank of Canada with any flotsam that washes in the door. This crew doesn't fit the governor's organizational plan at all. Give them a week's salary and clear them out."

There was a long silence. Finally, the burred steamboat spoke. "Is there anything worth my seeing here? We have to meet the governor at ten."

Frances's heart heaved. The door opened, and Dr. Grace ushered a great bear of a man into the office. Frances sprang to attention.

Dr. Grace put her at ease with a smile. "Frances, relax! It's not the King. Only Mr. Meldrum, the new secretary of the Bank of Canada. Mr. Meldrum, Miss McFadden, the secretary-treasurer of the Canadian Financial Resources Agency."

Mr. Meldrum was well over six feet tall, and his broad shoulders seemed even broader in his dark blue double-breasted suit. He held out a huge paw that engulfed Frances's hand. "Frances McFadden!" he exclaimed, rolling the name out through his thick Scottish burr. "Pleased to make your acquaintance. Now would that be the Glengarry McFaddens or the Aberdeenshire McFaddens?"

"Aberdeenshire, sir."

"What a good choice of ancestry! I was born not fifteen miles from Aberdeen myself. Fine highland stock!

Scots, wha hae wi' Wallace bled,

Scots, wham Bruce has aften led . . ."

Frances continued:

"Welcome to your gory bed,

Or to Victorie!"

"And ya know yer Robbie Burns!" beamed Scottie Meldrum.

"Father felt that the appreciation of our Scottish heritage was the hallmark of an educated mind."

"Och! What a wise man!" marvelled Mr. Meldrum. "Now, to business. Has Grace told you the Bank of Canada will set up offices in the Victoria Building on Wellington Street?"

Dr. Grace gave a low whistle. "That's quick."

"The governor and deputy governor have been shoehorned into borrowed space at the Department of Finance. Quite unsatisfactory. We can take possession of two entire floors January first. Some tidying and painting is needed, but we can move storage items over first thing in the new year. Is there anything here we should keep?" Mr. Meldrum turned and beheld the filing cabinets. "Lord almighty!" He swept his arm down the row. "What is this?"

"This," explained Dr. Grace, "is the excellent work that Miss McFadden and her staff have been hard at since May."

"Surely to God they're not all full!"

"Should I call on our archivist, sir?" Frances asked. "She can describe what we have on file."

"Briefly, then," said Mr. Meldrum, checking his watch.

Frances knocked on Mary's office door. "Miss O'Brien? Could you spare a moment?"

Mary stood up. Frances made eye contact and straightened her own shoulders. Mary lifted her shoulders, and her breasts strained against the tight blouse. Frances nodded her head imperceptibly, and stepped back to allow Mary out the door. Frances propelled her gently toward the bear-man and made introductions. Mary looked as though she had just straggled into the path of a runaway bus.

Mr. Meldrum was immediately captured by Mary's wistful face, and the canyon of cleavage that plunged down before him. "P-p-p-pleased to meet you, Miss—"

"O'Brien," said Frances and Dr. Grace in unison.

Mr. Meldrum's massive hand found Mary's. He blinked several times. Dr. Grace bit down on an escaping smile. Frances asked Mary to outline the archival collection. It was unlikely that Mr. Meldrum took in 10 percent of the presentation, but his eyes did not leave Mary for an instant. He was speechless even through her description of their file on the famous Johnson Gang's counterfeiting exploits.

"Thank you, Mary. Any questions, Mr. Meldrum?"

Mr. Meldrum looked like a sleeper awakening from a dream.

"No . . . no," he said, finally. "Very, very impressive."

Mary's breasts? The files?

"Grace, This is superb! I simply had no idea. Now there is one more staff member?"

"Yes, sir," said Frances. "Mr. Herbert Mueller is our translator. Many of these documents from foreign banks and news agencies were not in English, and he has done some remarkable renderings, anticipating that the Bank Executive might not be fluent in French or German or Spanish. Let me get him."

Mr. Mueller was cowering behind his desk. Frances picked up the three translations. She whispered, "I know this is hard for you, Musketeer, but we are doing very well. Just look him in the eye, and say, 'Good day, sir.' I'll look after the rest." Frances could hear his teeth chatter. "Take three deep breaths, and walk out. Shoulders back!"

"Mr. Meldrum, may I introduce Mr. Herbert Mueller, our translator?"

Mr. Mueller, in a great act of courage, stepped forward, took Mr. Meldrum's extended hand, and said: "Good day, sir."

Then Frances interceded with the three translations. "These are just a few things that Mr. Mueller has been working on lately. Here are press clippings on El Banco Nacional de España from the two main Madrid newspapers. Mr. Mueller usually just does a brief abstract, but is willing to do verbatim translations if requested. Here is a translation of the National Bank of Germany's Annual Report for 1933. This is a file on press releases from the Bank of Montreal in both French and English. There are some discrepancies that Mr. Mueller has noted for further reference."

"Discrepancies?" inquired Mr. Meldrum, looking at the file.

"Yes, sir — see here? The numbers are different in the balances in the English report and the French report. We're not sure which is accurate, not being bankers. Perhaps you'd be able to tell?"

Mr. Meldrum was not able to tell, and didn't mind admitting it. "I'd have to study the whole report to figure it out. And I don't understand a word of French outside '*bonjour*' and '*merci*.'" A sudden realization was dawning on Mr. Meldrum's face. "This place is a gold mine!"

Mr. Meldrum paced back and forth in front of them, deep in rumination, then he said: "Thank you, Mr. Mueller and Miss O'Brien. Please don't let me keep you from your work. Miss McFadden, may I have a private word with you and Grace before we leave?"

In the boardroom, Mr. Meldrum continued to pace. "Grace, I was hasty in my assessment of the work your people have done here. Six months of research, and it hasn't cost us a nickel! There is one fly in the ointment—these positions are outside the governor's organizational chart. If I can't win them over to hiring three employees, I need a fallback position. Miss McFadden, if they'll only allow me to hire one or two, who should it be? Could you think about that and give me a brief note by tomorrow?"

"I can tell you right now, Mr. Meldrum. Mary O'Brien would be the most valuable asset to the Bank. There are almost six thousand files out there. She has a photographic memory. She could find any file blindfolded. And she knows if there is a related file in another language, or if a subject is cross-filed under other topics.

"And if we could keep two employees?"

"There may be others who can cross-translate in four languages, but Mr. Mueller is absolutely meticulous. He finds errors in published documents that must have already been proofread twenty times. His expertise is invaluable."

"Ach—woman! But if you had to choose one?"

"Mr. Meldrum, if you had to go out in a blizzard, how would you choose between a coat and boots?"

"Well, Miss McFadden, it seems that ya don't have a very high opinion of yourself, if you'd insist that these two be hired ahead of you? Or are we listenin' to Saint Frances the Martyr here, who sacrifices herself for the welfare of others?"

Dr. Grace came to her rescue. "Mr. Meldrum, I think that's unfair. You asked Miss McFadden for a professional opinion on a difficult question. Should you fault her for giving good advice on short notice?"

Frances continued, "I am confident of my own skills, Mr. Meldrum. Dr. Grace put me in charge of this office. I don't feel I betrayed that trust—did I, Dr. Grace?"

"Absolutely not. Frances is an exemplary administrator and has unusually good judgment for one—" he veered from the precipice at the last moment, "—who has grown so quickly into the mastery of new tasks."

"Still," continued Frances, "I have a more general set of skills than those of Miss O'Brien or Mr. Mueller. That's why I would rank their talents ahead of my own."

Mr. Meldrum pursed his lips and narrowed his eyes. "Do you agree, Grace?"

"Oh, no," countered Dr. Grace. "Mr. Mueller and Miss O'Brien are exceptional, but Frances McFadden is the producer and director and stage manager here. The show would not go on without her. You wouldn't go out in a blizzard without a coat or boots, but you need a hat, too."

"Ahhh," moaned Mr. Meldrum, throwing his great head back and holding his temples in his hands. "Y're nae help to me a-tall!"

28

THE AXE

On Thursday morning, Scottie Meldrum stormed into the office with Dr. Grace. He collapsed into a chair in the conference room. "No sense beatin' around the bush," he said. "I could'na persuade their excellencies to keep you three on. I'm sorry. I did my damnedest, but there are too many forces contrivin' agin us. 'Tis a bloody shame." He smacked the table with his great fist.

"The governor wasn't against you on principle, but Frenchie and his lordship jumped on my head." He took his glasses off, running a hand through his receding hair. "Grace, you wouldna have the means to a wee dram?"

"Medicinals? Of course, Mr. Meldrum. Frances?"

Frances was back in three minutes with the decanter of Macallan's and the fixin's.

"Ach! Bless ye, lass!" said Scottie, pouring a huge tumbler of whiskey, and adding an eyedropper of water. He drained half the glass and took a deep breath.

"Sir Nigel Holmes, God's gift to central banking, put the kibosh to us. The goodly knight has taken an immediate dislike to me, which I'm pleased to reciprocate." He shook his head. "We need his central bank experience, but his arse is so tight, he couldna shit string. Ever' sentence begins with 'What we do at the Bank of England is . . .' failin' to comprehend that he isn't in England anymore. The B of E doesn't employ women, except as cleaning ladies and preparers of tea. Sir Nigel is clearly a man's man. He brought his valet with him as well as his secretary and cook. All male. If he weren't married, I'd be wonderin' about his gender preference in associates. Now he needs a driver. His valet used to drive him around in England, but is paralyzed by this frontier habit of driving on the right-hand side of the road."

"Can't Sir Nigel drive?" asked Frances.

Mr. Meldrum drained his glass and reached for the decanter. "Ach, Frances McFadden, you've obviously been spared contact with the British upper classes. Count your blessings! I'd be surprised if he can wipe his own arse. So now the Bank has to hire him a driver, and add all his servants to the payroll. Milord's advice is that you should all be dismissed today." Mr. Meldrum drained the second glass of Scotch, and slammed it down on the table.

"But the files . . . ?"

" 'Toss them down the garbage chute,' he says. He will teach us all we need to know about central banking. Then there's Frenchie to deal with. The prime minister wanted a francophone on the Bank Executive. Several good people declined. Monsieur Soulière was about the fifth choice, and poof!—he's the assistant deputy governor."

"A third of the country is French," said Dr. Grace.

"Agreed," said Mr. Meldrum. "But should their representative be a fifth-rate banker without a dram of imagination? His card is Frenchie-at-the-table, while Sir Nigel plays his Bank of England card. Which one will bore us to death first? He sided with Sir Nigel on dismissing you three. You're blessed to be out of it all, Miss McFadden.

"I did insist that Governor Towers come over here tomorrow to personally thank you all for services rendered." He looked longingly at the decanter, but resisted pouring a third tumbler.

Frances took a deep breath. "So we're finished. Well, Mr. Meldrum, thank you for trying. I'll notify the others." Frances closed the conference room door. As she walked down toward the washroom, her knees started to shake. Locking the bathroom door behind her, she sat on the toilet and sobbed.

Mary and Mr. Mueller took the news quietly. They had been on a cliff edge all week. "Remember, it is not our doing, and it is not our fault. If the King gave medals to office workers for valour, we'd all get one." Mary's eyes teared up. Mr. Mueller blinked blankly. After a minute of silence, Frances said, "Tomorrow will be our final day. Let's go out for a nice lunch at Murphy–Gamble's to celebrate."

They both stared at her, and she had to look away.

That night, Frances dreamed that she was on an elevator that didn't go down but wandered left and right with quick shifts and lurches, like a midway ride. Thankfully, her mother was working the evening shift at the hospital, and they didn't cross paths. Vera would somehow make this failure Frances's fault.

When Mary and Mr. Mueller arrived at 8:00 a.m., Frances outlined the plan. "This morning we write like mad, and after lunch we clean the place out. Dr. Grace said he'd bring the governor around about four to shake our hands. We have just over 150 contact names on my index cards. These people have been very helpful, and deserve a letter of thanks. Here is a draft:

December 7th, 1934

Dear_____:

Thank you for your invaluable assistance to the Canadian Financial Resources Agency over the past seven months.

The CFRA will close down as of 5:00 p.m. today as the Bank of Canada assumes full responsibility for central banking activities. Until their offices are operational, please direct any correspondence to

Dr. W. Grace,
Department of Finance,
East Block, Parliament Hill,
Ottawa

> *Yours sincerely,*
> *F.E. McFadden*
> *Secretary-Treasurer*
> *Canadian Financial Resources Agency*

"Add a personal note if you like, but keep it simple, or we'll be here until midnight. Here's a third for each of you. Type the letter and the envelope and return them to me when you have a dozen for signatures. Hopefully, we can get this done by noon, and we can all have a nice lunch before we pitch the files. Let's get cracking."

It was strange how motivated they each felt to get it over with quickly. At 11:30, there were voices in the hall. Dr. Grace and Mr. Meldrum walked in the door with three men. Frances looked up briefly, but continued typing. "Good morning, Mr. Meldrum, Dr. Grace. A delight to see you both. We're a little busy scuttling the ship, here, but there is coffee on in the back. I assure you we'll be done by five, and I'll leave my keys here in the top drawer. Our telephone line will be disconnected by six this afternoon. I've written the landlord. We're notifying all of our business contacts that we're closing for good today. Anything else?" She was impatient to type.

Mr. Meldrum spoke. "Miss McFadden, may I introduce Graham Towers, Governor of the Bank of Canada?"

Frances peered over at a clean-cut young man who looked like a Methodist minister. He had a gentle smile beneath wire-rimmed glasses. He stepped forward and extended his hand. "Pleased to meet you, Miss McFadden," he said in a sincere voice. His handshake was warm and firm. "Both Dr. Grace and Mr. Meldrum have praised the excellent work you've done here. I truly am sorry that we need to close the office down. It was nothing personal. It just didn't fit into our overall plan or, more importantly, our budget. May I introduce Sir Nigel Holmes, the deputy governor, and Monsieur Soulière, the assistant deputy governor?"

A silence followed, until Dr. Grace jumped in. "We were all meeting down the street with some deputy ministers, and Mr. Meldrum thought we could drop by on our way back to the East Block. Save troubling you later."

Another silence.

It was Mr. Meldrum's turn. With a sweep of his arm he said, "These thirty cabinets hold the archives Miss McFadden's team have built up."

"You don't mean they're all full!" exclaimed the governor.

"Pretty well," replied Frances.

Sir Nigel let his astonishment get the better of his disinterest. "Whatever could you possibly have in all this storage?"

"Dr. Grace wanted complete background information on the Canadian economy and the banking system on file, as he expected the first governor would be from England."

"Tsk," said Sir Nigel, like a benediction.

"This is all information on the Canadian banking system?" asked the governor.

"Partly, sir. We have a filing cabinet on each of the ten Canadian chartered banks, with their annual reports and policy statements going back twenty years."

"Not a bad idea," agreed the governor, "but would that fill four drawers for each bank?"

"Dr. Grace warned us that banks aren't always the most objective judges of their own performance. He told us to seek external reviews and collaboration. We have used three different clipping services to provide public comment on each bank, their stock and bond issues, and the market's response to their business activities. We prepared biographical files on the top officers in each bank, their board of directors, distribution of branches, organizational charts, et cetera."

The governor smiled. "You would have a file on me, then?"

"Yes, sir."

"What of the other twenty filing cabinets, then?" He walked down along the row of cabinets, and absently opened a drawer. He lifted up a file, and read the label. "This is a file on KCB29ARET4.10.1934? What does that mean?"

"Would you like Miss O'Brien, our archivist, to explain?"

"Is this really necessary?" asked Sir Nigel.

"I'm curious," said the governor.

Mary's typewriter had been thundering away in the background. She was nervous when Frances went to get her. "Relax," said Frances. "They've already fired us. What more harm can they do?"

"Gentlemen, Miss O'Brien, our archivist. She has the mastery of the thirty cabinets before you. Mary, I have reported on the ten Canadian chartered banks. Could you briefly explain what else we have on file here?"

Mary wet her lips. "Cer . . . cer . . . certainly. We have all their files on Lord Macmillan's Royal Commission on Banking and Currency. Not all concerns were addressed in Lord Macmillan's final report. Dr. Grace felt we should have records of who supported its general tone, and who didn't, and why. Two filing cabinets.

"Two more cabinets are filled with testimony and submissions to the House of Commons Committee on Banking and Commerce, when the Bank Act was debated.

"Dr. Grace also instructed us to set up files on the Bank of England and the U.S. Federal Reserve, as well as ten other central banks. We asked for their annual reports for the past twenty years. We also used clipping services to flesh out the economic, trade, and industrial concerns of the countries mentioned—government priorities, taxation policy, infrastructure funding, tariffs, anything that might influence their central banks. Twelve filing cabinets.

"Then, let's see—we also have two cabinets full of Canadian legislation, including budgets going back thirty years, describing economic policy, including trade and tariffs. And, of course, public comment in newspapers and periodicals on government policy."

"Thank you, Miss O'Brien," said the governor with a smile. "And your filing system?" he asked.

"The building security is not great. We thought it would be simplest just to code our files. For example, that file in your hand, KCB29ARET4.10.1934, came out of the top drawer of cabinet 17 near the front. 'K' is the code for Germany, and CB refers to 'Central Bank,' although they actually call it the National Bank of Germany. It is their 1929 Annual Report. 'E' is for 'external'—information, reviews, criticisms from outside the German Central Bank on their policy. 'T' means it has been translated into English, and the next number combination indicates that the whole file was summarized in October of 1934."

"And how many files are there here?" asked the governor.

"As of yesterday at five-thirty, there were 5,987."

Sir Nigel was incredulous. "Do you mean to tell me that you can find any one of six thousand files based on that silly code?"

"Yes, sir. I have a good memory." Mary blushed at this braggadocio.

"Where would you find the personal file on me from my days at the Royal Bank?" asked the governor.

"That would be in the second drawer from the bottom of the fourth cabinet from the far end, sir." Mary walked down the row of cabinets and opened the appropriate drawer. She pulled a file out. "Here it is, sir."

"Amazing!" exclaimed the governor, opening the file.

"Am I to understand that you have files on us all, then?" asked M. Soulière.

"Yes," said Mary. "We probably have two hundred files on Canadian bankers, including Mr. Meldrum and you, sir, and another two hundred or so on bankers from other countries."

The row of silent cabinets took on a new, personal interest.

"As a matter of fact," added Dr. Grace, "all of the press releases announcing your various appointments to the Bank of Canada were written by Miss McFadden. Neither the Finance Department nor the prime minister's office had anything like these resources."

"Here's another thing Miss O'Brien can do," added Mr. Meldrum. "Governor, take three bank notes from your billfold and pass them along to Miss O'Brien."

The governor smiled quizzically, but did as he was told. Mary studied each note front and back then returned them to the governor.

"What were the serial numbers on the three bills?" asked Mr. Meldrum.

"The Bank of Toronto five-dollar bill was CT997416."

"Amazing!" said the governor.

"The Bank of Montreal two-dollar bill was 79 . . . 796, no . . . 79964 . . . E . . . C . . . 7."

"E7C," corrected the governor, glancing down.

Mary swallowed. "E7C," she repeated, looking nervously at Frances.

"Exceptional!" said the governor. "And the last one?"

"The Dominion Bank ten-dollar note was . . ." A fearful blankness filled her face. There was a long pause. Humiliated, Mary stared at the floor.

Mr. Meldrum and Mr. Grace looked bleakly at the staff. The governor, ever polite, smiled. "Again, thank you all for your good work," he said. "I truly am impressed, and I'm sorry—"

In a trance-like voice, Mary cut the governor off. "The five-dollar bill was the better counterfeit," she said.

---- 29 ----

RECALLED TO LIFE

"**W**hat?" exclaimed Mr. Meldrum.

"A forgery? Let me see," said Monsieur Soulière.

The governor turned the bills over in his hand, examining them carefully, as the others crowded around.

Mary explained, "The paper is very good. The engraving is high quality, and the colouring is exceptional."

"So what makes you think it's fake, then?" asked the governor.

"A New York counterfeiting gang moved up to Montreal in the spring to lie low. It's probably their work. They were experimenting and just used that one serial number on all the bills they ran off," Mary answered.

"And how would you know that?" demanded Sir Nigel.

"We get information from all the banks regarding counterfeiting, fraud, and robberies. We also have regular correspondence with over a dozen police forces, including the Mounties. RCMP Inspector Hollingsworth has been particularly helpful."

"They share information freely with you?" asked the governor.

"One by one, the banks joined in, then the Mounties, as they understood the value of shared information."

"Which is the other forgery?" asked Monsieur Soulière. The four bankers examining the three bills carefully, rubbing them between their fingers and holding them up to the light.

Mary was unaware that her knowledge trumped that of all the men put together. "The blue ink on the Dominion bank note is at least two shades too dark. There is poor definition in the hairline of the King's picture. Probably the Johnson Gang."

"The Johnson Gang?" echoed Monsieur Soulière.

"You know, from Toronto?" said Mary. "The older brothers are still in Kingston Penitentiary, so one of the nephews must be learning to engrave, if they are still keeping the work in the family."

Scotty Meldrum fished a Dominion Bank ten-dollar bill out of his money clip. When he put it down beside the first note, the difference was obvious. "I'll be damned!" he said.

"Where do you get the counterfeit notes?" asked the governor.

"We have a few samples from banks, and every day I spend part of the morning going through the bank deposits of different businesses."

"They don't mind showing you their money?"

"Oh, no. If they turn a counterfeit note with their bank deposit, it's seized without being credited to their account. To build our collection, we exchange any counterfeit notes we find with authentic notes. Businesses are quite happy with the service."

"And what do you do with this information?" asked the governor.

"We mail out a securities information update every Friday on counterfeiting activities, robberies, and fraud. Frances! We have to send that out this afternoon before we close down!"

There was a long pause.

"Will any of you have trouble finding employment?" finally asked the governor.

"No," replied Frances. "The United States Federal Reserve has already offered Mr. Mueller a position in Washington, with a substantial raise."

"They know about Mr. Mueller?"

"Yes. Mr. Mueller has assisted them with some translation problems. They have four people doing the work he does."

"Four?"

"Yes. He translates both ways in four languages, and can cross-translate easily between any of those languages. The Americans have single-language experts only."

Monsieur Soulière snorted. "*Il parle quatre langages, mais il ne parle pas français dans un pays bilingue!*"

"Mr. Mueller is fluent in French, as well as German and Spanish and English," replied Frances.

Monsieur Soulière exhaled sharply in disbelief. "*Puis-je recontrer ce linguiste?*"

Frances walked down to his door. "Mr. Mueller, can you spare a moment, please?" He looked up at her. "Don't worry. This is our last day here. I will be with you all the time."

Frances performed the introductions. Only the governor offered a hand. The other two men eyed him suspiciously. Monsieur Soulière began. "*Quelles langues parlez-vous*, Monsieur Mueller?" he demanded.

Mr. Mueller looked at Monsieur Soulière's left ear. "*Je parle, lis, et écris l'allemand, l'español, et le français,* as well as English, of course. *Je lis un peu le russe et je parle un peu d'italien, aussi.*"

Monsieur Soulière was taken completely aback. "*Votre accent n'est pas canadien?*"

"*Non, monsieur. Je suis né en France, et j'ai habité divers pays, principalement l'Espagne. Mon père était dans le commerce des importations. J'habite au Canada depuis seulement quatre ans.*"

"And how are you with the French-Canadian idiom?"

"I'm learning, sir. *Il pleut a boire debout, ben oui.*"

Monsieur Soulière laughed.

Sir Nigel broke in. "That tie, sir. Did you pick it up in some second-hand shop?"

"Oh no, sir. It was a required part of my uniform. It's a school tie from Verties House at Charterhouse Public School in England."

"I know that! I have the same tie!" stated the deputy governor. "When were you there?"

"During the war, sir. I studied Moderns."

"Moderns? So did I. Who was your master?"

"Mr. Berkley for French and Spanish. Mr. Hartman taught German. Mr. Hines was my English master."

"Bloody Bunny Berkley? Is he still there? Must be as old as Methuselah," commented Sir Nigel. He worked his jaw hard in a reflective grimace, then asked, "How did you do, Mueller?"

"Firsts in Spanish and French, sir." Sir Nigel's mouth gaped. "Perhaps the competition was weaker with so many going off to war." Another pause. "And my mother insisted that I write to her once a week in each language."

"Oh, well, then!" exclaimed Sir Nigel, as if this were some form of cheating.

The governor looked at his wristwatch. "Gentlemen, we should go, or we'll be late for our afternoon meetings. Once again, thank you all."

Sir Nigel, once the proponent of a quick departure, spoke up. "Governor, could we have a word in private before we leave?"

"I think that would be most judicious," added Monsieur Soulière.

The five men filed into the conference room and closed the door. "Well, I'm proud of you both!" said Frances. "You presented very well. Now, let's grab a bit of lunch before our busy afternoon. Get your coats. I just have to powder my face."

Mr. Mueller and Mary were waiting in the hall for Frances when Mr. Meldrum rushed out of the conference room. "Where are O'Brien and Mueller?" he demanded.

Frances pointed. "We're heading out to lunch."

Mr. Meldrum went out into the hall and closed the office door, leaving Frances alone. She wandered back down the length of the outer office, taking a last long look at Mrs. Birchall's vibrant paintings of autumn landscapes. The hall door opened, and Mr. Meldrum threw Frances a grin and a wink. "Don't leave, lass!" he admonished as he re-entered the conference room.

Mary and Mr. Mueller slipped back in and scurried over to her. Mary whispered, "Mr. Meldrum offered us both jobs with the Bank of Canada! Said they were all fighting to get us! Sir Nigel wants both of us. Monsieur Soulière wants Mr. Mueller, and Mr. Meldrum wants me!"

Frances broke into a smile. "Wonderful!"

Mr. Mueller spoke softly. "We told him that we couldn't accept, of course."

"What?" exclaimed Frances. "Why not?"

Mr. Mueller became close to indignant. "They did not offer a position to you, Miss McFadden! We could not think of continuing without you. The Three Musketeers, Miss McFadden!"

"No, no!" replied Frances in horror. "You *must* take the jobs. Make sure our work isn't lost."

"Frances, we couldn't stay without you," said Mary.

"You *must* stay! You're missing the point! This is a great opportunity to . . ."

Mr. Mueller, jaw thrust out, interrupted, for likely the first time in his life. "Miss McFadden! We grew in the shelter of your encouragement. If those men—" he jerked his thumb toward the conference room, "—are so . . . so . . . stupid as not to see your role here, then I wash my hands of them."

"Me, too," said Mary. "Besides, it wouldn't be any fun."

Dr. Grace opened the door to the conference room, and the governor followed him out. The governor smiled and said, "Please don't leave." He and Dr. Grace went through the archway. Dr. Grace was back in seconds.

"Frances, have you got the account book of the office expenses?"

She drew out the ledger, and handed it to him.

"Did you do up that budget to see if we had enough money to get us to May?"

Frances handed a file over. He looked at it briefly, then smiled. "Come with me," he said. They both walked back to the little kitchen area, where the governor had just lit a cigarette.

"Miss McFadden," he said, "I apologize for the turmoil. Dr. Grace has just suggested a way to save the day.

"I am speechless with admiration for your work here. You would all be definite assets to the Bank of Canada. Here is my problem. We are operating on interim financing until the start of the new fiscal year next March. We are on a very tight budget. I did not anticipate that Sir Nigel would bring three staff with him from England. They incurred travel expenses as well, which I honestly don't know how I can cover. I'd love to have you and Miss O'Brien and Mr. Mueller on board, but I literally don't have a nickel extra until next April first.

"Dr. Grace has suggested that the budget of the CFRA might be called upon. Could you briefly explain your financial situation here?"

"Certainly, sir. Dr. Grace no doubt has told you that we have a budget of ten thousand dollars to last us to the end of May. He asked me to project salaries, rent, equipment, et cetera, until then."

"And you have complete discretionary control over how this money is spent?" inquired the governor.

"We do," said Dr. Grace.

"Dr. Grace cautioned me to keep a 10-percent contingency in reserve, which I thought was too little, so I have a 20-percent contingency, or two thousand, and we can still meet all foreseeable commitments."

"Wonderful!" exclaimed the governor. "What if you became employees of the Bank of Canada on April first, and all your expenses were then covered out of the Bank budget? How much would you have left over?"

Frances did some quick calculations. "About another five hundred dollars."

The governor smiled. "This just may work. If I can get that twenty-five hundred from you to cover my cost overruns between now and April first, I will hire you three then, and assume all your operating expenses."

"Sounds wonderful," said Dr. Grace, smiling. "What do you think, Frances?"

Frances was silent for a moment. "Governor Towers, surely I don't need to point out that with Dr. Grace's sign-off, you can just take the money and are not beholden to the CFRA staff for anything."

"Well, I won't sign it off," stated Dr. Grace.

"And I don't just want the money. I want you and Miss O'Brien and Mr. Mueller, but I can't afford you yet."

Frances gave a rueful little laugh. "Governor Towers, we've been battered about quite a bit this week. Dismissed by Mr. Meldrum, then thrown a lifeline. Dismissed by you and told to spike the cannons. We've been on a roller coaster. I really don't want to expose my staff to one more dashed hope."

The governor blinked rapidly for a few moments. "Miss McFadden, am I mistaken, or do you all wish to work for the Bank of Canada?"

"We do."

"And I'm offering to hire you as soon as I can pay you. Isn't that clear?"

"Governor Towers, what would be perfectly clear would be if you hired us today."

"But I don't have the money."

"If I'm going to give you twenty-five hundred dollars in April, I could give you enough to pay us from today until then. But I want signed contracts hiring the three of us as Bank of Canada employees starting today."

Dr. Grace winced, but Graham Towers took only a few seconds to consider.

"You're quite the negotiator, Miss McFadden," he said with a smile. "You get job security. I get bridging money to float me through to the new fiscal year."

"The old double coincidence of wants!" added Dr. Grace.

"Deal?" asked Frances.

"Deal," said the governor, reaching for her hand.

---- 30 ----

OUTSIDER

"To new beginnings," said Dr. Grace, raising a champagne flute to toast Frances across the linen tablecloth at the Château Laurier on the last Friday in December. They clinked glasses. The bubbles went up Frances's nose, and she laughed.

"Changes galore," continued Dr. Grace. "You start paying into a government pension plan, and we stop having weekly lunches in the Canadian Grill. I hope you'll keep in touch."

"Stop! You can't abandon me!" exclaimed Frances.

"Well, Scotty Meldrum starts co-signing the CFRA cheques on January first, and I think he'd look askance at this expensive little tradition. So 'Our revels are now ended.'"

Frances felt a sudden void. "But I still need you! Can't we . . ."

"Still be friends? Isn't that what they say in the movies at the end of a relationship?" He poured them both more champagne. "It's been a real roller coaster, and you've hung on for the ride. Now you're midwife at the birth of the Bank of Canada! How exciting for someone your age." He paused. "What is your age, by the way, now that it doesn't matter?"

"Now that it doesn't matter," Frances countered, "it doesn't matter, does it?"

"Touché," he grinned. "St. Frances, the patron saint of secrecy."

"You have been a wonderful mentor. Can't I still count on you for pearls of wisdom?"

"Certainly. You were top dog at the CFRA. You're going to be further down the food chain at the Bank. There'll be adjustments. Call if you need pearls."

Frustration overcame pride by the end of January. Mary was in tears daily, and Mr. Mueller was ready to resign. It was desperately close to a "Culloden File" emergency.

"Meet at the lunch counter in Woolworth's?" Dr. Grace repeated into the phone. "Has the Château Laurier burnt down? Does Woolworth's sommelier now have the best vintages in town?"

"I can't keep meeting you at the Château Laurier, for goodness sakes! What if somebody from the Bank saw us?"

"They'd think that we had discriminating taste and refined palates. How's the duck à l'orange at Woolworth's?"

"They do a very nice grilled cheese."

It was noisy at the crowded Woolworth's lunch counter when Dr. Grace slipped into the vacant seat beside Frances. "What's the problem?" he asked, after ordering a chicken salad sandwich.

"For starters, nobody at the Victoria Building seems to know what they're doing, or, more to the point, what to do with us," began Frances.

"Does Mrs. Birchall's art show to advantage in your new office?"

"We haven't even moved yet! Mr. Meldrum's secretary, Mrs. Hewitt, phoned up the first week of January and told me to prepare to move over immediately. I called a mover. He asked for a definite date and an exact location in the Victoria Building. I relayed these questions to Mrs. Hewitt. She said she'd get back to me. She did not.

"I sent a message over to the governor's secretary, a Miss Briscoe, giving some background on the Momsie Tuesday Tea meetings and suggesting that she should now attend to represent the Bank. No response.

"Suddenly, it was the middle of the month and I needed to have pay cheques co-signed for my crew and Sir Nigel's personal staff. I sent a memo over to Mr. Meldrum. Nothing."

"Finally, I marched up to the Victoria Building to see if I could find anyone alive. The Bank has rented the complete third and fourth floors. The third floor was a hive of carpenters and electricians running around, but no bankers. I went up to the fourth floor, but was stopped dead by a giant in formal dress. He could have been the headwaiter in heaven."

"Horatio Nelson Brooks," confirmed Dr. Grace. "He started as a boot boy in Buckingham Palace and worked his way up to being R.B. Bennett's butler before joining the Bank as Guardian of the Gate."

"He's very good at it," replied Frances. "'Your appointment, ma'am?' he asks, in this British accent. 'I don't have an appointment,' I begin, and he cuts me right off. 'No one is permitted on Bank of Canada premises without an appointment,' he says as he helpfully presses the elevator button to return me to the ground floor. I explain that I work for the Bank, and I'm looking for Mrs. Hewitt, but he only smiled blandly down at me as though I were a cranky child. I handed him the cheques, and asked him to pass them to Mr. Meldrum.

"Late that afternoon, Mrs. Hewitt called. Plans have changed. We are not to move until they figure out where we belong. Put the movers on hold. Further, she informs me, rather icily, that I should send all future correspondence directly to her, as Mr. Meldrum and Miss Briscoe are too busy to deal with minutiae. Then she grilled me on the memo I sent to Miss Briscoe about the Momsie Meetings. I sensed that Mrs. Hewitt and Miss Briscoe might not be close.

"I explained. I asked if she would like to attend the Tuesday meetings. She agreed, and as it was Tuesday, I met her in the lobby and took her up to the Hill. It seemed to work. I did the minutes as usual. Mrs. Hewitt enjoyed the cookies. She agreed to attend on behalf of the Bank. I bade my goodbyes and gave her all my files. I typed the minutes for the last time. Then this Tuesday, Rose Malone phoned me wondering where Mrs. Hewitt was, and who was to take the minutes.

"I called Mrs. Hewitt every ten minutes for well over an hour until she finally picked up. 'Was that meeting today?' she says absently. 'I couldn't get away.' So I felt caught, letting the Momsies down and throwing away a great channel into the government. I might have been a little brusque, but I asked Mrs. Hewitt if she thought she could get away next Tuesday at four. Then she got huffy and told me that the needs of Mr. Meldrum dictated her agenda, and not any tea party on Parliament Hill. We both hung up before things completely deteriorated."

"Very wise."

"Last week, Miss Briscoe phoned Mary to ask her to bring the counterfeiting file up to the governor's office. Mary leaves it there! Abandons the most important file we have! We have no duplicate. I could have killed her. I'm not allowed to phone Miss Briscoe anymore, but I do send Mary right back up with an emphatic note to Mrs. Hewitt asking for the file's return. No response.

"In the meantime, Mary has been summoned to the Victoria Building at least once a day to run messages or serve sandwiches."

"At least she's getting to know the giant," said Dr. Grace.

"Yesterday, she didn't come back for four hours. She'd been running files up to Finance, and shopping to buy fresh lemon for Sir Nigel's tea. Then she had to wash dishes! She was in tears because her regular work isn't getting done."

"Are they leaving Mr. Mueller alone?" Dr. Grace asked.

"Hah!" spat out Frances. "Monsieur Soulière wants him constantly to translate materials into French for his staff. And Sir Nigel's secretary,

Dodds, calls him virtually every day to rush up and render a document from German or Spanish into English. Dodds stands right at Mr. Mueller's elbow, waiting to race the translation in to his lordship.

"Mr. Mueller does a literal translation first, then, if the cadence isn't right, he polishes it until it sounds like it was written by a native speaker. This all takes time. Mr. Mueller is nervous with Dodds leering over his shoulder and frightened about making errors. On top of that, Sir Nigel is quite free with criticism of ambiguities in translations that were ambiguous in the first place.

"Mr. Mueller crawls back here, in the dead of winter, soaked in perspiration. He dreads going up there, or even getting a phone call. He told me yesterday that he loses so much sleep that he can't properly look after his invalid mother anymore. Like the canary in the coal mine, he could be the first to go down.

"The last straw was this article in yesterday's *Ottawa Journal*." She handed a clipping over to Dr. Grace.

Counterfeiting on the Rise in Canada

An anonymous source at the Bank of Canada confirmed yesterday that Canadian banks are suffering from a rise in the number of counterfeit bills in circulation.

Citizens need not worry, as The Bank of Canada will release new bill issues in March with security features designed specially to thwart further fraud.

"Isn't this a pat on the back?" asked Dr. Grace.

"Not when some anonymous source blabs to the *Journal*. The newspaper isn't on the streets five minutes when the phone starts to ring. Mr. Birchall at the Bank of Montreal is livid. 'I thought this was all confidential!' he complained. Then Superintendent Hollingsworth of the RCMP calls with the same message. All those people who worked quietly to clamp down on counterfeiting think I've double-crossed them.

"We started January full of hope, and now we're bleeding from multiple wounds. Mr. Mueller is on the brink of a nervous breakdown, and Mary goes home for dinner every night in tears. The Momsies, who opened to me so generously, feel insulted by Mrs. Hewitt's cavalier disregard. Frankly, I've had it."

Dr. Grace put a dollar down for the waitress and stood up. "I'm learning to love Woolworth's, but I think we need the Macallan to lift our spirits."

At the CFRA office, he pointed her into the conference room, and arranged the fixin's himself. After they both had a deep drink, he summarized, "You believe that you cannot protect your staff. You think you have let down your key contacts. You feel isolated from the institution that has become your life."

Frances nodded.

Dr. Grace drank deeply, then said, "This all must be very frustrating for you. I can see only two options. Option number one: You can tell them all to go to hell in a handbasket, and quit today. You said that the U.S. Fed would hire Mr. Mueller in a heartbeat, and the Mounties would love to have Mary join their fraud division. How about you? Would one of the Momsies take you on? Or one of the charter banks? Or Mr. Dubrofski? Or Huey Foo?"

For the first time, Frances smiled. "Yeah, I could get fitted up for brass knuckles and be Leather Jacket's assistant." She sighed. "What's option number two?"

"Option number two is tougher. Stay in the game and make it work."

"But I don't have any cards!"

"Ah, but you do," countered Dr. Grace. "You have a terrific work ethic, an excellent network, and a huge reservoir of information. The Bank brass all know that you're good, but they're in a popcorn popper right now trying to get the Bank airborne for their big opening March first."

"So who do I turn to? The governor? Mr. Meldrum?"

"The gatekeeper is Clara Hewitt. Scotty brought her along to a meeting at Finance last week. She looked very nervous. I think she's way out of her depth. She's probably great at being a private secretary, with only one child to coddle, but she hasn't a clue how to command the centre stage she's on now. Scotty must have confidence in her, or he wouldn't have brought her up here from Toronto. Unless," he added, "she has . . . other . . . assets that he values. Do you think?"

"I doubt it," replied Frances. "She does guard him like a jealous lover, but they flirt so shamelessly that there can't be anything behind it, or they'd be more discreet."

"Clara Hewitt holds the key to option two. Governor Towers and Miss Briscoe are building empire, but they don't get their shirt cuffs dirty with the day-to-day stuff. That's Scotty Meldrum's bailiwick. He's so busy that he needs Clara Hewitt to keep the hounds from the door while he works. Mrs. Hewitt is your gateway."

"But how do I get through? She sounds annoyed with me every time we talk."

"Send her a nice note. Acknowledge that she's your new boss."

"Surrender?"

Dr. Grace laughed. "In the army, they'd call it a tactical redeployment. There's no better way to overcome the fear she has of you."

"Fear? Of me?"

"Sure. You have a loyal team working for you. She's frantically trying to look after dozens of new issues all by herself. She's all alone in a strange town until her husband's transfer comes through. You've developed a great support network at the CFRA. She probably doesn't know where to buy a roll of toilet paper.

"Be generous with praise. Outline the dozen ways you can help her out. Elect Clara Hewitt your captain and join her team. Once you're in the Victoria Building, she won't be able to live without you.

"So, Miss McFadden? What'll it be? Option one or option two?"

31

THE VICTORIA BUILDING

February 1, 1935
> *Dear Mrs. Hewitt:*
> *I know you have your hands full helping Mr. Meldrum, but I need your advice. How can Mary and Herbert and I best assist you in serving the needs of the Bank?*
> *You know of Mr. Mueller's translation abilities. Mary and I have experience with typing, filing, minute-taking, and catering. We have a wide network including printers, suppliers, and caterers that we willingly place at your disposal.*
> *I ask one consideration. Recently we have had multiple demands from a variety of Bank departments, and have had difficulty prioritizing them. If all requests had the benefit of your counsel, we could provide continuity and quality service.*
> *Yours respectfully,*
> *Frances McFadden*

On Monday at 5:45 p.m., Frances's phone rang.

"Hello, Frances? It's Clara Hewitt. I'm just cleaning up some things, but I'd like to have a brief chat. Can you come up here at about six-fifteen?"

"Certainly, Mrs. Hewitt."

"That's not too late?"

"No, Mrs. Hewitt. I'm usually here until seven-thirty finishing up."

"Goodness! You're quite the workhorse!"

"Well, I hate to start a new day with a messy desk."

"We're birds of a feather! See you soon!"

Birds of a feather?

Clara Hewitt had a Rubenesque physique that she swathed in loose-fitting floral colours. Even with blonde highlights in her greying hair, she looked tired.

"Ah, Frances! Thank you for your note," she said, in a tone that might have been sincere. "I'm sorry that I haven't been in better touch. We seem to bounce from crisis to crisis, and I've been fighting just to keep afloat."

"We could move right up here tomorrow to help you out, if you like."

There was a pregnant moment of reflection. "The problem is, Frances, they have yet to finalize which department you'll all be in, and where you'll be located."

"But if we report directly to you, shouldn't we be nearby?"

"Well, I certainly think so, but all the offices on this floor have been allocated or else are—" she paused, "—contended for by various interests. You mentioned that you might be able to help with catering. That would be most appreciated. There can be half a dozen meetings a day here. The cafeteria in the basement will send up refreshments, but the service is indifferent. Mary has pitched in several times already."

"Mary and I could coordinate all of the catering for you. Dr. Grace had us test out a range of caterers last year, and we have detailed files. All we'd need is a table with a phone."

When Clara hesitated again, Frances walked back into the big outer office. Over twenty offices surrounded the perimeter of the huge third floor. Some now had names taped to the door. A dozen piles of desks and chairs dotted the landscape. Scattered around the floor were another dozen candlestick telephones sitting on phone books like baby birds reaching up out of their nests. One nest was against the wall by the back stairwell.

"If we set up back there," she pointed, "Mary or I could do the ordering, meet the caterers, and supervise cleanup."

Clara was weakening. "But there is no office for you, and we have no extra furniture."

"We don't need an office. All we need is a card table and a folding chair. I can bring them from home."

"You don't need an office?" Clara stared, as though Frances had said 'I don't need to wear underwear.'

"We need to be near enough to help, but not so close as to get in your way."

"Unfortunately not even this open area has all been assigned to departments yet," she demurred.

"If it's just temporary, we can move again when things sort themselves out. Meanwhile, it seems to be a waste of time for us to run back and forth from Queen Street whenever the coffee's late."

Clara was not accustomed to making decisions on her own. "Well, I could put your suggestion to the secretary to see what he thinks—"

"Of course," endorsed Frances.

Clara walked over to Scotty Meldrum's office door, tapped gently twice, then walked in. She was back out in a minute, smiling. "Mr. Meldrum thinks that arrangement will be fine for the time being," she said. "Oh, and until I get everything here under control, can you continue to do the minutes for those secretaries up on the Hill?"

The next day, Frances arrived at the Victoria Building at seven a.m. She set up the card table and folding chair that she had carted in on the streetcar. She had a clear view across fifty feet of open space to Scotty Meldrum's corner office and Clara Hewitt's office right next door. She checked the phone for a dial tone. A beachhead.

Frances spread the food and drink orders among the best caterers she had on file. Half the meetings were in the executive offices on the fourth floor, so Clara introduced her to Horatio Nelson Brooks, "the Guardian at the Gate." He was a large man with a large appetite. Frances invited him to be chief taster for executive meetings. He graciously accepted.

The third floor began filling up. The islands of furniture unfolded into work areas populated by new employees. Frances asked if she could bring over a filing cabinet to keep her accounts in. In the second week, as if by accident, her desk and typewriter appeared by the back wall.

When Frances was drafting the pay cheques in mid-February, she realized she was running short of money. Sir Nigel had insisted that his secretary, valet, and cook have their salaries bumped up to be commensurate with their service to a Deputy Governor. The catering was superior to the basement cafeteria, but more expensive, and Frances had been absorbing the additional costs from her own accounts. She was asking Clara's advice on the cash crunch when the elevator door opened and Scotty Meldrum stormed toward them. His face was red, and his jaw was set.

"We canna open the Bank of Canada for business on March first," he declared.

Clara's eyes widened. "My goodness! Why ever not? I thought we had everything ready."

"We have everything ready," blustered Scotty. "The goddamn printer doesn't have the money ready. They have used some new-fangled ink that is long-lasting but very slow to dry. The governor has been forced to push back the opening to March eleventh."

Scotty Meldrum stormed up quickly, but the act of speech seemed to relieve the pent-up pressure instantly. "Augh, it may be just as well. Another ten days' preparation just might save us some embarrassment."

"Mr. Meldrum," said Clara, "Miss McFadden fears she won't have enough money to cover salaries and expenses until the new fiscal year."

"Well, I don't have a spare cent," he said. "Can you economize?"

Frances plunged. "We are still leasing office space on Queen Street. If we could save the rent, I could balance the books."

"Fine. Move Miss O'Brien and Mr. Mueller right up here. I see them in the halls all the time anyway. Do it tomorrow, before anybody else notices."

"What about all our furniture?"

"Bring every stick. You can use the filing cabinets as room dividers."

Clara Hewitt looked overwrought. Things were moving too fast for her.

Frances said, "Mr. Meldrum, this would only be feasible if we can count on Mrs. Hewitt's direction, and she is terribly busy."

Mr. Meldrum smiled at Clara Hewitt. "Darlin', these youngsters can take a load off your desk if they're close at hand. And," he said, lowering his voice, "we need to squat on as much territory as possible before Frenchie and his lordship have pissed in all the corners. Excuse my French."

Frances raced back to the Blackburn Building. In light of all the improvements to the CFRA offices, Jake Kinkade felt there would be no difficulty getting new tenants and willingly cancelled their lease. Several frantic calls to movers got her nowhere, so she called Mr. Deavy, and rented the Yeoman's store truck and moving team for the evening. She didn't want to give Scotty Meldrum time to change his mind. They packed all afternoon. Mr. Mueller had to leave at six to tend to his mother, but Mary stayed on. Frances bought dinner for the driver and the two assistants. By seven p.m., the first load was on the truck. It took two trips, but by midnight, the back wall of the third floor was a labyrinth of filing cabinets and CFRA office furniture.

The next morning, Frances was going over the catering requests in Clara's office when Mr. Meldrum interrupted them. "Clara, the Executive are unhappy with the hiring process for their personal support staff.

Department heads don't want to sift through hundreds of applications. Until a personnel department is up and running, they want us to do their hiring legwork." His eyes moved over to Frances. "How did Grace hire your lot?"

"Dr. Grace interviewed me and gave me a shorthand and a précis-writing test."

"And the others?"

"I wrote up ads for the evening papers. We received about twenty applications for each job. I cut the list to six or seven on the strength of their applications. I did a preliminary interview and tested their skills. Dr. Grace interviewed the top two candidates for the final decision."

"Clara, set up a similar format. The Executive needs to hire at least twenty new support staff by the end of March."

Clara Hewitt was doing the math in her head. *Twenty hires, twenty applications each, four hundred files and phone calls and interviews . . .* "As you wish, Mr. Meldrum, but then I can't do your meetings and your minutes, and set up your files or handle your calls and appointments. There isn't time in the day."

Scotty looked back at Frances. "You did a grand job finding Mary and Mueller. Could you help Clara with this?"

"I'm sure the two of us can look after it, sir."

It was almost seven o'clock the next evening, and Frances was still trying to arrange all their furniture to best advantage, but there was too much of it, with the conference room table and chairs, and, of course, the art. Scotty Meldrum's thick Scottish burr startled her. "I didna ken you'd such a load of gear down there, lass." He sat down on the edge of the conference table with a sigh. "A wee dram of that good Macallan wouldn't have survived the trip, by any chance?"

Frances extracted a full bottle and a crystal tumbler from a drawer.

"Ah, lass!" he exclaimed. He untangled a chair that had been stacked on top of the conference table and sat down.

"I have no ice, but there's water in the washroom," Frances offered.

"I never challenged the good Doctor Grace on the topic," admitted Mr. Meldrum, "but single malt whiskey should be taken neat. Without pollutants or distractions." He drained a generous tumbler and poured another.

"Will you not join me, Frances McFadden? A respectable man shouldna drink alone."

Frances pulled out a second tumbler and handed it to him.

"A light hand, sir, if you please. I'm not sure of my limit—without distractions."

He laughed. "Well, here's to your safe landing in the Victoria Building. I've been trying to get you up here for a month, but there's been a civil war over who gets you and your crew, so we were stalemated until your money crisis. If Sir Nigel wanted his staff paid, we had to free up the rent money from your old offices. I don't know how long I can hold onto you all. Could be a week, could be thirty years."

He heard a noise and quickly hid his glass. It was a janitor emptying trash. "Clara Hewitt watches my drinking like a hawk. She's in cahoots with my wife to keep me perpetually sober." He picked up his tumbler again and a thought struck him. "Now, Nurse McFadden, how much medicinal lubricant do you still have in stores?"

Frances opened the filing cabinet and peered in. "We're down to eight bottles."

"That's long rations indeed," he pondered. "Clara would get quite suspicious if I began to prowl around your filing cabinet a lot." He paced a moment then snapped his fingers.

"Where would you be conducting the interviews for the new support staff, pray tell?"

"I was going to ask you about that, sir. Interviewees should have a little privacy, especially if we're giving them test pieces to type or transcribe."

He walked over to a closed office that had "G.D. Sedgley" taped to the door. Mr. Meldrum opened the door and looked inside. He ripped the taped sign off the door. "Now, lass, give me a hand, and we'll move the conference table and chairs in here right now. There should still be room for the Macallan filing cabinet in the corner."

In twenty minutes, they had it all snugged away. "Make a neat little sign that says 'Conference Room B' and tape it to the door. Move your desk over to guard the doorway. I'll tell Clara that you will use the "conference room" for interviews and, otherwise, it can be booked through you. I'll get us both keys. Leave it open and inviting when you're around; lock it up if you're out."

"Won't Mrs. Hewitt notice if you end up spending a lot of time there?" asked Frances.

He smiled like the Cheshire cat. "Coincidentally, the governor just asked me to superintend a new file on a permanent Bank of Canada headquarters. This is very hush-hush until we get board approval and the land purchased. I'll tell Clara that we're keeping those files locked out of sight in the new conference room. It's piddly little details that I don't want her to be bothering about. I may have to spend some time there planning the new building, undisturbed. The governor may join me occasionally. I may need you to take notes and draft contracts from time to time."

"And what about G.D. Sedgley?" asked Frances.

"He's some economist from British Columbia that the governor wants. Just heard today he broke his leg in four places skiing. May be in traction for months. The Bank could be out of this building before he even shows up."

32

SANDY SKELTON

On December 31, 1934, the Bank of Canada staff had numbered ten, including a cook, a valet, an introverted translator, and Frances McFadden. On March 11, 1935, the Bank officially opened for business with 213 employees. New staff arrived daily at the Victoria Building, unpacked their lives, and started work.

In the second week of April, Dr. Grace called Frances up. "Are you free for dinner tonight? There's someone I want you to meet."

"Matchmaking now, are we? Not busy enough in the Department of Finance?"

"No, no. This is not a match in the traditional sense, but you two do have some common interests. Can you meet me in the lobby of the Château Laurier at six-thirty? It'll be a treat."

"After twelve-hour days at the Bank, a treat for me is a hot bath and a good book."

"Still booking overtime?"

"Eight hundred and forty hours since last May."

"Good Lord! So what do they owe you?"

"At time and a half, plus interest on unpaid balances that comes out to seven hundred and seventy-eight dollars and forty cents."

"Almost a year's salary! Have you raised the overtime issue with Scotty Meldrum?"

"I have not. Mr. Meldrum recently issued a memo instructing staff not to work extra hours. It didn't seem like an opportune time to submit an invoice. His memo did not explain how to complete all the work we're supposed to do in eight hours."

"You've earned a free dinner, even if it cuts into your overtime. The Château at six-thirty?"

Frances sighed. "I don't think we should be seen eating together at the Château."

"Don't worry. Our host is not a public person. We'll be taking dinner in the privacy of his hotel suite."

That piqued Frances's curiosity: her strength and her weakness.

The lobby of the Château Laurier Hotel had been repainted a pleasant light cream colour since her last visit in December. Frances exchanged greetings and updates with Marcel, the head bellman, and Gib, the front desk clerk. They both missed the cookies. Dr. Grace arrived right on time.

"A word of caution. Our host is a bit eccentric, and his grasp of the social graces is not perfect. Please reserve judgment until you've had a chance to take his full measure."

The door to suite 814 was opened by a barefoot person of medium height in an expensive blue silk dressing gown and a white terrycloth towel turban. Only a pale, failed attempt at a moustache on the upper lip identified the delicate face as male. A cigarette smouldered like a slow fuse from the end of a long silver holder that he held in dramatic fashion in his left hand.

"Ah, Grace! So good to see you!" The man had an unusual slow speaking cadence. "Ahhhhh, Graaaacccccc! Sooooo gooood to seeeee youuuuu." He extended the long, delicate hand of a piano player to the taller man.

"Sandy! May I introduce Frances McFadden, or would you like to put some clothes on first?"

A radiant smile tilted toward Frances and the pale hand fluttered forward like an errant butterfly. "Miss McFadden! Alexander Spenser Skelton, at your service. Grace has told me so much about you, and I desperately need your help." He fixed her with a dramatic, beseeching stare. "Please excuse my attire. My entire wardrobe is in the hands of the hotel housekeeping department, getting purged of the reek from my transatlantic trek. Now, how about a libation to calm the nerves, and then we can order up dinner through room service. I hate dining rooms. They're so . . . public."

"And," put in Dr. Grace, "there is probably a dress code regarding turbans."

Cigarette holder clenched rakishly in his teeth, Sandy unwound his towel to reveal a dishevelled bouquet of damp blond hair. He shook his head like a dog coming out of water. Then he reached for an unlabelled bottle of reddish amber on the table. Sandy lifted ice from a silver bucket with tongs and filled three tumblers. "I hope you don't disapprove of rye whiskey, Miss McFadden. I know poor Grace is intransigently devoted to Scotch, but I am from Western Canada, a hearty land of endless fields of grain, where my father's daily eye-opener is a raw egg in a tumbler of rye. To the vastness of our Dominion," he said, toasting them both. The rye was sweeter than the malts they usually drank. It lacked the smoky flavour of peat, but was not unpleasant.

"Has Grace informed you that we are now colleagues?"

Frances's eyes shot up. "The ever-mysterious Dr. Grace has told me nothing."

"Yes!" exclaimed the silk dressing gown, which spilled open precariously high up a pale, nearly hairless thigh when the wearer turned to reach for an ashtray. "I was hired by the Bank of Canada this morning. Grace said it was essential that I speak to you at once, in that you virtually run the place."

Frances arched her eyebrows at Dr. Grace. "Dr. Grace is prone to exaggeration. I am so slight in the esteem of the Bank that I have neither an office nor a title."

"Both superficial and superfluous," responded Sandy disdainfully. "Much like clothes. But Sir Nigel has dubbed me 'Director of Research.' To humour him, I shall allow cards to be printed with that designation."

Frances blinked. The incongruity of the three-piece-suited British knight hiring a dressing gown and turban challenged credulity.

"I was surprised myself," Sandy confessed. "For some reason the old bastard has taken a shine to me."

"Where did you meet Sir Nigel?" asked Dr. Grace.

"Let's order dinner up, and I'll give you the sordid details while we wait."

Sandy sat back with a contented sigh. "The baronet rode with the Berkshire Hunt. Rode not very well, mind you, but he mounts a beautiful chestnut mare named Persephone. Two fellows I met at Cambridge, Kingsley and Southcott, are from Berkshire, and, knowing my affection for horseflesh, occasionally invited me to the country for a weekend ride. I was seated next to Sir Nigel at dinner one time and mentioned my admiration for Persephone. He immediately gave me a long dissertation on her bloodlines. 'Sired by Gallant out of Blue Bonnet' sort of thing. Tedious! He eventually got around to asking how I came to be a guest of Lord Kingsley, and found out his cousin Archie was my don at Cambridge. Well, now I was almost family! He gave me his card and insisted that I dine with him the next time I was in London."

Sandy grinned broadly. "My meagre scholarship did not extend to London supper clubs or box seats in the West End, so I graciously accepted. Several times. Sir Nigel is childless, and having no one to pass platitudes on to, he kind of adopted me. He enjoyed indulging his colonial waif at the Derby and Henley and the like. I was happy to give him such pleasure.

"Then, poof, he's off for Canada to take up the deputy governorship. When he discovered there was no research department, he urged me to apply. I had just finished my doctoral thesis in economics, and academic appointments are scarce, so here I am. Met with him this morning. He was embarrassingly keen to get me on board. Promised a generous wage and a free hand. It would have been uncharitable to refuse the poor fellow."

"So it's Dr. Skelton, Director of Research at the fledgling Bank of Canada, all on the strength of a romp over the Berkshire vale," summarized Dr. Grace.

"Exactly! Although I sit a horse pretty well, and think that had some contribution to his esteem."

"Your Rhodes Scholarship didn't count for anything?" asked Dr. Grace.

"Grace, I know nothing of that false god, modesty. I think it's all luck. Good or ill, it's too early to judge."

A knock at the door announced two men in hotel livery who wheeled in a table laden with white linen and silver domes and bottles and baskets and a single rose in a crystal vase. They set the dining room table, uncovered the steaming plates, poured the wine, and discreetly left.

The food lacked none of the flavour or vitality of dining room fare. Sandy Skelton attacked a large steak that was bloody and pink. "Texture at last!" he growled. "Ripping into raw meat gives the jaws a fine workout after they've gone slack from too many British stews.

"I told the old bastard I couldn't start for three weeks. Need to visit the ol' homestead in Alberta, and gallop in the foothills for a few days. In the meantime, I need to set some things in motion. Here, Miss McFadden, is where I need your help."

Frances smiled. "That's exactly the line Dr. Grace taught me to use when I'm about to blindside some hapless victim."

"I'm not one to feint before an attack, so here's the truth. I need support staff, and I'm told that your Miss O'Brien and Mr. Mueller are exactly the right people. I'm wondering if we can come to some sort of arrangement?" he said.

Frances met his gaze. "Dr. Skelton, if you're Sir Nigel's new boy wonder, you can likely poach any Bank employee you wish."

Sandy laughed and looked over at Dr. Grace. "I see what you mean about Miss McFadden! A razor mind and a superb grasp of politics!" He turned back to her. "Such a move would be a huge mistake. Remember, I am the newest hire; you were the first hire, I'm told, after the Big Four were in place. You have seniority."

Frances smiled back. "Dr. Skelton, a clerk, even with seniority, does not trump a director of research."

"Miss McFadden, it would be very foolish for me to try to trump in on you. I am told that both Miss O'Brien and Mr. Mueller are geniuses, but they have sensitive natures, and you run interference for them. I would need your help to continue to protect them. Scotty Meldrum tells me their skills are under-utilized serving tea and delivering messages."

"I have two concerns," said Frances. "First, I would want them to be secure. We have all been in limbo since moving to the Victoria Building. Could you create specific job descriptions that would cement their careers at the Bank?"

"I could. With your help."

"Second, while I agree that their talents haven't lately been put to best use, they have been invaluable to me. Replacements would take time to train and to bring up to speed. I'd need three new people to replace them. I now supervise three areas in the Secretary's department. There is the hiring of new administrative personnel—writing job descriptions, winnowing out the best candidates, administering competency tests, arranging interviews, and all the follow-up."

"So much for Flopsie. How about Mopsie and Cottontail?" asked Sandy.

"Catering is now also a full-time job. We might have a dozen meetings a day that need everything from coffee and juice to full meals. These have to be ordered, rooms booked, debris cleared up, invoices paid, and accounts kept. Several people have very specific food requests that must be tracked and respected."

"Another full-time job," added Dr. Grace.

"There's Mopsie," agreed Sandy. "And—?"

"Filing is a huge job that needs to be done promptly and correctly and cross-referenced if we ever want to retrieve anything. And, this may sound premature, with the Bank just launched, but we really should be starting an archive to track the history of the Bank's development, so in fifty years people can look back and see how we made it work."

"Brilliant idea!" exclaimed Sandy. "The top brass would certainly endorse tracking their place in history for future generations. I'll tell them you need three replacements and I'm sure they'll agree. They're all afraid of you up there."

"Really?"

"Really."

The next morning, Frances invited Mary and Mr. Mueller into Conference Room B and closed the door. "I met yesterday with a gentleman named Dr. Skelton who has just been hired to run the Research Department upstairs. The library is finally finished, and they want to get it functioning. Dr. Skelton wants both of you up on the fourth floor working for him. He has heard excellent reports of your work and says you're exactly what he needs.

"What impressed me about Dr. Skelton was that he took the trouble to ask for my permission to let you go, as if you both belonged to me."

"But we do!" said Mary.

"The Three Musketeers!" said Mr. Mueller.

"Dr. Skelton is ready to offer you both permanent positions with a raise. He wants Mary as Research Librarian, and Mr. Mueller as Head of Translation."

"What about you?" asked Mary. "You can't do everything here without us."

"Dr. Skelton will support three new hires to replace you two. Your skills really have not been fully utilized with catering and running errands. This Dr. Skelton is a little eccentric, but he's quite bright and likes fun."

"When would we start?"

"Dr. Skelton will be out of Ottawa for a few weeks. We have time to tie up loose ends here. He did suggest, Mary, that you drop over to the National Archives to see how they manage resources. Mr. Mueller, I explained the tug of war that has ensued over your translation services. Dr. Skelton has guaranteed that all requests must go through him, and he will only lend you out on terms that fit your workload.

"You'll each get a private office. With personally tailored job descriptions, you're set for life!"

33

CONSOLIDATION

At the freshly minted Bank of Canada, brand-new procedures were improvised as their functions formed. Traditions jelled in a moment. Scotty Meldrum magically melded the new structure into an organic whole. An Accounting Division was created, a Securities Section was instituted, and a Foreign Exchange Division was set up. Dominion banknotes were gradually replaced by new Bank of Canada notes, and the notes of the chartered banks were slowly retired from service.

Through all this, Frances strove to make progress while avoiding the whirlpools. The animosity between Scotty Meldrum and Sir Nigel Holmes simmered openly. The governor's secretary, Miss Briscoe, and Scotty Meldrum's secretary, Clara Hewitt, worked in a frosty détente. They communicated only by memo or intermediary.

As soon as Sandy Skelton's staffing requests were confirmed, Frances arranged for a two-week internship for Mary at the National Archives. She went reluctantly, but learned, and came back keen to recategorize seven thousand coded files for universal access. Mr. Mueller thrived in the solitude of his new private office next to Mary's.

Frances realized that she didn't need another Herbert Mueller or Mary O'Brien. She needed flexibility and initiative to deal with a Bank that seemed to recreate itself each day.

Gladys Gilhooly invited her in to recruit from the senior typing class. Frances liked a witty boy named Brendan Maguire the best. He could type fifty words a minute and take Pitman almost as fast as Frances.

"Brendan?" snorted Gladys. "He behaves in my class, but I've heard some wild stories in the teachers' lounge."

"The staff of the Bank of Canada is quite short on hell-raisers, so he may be just the spice we need," Frances replied.

"Cricket Crabtree didn't apply?" asked Gladys.

"Who's she?"

"She's a stick of a thing but she's the best typist I've ever seen."

"Better than me?" teased Frances.

"Better than *me*," replied Gladys. "She showed up out of the blue in November and was two months behind in everything. By Christmas she'd caught up to everyone, and she hasn't done a typing test since January that wasn't perfect. One hundred and eighteen words a minute. Error-free."

How about her steno skills?"

"Maude Faucet says Cricket can do two hundred and forty words of Pitman a minute, twice the class average. Neither Maude nor I have ever awarded perfect marks before, but it would be hard to justify giving Cricket Crabtree anything less than one hundred percent."

"So why isn't she interested in a job with the Bank of Canada?"

"I don't know. Why don't you talk to her yourself?"

Cricket Crabtree was Frances's height, but couldn't have weighed ninety pounds. She wore her brown hair in a pageboy style that looked home-cut. Her waifish face was thin and lightly freckled.

"Hi, Cricket. I'm Frances McFadden. Remember me from last week?"

The pale chin nodded.

"Miss Gilhooly says you're the best typist she's ever taught. Is there some reason you didn't apply to the Bank?"

"Miss. I need to . . . I can't work regular hours because I often have to look after my sister. And practise."

"Practise typing?"

"No, I practise piano. At least four hours a day."

"Ah," exclaimed Frances. "That would explain why you're so quick on the keyboard. Do you want to be a professional pianist?"

Cricket Crabtree looked down. "No, Miss. My father was a concert pianist, but he got arthritis in his hands. He can't play at all anymore, but loves piano music."

"What sort of flexibility do you need?"

"My father works shifts as a warehouse watchman. My mother . . . my mother passed away. My sister's only seven. She's too small to get her own meals or be home alone."

"What if I offered you flexible hours at the Bank of Canada? Would you consider working for us?"

Cricket Crabtree shrugged. "I'd have to talk to Dad."

"Here's my offer. I need you forty-four hours a week, anytime between six a.m. and nine p.m., Monday to Friday. Finish at one p.m. on

Saturday. No Sunday work. Your starting wage will be sixteen dollars a week. Every Saturday, I'll want to know what hours you can work the following week."

"What if there's an emergency with my sister?"

"The Bank of Canada is never more important than your sister."

Two down. Stella Stanton had mentioned that her younger sister, Bridget, was completing her final year at the Convent of Our Lady of the Sacred Heart on Rideau Street.

"Well, I'll tell ya the truth, Frances," said Stella, over a hotdog at the Honey Dew. "I love the kid, but she's a bit of a smarty-pants, and the nuns are barely passing her. They aren't known for their sense of humour. She is one tough nut, though. Living with our old man, you're either tough or you're Pablum. Gotta give him credit for that, at least."

"How's her typing and shorthand?"

"Good. And she's a whiz at guessing things! I'd say 'Hey, Brid, what time's it?' and she looks at the sun, or just the sky, if there's no sun, and says 'two-forty-five,' and twenty seconds later we hear the Peace Tower bell toll off a quarter to three. She's got the intuition, ya know, like an Injun, but those things don't count for much with the nuns."

Bridget came to the Victoria Building the next afternoon for an interview, self-conscious in her school uniform. She was cuter than her older sister, but her eyes had the wistful uncertainty of a motherless fawn. Frances sent her into the conference room for the typing test, followed by her standard dictation. Bridget did well.

"What do you like to laugh at?" asked Frances.

"Mostly at people that take themselves too seriously. And Charlie Chaplin, of course," she said with a grin.

"Can you come in Saturday morning? I've got a couple of people I'd like you to meet."

"Am I hired?"

"Not yet, but I'm impressed."

Bridget Stanton, Brendan Maguire, and Cricket Crabtree were all there before nine o'clock Saturday. Frances said, "I want you to do a group exercise. The people I hire have to work well together in a tight team with me. We have to be flexible and resourceful and deal with emergencies. Pitch in and help each other without being asked. So, I'm going to give you six Labours of Hercules to do by noon."

"Didn't Hercules have twelve labours?" asked Brendan.

"Correct, Brendan, but because you have yet to sin against the gods, I'm only going to give you six. Good luck!" Frances handed them each a sheet of paper.

The Six Labours of Hercules

Slip past the giant and find the library.

Break the filing system code (hint: it's not alphabetical).

Find the files on Sir Nigel Holmes, Scotty Meldrum, and Graham Towers.

Summarize each file in one hundred words.

Find three ways the Bank of England differs from the Bank of Canada.

Write one hundred words on why the Bank should hire you. Edit each other's work.

At 11:23, they were giggling as they sauntered back to Frances's desk. "All done," said Brendan, handing her a sheaf of papers. "What's next?"

By late November, Bank of Canada staff had grown to 312 souls. The Executive was considering a staff celebration of their first calendar year. As the lynchpin in the Bank's catering, Frances's expertise was called on.

"What if we did something informal, like a big cocktail party?" suggested Governor Towers. "On a budget of, say, a thousand dollars."

"If you don't need tables and chairs for a sit-down affair, we could have it right here on the fourth floor," suggested Frances.

"Wouldn't the staff prefer a change of venue?" asked Monsieur Soulière.

"Most of the staff never get past Mr. Brooks. This would be a real treat," replied Frances.

"But there isn't room for three hundred," exclaimed Monsieur Soulière.

"Well, if I understand what the governor means by informal—people walking around with a cup of tea and a sandwich—you don't need that much room. And a crowded space always makes an event seem more festive."

"Surely to God we can offer more than tea," interjected Scotty.

Frances continued. "If we used our own office space, the full budget could go to refreshments."

"I like the sound of it," said the governor, "but when would we have it?"

Frances looked at her calendar. "December twentieth is the last Friday before Christmas. If the Bank had an early closing, say about three, we could hold it then."

"Good idea," said the governor. "Everyone here works all sorts of overtime without any reward. They've earned a few hours' reprieve. In fact, I think we should close the office that Saturday as well. Give people a little extra time to prepare for Christmas."

There was stunned silence around the table. Close early, *and* a half-day off!

"You really think we could get three hundred people up here?" mused the governor, looking around the room.

"Well, sir, this boardroom, without the furniture, would easily hold a hundred. If we made use of the foyer and the hallways and the executive offices, I'm sure we could accommodate the entire staff."

Sir Nigel said, "Who will give the toast to the King?"

Scotty Meldrum and Monsieur Soulière exchanged glances. Their proud ancestors had both been conquered by the British Crown. While neither acknowledged any personal dislike of George V, and had accepted his appearance on Bank of Canada bills, both bore the sceptre's sway without joy. The less the King, any king, cast a shadow over their lives, the better.

"I was hoping we could get by without any ceremony at all," put in the governor. "Perhaps a sentence of congratulations and warm wishes for the festive season."

"I cannot imagine," continued Sir Nigel, "a public gathering anywhere in the British Empire where the King's health is not proposed. Mr. Secretary, who in your department administers the loyalty oath to the Crown? That would be the logical person to propose the toast."

"The Bank of Canada requires no oath to the Crown from its employees," Scotty snorted. He had fought valiantly against administering an oath of secrecy to each employee, but had lost that round, as the Finance Department required it. Scotty felt it an indignity to trusted employees. After two double tumblers of the Macallan, he had said to Frances, "Perhaps we should have everyone swear an oath not to piss in their wastepaper baskets."

Sir Nigel continued, "All public servants in the British Empire are de facto in His Majesty's Service, and swear an oath of loyalty on being hired. I cannot believe that you could let this organization function for a year without administering one!"

Scotty Meldrum stared daggers back at him. "I've been busy," he said.

Governor Towers diverted the issue with an even tone. "We've all been busy. It's understandable that some considerations may have slipped beneath our collective notice. I will seek clarification from the Minister of Finance and the prime minister on the custom in Canada regarding oaths of loyalty.

"Now back to the celebration. Miss McFadden, can I prevail upon you to come up with a plan to present to our executive meeting next week?"

"Certainly, sir," replied Frances, looking down at her notes. "The idea is to invite all Bank of Canada staff to a cocktail-type party to take place in the executive offices on Friday, December twentieth, between 3:00 and 5:00 p.m., on a budget not to exceed one thousand dollars?"

Nods all around the table. Frances was safely in the elevator before her knees began to shake. *Oh my Lord, what have I done!* She had provided catering for dozens of meetings and events since she had moved to the Victoria Building, but they had been a working breakfast for ten, a sandwich lunch for fifteen. And now, three hundred and twelve!

She called Dr. Grace as soon as she got back to her desk. He invited her to dinner at the Rideau Club at seven p.m.

"I thought the Rideau Club was a men's club."

"It is, but women guests are allowed on the premises after seven, if they behave. So, no swinging from the chandelier."

Over dinner, she outlined her predicament. He smiled. "Frances, this will be a cinch for you."

"But I have no idea what to order or how much. How do you craft a menu that will appeal to three hundred and twelve? And how much does that size of a crowd eat and drink?"

"Well, I'd craft many menus, and order lots. When food is free, people tend to graze like locusts. Gerard, the maître d' here, deals with these affairs all the time. He'll know all the details."

Gerard did. A month earlier, the Liberal Party had celebrated their election victory with a reception in the Rideau Club for two hundred and fifty. To cater to a variety of tastes, they had set up a series of "provincial" theme tables with delicacies from different parts of the country.

It had been a great success.

At the next executive meeting, Frances presented a typed report with scale diagrams of the layout for the celebration. What to call the event was an early concern. "Party" sounded too un-Bank-like, and "cocktails" sounded racy. It was too early for dinner and too late for lunch. It wasn't really a meal at all. "The Governor's Tea" was agreed upon as nicely understating the festive occasion.

Graham Towers checked on protocol, and found that if speeches were not given at a reception, a toast to the King was not necessary. Instead of a formal group welcome, two reception lines were to be set up in the foyer, and department heads would introduce their staff to either the governor or the deputy governor.

"So, how did it go?" asked Dr. Grace, when they met for their end-of-year lunch at the Château.

Frances beamed. "It was a smash! I asked for two volunteers from each department to act as hostesses—the "carnation girls." They were a great bunch, full of ideas and solutions. We met several times to sort out the logistics.

"We canvassed for menu ideas—'Quality, variety, and not too messy' were the main responses. The Rideau Club had a line on Pacific salmon, which they offered with capers and fennel wisps on toast wedges. Their pastry chef is a master at tiny tart-like cheese and mushroom quiches. The Château provided a pair of shrimp trees: three-foot-high ice cones, wrapped in wire to which hundreds of jumbo shrimp could be hung between parsley sprigs. Six other caterers were asked to provide specialty foods for fifty people at individual stations. They competed to outdo each other.

"Each hostess wore a white blouse and pinned on a red carnation as identification. When the crowd arrived, the carnation girls whirled through the crowd with trays of drinks and food. We turned off all of the overhead lights and used hundreds of candles on every horizontal surface. Some pine boughs and a few red and green streamers made it into a cosy fairyland.

"I'm glad you advised me to over-order. About two hundred and eighty showed up, and they ate enough for four hundred. I had ordered for four hundred and fifty, so afterward we were able to send several cartons along to the Men's Mission and the Salvation Army Hostel."

"Did people stay until midnight?"

"No. By six-thirty, the last stragglers had departed. By seven, the caterers were packed up and gone."

"Have you had a post-mortem?"

"Yes. I held back Brendan and Cricket to circulate and take notes on everything—congestion, traffic flow, bottlenecks, food successes, et cetera. We've got a dozen suggestions on how to improve things next time."

"Next time?"

"Yes! I had a lovely note from Governor Towers congratulating me for an exemplary event. He was kind enough to point out that I had set every single parameter for the Tea, so the party was really my success. He said it was the finest event of the Bank's first year and asked if I'd undertake to make it an annual tradition."

"That sounds like a life sinecure. And to think just months ago you were scrambling to get a toehold in the Victoria Building."

"I'd still rather have my picture on the ten-dollar bill," smiled Frances.

"One step at a time, Miss McFadden," winked Dr. Grace.

34

1936

In the new year, Sir Nigel Holmes pressed for an oath of loyalty to the Sovereign. The duress brought Scotty Meldrum to Conference Room B and the solace of the Macallan.

"This pissant knight will be the death of me," he muttered.

"Does the governor know your feelings?" asked Frances.

"Soulière and I have aired our concerns, but they sound petty and personal. It is customary in the broad dominions on which the sun never sets that civil servants swear such an oath. It has fallen to me to organize a mass oath-swearing to His Majesty, King George V of Great Britain, Ireland, the British Dominions, Defender of the Faith, blah, blah, blah . . . by the end of the week. Such logistics are not in Clara Hewitt's bailiwick. Can you help me, Frances McFadden?"

Bank of Canada employees came in small groups to the boardroom, where names were checked and oaths were sworn. In a memo dated January 17, Scotty reported the task done and finished forever, amen.

On January 20, George V slipped from a coma into death without ever becoming aware of the allegiance of his loyal subjects at the Bank of Canada. Sir Nigel wore a black armband for a week. He attended commemorative services at the British High Commission, the Governor General's residence, and Christ Church Cathedral. In early February, Scotty Meldrum showed Frances the memo from Sir Nigel asking when an oath of loyalty would be sworn to the new King, Edward VIII.

"I canna go through this charade again. I do no' believe in swearing oaths to monarchs across the seas, and I'm damned if I'm going to ask Bank staff to humiliate themselves again."

Scotty Meldrum looked into the depths of his Macallan for a long moment and said, "Just between you, me, and the Macallan, I've been offered the vice-presidency of the Bank of Nova Scotia in Toronto."

Frances was stunned. "But you love it here!"

"I would indeed miss the excellent people who have transformed the Bank from an Act of Parliament into a vibrant entity. But, no baronets. No foolish oaths to distant kings. And a hefty pay hike. Not a bad package." He took a long drink. "I have until next Wednesday to decide."

"What does Mrs. Hewitt think?"

"Oh, I haven't told Clara. She'd be too distraught. She and her husband have just bought a house in Ottawa."

Frances ached. It was after seven when she took the stairs to the fourth floor. The foyer was dark. Light cascaded from Miss Briscoe's open door, but her office was empty. Through the connecting door, Frances could see the governor working at his desk in shirtsleeves. There was no sign of Miss Briscoe. Frances knocked on the doorframe, and the governor looked up.

"Oh, hello, Miss McFadden. Goodness, you're working late! Miss Briscoe just stepped out to fetch us a bite to eat. We have to get the annual report off to the printer first thing tomorrow. She should be back in fifteen minutes."

"I was wondering if I could speak to you, sir. About a confidential matter."

The governor looked at her for a long moment, then stood up and stretched. "Certainly."

Frances went through a panicked fifteen seconds. "Governor Towers, something has been told to me in confidence. I respect confidences, but I also respect the institution of the Bank."

The governor took a cigarette out of a silver box on his desk and lit it. "Well, I must confess that you have raised my curiosity. Do you think that sharing this information would benefit the Bank?"

"Yes, sir."

"But you don't wish to betray a confidence?"

"No, sir."

"A moral dilemma," he said thoughtfully. He walked over and looked out the window at the Parliament Buildings. "Suppose you gave me some general information about a hypothetical situation, without naming any names. Would that work?"

"Maybe."

"I have great respect for people who respect confidences, but I also respect people who can find solutions to difficult problems. Give it a try, but don't cross a line that would trouble your conscience."

"Well, sir, there is a . . . certain party . . . who gives his heart and soul to making this the best central bank on earth. Lately, certain circumstances . . . have frustrated him, as much as he loves working here." She paused. "And now he's had an attractive employment offer elsewhere. He has until the middle of next week to decide."

"Ah, a push and a pull," said the governor, with a faint smile. "Would anything entice this party to stay at the Bank?"

"It's hard to say, sir. This party works mostly for the pleasure of work well done, so I don't think it's a question of a reward. Still . . ."

"Still?"

"Perhaps some recognition of his considerable contributions, and maybe some . . . hope of things to come would hold him. It would have to be indirect, so he didn't suspect."

"That we had spoken?"

"Yes, sir."

On Tuesday, Frances had lunch with Rebecca Hall, the payroll clerk, and Janet Berkman from Public Relations.

"Well, your Mr. Meldrum is certainly the apple of somebody's eye," said Rebecca.

"Oh?"

"I just processed a salary change that went through Executive last night. "He's getting a 50 percent raise retroactive to the first of the year."

"What a coincidence!" put in Miss Berkman. "This morning I was asked to draft up the terms of reference for 'The Duncan Meldrum Awards of Excellence' which will be inaugurated on the Bank's anniversary, March eleventh. Three awards of one hundred dollars each are to be presented annually to deserving staff."

September was unusually cold and wet, but the four girls weren't going to let weather thwart their annual weekend retreat to Kingsmere Lake. The rain kept them indoors around the fire, which added heat to the warmth of the wine from L'Épicier Laframboise. They quickly fell into the game of "Truth or Consequences."

Frances confessed to being clutched and kissed a couple of times by Buddy Drury, the grocery boy, when he was making home deliveries to Rochester Street.

"Buddy Drury sure has a tight little bum," mused Katie Deavy. "Exactly who was the clutcher and who the clutchee?"

Frances made a show of indignation. "Buddy Drury can hardly spell his name. If you think I'd grab his —"

"Frances McFadden!" cut in Dorothy Deavy. "I thought you were a socialist! Where is your compassion for the plight of the masses?"

"I don't think a grocery boy working in his parents' store quite qualifies him as 'a worker of the world.' Even Lenin would draw the line at Buddy Drury."

"But his bum—"

"And he has bad breath—"

"But his bum, but his bum, but his bumbumbum . . ." sang the giggling chorus, which now included even that traitor Mary O'Brien.

Dorothy Deavy was the real surprise. "Well," she said, draining her fourth glass of wine, "a man once asked me to touch his penis, and I did."

"You didn't!" came a chorus of awe.

"Funny, I thought I did. Then I guess I have no truth to share."

"Who was it?"

"Tell us! Tell us!"

"Mr. Pemberton."

"The druggist? From Pemberton's Pharmacy?"

"Where?"

" When?"

"Where was his penis? About where you'd expect it to be. When? Well, he left Ottawa when his wife died last year, so it was before that."

"Not 'where's his penis,' moron. Where did you do it?"

"We didn't 'do it.' He just asked me to touch his penis, and I did. He was very polite about it."

"Polite?" snorted Katie. "Like, he said, 'Kindly pass the cucumber sandwiches. And, oh, could you please touch my penis?' "

"He's so old!" exclaimed Mary.

"In his early thirties," said Dorothy. "Quite youthful, actually. Like a teddy bear with a moustache."

"That's disgusting!" said Frances.

"Have you ever touched a man's penis?" asked Dorothy.

"No!" cried Frances and Mary in chorus.

"Then perhaps you shouldn't comment on things you know not of. Doesn't the Bible say, 'Judge not that ye be not judged'?"

"The Bible!"

"I've read the Bible quite extensively," said Katie Deavy, while applying red polish to the thumbnail of her left hand. "I don't recall that it takes a position on penises."

"If you're going to be all hysterical, maybe we should just forget it," said Dorothy, yawning.

"Please! We'll behave!" said Frances.

"Promise?"

"Promise!" the three echoed.

"Well, you remember that Mrs. Pemberton used to help out in the drugstore until she got the TB? I guess I was seventeen when I started working there Friday nights and Saturdays.

"One night, I was in the back, stocking the dispensary shelves. The aisles were quite narrow, and if Mr. Pemberton needed to get by, we squished against each other. I didn't mind. I liked his aftershave.

"So, he brushes me like he's trying to get by. I squeeze forward, and then he stops and says, 'Dorothy?' just above my ear. I turned around, and his arms sort of fell around me. It was comforting, like a cradle. We stood there holding each other for a bit, then he takes my hand and kisses it, and says, 'Will you touch me?'

"Well, I'm a little confused, because I'm holding him, right? So I say, 'sure.' Then he guides my hand down between his legs. I could have taken my hand away, but I was curious. He began breathing in short gasps, then he suddenly let go and turned away. He told me to go out front and close the cash."

"And that was it?" asked Katie. "Howdja know it was his penis?"

"Well, there's not much else bulging out down there."

"I don't think that counts," added Frances.

"You weren't sure for sure, were you?" queried Mary.

"Well, I was pretty sure. The next Friday, I was sure-for-sure."

"The next Friday!"

"Yeah. Started the same way."

"You didn't push him away."

"No."

"So we're holding each other and he moves my hand down, and I feel him. Then he unbuttons his fly, and puts my hand inside his pants."

"No!"

"Why didn't you run or scream or something?"

"It wasn't scary. It was like being an explorer. He guided my hand with his own."

"What did it feel like?"

"It was sort of like milking a cow."

"Milking a cow!"

"And then what?"

"He started to cry. I guess with his wife so sick, he wasn't getting much attention. Then we heard the bell as the store door opened. "Wash your hands before you go out," he said.

"And the next Friday?" asked Mary.

"There was no next Friday. When he paid me for my hours on Saturday afternoon, he counted out the correct change, then he gave me a smile and an extra fifty-cent piece.

"He might as well have slapped me in the face. I quit the next day. Told his wife that I had to concentrate on my schoolwork."

In early December, Dr. Grace phoned up. "It's your anniversary. We have to celebrate."

"Anniversary?" reflected Frances.

"Yes! Two years to the day since you put the gun to Governor Towers's head and insisted on a permanent contract. Let's celebrate your two years of paying into the Bank of Canada pension plan."

Frances wore the cocktail dress he had bought for her in Toronto. "Just look at you!" he exclaimed. "I'm amazed that those old rags still fit."

" 'Quality lasts.' Remember?"

"So tell me, Frances McFadden, any surprises in two years before the mast?"

"Surprises?" Frances reflected. "Hmm. Remember when you asked me to dress a bit 'older' for the office?"

"Yes. And how offended you were."

"Well, you were right; I was wrong. People began to defer to me, or more accurately, to my wardrobe." She laughed. "That was a surprise! Mary O'Brien told me that my clothes were a regular topic around the water cooler. Clara Hewitt must spend a fortune on her wardrobe, but she always looks garish, like a peacock at a funeral. Miss Briscoe favours black, and looks like a nun most of the time. They're both politely aghast at each other's taste."

"So you're somewhere between the poles?" Dr. Grace asked.

"Well, I dress to help get things done, and this has magically vested me with some kind of authority with the Executive. I'm sure it's because I *look* efficient rather than that I *am* efficient, that I get listened to."

"Or a sad comment on how poorly most people dress for work. Well, that gives you upward leverage. How about down the ladder?"

"Another surprise! The administrative support staff have no union, so we're leaderless. That role rightfully belongs to either Miss Briscoe or Clara Hewitt, our queens, but neither wants the job, so people come to me with their problems."

"Because you dress well?"

"Partly, I suppose. Partly because I know all the department heads, and I can put in 'a quiet word.' Partly because I was the clerk that handled all the interviews for the Executive support staff. They think I hired them personally!

"I would check in on them to see how they were settling in. I try to have lunch with a different bunch every day, or sit down with anyone who is alone in the dining room. Just Christian courtesy, really. But they look at me with these puppy eyes like I've saved them from the *Titanic*. It took me the longest while to figure it out."

"Now you're the power behind the throne."

"Oh, right!" she laughed. "And the 'carnation girls' who help out at the Governor's Christmas Tea are amazingly loyal to me. To me!"

"So, the Executive defer to your judgment and the support staff think you're Florence Nightingale. You've come a long way for a high school dropout."

"The new Bank Headquarters file is another surprise. It's fascinating, but neither Clara nor Miss Briscoe wanted anything to do with it. When Mackenzie King gave the governor the go-ahead back in January, Mr. Meldrum handed the file to me."

"What's so special about it?"

"Well, it's so different! I'm talking to architects and real estate agents and engineers, learning something new every day. And it's such a hopeful thing to be working toward a real home for the Bank. I see the governor and Mr. Meldrum regularly when they come down to check on progress. The governor is like a kid in a candy store over the new headquarters."

"He has no children of his own, so this is his baby," suggested Dr. Grace.

"I guess. He clearly doesn't like operating out of rented space in the Victoria Building. He wants a home where the gold and all the staff can shelter under one roof. In April, we got a deal on the property at 234 Wellington Street. The Bank headquarters will look out on the Ottawa River and the Gatineau Hills. For a hard-nosed banker, scenic views are surprisingly important to Graham Towers."

35

CORNERSTONE

Canadian Banker, March 1937
Bank Chooses Classical Design
A neo-classical style has been chosen for the new Bank of Canada Headquarters. The design expresses a morning-coat respectability, as well as stability and a restrained opulence.

Ottawa Citizen, June 22, 1937
Bank Vault Nearing Completion in Ottawa
The greatest vault in Canada is nearing completion on the site of the new Bank of Canada Building. It will become the home of the country's two hundred million dollars' worth of gold.

The exact nature of the vault's walls and the elaborate system of alarms will be known only to a few bank officials.

Ottawa Journal, July 14, 1937
PM to Lay Cornerstone for Bank of Canada
The cornerstone for the new Bank of Canada head office building will be laid in a formal ceremony on Tuesday, August 10, with Prime Minister Mackenzie King officiating.

At four in the morning of August 10, Frances woke with a splitting headache. Migraines debilitated her half a dozen times a year. Aspirin would numb her body, but did not diminish the throbbing. The only recipe for relief was a cold compress and a dark, quiet room for fourteen hours. However, the thought of taking a day off work never occurred to her. Vera McFadden, who was a nurse, set the household standard for pain endurance. Inconvenient health issues were never to interfere with one's "duty." Through colds and fevers, Frances had not missed a day of school in her life.

Frances retreated to Conference Room B and kept the overhead lights off. A focused awareness of the compelling presence of pain allowed her to work gingerly around it.

Things started to unravel shortly after nine a.m. Fenton's Fine Foods had the contract for the day's pre-ceremony gathering and the board of directors' meeting afterward. However, a cockroach infestation in the restaurant next door had seeped through the old walls of the Fenton kitchen and the city health department had closed both businesses down that morning. Frances consoled a distraught Mr. Fenton, then turned her pounding head toward a solution.

By ten, she had a commitment from Shirley's Bakery for three platters of crustless sandwiches and a dry bar for the two o'clock reception with Mackenzie King. While not completely abstemious, as had been R.B. Bennett, the prime minister was known to frown on conspicuous imbibing. By eleven a.m., she had browbeaten Maisie's Bits and Bites into providing assorted hors d'oeuvres and a wet bar for the board meeting that was tucked in between the cornerstone ceremony and the evening banquet at the Château Laurier.

Miss Briscoe and Clara Hewitt, who did not share well, were at the Château Laurier all day, sharing the logistics of the Bank's celebratory dinner for one hundred and fifty guests. The phone rang constantly with inquiries from rude reporters about dignitaries, building costs, and completion dates. Each shrill peal of the telephone set Frances's head reeling.

It had been a coup to get Prime Minister Mackenzie King to officiate at the laying of the cornerstone. He would be received by the Bank directors in the boardroom at 2:00 p.m. They would all walk the two blocks down Wellington Street for the 3:00 p.m. ceremony.

Horatio Nelson Brooks, dressed like first footman to God, met the elevator and escorted guests into the boardroom to be received by the governor and Sir Nigel. Everyone was caught up in the celebratory mood, and the room filled with convivial banter and cigar smoke. Frances and Mary darted about emptying ashtrays and topping up sandwich platters. Brendan Maguire dispensed coffee, tea, and ginger ale from the dry bar.

"Oh, no! It's starting to rain!" Mary noticed. "They'll all get soaked at the ceremony!"

A quick glance out the window confirmed the worst. Frances grabbed Mary's elbow and hustled her out the service door into the hallway. "Get right down to Murphy–Gamble's and buy fifteen umbrellas."

"Fifteen umbrellas! With what? I don't have more than a dollar in my purse."

"Charge them to your mother's account. We'll pay her back. Grab Bridget on your way through the office. Get back as fast as you can."

It was only a block and a half to Murphy–Gamble's on Sparks Street, and Mary and Bridget were back, soaked and breathless, by 2:45. *You might have used one of the umbrellas, ladies,* thought Frances, while migraine lightning flashed.

As guests headed to the elevator, Mary and Frances doled out the umbrellas. Sir Nigel exited the boardroom last, in animated conversation with Mackenzie King.

"Excuse me, gentlemen," said Frances. "It's raining outside. Would you care for an umbrella?"

Sir Nigel snatched one from Mary without a break in his conversation. Frances handed the last umbrella to the Prime Minister with a polite smile. Mackenzie King stopped and looked at her intently.

"Have we met before, ma'am?" he inquired.

"I don't believe so, sir," replied Frances, through her veil of pain.

The ever-genial governor performed introductions and hands were shaken.

"Frances McFadden," puzzled the prime minister. He squinted his eyes and looked off in the distance for a moment. "Oh, yes!" he said with a smile. "You visit the Deavy cottage on Kingsmere Lake, don't you?"

"Yes, sir. The Deavy sisters are good friends. Do you know them?"

"It's a small lake. I know all the cottages. I watched Mr. Deavy's father build that place many years ago." He looked at Mary O'Brien. "You've been up there, too!"

Mary nodded.

"You have a red bathing suit, don't you?" said the prime minister, wagging his finger at her. Mary turned beet red.

The governor was holding the elevator door open for the prime minister. "Sir, you'll be late for the ceremony," said Frances.

"Do come along, Miss McFadden. Don't you want to hear my speech?"

It was a sore point, but few of the administrative staff had been invited to the ceremony. "I'd love to, sir, but we're out of umbrellas," she said as gaily as possible.

"Well, share mine, then, girl," said McKenzie King, taking her by the elbow and whisking her into the elevator.

A light drizzle was falling as they left the Victoria Building and headed down Wellington. Mackenzie King was filled with lively banter. Frances could tell that Sir Nigel, who limped along behind them thwacking his cane on the sidewalk, wanted very much to be limping alongside the prime minister. The parade of umbrellas mounted the platform, to a steady applause from the damp assembly.

"If you'll excuse me, sir," Frances said, "I'll just get something to wipe off the chairs."

Mackenzie King checkmated Frances. "Let someone else attend to that. I need you to hold the umbrella while I go over my speaking notes." As the Peace Tower clock struck 3:00 p.m., the shower stopped, and the sun came out, creating a rainbow over the Gatineau Hills. Graham Towers stepped to the microphone to introduce the prime minister. The speech was long on metaphor about cornerstones. A silver trowel was handed to Mackenzie King for the official laying of the stone, and photographers closed in.

Frances was gathering up the umbrellas when the prime minister returned.

"Did you like the speech?" he asked her with a boyish grin.

"Oh, yes, sir," replied Frances. "Fiscal responsibility being the cornerstone of nations was right on the mark." It was the only line she could recall in the echoing chamber of her mind.

"Thank you!" he said with genuine pleasure. "My car is here; why don't I give you a ride to the reception?"

Frances's arms were full of dripping umbrellas. None of the administrative staff had been invited to the reception, either, but Frances did not know how to phrase this to the prime minister. "Thank you, Prime Minister, but I have duties back at the Victoria Building for the board of directors' meeting."

"Oh," said Mackenzie King, a little disappointed, but respectful of duty. "Well, at least let me give you a lift back up the street."

"Why, thank you, sir," Frances said, "but couldn't you take Sir Nigel? I can walk."

"Sir Nigel can ride with Dunning," he replied curtly, jerking a thumb at the Finance Minister. Mackenzie King whisked Frances down the platform steps, and a Royal Canadian Mounted Policeman opened the rear door of a black limousine to receive them.

He chatted cheerfully to her on the short trip up Wellington Street. Frances wondered if important men crave neutral audiences where they don't need to watch every word. The Mountie opened the back door for her, and she exited as gracefully as she could with an armload of wet umbrellas. The governor and Sir Nigel caught up to her in the lobby.

"Sorry, sir," she stammered, "I was caught off-guard."

"Miss McFadden," smiled the governor, "when prime ministers crave the company of Bank of Canada employees, it is our duty to comply."

"You didn't tell him anything, did you?" rasped Sir Nigel.

"The prime minister pretty well carried the conversation," replied Frances.

Sir Nigel looked faintly relieved, and the governor smiled his lovely urbane smile. "Wonderful!" he said.

The uneven ascent in the stuffy elevator followed by a bumpy stop added a sudden nausea to Frances's other concerns. She broke for the bathroom down the hall and shouldered the heavy oak door aside just in time to fling the umbrellas on the sink and lunge for the toilet. She had had little to eat all day, a small blessing. As she was mopping up in front of the bathroom mirror, there was a pounding at the door.

"Frances? Are you in there?" came Mary's muffled voice. "Emergency! I need to talk to you!"

Frances, still dazed, picked up the umbrellas and opened the door. She heard herself saying, "What's wrong?" but she could barely focus on Mary's face.

"That voice! That voice!" repeated Mary frantically. "Didn't you recognize that voice?"

What voice? Whose voice? When? Where? Frances could only manage a stunned silence.

"Remember that night when we all went swimming naked at the Deavys' cottage? And the Laframboise boys wanted to take us to a dance and wouldn't leave? And a man in a canoe told them to run along? That was the prime minister! I recognized his voice when we were handing out the umbrellas!"

"Oh," said Frances. "Could be. So?"

"Frances! The Prime Minister of Canada saw us naked!" Mary was torturing a handkerchief in her humiliated hands.

"Mary, this is not an emergency. He saw our heads in the water. Naked, perhaps, but only our heads. It was dark, remember? We could only see a vague silhouette of him. He commented on your red bathing suit, not on any aspect of your anatomy. Here, take these umbrellas, I've got to get to the board meeting."

For the first time, Mary noticed Frances's paleness and wincing eyes. "Frances, you look awful!"

"Just a headache. Can you do something with these umbrellas and cover my desk while I'm in the boardroom? I won't be long. They'll need to leave for the banquet by five-thirty."

"Should I take the umbrellas back to Murphy–Gamble's and ask for a refund?"

"That would be unethical, Mary. We have used them, and they are no longer in new condition. Store them somewhere safe. For a rainy day."

Mary giggled.

There were eleven directors present plus the governor, Sir Nigel, and Scotty Meldrum. The wet bar was set up on a side table under the windows, beside platters of canapés. On the opposite side of the room was a small writing desk, where Miss Briscoe normally sat to take notes. The minutes of the last meeting plus agendas for today lay on the desk. Frances was distributing them when she heard a gruff snort from the wet bar.

"What sort of nonsense is this?" said a bald man with a walrus moustache. "Nothing but sherry and port?"

The governor smiled over toward Frances. "We usually have assorted liquors available for board of directors' meetings. We did order a wet bar, didn't we, Miss McFadden?"

"We did, sir, but we had a change of caterer this morning. Perhaps their interpretation of 'wet bar' is not the same as ours."

There was general consternation. Frances walked over to whisper in Scotty Meldrum's ear. He laughed and whispered back, "Nay, lass, we will not be wasting the Macallan on this scurvy lot. Let them drink sherry."

Frances returned to her seat, and took attendance. Each director had a brass nameplate on a polished wooden block in front of him. Two of the elected directors, whose terms were about to expire, were extracting every ounce of influence they could in their dying days around the table.

The bald man, Hiram Marsden, took the lead in this, assisted by a lean man named Dupuis. "I don't like the design for the new King George VI series of bills," said Marsden. "The colours are washed out."

"Having French and English on the same bill is going to be confusing for the public," put in Dupuis.

The afternoon droned on through a haze of cigar and cigarette smoke that did nothing to alleviate Frances's headache. Rebuttals came from other directors in a patient manner, until the governor would sum up, with a pointed look at Frances. "Although some directors expressed concerns about the design of the George VI notes, in light of expediency, the board held to its design decision of the May meeting."

Dupuis attacked on a new topic. "Why is the Bank Research Department doing consulting work gratis for other government departments? Why the devil don't they hire their own researchers?"

"If it's such good advice, why the hell aren't they paying us for it?" snapped Marsden.

The governor's face darkened. He was staring Marsden down when the door behind his shoulder silently opened, and Mary O'Brien's anxious head peeked in.

No, Mary! Please—not now!

When she located Frances, Mary cautiously closed the door and scurried over to her, bending to speak in her ear.

"Mary! The board can't be disturbed!" Frances whispered vehemently.

Mary whispered back, "It's an emergency, Frances! You must come immediately! I can take the meeting notes."

"*Another* emergency, Mary? Look after it! I can't leave."

"Frances, there are two men outside who need to speak with you."

"Who, for pity's sake? Tell them to wait."

"Frances you *must* come." Mary insisted, tearing up. She took a deep breath. "It's Culloden File, Frances!" she declared.

Frances winced at her through the pain. "Culloden File?"

"It's the police."

PART
THREE

36

MEMORIAL

Ottawa Journal, Wednesday, August 11, 1937

McFadden, Vera Alice *(nee Fields) accidentally on Tuesday, August 10th, 1937, age 47. Predeceased by daughter Alsa Louise, parents Margaret and George Fields and sister Alma of Strathroy, Ontario. Survived by brother Arthur, of Strathroy, and daughter Frances Elizabeth McFadden of Ottawa. Funeral service at Erskine Presbyterian Church on Bronson Avenue at 11:00 a.m. on Friday, August 13.*

The great arches of the Gothic church dwarfed the scattered clusters of mourners. The Casavant organ's lament echoed numbly off the stained-glass windows. It was a meagre observation of even a modest life.

Frances had telegraphed her uncle Arthur in Strathroy, where he tended the family hardware store. "Tended" was Vera's verb. Arthur did not "run" the store the way their father had. George Fields had started out as an itinerant piano salesman travelling the back concessions of Southern Ontario in a one-horse shay, charming newly prosperous farmers into cultural ascendancy through the purchase of a parlour piano. He built that entrepreneurial knack into a thriving hardware business. There was profit enough to send Vera away to London for training as a nurse.

Condolences were wired back from Strathroy. "Circumstances" prevented Arthur and family from making the long journey to Ottawa in time for the funeral. Closeness had never defined the Fields' siblings, although perfunctory Christmas and birthday cards were exchanged. Frances had a vague childhood memory of visiting the family store, George Fields & Son, Hardware. It must have been on a Sunday, because there were no customers. Frances and Alsa raced breathlessly over the oiled hardwood floors between the kegs of nails and bags of seed grain, playing hide-and-seek with no adult admonitions. Her Fields cousins, Keith and Bruce, were lanky older boys detached from the frivolity of girls' games. She remembered only their reddish hair and the calloused hands they tickled her with, and the smell of leather.

The most recent address Frances had for her father was the St. Louis YMCA, where Lionel McFadden had worked after leaving Toronto. His last letter had been a brief note three years earlier when Alsa succumbed to tuberculosis. Lionel did not return for his daughter's funeral. Vera had rationalized that the distance was great and the train expensive. From then on, questions about her father had been brushed obliquely aside. Frances sent a telegram to Lionel McFadden care of the St. Louis YMCA. The next day, the Canadian Pacific Telegraph Company notified her that the message had been undeliverable. No Lionel McFadden resided there, and no forwarding address was known. Frances was first disheartened, and then angry at being left alone to deal with everything.

Half a dozen neighbours came to the funeral. A clutch of Vera's nursing colleagues from the Civic Hospital sat together in a tightly uniformed phalanx. There was a smattering of elderly Erskine Presbyterians who attended all funerals as a matter of course.

Added to this sparse homage for Vera was the surprising support for Frances. The Deavys and the O'Briens were there in Sunday best. The Bank of Canada was represented by Mr. Meldrum and Clara Hewitt. Sandy Skelton, in an ill-fitting sports coat, sat with Dr. Grace, Cricket Crabtree, Brendan Maguire, and Mr. Mueller. Mr. Forestall came from the High School of Commerce. Stella Stanton had abandoned the elevator at the Blackburn Building to be there. Lolly O'Byrne from Imperial Printing had shut down the presses. Raymond, the head bellman, and Marcel, the maître d' from the Château Laurier, attended in hotel livery. Huey Foo and Leather Jacket sat in a rear pew, as inconspicuous as chopsticks at a Victorian tea. All the Momsies were present, dressed to the nines. Betsy Knowles led a contingent of two tables from the Metcalfe Street Bridge Club. Mr. Birchall, from the Bank of Montreal, was accompanied by his artiste wife. Frances's old contact from the counterfeiting days, Detective Hollingsworth of the Mounted Police Fraud Squad, sat with her new acquaintance, Sergeant Robson of the Ottawa Police Traffic Division.

Sergeant Robson, a family man, had been quietly calm and direct when he came to the Bank of Canada to break the news. His companion, a young constable named Scobie, was nervously new to the bereavement aspect of policing. Frances's headache that day had left her disoriented, and she had not the faintest clue as to why the Ottawa Police would want to talk to her.

"Sorry to disturb you at work, Miss McFadden," Sergeant Robson had said after the introductions. He came right to the point. "Your mother is Vera McFadden?" Frances nodded. "She's had an unfortunate accident."

"Oh," replied Frances impatiently, still buffeted by the headache and the uncongenial meeting she had just left. "Is she hurt?"

Sergeant Robson took Frances by the arm and guided her to a pair of chairs against the wall. *Not a good sign.* He sat, and gently drew her down into the other chair.

He took a deep breath. "She's dead," he said simply. "I'm sorry."

Frances was incredulous. "What . . . ?"

"She was hit by a streetcar in front of Union Station about three this afternoon. Killed instantly."

"Killed?" echoed Frances as every other concern dissolved.

"Yes." He consulted a small notebook. "Car number 815, eastbound on the Bronson Line, was pulling in to stop in front of the train station where car number 822 from the Rideau Line was parked discharging passengers. Your mother stepped from the curb behind the parked streetcar. Car 815 failed to brake in time. Your mother was crushed between the streetcars. Constable Scobie, here," he pointed with his notebook at the fidgeting policeman, "was directing traffic at the corner of Rideau and Sussex and raced over. The cars were pushed apart by bystanders. Constable Scobie was unable to find a pulse on your mother and immediately called for an ambulance, which rushed her to the General Hospital. The doctor on duty in the emergency ward," he squinted at his handwriting, "a Dr. Seydegart, pronounced her dead on arrival at 3:22 p.m. I'm sorry."

Frances couldn't believe it. Her mother was such a careful soul. Wasn't the strict adherence to a mannered decorum insurance against the unexpected? "How did you find me?" she asked, as if it mattered.

"No one in the crowd of bystanders recognized your mother. I took the liberty of looking in her purse. There was a torn envelope with the word 'Frances' and a phone number on it. I was told you were in a meeting with the governor of the Bank of Canada and could not be disturbed. I came right over. There was also a lawyer's business card for a Mr. Morningstar in the purse, and I called that number to see if your mother was a client. Mr. Morningstar was out of the city, but his partner, Mr. Mowbray, confirmed that Mr. Morningstar is the executor of your mother's estate."

Frances was completely disoriented, like Alice in Wonderland. She finally murmured, "What now?"

"You'll need to come down to the General Hospital to identify the body," said the sergeant, "and then if you call Mr. Mowbray, he'll have your mother released to the funeral home of your choice. There were no instructions regarding a funeral in your mother's will, so the executor would defer to the wishes of the family."

Vera McFadden was difficult to recognize in the hospital morgue. Her face was not relaxed, but tightly drawn over her shallow cheekbones, as though gravity was already pulling her features down into the earth. Her hair was dishevelled. In the dim light that reflected poorly off the green tiled walls, Frances could barely distinguish her own mother. The dress, a flowered green calico in which Vera took much pride, was much easier to identify. And the purse, of course.

Reverend Grisham conducted a simple yet dignified service. The deep timbre of his voice, which set babies crying at baptisms and seemed sombrely downcast at weddings, was perfect for funeral orations. Afterward, he escorted Frances out of the sanctuary and down the stairs to the church hall. The Erskine Presbyterian Ladies' Auxiliary had laid on a spread of crustless sandwiches, assorted cookies, coffee, tea, and a fruit punch. It was entirely satisfactory. A line formed to approach Frances. She was offered firm handshakes and the occasional hug, as though she had won a prize. Many choked back tears in their messages of solace, although they barely knew Vera McFadden at all. It was entirely mystifying.

Cricket Crabtree and Brendan Maguire were quick to explain that Bridget Stanton had wanted desperately to come, but they were unanimous that Frances would want her desk covered at the Bank, and straws had been drawn. Marcel explained in his charming French accent that all her friends at the Château Laurier wished to be there, but the manager had drawn the line at two representatives. Mr. Forestall had telegraphed Miss Gilhooly in Nova Scotia with the news. The Bank of Canada did not officially have anything called compassionate leave; still, Mr. Meldrum told Frances to take a week off work if she needed it to "wrap things up" and "get her footing."

Sandy Skelton, completely out of his element, fumbled for words. Dr. Grace bit his lip silently and gave her a hug. Huey Foo was perfunctory and businesslike. "Death part of life, Miss Fran. Need help? Please call."

The Momsies had all brought food. "Is your house key still under the back stoop?" asked Rose Malone. "Good. We've got three casseroles and a cold roast of beef and enough baking to last you to Christmas. We'll take it right over."

Betsy Knowles, gracefully attired in a lavender linen dress with black accents, was also a trifle awkward when she extended a black-gloved hand. Frances was now a regular with the Metcalfe Street Bridge Club. "I'm so sorry, my dear," Betsy said. "I wish you all the best through this turmoil, and hope your friends won't be deprived of your companionship for long." *Translation: "A little thing like being orphaned won't keep you from bridge club next week, will it?"*

A bearded man who said he was the vice-president of the Ottawa Electric Railway Company extended his condolences on behalf of their staff. "Our first tragedy in two years," he said. As the reception began to thin out, a very young man in a grey suit entered the church hall, asked a question of one of the ladies of the auxiliary, and followed a hand pointed her way. "You Miz McFadden?"

Frances nodded.

"Sorry about your mother. Name's West. From the *Ottawa Evening Citizen*. Investigating reporter," he added, with a light glow of pride. "I'm trying to clear up some things about your mother's accident. Sorry to disturb you here, but I've called your home a few times without any luck. I'd like to ask you a few questions."

Frances blinked.

A distinguished-looking grey-haired man joined them with a teacup in his hand. "Mr. West, have you no sense of decorum? I don't think the publisher of the *Ottawa Citizen* would like to hear that his employee has been badgering the bereaved before the body is even in the ground."

"Begging your pardon, Mr. Morningstar," said young West, "but the editor of the city desk sent me here to get some facts. A few things don't add up, and we don't want the *Ottawa Journal* to scoop us."

"I think you journalists could find a crisis in a laundry list," said the grey-haired man. "Miss McFadden won't speak to any reporters before she speaks to you. Will that do?"

"I guess," young West said reluctantly.

"Good. Help yourself to a sandwich on your way out."

The older man turned to Frances. "Miss McFadden?" he confirmed, with a slight bow. "I'm Charles Morningstar. Please accept my sympathies. I'm your mother's lawyer and the executor of her will. I should have been in touch earlier, but was in Halifax on business and only just returned to Ottawa this morning.

"The police contacted our office on Tuesday afternoon, and my partner, Ed Mowbray, released the body to Matthews & Sons Funeral Directors as per your wishes. I imagine you are quite overwhelmed, but we really should have a reading of the will as soon as you feel up to it. Here's my card."

Frances had no concept of lawyers or executors or wills. What with all the funeral arrangements, she had not given a single thought to her mother's having a will. Vera had been particularly discreet about money. Frances had no idea about the expenses incurred in running their home. The reality of being a single wage earner hit her suddenly. She had paid a dollar fifty a day to her mother for room and board, and directed the rest of her salary to her business wardrobe. There was fourteen dollars in her bank account to show for three years' work. It suddenly dawned on her that she probably could no longer afford to live in her own home.

The morning after the funeral, Frances phoned the number on Charles Morningstar's card, and the lawyer cleared his daybook at 1:00 p.m. that afternoon for an appointment.

— 37 —

MR. MORNINGSTAR

M r. Morningstar had a kind handshake and did not waste her time. "With no extended family in the vicinity, your mother appointed me executor of her estate, and guardian of her legal issue who are not yet of age. How old are you?"

"Twenty. I'll be twenty-one next January."

"Then you are still a minor under Ontario law. I'll be your legal guardian until your birthday."

"What exactly does that mean?"

"A legal guardian acts kind of like a parent." He reflected. "Miss McFadden, you have carried on your life essentially as a working adult for several years. However, by law, you cannot enter into contracts yet, so I will act on your behalf. Your mother's estate will be held in trust until you reach the age of majority."

"It sounds like a lot of paperwork," said Frances. "Wasn't my father mentioned in Mother's will?"

"No. Your mother directed me to leave her entire estate to you and your sister equally back in 1934 when your father requested the divorce."

Frances was struck dumb. She did not know one person who was divorced. "My father wanted a divorce? Mother never mentioned it."

"Well, I don't think it was an easy time for her. Many people feel shamed by the concept of divorce. View it as a personal failure. The only grounds for divorce in Canada are insanity, cruelty or adultery. Your mother assured me that none of those was applicable to her, and she refused the divorce request."

"Did she say why Father wanted a divorce?"

"She did not. One could speculate, although the courts of law deal with fact, not speculation."

"Well, Mr. Morningstar, this is all quite surprising news to me. I'd welcome your opinion."

"Your father likely wanted to remarry."

"Remarry! *My* father?"

"He had lived in the United States for several years. In the state of Nevada it is possible to get a unilateral divorce—by which I mean one without the participation or consent of a spouse—after a very brief residency. If he did remarry and ever returned here, he could be charged with bigamy, because Canadian law would not recognize a Nevada divorce. However, if he stayed in the United States, it's unlikely anyone would ever know."

Frances was stunned at this representation of her timorous father *romantically involved with another woman? Demanding a divorce?*

"Let's leave it for now," said Mr. Morningstar, returning to his files. "Your mother's will dates from January 15, 1934. You and your sister Alsa are named as equal beneficiaries. I understand from the obituary notice that she passed away?"

"Yes, she died in the Ottawa Sanatorium in March of 1934."

"Your mother's will is straightforward. It directs the executor to pay any debts against the estate and then to divide the balance equally between you and your sister. You are now the sole beneficiary. Could you please get me a copy of your sister's death certificate for my files?" He made further notes before asking, "Would you have any idea what assets your mother owned?"

"No. There's our home on Rochester Street. I know she had an account at the Bank of Nova Scotia."

"Did she have any outstanding debts?"

"I doubt it. She hated debt. She was the only one on our street who didn't run a tab at Drury's Grocery Store."

"Did she own any stocks or bonds?"

"I really don't know, Mr. Morningstar. My mother never discussed money. There was always five dollars in the kitchen cookie jar to pay for grocery deliveries, but that was all I knew of household finances."

"You'll have to go through her papers. I could come over to the house and help you understand what is pertinent, if you like."

Frances gathered up her purse and gloves and rose to go. "Thank you so much, Mr. Morningstar. I'll search the house. It would be wonderful if you could look over the findings."

"Certainly." He paused. "There is one other thing. Has anyone from the Ottawa Electric Railway Company contacted you since your mother's accident?"

"A man at the funeral offered condolences on behalf of the company. I don't remember his name. Why?"

"There will be a police investigation into your mother's death. It is possible that the Ottawa Electric Railway, or the streetcar driver, or both, might be found negligent in her death. You could be in a position to sue them for damages."

Frances was horrified. "For *damages*? Death is a *damage*?"

"Sorry. I know these legal terms can sound quite heartless. But, in law, negligence resulting in injury or death leaves the negligent party, in this case the OERC—who owns the streetcar—and the driver, who actually propelled the car into your mother—excuse my bluntness—liable for damages."

"And someone has placed a value on the loss of a mother?" Frances felt nauseated.

"Miss McFadden, it must sound like the height of disrespect to put a cash equivalence on the death of a human being. However, English common law is built on precedent. Sadly, you are not the first to lose a mother by accidental death. Such cases have been argued before the courts many times. No two cases are exactly alike, but to make the legal system expeditious, precedents are referred to, and values are assigned."

"It seems ghastly to think of profiting from a mother's death," said Frances. "I'm sure the poor driver must feel terrible."

"According to the police report on the accident," said Mr. Morningstar, flipping open a file on his desk, "the driver, a man named John Wyatt, was quite distraught. In testimony taken down by the police, he claimed that he had told his supervisor several times that the brakes on streetcar number 817 were faulty. There were three passengers on the streetcar who gave statements that the driver smelled strongly of alcohol when the accident occurred. Apparently this particular driver has a record of similar infractions. The OERC has suspended him pending an investigation. He will likely be fired."

"Well, an unemployed streetcar driver is not going to have any money even if I did sue him."

"True," replied Mr. Morningstar. "However, the OERC makes a handsome profit every year. It was their streetcar. It was their employee. There is a principle in common law known as vicarious liability. This means that a company has a shared responsibility in ensuring that its employees, in acting as their agents, behave according to law in the safe discharge of their duties."

"Do you think I should sue the streetcar company?"

"That's an option. Suits do take time to work through the court system, and they can be costly. The OERC is a prosperous entity and can afford to hire the best legal counsel available."

Frances thought for a moment. "I don't suppose the publicity around a trial would be very good for the streetcar business."

Mr. Morningstar nodded. "Very insightful, Miss McFadden."

"I still don't see—"

"This is precisely why they might contact you. The success of the Ottawa Electric Railway Company depends on the confidence of the public. If it comes to light that their driver was drunk on duty, and that they fail to keep their cars in good repair, their reputation and ridership could decline precipitously.

"Furthermore, the OERC has a monopoly on operating streetcars in Ottawa, for which they pay the city an annual licensing fee. Monopolies generate suspicion in a free-market economy. In order for city council to justify granting it, the recipient must be held to very high standards of service delivery. Coincidentally, the OERC's licence is up for renewal this year—in November, I believe. They would not want any blemish on their record as they go through the reapplication process. So they might approach you about an out-of-court settlement."

"What's that?"

"It's a resolution arrived at by disputing parties to avoid the need for a trial."

"I don't understand. If I don't sue, why would the streetcar company offer me any money at all?"

"Because they know you *could* sue. You have a strong case. They don't want the publicity. All court cases are public, and the newspapers would follow this very closely. The reading public loves the story of an underdog battling big business."

"But they could hire a big-shot lawyer who could easily win the case."

"The OERC could hire an experienced litigation lawyer. However, such lawyers are expensive to retain, and the bad publicity might cost them lost revenue worth many times what a respectable settlement would have cost them."

"And exactly how much is respectability worth these days?" asked Frances.

"It would be easy to check precedents. I daresay that the OERC has already done this. My guess is that they will be in touch with you shortly to make an offer."

"What should I do?"

"You have three options. You can accept the offer, you can counter the offer, or you can decline the offer and commence an action against them."

"There is a fourth option. I can find the whole thing so distasteful that I shun it completely."

There was a long silence before Mr. Morningstar replied. "Miss Mc-Fadden, I am not your lawyer. I was your mother's lawyer, and am acting on her directions in executing her will. Likely you need a little time to think about any potential dealing with the OERC, and I recommend that you obtain legal counsel to advise you."

"Would you act as my legal counsel, Mr. Morningstar?"

"You could retain me, or you could select from any number of good lawyers listed in the phone book."

"Are you reluctant to take me as a client?"

"What I am reluctant to do, Miss McFadden, is to take advantage of you in the midst of your bereavement. It would be unethical for me to suggest that you engage me, because I would obviously gain financially from the relationship. And, as your legal guardian, I would be hiring myself on your behalf. This borders on a conflict of interest."

Frances processed this slowly, like the riddle it was. "Mr. Morningstar. I have never had to deal with a lawyer in my life until today, but I like the way you do business. You came to my mother's funeral. You explained all these legal details in a way that was easy to understand. You have given me good, solid advice, and have not thrust your services upon me. I would like to engage you to represent me in any dealings with the OERC, if you will have me as a client." She paused. "I don't suppose it's unethical if we both benefit from the relationship?"

Mr. Morningstar came as close to laughing out loud as he had ever done in a professional meeting. "Miss McFadden, you have a wonderful understanding of life for someone so young. As your guardian, might I suggest that my law partner, Roger Mowbray, be engaged to defend your interests with the OERC? He does the litigation work for our law firm, and is quite experienced in personal injury cases."

"That would be fine."

"Good. I'll instruct Mr. Mowbray to check precedents. If the OERC *is* in touch with you, please direct them to our firm. I would be quite surprised if you don't hear from them this week. Lou Quain usually handles their litigation. Nice enough. A little aggressive."

"Do I have to see him at all? This sounds quite confrontational."

"You don't need to get drawn into any discussion. Direct any calls to our office. Mr. Mowbray can meet with Mr. Quain on your behalf. If Mr. Quain does call, he likely will offer a lowball settlement, hoping that you will take it, and his client will not be out of pocket much. We will need your instructions on what we should accept on your behalf, or how hard you would like to bargain. There would be a point where Mr. Quain might withdraw his offer and invite you to sue."

"This Mr. Quain will have instructions from the Ottawa Electric Railway Company on how high to go?"

"He will."

"Mr. Quain will have the same access to legal precedents that you do?"

"He will."

"Then shouldn't you two be in the same ballpark as far as a settlement goes?"

"We should be. However, there likely isn't an exact precedent for an exactly similar situation. Also, a judge might deem that your mother's stepping into the street without noticing the traffic makes her at least partly responsible for her own death, thus reducing the liability of the OERC."

"Mr. Morningstar, I honestly have no desire to sue this company. I use their streetcars all the time. They give great service for a nickel ticket. I feel the whole discussion of benefiting from the death of my mother extremely distasteful. The publicity of a court trial is unappealing."

Mr. Morningstar folded his hands neutrally, but did not speak.

After a thirty-second reflection, Frances added, "Still, I now have responsibilities that I have never faced before. I'm an orphan. It may be too expensive for me to keep living at 180 Rochester Street. I guess I need you and Mr. Mowbray to do your best for me here with a minimum of fuss. Is that direction enough for now?"

"It is."

38

ROCHESTER STREET

The only home Frances had ever known was 180 Rochester Street. Her parents had rented the house just before she was born in 1917. The neighbourhood was a little rough for Vera's taste, but during the war, housing was hard to find for a growing family. When Vera's father died, she inherited enough to purchase the house and patch it up.

Although Frances was not superstitious, the house had all the hallmarks of "unlucky." From here, Lionel McFadden had walked out of her life, Alsa had contracted tuberculosis, and Vera left for her destiny with the streetcar. The rustic charm of the old farmhouse had been overwhelmed by circumstance. The atmosphere was hauntingly empty of comfort, a husk without a kernel.

The night of the tragedy, Frances had accepted Mrs. O'Brien's offer to stay with their family. It was reassuring to have the sounds of the living around her. Pans clanging in the kitchen, Robbie running on the stairs, Mr. O'Brien whistling while he shaved. The banter around the O'Brien dinner table was lively. Halfway through every meal, Mrs. O'Brien would exclaim "Oh! Good night!" and would jump up to retrieve some forgotten tomato aspic or cabbage salad from the icebox. Mary's reticent nature bloomed with the confidence of familiar surroundings. She exchanged teasing jibes with her brother about their father's matchbox collection, or their mother's adoration of Clark Gable.

Frances was grateful. However, sharing a bed with Mary was another matter. She had always had her own bed. She had not even shared a room since Alsa left for the Ottawa Sanatorium four years ago. Mary was an animated sleeper, thrashing arms and legs about like an octopus in heat, yet woke each morning radiant and beautiful. Frances barely slept at all.

Frances had made brief visits to 180 Rochester to pick up clothes or collect the mail, although the vacant house repelled her. She dashed in to her task and dashed out again. On Sunday after church, she phoned the Deavy sisters and invited them to a scavenger hunt.

"This lawyer says that I've got to find all of Mother's pertinent papers. It's kind of spooky in the house all alone. Do you want to help me search the place? We could have supper afterward with all this food the Momsies left for me."

"A treasure hunt and a picnic!" delighted Katie. "No adults! Count us in!" Katie and Dorothy were sitting on the front porch when Mary and Frances arrived. "Some cute guy was just around looking for you," said Katie, eyebrows raised. "Said he was a cub reporter from the *Ottawa Journal*, but he looked hardly old enough to be into long pants. A new romantic interest?"

"He left his card," said Dorothy, "if you're interested. He had a cowlick and dimples. Might be your type."

Frances took the card. It was reassuring to be teased again, her friends no longer intimidated by the sanctity of her bereavement. "You could have used the secret key to let yourself in, ladies."

"That key is about as secret as Christmas," said Dorothy.

Frances opened the door into the stale smell of furniture polish and her mother's lavender perfume. "Okay, sleuths. We're looking for papers, files, letters, anything that looks official. Dorothy, can you check the basement? Mary, take the kitchen, and Katie, you do the dining and living rooms. I'll do Mother's room upstairs. Bring any booty to the dining room table, and we'll sort it out later."

Frances had never opened a drawer in her mother's room without specific direction. "Frances, can you go up and get me the Nivea cream out of the top drawer in my dresser?" The invasion of private space felt strangely illicit. At the back of the underwear drawer was a satchel of coins, mostly old and foreign. In the drawer of her mother's dressing table were three bankbooks. On the top shelf of the bedroom closet was a series of shoe boxes tied up with string. Each had a date on the end: 1927, 1928, 1929, et cetera. On the floor of the closet at the back behind several pairs of old shoes was a locked green metal box. She took several trips down to the dining room table. "Keep your eyes open for keys," she shouted to her friends.

At four p.m., they switched venues and in teams re-sifted each area with new eyes. The linen closet yielded two bankbooks from the Bank of Nova Scotia, and a bottle of brandy. A can of creamed corn stored in the fruit cellar had been emptied from the bottom, cleaned carefully, and stuffed with a wad of one-dollar bills.

At five p.m., the girls gathered for show-and-tell and supper.

They had located a total of six bankbooks with active accounts and surprising balances. *Six bank accounts? For a shift-duty nurse?* When shaken, something inside the locked green box slid around like paper, and something jingled with a metallic rattle. Including a jar of coins from behind the furnace, they had $74 in bills and $29.27 in coins.

"Your lawyer friend should be pleased," said Mary.

The next morning after breakfast, Frances walked around the corner to 180 Rochester and lingered on the porch until Mr. Morningstar arrived sharp at 9:00 a.m.

"Very good work, Miss McFadden," he declared, on surveying the dining room table. "This locked box is a conundrum. Still no sign of the key?"

"We found several keys, but none fit."

"Anything in your mother's handbag?"

Mother's . . . handbag? Frances had hung it on its regular hook on the hallstand when she came home from identifying the body. Hidden in the open, the girls had overlooked it. Frances emptied it out on the dining room table. Two handkerchiefs, bus tickets, another bankbook from the Ontario Savings and Loan, a clasped change purse containing $2.19. There was a Canadian Pacific Railway money order made out to Vera McFadden for forty dollars. It had been wired from Chicago on August 1. *Chicago?* When Frances shook the bag upside down over the table, two small brass keys on a little chain fell out. Mr. Morningstar picked them up and tried one in the lock of the green box. It opened with a click.

Inside was the deed to the house, a copy of Vera's will, and two keys wired together.

"Those are safety deposit box keys," said Mr. Morningstar. "I have to write to every bank where your mother had an account for final statements, so I can ask if she had a safety deposit box as well. Your mother certainly did not put all her eggs in one basket.

"I need to run an ad for three days in the local papers in case there are outstanding debts against your mother's estate. We should be able to clear probate by the middle of September," he said, sliding the pertinent papers and bankbooks into his briefcase. "Has the streetcar company been in touch?"

"No, but neighbours say another reporter was around yesterday." Just then the telephone rang. The caller identified himself as Louis

Quain, counsel for the Ottawa Electric Railway Company, calling to offer his condolences.

"Thank you," said Frances.

"And my client, the OERC, would like to extend their heartfelt sympathy as well."

"Much appreciated."

"The OERC has instructed me to offer you some token of support to help you get through your grieving."

"That's very kind," said Frances. "Why don't I hand you right over to my lawyer, Mr. Morningstar?" She covered the receiver with her hand. "A Mr. Quain wishes to offer me a token on behalf of the OERC."

Mr. Morningstar chuckled silently as he took the receiver.

"Hello, Lou. How's the golf? Yes, I've been down in Halifax for over a week wrapping up that Murchinson bankruptcy. Just got back.

"Very thoughtful of you to call, Lou. I can imagine the OERC doesn't want this accident to blow up in their face. Yes, as a matter of fact, I'm executor of Vera McFadden's estate, and legal guardian of her daughter, so we're here going over the papers now. Frances McFadden has retained our firm to represent her interests. Roger will likely handle the litigation, if it comes to that. He's checking precedents right now." Mr. Morningstar listened and shook his head with a knowing smile to Frances.

"Well, Lou, the city newspapers have had people around looking to talk to Miss McFadden, and they're just spoiling—" He stopped to listen.

"No, she hasn't, yet, but there seems to be considerable interest. 'Orphan Left Destitute'—just the kind of thing the papers love." He listened.

"I *could* advise that, but it is flattering to have the newspapers tripping over each other to get an exclusive. She's just a girl of twenty, quite young and impressionable." Mr. Morningstar was clearly enjoying this little game.

"Lou, if I asked her to forgo the flattering attention of the press, she might well ask for something in return.

"Yes, well, 'reasonable' works both ways, doesn't it? And if this dispute gets fought out in the newspapers, the public forum isn't likely to damage *my* client's reputation much. So she hasn't much to lose, compared to the OERC. Their licence is up for renewal this November, isn't it?" He listened.

"Well, they're not paupers, Lou. I guess the question is, are they *good* businessmen? City council reads the papers, too, and a lot of voters don't like monopolies one bit. The OERC management is going to have to consider whether it's worth putting a five-year licence renewal in jeopardy over some nickel-and-dime litigation."

"Fine. Get your instructions, and I'll get mine. What say we meet later this week? Is Thursday good? Our office at two? If we wrap it up quickly, we might have time for nine holes before we lose the light. See you then."

Mr. Morningstar hung up, and smiled. "I believe Mr. Quain was caught off guard to find that you already had legal counsel in your corner. He claims that the Ottawa Electric Railway Company highly values 'quick and quiet.' Quiet means no statements to the newspapers and quick means a deal inked within two weeks. What do you want?"

"Quiet and quick would suit me fine," replied Frances.

"If the OERC values their reputation and their negotiating position for their licence renewal, they may be much more reasonable in negotiations. They've bullied their way to a couple of favourable settlements recently because they've threatened to take cases all the way to the British Privy Council. That's expensive, and takes years, and frightens most individuals with shallow pockets."

"So how do things look?" asked Frances.

"I think they look good if you're not greedy. What is the minimum you would settle for?"

"I'm not greedy. However, I'm now a single wage earner, and will need cheaper accommodation. After you check precedents just use your best judgment."

"I'll know by Mr. Quain's opening offer how interested the OERC really is in 'quick and quiet.' The streetcar company is much more vulnerable to the court of public opinion than you are. Public sympathy goes with the orphan every time. Oh, do you mind referring all inquiries from the newspapers to me until this is settled?"

"Certainly not," said Frances.

"You have three aces, as I see it. The moral high ground in a public contest, their upcoming licence renewal, and a police report that shows their streetcar had faulty brakes and a driver who had been drinking."

"But they have deep pockets."

"They do. And they want to keep money in those pockets, so the smart bet is they'll wager a little to save a lot. Leave it with me. I'll consult back if they make an offer."

As he rose to leave, Frances said, "How much do you think this house is worth?"

Mr. Morningstar looked around. "You should get it professionally appraised. Unfortunately, many Ottawa homes were sold for taxes after the crash, pulling prices down. I handle a few real estate closings, so I'd guess a three-bedroom brick house on Rochester Street would fetch somewhere in the $4,000 range."

"I doubt my Bank salary will cover the upkeep here," said Frances.

"Without some help from the Ottawa Electric Railway Company?" Mr. Morningstar smiled again. "I'll just draw that to the attention of their legal counsel."

---- 39 ----

OPTIONS

When she returned to work, Frances's young team were awkwardly deferential to her, smiling briefly before quickly looking away. It was unnerving. She called them into Conference Room B and closed the door. "I've had a shock. I've needed a week to put things in order at home, but it's back to business now. I'm so pleased you did so well without me! So good, and so young!"

Toothy grins like Halloween pumpkins.

"You're not exactly Methuselah, Miss," said Bridget.

"It was a real eye-opener to see how much work crosses your desk," said Cricket.

"Yeah," added Brendan. "I guess you're not overpaid after all."

Mr. Morningstar phoned late on Thursday. "I've had quite the interesting afternoon with Mr. Quain."

"Bad news?"

"*Not at all*. Ed Mowbray and I met this morning to go over precedents. The cash settlements ranged from three thousand to fifteen thousand dollars in accidental deaths 'with cause,' as they say. We expected Lou, who would have read through the same cases, to come in with an offer of three thousand five hundred and we would gradually whittle to a middle ground in the eight thousand dollar range."

"And?"

"Well, the OERC obviously values 'quick and quiet' over *all* other considerations. They want a settlement by *this* weekend. They want *no* publicity other than a brief release from their office stating: '*A settlement between the Ottawa Electric Railway Company and the estate of the late Vera McFadden has been reached concerning the unfortunate accident of August 10, 1937. Details are confidential out of respect for the parties involved.*'"

"And the settlement?"

"The OERC will pay the estate of Vera McFadden twelve thousand dollars."

"Wow!" exclaimed Frances. "That sounds pretty good without a fight."

"Ed and I agree."

"Do you think I should accept?"

"Well, if you accept, the settlement is confidential. No bragging."

"No problem."

"And they want a decision by Saturday noon."

"Suits me."

"Then my advice would be to take the twelve thousand and run. Cash in hand is far better than the potential of a multi-year battle."

"Jarndyce versus Jarndyce," said Frances.

"Exactly!"

"Let's take it."

On Friday, Dr. Grace called up with an invitation to dinner at the Rideau Club with Sandy Skelton. It was a pleasant relief from the O'Brien kitchen table.

"Well, can't you just move back to Rochester Street?" asked Sandy, settling into his rye and water.

"I know," confessed Frances. "I harp about too much family at the O'Briens', who are generous, loving souls, and I complain about an echoing emptiness at 180 Rochester Street. However, Mary thrashes around so much, I can barely sleep."

"I can suggest a short-term solution," Sandy said. Remember that charming little suite where we first met at the Château Laurier? That was lent to me by my lawyer uncle Wallace. His firm's senior partners are often up in Ottawa to present cases before the Supreme Court. They keep that suite booked year-round, but they won't likely be using it until the fall assizes in October. Interested?"

"It's way out of my price range," Frances said.

"They didn't charge me a cent. I did pay for meals and tipped the staff out of my own pocket." He smiled. "Not a bad deal for an orphan."

"The perfect solution!" concluded Dr. Grace. "And I know someone who might be interested in buying your home. An Austrian fellow I met at the Sorbonne, Karl Morton, has just arrived in town with his family. He starts teaching physics at the University of Ottawa this fall. They're camping out in rented rooms in Sandy Hill until they find a furnished house. They left Austria very quickly. Would a Jewish professor fit in on Rochester Street?"

"What matters the most on Rochester Street is whether you cheer for the Toronto Maple Leafs or the Montreal Canadiens. Have them come for a look. It's a nice house, really, it just doesn't feel like home anymore."

Gladys Gilhooly had sent a condolence note from the Annapolis Valley inviting Frances to Saturday lunch at Murphy-Gamble's on her return.

"You poor dear girl," she said, giving Frances a big hug. "I'm so sorry I couldn't be here for you."

"Everyone has been very considerate," replied Frances. "My friends, the people at the Bank, my guardian—"

"*Guardian?*" echoed Gladys. "You are now the *ward* of a *guardian?*"

"Yes," Frances smiled. "Doesn't it sound like a Victorian novel? I'm still a minor, and legally need a guardian to act on my behalf. My mother named her lawyer, Mr. Morningstar, as both her executor and 'guardian of legal issue during minority,' as they so quaintly put it. He's most respectful. He explains the Byzantine aspects of the law and goes over my options. Now how about you? You look tanned and vibrant."

"It was just a delight being down east with the boys," Gladys laughed. "The farm prospers, and the bachelor brothers have installed electricity, indoor plumbing, *and* a telephone, and still have money in the bank. Oh!" she said, dropping her voice to draw Frances toward her, "but the big news is at the Balmoral!

"Remember when I moved in three years ago? Long waiting lists, and only Betsy Knowles and Divine intercession shoehorned me in? Well, the Balmoral Arms has fallen victim to the times! There are now several empty apartments with no takers! And Miles, the doorman, who knows *everything*, tells me that several tenants are in arrears with their rent. *Quelle* surprise for 'the carriage trade,' *n'est-ce pas?* Remember Mr. Carlyle, the building manager?"

"The one who feared teachers and bank clerks might steal the brass plates off the light switches?" replied Frances.

Gladys chortled. "Well, I wasn't back an hour when he was around, hat in hand, to ask if I knew any other teachers who might like to rent there. He looked so downcast it was comic! But Frances! I hadn't thought about you! Betsy would love to have another bridge player at close quarters. If Rochester Street has lost its appeal, the Balmoral Arms might be just the ticket!"

"Goodness, Gladys. What an idea! I feel absolutely no attachment to the old house. The emptiness mocks me every time I open the door. A friend of Dr. Grace's is interested in buying the place furnished. Sandy Skelton got me the loan of his uncle's unused suite at the Château Laurier until October. After that, I don't know."

"Why don't I ask Mr. Carlyle to show you what's available? Even if nothing suits you, it would be worth the experience to see him eating humble pie before a bank clerk!"

Mr. Carlyle was hardly recognizable. His face was pasty, and he was at least thirty pounds lighter. His suit collapsed over his body like a blown tent.

"I'm sorry to hear of your mother's passing, Miss McFadden," he said, as he fumbled with a great tangle of keys. "We have a bachelorette, quite similar to Miss Gilhooly's spot, but higher up with a better view." They took the elevator to the third floor. "It rents for sixty-four dollars a month." Mr. Carlyle watched hopefully as she opened closet and cupboard doors.

"Very nice," Frances said with a weak smile. "I know that Gladys is quite happy in a similar space, but it does seem a trifle tight after a three-bedroom house."

"Would you like to have a look at a one-bedroom apartment? We have two empty at the moment at eighty-five dollars a month."

That was exactly how much Frances earned in a month, but she kept mum and took the tour. The one-bedrooms had fake fireplaces beneath plaster mantels in the living rooms. The hardwood floors gleamed. One apartment faced south and caught the light nicely, but neither excited Frances's interest. While they waited for the elevator, Mr. Carlyle seemed so crestfallen that Frances felt sorry for him.

"I appreciate the quality that the Balmoral offers, Mr. Carlyle, but I've come through a lot lately and I don't want to rush into any decisions."

"Well, you've certainly got your feet on the ground, Miss McFadden. I commend you for not doing anything foolish." He snorted derisively. "You want to see what foolish looks like? Let me show you something."

When the elevator arrived he pressed seven and the car took them to the top floor. On Gladys Gilhooly's floor, there were sixteen apartments, but dwelling size grew with elevation. On the top floor, a single large apartment occupied each of the four wings.

"Ever heard of Mitzie Gibson?" Frances shook her head. "She moved in here when the Balmoral first opened. Her mother was from lumber money, and her father was from Park Avenue in New York. The mother died when Mitzie was about fourteen. The father was an alcoholic. She was mostly raised by maiden aunts who had a pretty rough time with her. They didn't want to put her on the street, so to get her out of her grandfather's house, she got a big cheque to set up here. A *big* cheque. Then she turned twenty-one, and came into some real money from her mother's estate.

"The building was still under construction then, and the owners were so happy to have an old Ottawa name in here that they let her get away with murder. She brought this flashy *Eye-talian* interior designer up from New York with all sorts of ideas. Special panelling from England, and inlaid designs in the hardwood floors. Wanted plate glass windows like a department store. *Had* to have a terrace. No Fifth Avenue resident can exist without a terrace. He drove the building contractor nuts.

"Well, they wouldn't let him change the exterior walls. He complained so much they finally let him put in skylights, and allowed a terrace out of sight on the roof space above the apartment. Miss Gibson had to pay for extra steel girders to support the landscaping on the roof. The money flowed like water.

"The place is still filled with Miss Gibson's stuff," he said, fumbling with the lock. "She winters in Florida, so she hasn't been here since New Year's Day. The rent cheques stopped coming in March. In May, the *Ottawa Journal* Social Pages noted that Miss Gibson had married some European count and was touring the continent. I called the family solicitor about the rent and the furniture, and he told me the family had washed their hands of her. When I threatened to auction the furniture to recoup the rent, he told me to go right ahead.

"And you'll have to forgive this Eye-talian's idea about furniture. He convinced Miss Gibson to go whole hog for this new art deco look. Crates of the stuff came over from France."

Mr. Carlyle finally found a key to open 7SW. A large, square skylight bathed the entrance vestibule in warm sunlight. Through an open doorway to the left, Frances could see a spiral staircase. Mr. Carlyle rolled his eyes. "Access to the *terrace*," he said.

An oak-panelled study with built-in bookcases contained an ornate Chinese desk, a backless sofa, and two wing chairs. A gigantic polar bear skin rug covered the floor. The kitchen cupboard doors were leaded with designs in coloured glass. In the master bedroom a four-poster bed faced a marble fireplace across the room. A doorway led into a large ensuite bathroom where an immense tub sat in a bay window. In the right corner was a large shower stall tiled in a brilliant golden dragon mosaic. Sunlight cascaded into the bathroom and a dressing room next door through another skylight.

The living room was as large as Betsy Knowles's. Sliding French doors led into the dining room. A bay window cast sunlight onto a dining room suite accented with wood inlays.

"I asked Tackaberry, the auctioneer, to have a look at the lot, and he says we'll be lucky to get five cents on the dollar for this stuff in Ottawa. Nobody's buying *anything* since the recent downturn. And old Ottawa money, the type that's always flush, likes antiques with a British flavour. Tackaberry doubts we can raise enough to cover the back rent. Add his fee, and the hassle of tying up an elevator for a day moving everything, and it's a nightmare. Can you imagine anything more scatterbrained?" He swatted his hat against his thigh twice for emphasis.

Frances thought it was the most beautiful place she had ever seen in her life.

— 40 —

LONG TERM

In mid-September, Mr. Morningstar invited Frances down to his office. "Your mother's will has cleared probate," he said. "All expenses have been paid, including legal work on the sale of your house and furniture. That was timely!"

Frances nodded. "The Mortons needed a home, and I needed to be free from the memories. In economics, that's called a double coincidence of wants."

"This leaves quite a trust fund for you, young lady," continued Mr. Morningstar. "Including the Ottawa Electric Railway Company settlement, the house sale, your mother's life insurance policy, and her seven bank accounts, it's just shy of thirty-two thousand dollars. Not quite enough to retire on, but a nice nest egg. What would you like done with it?"

"Beats me. What do you suggest?"

"The economy is stumbling again, so the stock market's out. Government bonds are safe and pay a respectable 3 percent. Or there's real estate. You could purchase a small apartment building."

"Who looks after the leaky roofs?"

"You can, or you can hire a manager."

"It sounds like more headaches," concluded Frances, then she laughed. "This living in a hotel is quite nice. Maid service. Room service. Dry cleaning and laundry picked up. A woman could grow accustomed to it."

"Remember, you're *not* paying rent at the Château Laurier. My guess is that suite would cost at least fifteen dollars a day." Mr. Morningstar did some quick calculations. "You could probably live there for about five years if you wanted to run through all your inheritance."

"Would you let me be so foolish?"

"I'd advise against it, but it's your money."

"What if I wanted to give it all to the Salvation Army?"

"Again, I'd advise against it."

"You don't think the Salvation Army is a worthy cause?"

"One of the worthiest, but they aren't my client. *You* are my client."

Late for bridge club the following week, Frances sprinted down Metcalfe Street to mitigate the wrath of Betsy Knowles. When the French maid opened the door to her breathless face, Frances could hear a lively argument coming from the living room.

"I don't believe it," trebled Clarissa Semple.

"It's true, isn't it, Betsy?" responded Gladys Gilhooly.

"We received the notice this morning," confirmed Betsy. "Apparently, the Balmoral owners—the Perleys from Toronto—are experiencing something called 'liquidity issues.' They've offered any tenant a second year's rent free if they can pay one year's rent in advance."

"Two years for the price of one?" asked Marjory Dawes, as Frances walked into the room and took a glass of sherry from the maid.

"Yes!" exclaimed Gladys. "Mr. Carlyle claims the Perleys have mortgaged the place to the hilt. What with arrears and vacant apartments, something they *never* expected, they're on the brink of defaulting on their mortgage. They need thirty-five thousand dollars hard cash by the end of September, or they could lose the Balmoral to creditors."

"Would you all be out on the street then?" blinked Debra Semple.

"Oh no," said Betsy. "The creditors would just take over our leases. Carlyle would certainly lose his job."

"Goodness! This sounds like great luck for you all," chimed Nora Ray.

"Hah!" exclaimed Gladys. "I live hand-to-mouth on my teacher's salary. I could hardly come up with an extra month's rent in cash."

"Well, surely the affluent crowd here will be delighted, won't they?" asked Clarissa.

It was Betsy's turn for a dismissive scoff. "The millionaires live in Rockcliffe, Clarissa, not the Balmoral. I doubt there are five tenants here who could come up with a year's rent in advance." She stubbed out her cigarette. "We're all tied up in long-term investments. Stock portfolios and real estate have lost value since the crash. No one wants to sell at a loss. It isn't just the Perleys who are 'cash poor.'"

"Money is such a sordid topic," said Marjory Dawes. "Can we play bridge?"

Frances did her homework carefully before meeting Mr. Morningstar on the last Monday of September. For an incredulous man, he listened very patiently. "You want me to arrange a long-term lease on apartment seven south-west at the Balmoral Arms? How long?"

"As long as I can afford," answered Frances.

Mr. Morningstar's fountain pen raced. "The rent is one hundred and seventy dollars a month, or two thousand and forty dollars a year?" he asked.

"Correct," said Frances.

"And the management will give you two years for the price of one if you pay up front?"

"Right," continued Frances. "Making the effective monthly rent eighty-five dollars, which is just a little more than Gladys Gilhooly pays for her bachelorette. Apartment seven south-west must be four times as large."

Mr. Morningstar paused. "I mean no disrespect, Miss McFadden, but I pay less rent for my three-bedroom house in Sandy Hill. Does a bank clerk need such a large apartment?"

Frances silently remembered King Lear rashly begging his daughter, "Oh, reason not the need!"

Mr. Morningstar scribbled on. "If you emptied the trust fund, you could afford just over thirty-one years." He laid down his pen. "Do you want to tie yourself to the place until you're fifty-one?"

"The apartment is breathtaking," replied Frances. "I love my life at the Bank, but it leaves me time for few pleasures. I'd just like to retreat to a little comfort after a long day. Is that irresponsible?"

Mr. Morningstar shook his head ruefully. "It is certainly a different investment philosophy from your mother's."

"Yes, but I won't have to worry about the eavestroughing or mowing the lawn."

"What if you were to marry and start a family?"

Good point. Frances's silent lust for Buddy Drury had never aspired to marriage, but both Mary O'Brien and Katie Deavy were beginning to hint at matrimonial interests. "If my circumstances did change, would I be allowed to lease the apartment out?"

"A sublet?" Mr. Morningstar, jotting notes. "We could inquire." He continued, trying not to sound judgmental. "We'd want to check their mortgage to ensure that a long-term lease would be guaranteed against the title."

"Pardon?"

"Well, if the Perleys do go bankrupt, will the new owner guarantee the leases? Mr. Carlyle would know the details, and if they'd be interested in a thirty-one-year lease."

"Can you inquire for me?"

"Certainly."

"How much is left in the trust fund if we pay out thirty-one years' rent?"

More calculating. "Just under three hundred dollars."

Frances smiled. "That's cutting it tight. What if we back off to a round thirty years?"

"That would leave nearly thirteen hundred in the trust account."

"Miss Gibson stopped paying the rent six months ago. They're going to sell the furniture to recoup the lost revenue. Offer Mr. Carlyle thirteen hundred for all of it. That'll cover his loss and save him the trouble of moving it."

"And clean out the trust fund completely," cautioned Mr. Morningstar.

"Well, I had nothing two weeks ago, so what's the difference? This way, I'm housed and worry-free for thirty years. I think it's a good trade."

"Might as well call Carlyle right now," said Mr. Morningstar, "and see if he's interested."

"Mr. Carlyle? It's Charles Morningstar of the law firm Mowbray & Morningstar. I have a client interested in a long-term lease on one of your apartments. Is seven south-west still available? Good. And I understand you're offering a free year's rent for every year's rent paid up front? The current full rent is two thousand and forty dollars annually? My client would like to lease seven south-west for thirty years."

He listened for a minute. "Well, you have a promotion, or you don't, Mr. Carlyle. I'm not asking for any favours. Oh, and I understand that you plan to auction the apartment contents to cover arrears? My client will take the furniture as is in return for paying the six months' back rent. Yes, that's the total I get, thirty-one thousand six hundred and twenty dollars. Interested?"

"I'll need to check your lease to make sure my client's investment is protected. And I'll need a sublet clause. What other inclusions are there? Fine. Why don't I drop by this afternoon about four-ish? If all the legal details check out, we can get a certified cheque to you on signing the lease. We could do it by Thursday, if there are no complications." He looked over to Frances, and she nodded enthusiastically. "Fine, then. See you at four."

When he hung up, Frances said, "I know you're unsure about this, Mr. Morningstar. Why don't you look at the apartment this afternoon while you're there? I've invited two friends to see it, as well."

Doctors Grace and Skelton were as skittish as schoolboys playing hooky as they escorted Frances down Metcalfe Street on a fine fall day.

"It is awfully good of you two," said Frances. "My lawyer thinks that I'm loony."

"You don't want to live at the Château forever?" asked Sandy.

"I'd love to live there forever. I've grown especially fond of the Eggs Benedict from Emile in room service, but I'm not sure the generosity of your uncle's law firm would extend to 'forever.'"

"Why don't you just buy yourself a little cottage?" asked Dr. Grace. "Have some equity?"

"I don't want to worry about the furnace breaking down, or the pipes freezing. Running the Bank of Canada is exhausting enough." She grinned. "My lawyer . . . my guardian, Mr. Morningstar, is very polite, but he thinks this is a crazy thing to do with my inheritance. Maybe he's right. What do I know? I'll probably die at the Bank of Canada beside my typewriter. In the meantime, I just want some calm place to crawl home to."

"And you said this was the deal of a lifetime?" asked Sandy.

"Yes! Two months' rent for the price of one for cash up front. The offer ends Thursday."

"How many months are you interested in?" asked Dr. Grace.

"If I pay for one hundred and eighty months, I'll get the same for free."

Sandy Skelton slapped his forehead. "Three hundred and sixty months! You want this place for thirty years?"

"Well, if it's a good deal for one month, it's a better deal for three hundred and sixty months, wouldn't you say?"

Mr. Carlyle's desk was littered with papers and files. "Oh, hello, Miss McFadden. You'll have to excuse me—I'm very busy this afternoon. I have a potential tenant for the Gibson apartment, and a lawyer is coming down to see that all the paperwork is in order. Can you come back tomorrow?"

"I'd like to have another look at seven south-west, if you don't mind. May I have the key? I can find my way up."

"I'm sorry, Miss McFadden. There's a conditional offer on seven south-west, so I can't let you in."

"That's *my* offer, Mr. Carlyle. For thirty years and for all of the furniture. My lawyer, Mr. Morningstar, is coming down to check the lease. I'd just like to show it to my friends. Oh, this is Dr. Grace from the Department of Finance, and Dr. Skelton, from the Bank of Canada."

Mr. Carlyle slowly sank into his seat. A huge ash from his cigar dropped onto his vest. "Miss McFadden . . . *you* have thirty-one thousand dollars in cash?"

"I believe thirty-one thousand six hundred and twenty was the exact amount. I don't have it with me. Mr. Morningstar looks after that sort of thing. He'll be here shortly. He's not very keen on this lease idea. I'd appreciate your help convincing him. The key?"

Dr. Grace strolled leisurely through the apartment, whistling "Danny Boy." He looked out all the windows as though the view was the apartment's most interesting feature. Sandy Skelton was more tactile. He silently picked up vases and got down on the dining room carpet to finger the weave. He flipped a side chair upside down to look at the bottom. Only when he found the circular staircase did he speak.

"Hello? What's this?"

"The previous tenant had a terrace built up on the roof," answered Frances.

He started up the stairs, followed by Frances and Dr. Grace. At the top was a small greenhouse with a tap in the corner beside a dusty watering can. A covered walkway led to a glass gazebo that housed half a dozen chairs and two couches cloaked in faded dust covers.

Running west from the gazebo was a narrow reflecting pool, between neglected boxwood hedges. At the far end of the pool was a large metal disc containing ashes and a few charred logs. Solid wood cube-stools surrounded the fire pit. In the four corners of the garden were life-sized nubile statues. The golden afternoon sun dazzled in the wind-rippled reflective pool and set the glass gazebo on fire.

They retreated down the spiral staircase to find Mr. Morningstar. Frances made introductions, and they all sat down around the oblong dining room table. Frances ran her finger over the seamless inlay in the tabletop.

"It's walnut with cherry and maple inlay," said Dr. Skelton. "As are the matching side chairs. All by Bouchard et fils of Paris."

Mr. Morningstar removed several files from his battered briefcase. He smiled gamely at Frances. "Quite the place," he said.

"Any problems with Mr. Carlyle?" Frances asked.

"He was a little stupefied about your being the client, but his primary concern was getting the cash by Thursday. I assured him a certified cheque could be provided on signing the lease." Mr. Morningstar checked over a document. "The rent includes heat, hydro, water, and taxes. You also get one underground parking spot and three hours of maid service a week. Sublet privileges have been added, as well as a first refusal on extending the lease when the contract expires in nineteen sixty-seven."

"Hey!" noted Dr. Grace. "Canada will be a hundred years old in nineteen sixty-seven."

"What do you think?" asked Frances.

Mr. Morningstar hesitated. "I think that for what it is — an apartment lease on a first-class residence — it's an excellent deal. Whether it's the best use of your inheritance, I'm not so sure if it's . . . well, prudent." He grimaced at sounding judgmental.

"Legally, is it sound?" asked Dr. Grace.

"Oh, yes. The prepaid lease is like a second mortgage against the building. It's guaranteed, regardless of owner."

"And the furniture?" asked Sandy Skelton.

"Mr. Carlyle was delighted to recoup the missing rent."

"Is the furniture Mr. Carlyle's to sell?" continued Sandy.

"Yes. He showed me his correspondence with Miss Gibson's lawyer. The building owners are within their rights to seize the furniture against the unpaid rent. I have it all in writing." He passed a sheet of paper to Sandy.

"Well, I say snap the place up," said Sandy. "This dining room suite" — his knuckles knocked on the table — "is identical to the one Lord Northcott's wife purchased for their townhouse in Mayfair. For a thousand pounds. That's five thousand Canadian. The kitchen cabinet doors are all signed by Tiffany, and would get you two hundred dollars apiece without the bat of an eye. The wing chairs and sofa in the library are by Sue et Mare and would fetch two thousand dollars at Christie's. That is not to mention this Persian rug or those four nude nymphs on the roof signed by Eric Gill. Miss Gibson's collection would easily bring thirty thousand dollars at auction in London or New York."

"But we're not in London or New York," replied Mr. Morningstar.

"Fortunately," said Sandy, "making it quite the bargain. You could have it all packed, insured and shipped for under $500."

"I like the place," mused Dr. Grace, "although my Spartan tastes run more to YMCA décor."

"They'll still be short of the thirty-five thousand dollars they need for the mortgage," Mr. Morningstar said.

"Not anymore," replied Frances. "I browbeat Gladys Gilhooly into borrowing four thousand from her farmer brothers. She was loath to impose, but I told her she'd be doing them a favour. Their savings are in government bonds at 3 percent. She could offer them 5 percent and still get three years of free accommodation."

Mr. Morningstar surrendered. "Well, Miss McFadden, what are your directions?"

MRS. DELOITTE

Frances looked down from her dining room bay window on a blustery Sunday morning in late November. A milky sun shone intermittently through a scud of clouds. The wind whirled last night's snowfall into drifts. She felt the need for church. The spiritual nature of the sanctuary, the hymns and the sermon always cleansed her. Still, it was two wintry miles to Erskine Presbyterian Church from her new apartment. The phone book revealed Knox Presbyterian on Elgin Street, a few blocks away. She bundled up and headed out.

She had been putting in seventy-hour weeks at the Bank all fall. Tracking the details for the new Bank headquarters had been consuming. Like proud parents, Scotty Meldrum and Graham Towers dropped down to Conference Room B regularly to check on progress and tweak the plans. "Frances, cost out marble floors in the executive washrooms instead of tile." "Frances, what about Cuban mahogany trim in the boardroom?"

The sanctuary at Knox Presbyterian had a craftsman style of clean lines and exposed wooden beams that gave it a cottage-like intimacy. Fifty children and a scattering of adults gathered at the chancel for a blessing before exiting for Sunday school. The teachers were young mothers or spinsters except for a handsome woman in a lavender coat and stylish hat.

The service was the perfect tonic. Frances went home with a lighter step through the drifting snow. She suddenly noticed the lavender coat just ahead of her, turning into the Balmoral Arms. When Frances entered the lobby, Miles was brushing snow off the stranger.

"It's bitter, but it's beautiful, too," smiled the woman.

"Hello, Miss McFadden, can I brush you down?" asked Miles. Frances held her arms wide, like a scarecrow, and was quickly dusted. The elevator arrived, and both women entered.

"Floor?"

"Seven, please," replied Frances.

"Ah! The new tenant in seven south-west!" said the woman with a welcoming smile.

"Yes. I'm Frances McFadden."

"Pleased to meet you at last! I'm Anna Deloitte," she said, grasping Frances's hand warmly. "How have we lived just a floor apart for two months and never crossed paths?"

"Did I see you at church this morning?"

"Yes. I don't remember seeing you at Knox before."

"I belong to Erskine, which used to be my neighbourhood church." Frances shook her head. "I'm afraid my faith wasn't strong enough to get me all the way over there in this weather."

"Taking a shortcut to salvation, are we?" teased Anna. "Exactly my kind of woman. Would some hot coffee interest you?"

"Wonderful!" returned Frances.

Anna Deloitte had a charming two-bedroom place on the sixth floor. The furniture was a comfortable eclectic mixture. The smaller bedroom was set up as an office with a desk and typewriter under the window. "I work from home," Anna explained.

Frances had never met anyone before who worked from home. Over coffee served in delicate blue Dresden cups and some delicious banana loaf, Anna's story came out.

"My parents were medical missionaries serving the Hunan Mission in Western China. Father was a doctor and Mother was a nurse. I was born in the mission hospital and went to the mission school until I turned thirteen."

"Do you speak Chinese?"

"I do. There were French and German students there, too, and we learned each other's language like a game."

"And when you turned thirteen?"

"I was sent abroad to continue my education. The Canadian Missionary Society arranged for me to go to boarding school in Switzerland. They saw me as a missionary-in-training, and wanted me well grounded."

"A career path so young?" asked Frances.

"I had good qualifications. I was fluent in Mandarin and had endured the hardships of the west China plain for a dozen years. My parents had imbued me with a sense of social responsibility and Christian ethics." Anna Deloitte had a self-deprecating smile. "But I lacked the temperament."

"It must have been hard to leave China."

"Terribly. I missed my friends and parents. And the servants. Even missionaries could afford a cook, a maid, my ayi, and a gardener. It was like having six guardian angels."

"Why Switzerland?"

"Canada was essentially a foreign country for me. Mother and Father received home leave every five years, so I had been back only twice. These trips were hardly a holiday for my parents. They spent all their time fundraising for the missionary society. Both were shy. They would have preferred seeing a hundred patients a day in their dirt-floored hospital to the round of teas and guest-preaching that was organized for them in Canada.

"So at thirteen, they packed me off to The Neuchâtel Ladies' Academy."

"Can missionaries afford boarding schools?"

"No. However, a CMS patron from Toronto paid half the fee, and two missionary children a year were taken in with the understanding that they would 'work their passage' for the other half of the fee. Everyone called us 'the Charities,' reminding us daily that we were out of our social class. The other girls were from all over Europe, but mostly British."

"How did 'the Charities' pay their way?"

"Scrubbing bathrooms. Cleaning classrooms. Gardening. Kitchen work. I liked the kitchen. There was a wonderful Scottish cook named Mrs. Douglas. She couldn't abide the snobbishness of the fee-payers and took the Charities under her wing. She started us cleaning the pots and peeling vegetables, but moved us up if we showed promise." Anna laughed. "She would pretend that she was testing out the food on us. 'Taste the bread pudding, girl, to see if it's fit for real humans.' It was always good. 'Are ye sure, girl? Better taste it again.'"

"Did you get back to China much?"

"Just once. It was expensive to travel, and of course young girls couldn't travel alone. In the summer of 1916, two Swiss nuns were being sent out to the China mission and agreed to escort me. Two retiring nuns brought me back. It was the last time I saw my parents. They died in the Spanish 'Flu epidemic in 1918."

"Weren't you lonesome on holidays?"

"There was quite a focus on athletics at the school, or as much athletics as could be accomplished in long dresses. They considered me to be 'rigorous' because I didn't swoon if I scraped a knee. Girls began to

invite me home for Christmas or summer holidays. I met Rodney Deloitte at Laura Camden's family estate in Yorkshire."

"Your husband?"

"Yes. Ever so briefly, war being what it is. We met at Christmas,
1917. He was in the RAF with Laura's brother, and had been invited to
Lord Camden's estate for the holiday. He proposed at Easter, and we
were married in June of 1918, the week after I graduated."

"Ever so briefly?" repeated Frances.

"Yes. War bride. War widow in less than four months. We had a
lovely honeymoon in the Lake District, but then Roddy's leave ended,
and he returned to France. His plane went down near Le Hamel in mid-
October. He survived the crash, but died two days later from his burns."

"An orphan and a widow within a few months! What then?"

"Well, I had no sisters or cousins or aunts, but I did have a new
connection in Mrs. Edgar Deloitte, my mother-in-law. A wonderful
woman! She invited me, sight unseen, to live with her in Ottawa. School
was over. The war was soon over. My marriage was over. It was the only
offer I had.

"One of the boons of missionary work was a survivor's pension. I
also received a tiny annuity because Roddy had died in uniform. Then
there was a small inheritance from my father's parents' estate. So I settled in with Mrs. Deloitte senior with enough means to keep me present-
ably dressed. Mrs. Deloitte was a widow with a smallish house in New
Edinburgh."

"So what did you do?"

"Well, at first, I was 'in mourning,' so I didn't do much but wear
black. While I had been officially 'finished' at the Neuchâtel Ladies'
Academy, I really didn't have any skills. I took a typing course, thinking
I might be able to get an office job, but all the soldiers were returning
home and there were no openings for women. To tell the truth, I'm not
much of a nine-to-five type anyway. Mrs. Deloitte was well connected
socially, so she introduced me around, and suggested I do some charity
work to fill in my time. I joined the May Court, and volunteered at the
Red Cross and the Good Will. I had something on almost every day.

"Then I started to get invited to Government House. I had been
presented to Lady Evelyn, the Duchess of Devonshire, in England at
Lord Camden's estate. She was honorary chair of the May Court, and
we were reintroduced.

"At the time, there was a funny kind of crisis in the local social scene because Ottawa is such a man's town. Diplomats, military attachés, Members of Parliament, businessmen abounded. Every hostess wanted to snag them to their tea or dinner, but there was a dearth of unattached ladies to balance the field. So Charity Girl Anna Deloitte entered the social circuit as 'suitable escort.' Respectably connected. Still in widow's weeds, not seeking an entanglement. And charmingly finished in Neuchâtel. I could converse in four languages, ride horseback, play tennis, golf, and bridge."

"A paragon!" exclaimed Frances.

"Exactly!" laughed Anna. "And so I parlayed all that into my own little business, once Mrs. Deloitte senior passed to her final reward."

"Business?"

Anna smiled a delicious smile. "I'm a professional escort and personal assistant," she said.

"Professional escort?"

"Yes. Men pay me to escort them to various social events." She drained her coffee. "Now I know what you're thinking. When men pay for a woman's services, there are assumptions about what those services extend to. However, it is paramount to my business reputation that all my services be provided in public places."

"It's really no different from what I do for a living," said Frances. "I get paid for public services, too. How did you make this transition from socialite to businesswoman?"

"As immodest as it may sound, I was in too great demand. Mind you, the competition consisted of awkward younger daughters or spinster cousins. I didn't know how to ration myself without appearing rude. Charlie Dobbs asked me to the Hunt Club Ball, and I accepted, even though I usually escorted Alex Hope to Hunt Club events. Alex was quite annoyed. He didn't wish to be stranded again, so he offered me a retainer if I reserved time for him each week. Word quickly got around.

"I was worried about appearances. Scandal closes doors quickly in Ottawa, so I sought the advice of the Duchess of Devonshire, who was the doyen of the local social scene. She knew I had limited resources. She spoke to the other leading hostesses in Ottawa—all married women, of course. I think they admired my gumption. The suffragette movement was afoot after the war. Anyhow, they all agreed that a professional relationship was perfectly acceptable as long as there was no hint of disgrace and no money passed hands in public."

"How much 'business' was there?"

"Oh, there are dozens of social events in Ottawa—luncheons, dinners, charity fundraisers, and galas at the sports clubs. There are bridge nights, skating parties, military balls, weddings, christenings, and Parliament Hill occasions. I've had a dozen events a week."

"How ever did you keep track of it all?"

"I became a very good bookkeeper. Requests came in. I confirmed my availability and sent out invoices."

"Men paid in advance?"

"Yes indeed. Lady Evelyn's suggestion. 'Your time is your money, Anna,' she said, 'and you can't afford to be seen with deadbeats.' So they prepay their bookings by return mail."

"Do you charge them all the same rate?"

Anna Deloitte smiled her mischievous smile. "Men who show special appreciation earn a discount. Occasionally, I'm bought a new outfit by a style-conscious client."

"Goodness! Where do men get all this money?"

"Some are from old money, and some are remittance men, and some are successful at cards, I suppose. The businessmen all have expense accounts. As 'personal assistant,' I often do accounts for them. They bring me all their bills and receipts in a shoebox and I put it in order and draft cheques for them to sign. I type correspondence as well."

"Wouldn't you like to settle down and raise a family?"

"I enjoy the freedom," Anna Deloitte replied. "And, I can't have children. A medical condition. It would be unfair to offer myself as a wife who could never produce an heir. Besides, these men are clients, and I maintain a professional distance. Does a doctor look at a patient with 'romantic' interest? It would be unethical."

"Anna Deloitte!" laughed Frances. "You socialized with countless men over a dozen years and no one came to your attention beyond a 'professional interest'?"

Anna smiled. "There was one man who fascinated me. He had suffered greatly in the war, physically and emotionally, yet he bore it all like a mantle of grace. His left arm had been amputated, but he could play tennis or golf or ride a horse with the best of them. He danced divinely, without any self-consciousness. He was German, but he had that delightful self-deprecating humour that is so Canadian."

Frances blinked. "He fought for Germany?"

"Yes," sighed Anna. "I know, the enemy. The enemy that plucked my fresh husband from me. Maybe that was why he fascinated me."

"How did you meet him?"

"He works for the farm implement division of Krupp. The Canadian government is a major purchaser of agricultural machinery. He comes over for a month or two every year. I met him at the British High Commission. He has many friends there. He went to public school in England and studied at Cambridge for two years before the war.

"So you see, he didn't hate the enemy. Nor do I, and that might have been another attraction. The war that cost him so much was like a game. His team lost and, ever the good sportsman, he congratulates the victors and stands them a drink. He was not diminished by his loss, although I think his view of war changed, and now he'd rather play tennis and sell tractors."

"Did you say you played bridge? Why haven't I seen you at the Metcalfe Street Bridge Club? You practically live in the clubhouse."

"Yes, dear Betsy," said Anna with a sigh. "She doesn't fully approve of me, although she has been reduced to calling a few times when desperate. However, I usually work nights, and when I'm not working, I don't really want to sit down with a dozen women for three hours. Are you a regular?"

"I am," Frances laughed, "which should give you an idea of *my* social life."

"Well, this puts the Metcalfe Street Bridge Club in a whole new light," replied Anna Deloitte. "I might just find myself available at Betsy's next invitation."

——— 42 ———

LADY MARGARET

In late April of 1938, Scotty Meldrum superintended the move into the new Bank of Canada Headquarters building. It was a masterpiece of logistics that would rival any campaign of Napoleon's. Beginning in February, detailed instructions were bulletined to all departments weekly with updates and a calendar countdown to April 29. Two weeks before the move, floor plans were distributed, with each employee's destination clearly marked in red. Colour-coded shipping labels were printed to designate floor destination and office number.

Banking activities on the fourth and fifth floors of the Victoria Building came to a halt at noon on the final Friday. A huge smorgasbord lunch was set up on each floor, creating a festive atmosphere for the packing and labelling that continued all afternoon.

At three o'clock sharp, an army of movers swarmed in, siphoning boxes and furniture down the elevators to a fleet of trucks. Bank staff bade final adieus in the Victoria Building Friday night and reported for duty at 234 Wellington Street on Saturday morning. An archipelago of neatly labelled furniture islands floated throughout the five floors of headquarters. By one o'clock, everyone had unpacked. May 1938 began with no disruption of Bank service.

The clean art deco design of the new headquarters exuded confidence. The governor, who worked relentless hours, even had a bedroom off his office. The only fly in the ointment was the central air conditioning, a first in Ottawa. It failed when tested by a sultry July. Scotty's polite inquiries turned to passion as he relentlessly hunted down manufacturers and contractors, trying to find someone to take responsibility, and "fix the damn thing."

Marriner Eccles, the chairman of the U.S. Federal Reserve, was due in Ottawa in early September with his entourage. He had hosted Bank of Canada officials in Washington during the winter, and Graham Towers was anxious to return the favour.

"It's hotter than a firecracker," said Scotty Meldrum. "Why don't we treat the Americans to a few days up in the Gatineau Hills? We'd get more sorted out around a campfire than we would sweating away here."

Miss Briscoe was away on summer holidays, and Frances was taking notes at Executive meetings. She could not call up an image of Sir Nigel Holmes swatting mosquitoes in his three-piece Savile Row pinstripe.

"Barter all day around the campfire like Hiawatha?" inquired Sir Nigel. "I doubt Marriner Eccles has seen more wilderness than one would find in a stroll through Central Park." He rapped his pipe dismissively into an ashtray.

"Well," said Graham Towers, "there wouldn't be any distractions, other than the deerflies. It would be nice to have his undivided attention."

"After Labour Day, no one uses the Five Lakes Fishing Club," said Scotty. "I could book the whole place. Sleeps twenty comfortably."

"In tents?" asked Sir Nigel.

"No. It's the old Gilmour family cottage—a castle of white pine and cedar shakes set on twelve hundred acres. It's only an hour's drive away."

"What are the servants' quarters like?" inquired the baronet. "My people are very fastidious."

"Doesn't your wife need the servants in town?" countered Scotty. "Manx, the caretaker, can look after us, with his wife Trixie, the cook."

"Lady Margaret is quite independent," insisted Sir Nigel. "And I'm on doctor's orders about diet. I can't have some woodsman's wife frying everything in bacon grease. And I never travel without my valet, secretary, and driver."

Scotty throttled his rage and made all the arrangements. The Americans would arrive by train Monday, in time for a dinner reception at the Château Laurier. Tuesday morning, the safari would depart for three nights in the woods. The senior Executive gave their secretaries the week off. Frances was to provide desk coverage for their offices. She took the governor's office; Cricket covered Scotty; Bridget, whose French was the best, went to Monsieur Soulière. Brendan looked after Sir Nigel.

Tuesday morning, Frances was in early checking over the briefing cases for a last time with Scotty. "There is no phone up at Five Lakes," he said. "In case of a Culloden File event, like an invasion by Martians, call Ruggles' General Store in Wakefield, and ask them to send the delivery truck up to Five Lakes."

Sir Nigel was reluctant to give a stranger access to his secretary's desk. "Tell the boy not to touch a thing besides the phone," he warned Frances. "Lady Margaret might call," he added elliptically.

Sir Nigel's wife was almost unknown to Frances. He observed the Bank of England tradition of keeping personal life divorced from professional activities. When spouses were occasionally required "to show the flag," duty was served by Lady Margaret, then the flag was quickly re-furled and closeted.

Each morning, Frances did a round of the executive offices. Brendan Maguire was doing a crossword when Frances walked into Sir Nigel's outer office.

"And does the Bank of Canada pay employees to do puzzles, Mr. Maguire?" she asked.

"Just improving my vocabulary to better serve the Bank, miss."

"Nice try, Brendan," Frances reached for his phone log. "Much coming in?"

"No. An invitation to a garden party at the Governor General's next week to observe the Queen's birthday. A delivery from the High Commissioner's Office."

"What's this?" asked Frances, pointing to the initials W.N. in the log.

"Oh, three wrong numbers at 9:05, 9:16, and 9:27 this morning."

"Wrong numbers?"

"Well," said Brendan, "the phone rang. I answered, ever politely, and after a few seconds, the phone line went dead. Must have been wrong numbers."

"No voice on the line?"

"I could hear breathing, but no words."

"Brendan, have you ever had a wrong number in the three years you've been working at the Bank of Canada?" Frances asked.

"Maybe once."

"Sir Nigel is not exactly the chummy sort. Who would have his office number?" Frances wondered out loud. She reached for the index card box on the corner of Jenkins's desk. Contacts at Government House, the British High Commission, names from half a dozen legations. The barber at the Château Laurier. The home number of Graham Towers. Then, under H, was the single entry: Lady Margaret: 4735, 301 Lansdowne Road, Rockcliffe.

"Lady Margaret might call."

Frances asked the operator to put her through to 4735. It rang ten times, but there was no answer. She hung up and called again after two minutes. After eight rings, the phone receiver at the other end was picked up.

"Hello?" said Frances. "Lady Margaret?" No response. "Lady Margaret, this is Frances McFadden in Sir Nigel's office. Did you call here earlier this morning?"

Frances heard a laboured breath before the line went dead. She called Murray at Red Line taxi. "Can you get down to the Bank of Canada right away? I'll meet you at the Sparks Street entrance."

She ran down the hall to Mr. Mueller's hideaway in the Research Library.

"Something's come up. Could you take my desk for an hour? My staff are spread all over covering for the Executive Retreat."

Mr. Mueller had stood up in that old-fashioned polite way when Frances burst into his office. "Certainly, Miss McFadden." He smiled.

Murray was prompt and traffic was light. They were at 301 Lansdowne Road in ten minutes. "Can you come with me?" Frances asked, as they parked in the laneway.

She rang the front doorbell twice. They could clearly hear the chimes echoing away inside, but there was no response. The door was locked. The curtains on the front windows were closed. A side door off the laneway was also locked. Around the back, there were French doors leading out onto a flagstone patio. Locked. More knocking, but no response until they heard a loud crash from inside the house.

"Murray, go that way and see if any windows are open. I'll check this way."

Seconds later, Murray shouted. Frances raced across the wet garden earth to find him at the side door pointing at the milk box. He opened the outer door to reveal two quarts of homogenized milk with the cream bubble on top from Clark's Dairy. The inside door of the milk box was ajar.

"Can you squeeze through that little opening?" Frances asked.

"Not a chance! It's up to you."

"I can't squirm through there in a dress! It'd be indecent!"

"Well," said Murray, "it's you through the milk box, or we break down the door on a hunch. Which would you rather explain to the police? And Sir Nigel?"

Murray removed the milk bottles and bent down to give her a boost, forming a stirrup with his locked fingers. Frances hesitated. "Don't give yourself airs, Frances McFadden," he said. "Your legs aren't that good-lookin'. And take off your shoes so I don't get my hands dirty. It looks like you've been muckin' out a barn."

Frances slid inside and found herself on the landing of the basement stairs. She called out "hello" to no response before unlocking the door for Murray.

"Should we split up and see what we can find?" he whispered.

"You are not leaving me in here alone," Frances whispered fiercely back. Then she said in a normal voice, "Why are we whispering?"

The kitchen was sun-filled, but empty. A half-eaten breakfast of poached eggs and peameal bacon sat beside a cold mug of tea. Beyond the kitchen was a large formal dining room, also empty. A wide archway led into a deserted living room which they traversed at an angle toward the front hall. On the hall floor lay a candlestick telephone with the receiver off the hook. Through a doorway beyond the staircase, they could see the slippered foot of a leg. Lady Margaret Holmes was face down on the Persian carpet in the den. Her right hand still grasped the end of a table runner. Shards of a porcelain flower vase sat in a puddle a foot from her head. The flower water had drenched her hair.

"Lady Margaret!" Frances called, bending down. "Are you all right?" She helped Murray roll the motionless woman out of the puddle. Lady Margaret's eyes fluttered open. She smiled. She opened her mouth and moved wordless lips. The taut cords of her neck muscles strained mightily, silently. Sweat glistened on her brow. Her eyes darted down to her left, then back at Frances, and then down again to her left. Clutched in her fingers was an index card.

Dr. Norris Eldredge, M.D. Heart Specialist
Medical Arts Building
216 Metcalfe Street
Carling 7639

Dr. Eldredge was a man of action. "Call an ambulance and get Lady Margaret to the emergency ward at the General Hospital. I'll meet you there."

An ambulance arrived quickly, and two muscular attendants strapped Lady Margaret onto a stretcher and carefully lifted her in.

"I'll go with them to the hospital," Frances told Murray, more calm-ly than she felt. "Take this note for Sir Nigel back to Brendan Maguire at the Bank. He's to talk to no one. Drive him straight up to the Five Lakes Fishing Camp and tell him to deliver the note personally. Stop at Ruggles' General Store in Wakefield for directions. Hurry."

Dr. Eldredge was waiting at the emergency ward when the ambulance arrived. He whisked Lady Margaret right into an examination room. "Don't go away," he said.

Frances phoned the Bank. "Mr. Mueller, circumstances are going to keep me out of the office for a while yet. Could you continue to cover my desk?"

"Of course, Miss McFadden."

"It might take the rest of the afternoon."

"Take all the time you wish. I can work right here by your phone."

"I'm sorry to impose."

"Miss McFadden, I'd cover you for the rest of the month, if you needed it."

Frances choked up. "Thank you, Musketeer," she said when her voice firmed.

"One for all. All for one," he replied.

Dr. Eldredge was circumspect, but concerned. "Lady Margaret is resting comfortably. She's conscious, but has obviously had a stroke, and is at least temporarily paralyzed. Sir Nigel should be informed at once."

"Sir Nigel is in the Gatineau Hills at a bankers' meeting. I've sent him a message," replied Frances.

"Good," said Dr. Eldredge, looking at his watch. "I have other patients. I might be able to hunt up a private duty nurse."

"I can stay with Lady Margaret," said Frances.

"Are you good friends?"

"No. I work at the Bank of Canada with Sir Nigel. If our situations were exchanged, I'd appreciate some company," Frances said simply.

Even though the shades were drawn, it was hot in the private room where Lady Margaret rested. She had been sedated, but at about two p.m., she opened her eyes and smiled. She looked at Frances, and looked down at her own left hand lying on the sheet, and looked back at Frances. Frances moved her chair closer to the bedside and took Lady Margaret's warm hand in her own. The smile grew, the jaw trembled, and a tear trailed down the older woman's cheek.

Frances nodded off in the dark room, and barely heard the door click open when Sir Nigel entered shortly after four. He tiptoed to Lady Margaret's side and silently put his hand on her brow. She opened her eyes and smiled.

"Oh, my dearest," he gasped. "Oh, my dearest," He leaned down and kissed her tenderly on the cheek. He started to weep, and laid his head beside his wife's on the pillow.

Frances was too startled to be embarrassed. She sat absolutely still until he recovered.

"Excuse me, Sir Nigel. I should get back to the Bank unless I can do anything else here."

Sir Nigel looked across his prone wife, blinking wildly. Frances wondered if he even recognized her.

"Thank you," he said.

Near midnight, Lady Margaret Holmes died of a cerebral haemorrhage.

Lord and Lady Tweedsmuir hosted a small, private funeral at Government House. Frances received a formal invitation on the Baronet's gold embossed stationery. She called Anna Deloitte for etiquette pointers, never having met a governor general.

"They're very nice, but his health is poor. It's 'My Lord' and 'My Lady.' I can lend you a long black dress with matching gloves. Wear a black hat with veil."

"I don't know any small talk for Lords," Frances fretted. "Wait! Didn't Lord Tweedsmuir write that Richard Hannay mystery, *The Thirty-nine Steps*? Should I ask if he liked the Alfred Hitchcock film?"

"One answers questions of the G-G, one does not ask them. Anyway, he hated it."

The governor, associate deputy governor, and secretary were the only other Bank employees in attendance. Sir Nigel Holmes sat gauntly through the service like a man poleaxed. On September 12, he resigned from the Bank to accompany his wife's body back to England for interment in the family crypt.

On Monday, September 15, Scotty Meldrum was appointed Deputy Governor of the Bank of Canada.

43

PERSONS OF INTEREST

The freshly minted deputy governor wheeled into Frances's office and closed the door. Wordlessly, he ransacked her bottom filing cabinet drawer like a dog after a bone.

Without looking up from her typing, Frances said, "You took the last of the Macallan up to Five Lakes. Oh, and congratulations."

Scotty looked emptily around, like a child who has dropped his candy in the dirt. "Order two more cases of the Macallan immediately, Miss McFadden. And never again let us run out of liquid sustenance. I'm in the front line now, and will need succour more than ever."

"Whose budget should these medicinal supplies come out of now that I no longer report to you?" asked Frances.

"You are remarkably well informed, Miss McFadden. Doug Marble's down in New York meeting bankers and just heard of his promotion last night."

"Will he sign for the Macallan invoice, then?"

"For God's sake, lass! Marble is a Free Methodist and regards weak tea as morally questionable. A Macallan invoice would horrify him."

"Well, then . . . ?"

"Marble was quite surprised by his promotion. He asked if he could pick a new executive secretary as Clara will be moving upstairs with me."

"That's not unreasonable, is it? Lily Gilchrist has served him well in Public Accounts, but now he'll need someone with a wider range of skills."

"Yes. That's why he wants you."

"Me?" said Frances. "I barely know him!"

"Your reputation has apparently preceded you to New York. Including your rescue of Lady Holmes."

"Didn't do her much good."

"Sir Nigel was filled with self-recrimination for taking all the servants up to Five Lakes. You saw him at the memorial service. Haggard as a witch from Macbeth. Now, I never much fancied his lordship, but we did need a central banking man to get us launched, and he certainly greased the skids. However, now we're under full steam, and the pilot has served his purpose," said Scotty.

"So I'm to move into Mrs. Hewitt's office as the secretary's secretary?" asked Frances. "That's quite an honour."

"No, lass. I told Marble that you couldna take the job."

Frances's eyes narrowed. "You turned down my promotion? Without consulting me?" Frances could feel the old red terror rising within. "That's . . . that's . . ." Fortunately, words failed her.

"I should have talked to you, but I didna have time. I'm sorry."

Frances had never ever heard the words "I'm sorry" come from Scotty Meldrum's mouth in four years, and her anger eddied away.

"The plain truth is that I need you on the fifth floor," Scotty continued.

"But you're taking Clara up with you." Frances had never referred to Mrs. Hewitt as "Clara" in her life. Times were changing.

Scotty took a deep breath. "Clara Hewitt is a *wonderful* woman. Keeps my desk neat, my appointments organized, and picks out birthday presents for my wife and the boys. Her talents are deep." He paused. "But not wide. That's the simple truth, not a judgment. I need her, but I need other assistance as well. You, Frances McFadden, could fill the bill. Will you stay with me?" he asked.

Frances smiled at his contriteness. "Well, this is all quite sudden, Mr. Meldrum. Sorry, Deputy Governor Meldrum. What did you have in mind?"

"As secretary, I was completely engrossed with the internal functions of the Bank. Leases, organization charts, the new headquarters building. That damn air conditioning. Well, it's a new game. Senior executive portfolios have all been reorganized. Governor Towers wants the job descriptions of the governor and the deputy governor to be identical. We will both sit on every committee and be privy to all correspondence, in case any unforeseen circumstance should befall him.

"It's the greatest possible privilege to work in harness with Graham Towers. He's the only genius I've ever met. Perceptive, balanced, commanding, genial. And all without a hint of ego. He has only one goal: to build the best central bank in the world."

Frances asked, "And where does Frances McFadden fit in?"

"Frances McFadden is to become special assistant to the Executive Committee, reporting directly to me. We must be mindful that your work steers clear of Clara Hewitt and Miss Briscoe, who both have their hands full."

Frances was puzzled. "What kind of work are you thinking about?"

"The first task is preparing the Bank of Canada for war in Europe. That was the complete agenda of our Gatineau retreat with the Federal Reserve. Hitler is positively lusting to annex the Sudetenland in Czechoslovakia. By treaty, if possible; by other means, if necessary.

"The Bank of Canada will face a host of issues if war breaks out. We need a strategy for foreign exchange. We need to prevent a run on the Canadian dollar. We need to raise money for a war effort. The Bank of Canada is only four years old—a child in the world of central banking. We have to grow up in a hurry.

"Interested? Or would you rather work for Marble?"

"Can I think it over?" asked Frances.

Scotty frowned. "I need a person who can act instinctively."

"This sounds like blackmail, but not as subtle," said Frances. She paused. "Okay. I'll do it."

"Good lass!" smiled the deputy governor. "And we have to operate with the utmost secrecy."

"Secrecy?"

"Of course. We have diplomatic relations with all the potential belligerents. We cannot be seen to be preparing for warfare against them. And Canadians are still struggling with this Depression. They're worried about their next meal. They are not ready for war. We cannot appear to be rattling the sabre.

"Now, I am not in favour of war. It is an unhealthy state for man or beast. But if war comes to us, and we are not prepared, we're in a fix. English Canada will not sit on the sidelines if the United Kingdom is threatened. And, here's the rub: French Canada has no wish to be taxed in kind or in manpower to support a European war."

"Even to defend France?"

"France abandoned Quebec in 1763. They share a language, but there is no visceral tie, as there is between English Canada and Great Britain."

Frances mulled this over. "Do I understand, then, that even Monsieur Soulière won't be party to these preparations?"

"Correct. Nor will Marble. Just a scant few of us. Do you know Sydney Turk in the Foreign Exchange Division? Slim fellow with a narrow moustache?"

"I've met him. Come to think of it, I haven't seen him around much lately."

"Exactly. His secretary doesn't even know where he is, and I didn't know this until yesterday. He's been working for several months 'on special assignment.' You'll be doing much the same, along with Sandy Skelton from Research."

"If I move up to the fifth floor, what about my team? Cricket and Brendan and Bridget?"

"They can't come. Security issue," said Scotty. After a pause, he asked, "Could one of them become Marble's secretary?"

Frances thought. "Cricket could. There's nobody in Ottawa that types or takes dictation faster. She's smart as a whip."

"Sir Nigel left his office closets and cabinets packed full of materials that need to be sorted, then shredded or archived. It might take a year. Could one of your lot help Mary with that?"

"Bridget would be the one. She's strong on details. Brendan will still have his hands full looking after the catering. He could easily work under Cricket, if she becomes Secretary Marble's secretary."

"The governor is sending me to Europe next week to look over the situation and introduce myself to the bankers. While I'm gone, you need to help Doug Marble set up shop. Oh. Do you have a passport?"

"No."

"Well, get one. You may be travelling. Do you know anything about coded messages?" Frances shook her head. "Read up on them. That's it. When I return in October, we'll start up full bore.

"A new coordinating committee for contingencies, or the CCC, is to be set up with other key government departments. Your friend Grace from Finance will be on it, along with representatives from Trade, External Affairs, and Defence."

"Just like the Momsies!" said Frances.

"Yes, but all hush-hush. The prime minister doesn't even want to know the details, so he won't have to answer any embarrassing questions in the House. The governor will chair both the internal Preparation Committee and the external CCC. You'll be secretary for both."

"Are conditions of work top secret as well?" asked Frances.

"You'll get to work your fingers to the bone, sixteen hours a day, with no formal recognition. We'll bump your salary to the same level as Clara Hewitt's and Miss Briscoe's, but you must keep that quiet. No jealousies. Anybody asks what you're doing, just grimace and say 'special assignment work,' as though we have you cleaning the toilets."

"One request."

"Yes?"

"That memo you send out regularly to all staff cautioning us against working overtime? Take me off the mailing list."

Scotty Meldrum laughed his deep barrelhouse laugh, and slapped the table as he rose.

Once the Munich Crisis made headlines in the Ottawa newspapers, people began to talk about the future. Anna Deloitte was strangely philosophical for a war widow. "Kings declare war but they don't lead their men into battle anymore," she said as they walked to church for Thanksgiving services. "Politics killed my husband, not 'the enemy.' You could no more blame the German people for the war than you could blame the Spanish people for the Spanish 'Flu."

Then she let a name slip. "Herr Kessler is the first to condemn the folly of war, although he was a professional soldier. War crippled him, and the inflation that followed bankrupted his parents. He's been working in Ottawa for the last two months trying to close a large government contract caught up in a bureaucratic tangle."

"What does Herr Kessler think about the Nazi regime?" asked Frances.

"Oh, he's not political at all. He just rolls his eyes and quotes Voltaire about every country getting the government it deserves. Tractors still need to be sold, he says, and wheat needs to be harvested, no matter how badly we're governed."

The Metcalfe Street Bridge Club held every possible opinion about the European situation. Nora Ray loved German music and thought that a country that produced Mozart and Wagner held the world in its debt. Debra Semple didn't like the Germans, but didn't like the French, either, and thought that if they were foolish enough to go to war, we should stay well out of it. Margery Davies, who had a picture of George VI over her mantel, felt that any threat to England was a threat to civilization, and duty calls us to stand by the Union Jack. Clarissa Semple said the real peril was the Communist menace, and any country with the courage to stand up to the Russians should be supported. Audrey Beauchamp, the lone French Canadian, said that she liked the British better than the Germans, but not enough to go to war for them. Sarah Dawes was a

Quaker, and thought that any war was immoral. Gladys Gilhooly felt that war unjustly punished the poor soldiers, and profited the rich who owned the munitions factories. Betsy Knowles viewed the whole topic as infinitely less important than bridge.

The restlessness in Europe stressed the Momsies. Three of them had lost husbands in the last war. Contingencies were clearly being considered in their various departments, although they did not openly discuss them. However, veiled references were thin. "Our diplomatic missions are being advised on evacuation procedures, in case." "Are you laying in extra office supplies, in case of rationing?" It cast a deep pall over Tuesday tea.

Inspector Hollingsworth, Frances's RCMP contact from the old days of the famous counterfeiting file, walked back into her life with a Jack Russell terrier named Beauregard. Man and dog lived just down the street from the Balmoral, and they took brisk round-the-block constitutionals twice a day.

"Well, Frances, wonderful to hear that you're still in the service of the country," said Inspector Hollingsworth. "How does the banking community feel about the European situation?"

"Bankers are not much given to expressions of emotion, Inspector," Frances admitted, "but of all economic conditions, good, bad, or indifferent, 'disruptions' are the most feared. Suspense," she continued, "is great in fiction, but it creates havoc with the foreign exchange rate. How does the Mounted Police Fraud Division feel about it?"

"We've gone through a reorganization over at headquarters," he said. "I'm on the International Desk now, but counterfeiting is still a big concern."

"International counterfeiting?"

"Holding a war is very expensive. It's far more economical if you can finance it with someone else's currency. Print up a bunch of American dollars or British pounds and pass them in another country. No one would waste time counterfeiting Canadian dollars on a large scale, but our American and British colleagues feel vulnerable, and have asked us to be vigilant."

"That's all you need to be vigilant about?"

"We keep our eyes open for persons of interest. Speaking of which, there is a very regular visitor to the Balmoral, a Herr Kessler. German National. Agricultural implement salesman. Ever run into him?"

"I haven't met him personally, but my neighbour, Anna Deloitte, has mentioned him." She paused. "A person of interest?"

"Perhaps. He has a few curious traits. Quite an accomplished amateur photographer. Always has a camera with him. Never visits the German Embassy, but is frequently at the British High Commission. Seems to be quite the social butterfly for a tractor salesman. Spends a great deal of time in the company of your Mrs. Deloitte."

Frances smiled. "One would almost think you're following him, Inspector." Inspector Hollingsworth smiled wordlessly back. "Does taking pictures and squiring an attractive widow to social functions qualify as suspicious behaviour?"

"Suspicious? Not necessarily. But curious," said the Inspector. "Like Mrs. Deloitte herself."

Frances was taken aback. "Do you also think Anna Deloitte might be 'a person of interest'?"

"She certainly has close access to a great number of well-connected people."

Frances laughed. "Of course! That's how she earns a living. But Anna couldn't possibly be involved with any intrigue. She's too ..." She thought a moment. "Guileless. That's it. She told me her entire life story ten minutes after I met her. She's a Sunday school teacher, for goodness sakes!"

"Just keep your ears open, Miss McFadden, if you don't mind."

Frances smiled. "Should I give you a call if I notice any coded messages in her purse?"

"Never telephone me on business. I walk Beauregard twice a day, at seven-thirty in the morning and seven-thirty in the evening. We are creatures of habit, and you can always find us walking the block, rain or shine."

"Never call? Surely you don't suspect the Bell Canada telephone operators of being enemy agents?"

"I don't know any telephone operators personally, and maybe they all teach Sunday school, too. However, they can listen in on any conversation in Ottawa. Undetected. Would they sell that information, or provide it free to a sympathetic cause? Hard to tell. Our department has been advised to never say anything over the phone that we wouldn't want published on the front page of the *Ottawa Citizen*. The same applies to telegrams. We sometimes send coded messages when we have no other choice, but codes attract attention, too.

"Meanwhile, Miss McFadden, you're welcome to join Beauregard and me for a walk anytime."

—— 44 ——

END OF INNOCENCE

It was not surprising that Katie Deavy was the first friend to succumb to matrimony. She was the hunter of the pack and brought home the first trophy. She was about to turn twenty-one, and was set to marry Kevin Warren on June 10. Frances and Dorothy were downtown purchasing two small crystal salt and pepper shakers from Birks for Katie's trousseau.

"Have you noticed something fishy about Mary lately?" asked Dorothy.

Frances reflected. She and Mary used to get together for lunch regularly, but that had been Mary's initiative, and the initiative had lapsed lately. "Haven't noticed anything, but life is a whirlwind for both of us at the Bank these days. Why?"

"Oh, just little stuff. Mary and I were supposed to go to the library together a couple of times, and she cancelled at the last minute—very apologetic, but without giving any reason. Last week I saw her in the men's section at Ogilvy's picking out socks. When I bounced over to say 'hi,' she hid them behind her back. The girl cannot tell a lie, but she wouldn't meet my eye and was as nervous as a shoplifter."

"Time for 'Truth or Consequences'?"

"I think so," agreed Dorothy.

Katie Deavy had gone to work at D. Kemp Edwards' Lumber Yard after graduating from the High School of Commerce. That's where she met Kevin. She had rebuffed Frances's offer of a job at the Bank of Canada.

"No offence, Frannie, but there just aren't enough fringe benefits down there for me."

"What do you mean? There's a subsidized cafeteria and a good pension plan."

"I mean men," said Katie.

"Men work there."

"Yeah, but they're all bookish, college types. I'm in the market for something more down-to-earth."

"Katie Deavy! What kind of reverse snobbery is this? You have read more of the Bible and more of the dictionary and more fiction than anyone I've met at the Bank of Canada. You could hold your own with any of them."

Katie raised her eyebrows. "I'd kind of like to be holding somebody else's. If you catch my drift."

"Truth or Consequences" required completely different strategies for Katie and Mary. It was unclear how much Katie's racy comments were seated in experience. It was absolutely clear that Mary O'Brien had no experience at all.

Dorothy opened with a feint at Frances. "Are you seeing much of your old sweetheart, Dr. Grace, these days?"

"Lookit, Dr. Grace is not now, nor never has been, my 'sweetheart.'"

"But there's such adoration in your eyes when you mention him!"

"I like him. Is that a crime?"

"Don't you love him?" asked Mary. "Even a little bit?"

"I love him like a brother."

"Like a brother, is it?" retorted Katie. "Well, there's a word in the dictionary for that!"

"Will you stop this?" Frances demanded. "Dr. Grace hired me into a job I love. He's my trusted confidant for professional problems. He is not a romantic interest. The end."

"Why not?" pursued Dorothy. "If he's so perfect?"

"The plain truth is that I need him too much in the relationship we have. I wouldn't want anything romantic to come between our closeness. If things went wrong, I'd be miserable."

"But things could go right. Then you'd have everything in one package."

"But they could go wrong. And it's not worth the risk."

"Nothing ventured . . ." teased Katie.

"Nothing lost," said Frances, switching topics. "Now, Mary, I'm noticing a lot less of you down at the Bank lately. You used to drop in for lunch all the time. Have I got body odour or something?"

Mary's eyes darted around frantically. "No. I know how busy you are, and I'm busy helping Bridget with the new Bank Archives . . ."

"But you still eat lunch?"

"I often take it at my desk."

"Alone?"

Mary swallowed and looked down.

"And our Thursday night visits to the library, Mary?" prodded Dorothy. "You haven't been available for over a month. Given up reading?"

It was Katie's turn. "I saw you last Sunday afternoon get on the Britannia Beach streetcar. With a large picnic hamper. All alone. I would have enjoyed a picnic at Britannia, had anyone invited me."

Mary was trapped. "I . . . I'm . . . I'm sorry!" was all she could say before she burst into tears.

"Truth or Consequences" was intended to relieve tension by sharing secrets with trusted companions. It was licensed bragging. "You asked, so I had to tell you." It was not intended to reduce friends to tears.

Dorothy gave Mary a hug. "Hey, kiddo, it's only us."

"Playing a game," added Katie.

"Are you in any kind of trouble, Mary?" asked Frances.

"Oh, no! No trouble at all," sobbed Mary.

After Mary regained her composure, Frances said, "Well, we don't want to pry, but clearly something is on your mind lately. Perhaps a confidence with another party . . ." Mary's face lit up. "That you're not at liberty to share—"

"Even with your best friends," continued Dorothy.

"We're happy to know that this distraction is not in the 'trouble' category—"

"And we're here for you if we can help," added Katie.

"Oh, thank you!" sighed Mary, tearing up again. "You are the best friends a person could ever have!"

Two weeks later, Mary bounced radiantly into Frances's office. "Can we have lunch together today?" she asked with as much coyness as innocence could muster.

"Love to Mar, but I'm taking minutes for the governor at a noon meeting. How about tomorrow?"

Mary reached around to close the door. She grabbed both of Frances's hands in her own. She was bursting. "Have you ever met Nathan Bedford in the Securities Department?"

"Junior officer? Joined the Bank last August fresh out of grad school at McGill?" Mary nodded. "Good-looking in a quiet, confident way?"

"Yes!" Mary exclaimed. "Nat proposed and I've accepted!" Frances gave her a joyous hug. "Nat came over last night to ask my father's permission. Mother and I had Father all prepared with the right answer!"

"Congratulations! But why all the secrecy?"

"Nat popped the question two months ago, and I accepted immediately. But of course he had to ask his department head's permission to marry. Mr. Henderson told Nat that he has a great future at the Bank, but he didn't earn enough to get married. Well, yesterday, all the raises were passed by the Executive Committee, and Mr. Henderson called Nat right in. He'll be making two hundred dollars a month starting the first of May, and Mr. Henderson feels that's enough to support a family. So he's given us his blessing, and we're getting married June twenty-fourth. Will you be my maid of honour?"

"Of course!" said Frances. Her mind was churning with the news and a random thought struck her. "Junior securities officers start at $160 a month, don't they?"

"That's right. And Nat's very careful with it."

"And you make seventy a month, so together you earn $230. If Mr. Henderson thinks you only need $200 a month, why the holdup?"

"Oh, I'll have to resign as librarian once I'm a homemaker."

"Do you want to resign?"

"Oh, no! I love my job! But it's the rules."

"This is a rule for the Bank of Canada?"

"That's what Mr. Meldrum says. I'm so excited!"

When Mary left, Frances got out her copy of the Bank of Canada Employees' Rules and Procedures. She had worked on the final draft two years earlier, and her memory served her well. She phoned Clara Hewitt and asked for ten minutes with the deputy governor to clarify a procedures issue.

In four years at the Bank of Canada, Frances had never requested a personal meeting with Scotty Meldrum. They usually did their business on the fly, or he came her way for discussions over the Macallan.

"So, lass," he said jovially, "Clara says you 'need a procedure clarified.' I thought you knew them backwards."

"So did I. You've heard that Mary O'Brien has accepted a marriage proposal?"

"Yes! Wonderful news. Young Bedford is a comer. He'll be a department head in no time. Delighted that he's marrying inside the Bank. Mary will understand why he's often late for dinner."

"Mary says she has to resign as librarian in order to get married."

"Yes. Married women need to guard the hearth and home. And before you know it, she'll have wee bairns scampering about. The next generation for the Bank of Canada, let's hope! Now what are you struggling with?"

"What I'm struggling with, is why Mary O'Brien has to retire just because she's getting married."

"It's the rules. Can't be helped."

Frances held up her copy of Bank of Canada Rules and Procedures. "Perhaps you can help me, sir, because I was unable to locate it in the rules book."

Scotty Meldrum sighed. "It's not in *those* rules, but it's . . . you know . . . customary. Surely you agree."

"Since you ask, I certainly do not agree. How does getting married possibly affect Mary's work at the Bank?"

"It's not Mary's work that's the issue. A wife has responsibilities."

"What? To cook and clean house? She does that in her parents' home right now. It will take her *less* time to look after just the two of them."

"But she'll be starting a family soon—"

"But she doesn't have a family *yet*. Only Mr. Bedford to look after. He is a McGill graduate, and can likely feed himself and wash his own socks."

"D'ya think Mary should have divided loyalties between the Bank and her husband? D'ya want to put her in that position?"

"You and the governor are both married. Do you have divided loyalties?"

"Ach! Apples and oranges, lass. It's a man's lot to bring home the bacon. Any woman should be happy to be so taken care of."

"And did you ask Mary if she'd be happier at home?"

"No," Scotty replied with exasperation, "but I'm sure—"

"Well, begging your pardon, I did ask her. She'd be happy to stay as librarian after her marriage, but she can't because it's against the rules." Frances wagged the rule book at him.

Scotty's face turned crimson. "Are you telling me Mary is unhappy to be getting married to young Bedford?"

"She is delighted to be marrying Mr. Bedford. That's not the point!"

"What is the point?"

"There are actually two points, Deputy Governor. First, if it is a Bank of Canada rule that employees must resign to get married, why isn't it in the rule book?"

"Well, it's the custom, for God's sake. Do we have to put every custom in the rule book? Should there be a rule to flush the toilet after use?"

"And secondly, why is it customary for women to resign on getting married but not for men? Is the work of women here less worthy than the work of men?"

"Don't be ridiculous!"

"Who's being ridiculous? Whose ridiculous rule—"

"Ach, lass, you're just in a tizzy because Mary O'Brien's your friend. I can't believe she put you up to this."

Frances's cheeks reddened. "That is untrue, and unfair! Mary did not put me up to anything! She is far too ethical. Unlike the rules of some organizations.

"And, I'm embarrassed to admit, it is *not* my friendship that has brought me here. It's the Bank of Canada that will suffer if Mary goes. Mary has a unique talent for archival work and librarianship, carefully honed to our specific situation. There isn't a person in Canada who could do her job. Even an excellent replacement would take a year to train. The whole research function of the Bank will be crippled in the meantime."

"Listen, Miss McFadden," said Scotty Meldrum, now beet-red. "You need to be reminded occasionally that you do not run the Bank of Canada. You're a damn fine employee. People who are right most of the time sometimes think that they're right all of the time. And they're not."

"Clara Hewitt is married, isn't she?"

"Yes, but she was hired before the Bank of Canada rules were set up."

"Rules? Or do you mean discriminatory customs?"

"Clara was working for me at the Bank of Nova Scotia before I joined the Bank. The Bank of Nova Scotia had no policy on the employment of married woman."

"What an enlightened attitude," said Frances. She wheeled around and stormed out of the room.

Three days later, Mary O'Brien dropped into Frances's office with a big smile. "Guess what!" she said. "Mr. Marble just told me that I can stay as librarian until my replacement is trained. Nat thinks it's great! We'll be able to put away some money before we start a family." Mary could not even say "start a family" without blushing at the intimacy it suggested.

"And who's to hire and train the new librarian?" asked Frances.

"Mr. Marble wants to see you about that."

"Miss McFadden!" Mr. Marble said with a smile. "The deputy governor just spoke to me. He doesn't wish to leave our library vulnerable when Mary gets married, so he wants her to stay on while we train a replacement. Could you and Mary look after the selection process?"

Frances reflected. "That might take some time. Mary will be very hard to replace."

"I appreciate that. No hurry."

"And I have many priorities now on this special assignment work."

"I'm sure you do, Frances."

"And once a candidate is hired, it will take Mary a while to train her."

Mr. Marble nodded. "Absolutely. Use your own good judgment. We don't want to disable the Bank's research capabilities. That's what the deputy governor insists on, and I have to agree with him."

"Mr. Meldrum wants Mary to stay with us as long as it takes?"

"That's what he told me this morning."

Frances was silent for a moment. "Well, we want to keep the deputy governor happy."

"Indeed we do, Frances. We certainly do."

45

THE POLISH DILEMMA

Both June weddings went off splendidly. Mary and Nathan Bedford solemnized their vows in the cavernous sanctuary of St. Patrick's Basilica and left by train for their honeymoon in Niagara Falls. Katie Deavy tied the knot with Kevin Warren in a simpler morning ceremony in the chapel at St. Luke's Anglican, then headed up the Ottawa Valley in a D. Kemp Edwards pickup truck. Kevin had risen from stock boy to assistant buyer in the lumberyard, and Mr. Edwards loaned him the truck if Kevin would check out the lumber mills between Fort Coulonge and Kirkland Lake.

In the balmy summer evenings, Frances often saw Inspector Hollingsworth and Beauregard on her way home. One evening, the inspector observed, "Your Sunday school teacher is very tight with a certain tractor salesman these days."

"Is that a concern?"

"Not necessarily. Beauregard and I are creatures of habit ourselves, and I like the predictability of Herr Kessler's activities. Sudden changes in routine would cause concern.

"Tell me, is Mrs. Deloitte chatty?"

"Well, she's not secretive. She has a guileless nature that's quite refreshing, compared to the politics at the Bank. That's why I can't believe that Anna is, well, a person of interest."

"Could she be unwittingly compromised?"

Frances reflected. "Anna is not innocent the way my friend Mary O'Brien—I mean Mary Bedford—is. Born in China, schooled in Switzerland, and having a husband die young has matured her through a wider range of experiences. Still . . . she has no affectations and she might not see them in others."

"Does she ever mention Herr Kessler?"

"Occasionally. Herr Kessler took some pictures that Anna had framed. He's clearly an accomplished photographer."

Inspector Hollingsworth lit his pipe. "He is also quite a prolific photographer. He takes several rolls of film in to Gould's Camera Art every week to be developed. He also mails film to Diebel Photography Laboratory in Düsseldorf, Germany. Coincidentally, my FBI contacts tell me, the German military attaché in Washington, a Major Ziegler, also a photographic enthusiast, regularly sends film to Diebel."

"Coincidentally?" smiled Frances. "Have you checked Diebel out?"

"It's difficult," replied the inspector. "We have working relationships with the FBI and Scotland Yard, but we can't really ask the Gestapo about Diebel Laboratories."

"Diebel of Düsseldorf may *be* the Gestapo," conjectured Frances.

Inspector Hollingsworth just smiled.

The wilt of August fell upon Ottawa. On the Civic Holiday weekend, Miss Briscoe ate a warm egg salad sandwich at the Glebe United Church Sunday school picnic and came down with amoebic dysentery so severe that she had to be hospitalized. Governor Towers asked Frances to step in as his secretary. Scotty Meldrum was heading to Basel, Switzerland, to represent Canada at a meeting of the Bank of International Settlements, and wouldn't be needing Frances much.

Every Tuesday morning at eight, the Bank Executive Committee met in the fifth floor boardroom. Sandy Skelton was sitting in at Exec in preparation for covering off any Contingency Coordinating Committee tasks when Scotty left. At the August 8 meeting, Sir Randolph Buckley, the British High Commissioner to Canada, made a surprise appearance. Frances noticed that he was not on the agenda that Miss Briscoe had prepared in advance. A faint odour of Sir Nigel Holmes wafted from the high commissioner.

"A European country," Sir Randolph articulated slowly, "has concerns about its gold reserves. The times are uncertain, and bordering states are perceived to be restless. The Bank of England has been approached for safe refuge. However, having already extended a similar courtesy to a number of nations, they have no room left. Montague Norman has asked, off the record, if the Bank of Canada could offer assistance."

"Comments?" asked the governor, looking around the table.

"Well, what country? And when do they want to make the transfer?" asked Douglas Marble, who would have to handle the logistics.

"Really not my place to bandy about details without a commitment here," replied Sir Randolph. "No offence. Scotland Yard is always tweaking us about spies and Mata Hari types. Bloody annoying.

"Just last week they asked us to keep an eye on a German tractor salesman. It's hard to keep him out of our sight. He virtually lives at the High Commission. A friend of Williams, my first secretary. Drops in for tennis or the occasional gin and tonic. Sterling chap, actually. Yes, he's German, but so is the Royal Family, for God's sake. And he's *practically* English. Went to Harrow. Went to Cambridge. Helped win the fours at Henley before the war. Comes from an old aristocratic Rhineland family. As likely to have truck with the Nazis as I am with the Labour Party."

"How large are the gold reserves?" asked Scotty.

"Just under nine million pounds sterling."

Mr. Marble did some scribbling. "That would be about forty million Canadian, or less than three thousand bars. We have the space."

"This country would pay transportation and security costs to get the gold to Ottawa?" asked Monsieur Soulière.

"Certainly," replied Sir Randolph.

"Why not, then?" said Scotty. "We have the room. It will cost us nothing. We make a friend."

Nods around the table.

"Fine," said the governor. "Sir Randolph, please convey our willingness to Governor Norman at the Bank of England. Final details can be worked out through direct contact with me."

The Metcalfe Street Bridge Club was struggling to keep three tables afloat with several regulars out of Ottawa to escape the heat. Betsy Knowles had to call on Anna Deloitte to round out the twelfth seat. It was the dog days of summer, and everyone was a-twitter with gossip to relieve the ennui.

"Jenkins, the Minister of Labour, has a local paramour, apparently, as his wife refuses to leave Winnipeg to join him here," ventured Audrey Beauchamp over the pre-game sherry.

"I hear that Lawrence Cromwell, a thoroughly nasty man, is about to be appointed to the Supreme Court, over Sir Lyman Duff's strenuous objection," threw in Margery Davies. "The court needs a representative from Western Canada since Jack Kingsway died, and the pickings are slim."

"Father's dentist told him the Polish government is scared to death that the German army will invade any day now. They want to move their gold reserves to the Bank of England for safekeeping," declared Clarissa Semple.

"What foolishness," snorted Nora Ray. "Why would an educated nation like the Germans want anything to do with the Poles?"

"I suspect it's true, though," added Betsy Knowles while lighting a cigarette. "I had tea at the British High Commission yesterday. They were bragging they were the safety deposit box of Europe, with more goodies on the way by mid-September."

"You'd think the Bank of Canada vaults would be a lot safer than the Bank of England, if things get testy in Europe. Does your Bank deal with these requests, Frances?"

Frances gave a doe-eyed glance around the assembly. "Ladies," she said, "I am a clerk-typist at the Bank of Canada. For some reason, Governor Towers seldom solicits my opinion on international gold shipments." Laughter rippled through the room. "However, I will insist on being apprised of the situation the next time we meet in the elevator."

With Scotty Meldrum in Switzerland, Frances was unsure what to do. Next morning, she dropped in to Sandy Skelton's office and closed the door.

Sandy's eyebrows shot up. "Ah, Miss McFadden seeks a private encounter with the Director of Research, behind closed doors. I'd always suspected that you found me unbearably attractive, but isn't it a little early in the day for a romantic adventure?"

Frances shook her finger at him. "Sandy, the Scotsman is gone, and I need advice. Remember that allusive reference Sir Randolph Buckley made last week to the potential peril facing a certain country's gold reserves?"

"Right. The top secret event of the century?"

"Yes. Well, I was playing bridge last night, and people were gossiping about a gold shipment from Europe as though it were a new movie in town."

"Who was being so indiscreet?"

"I need not name these ladies, but they're very well connected in Ottawa. They enjoy scoring points with the best gossip as much as they do with the best bridge hand. The rumour was that the Polish gold reserves were going to be moved to England by the middle of September."

"You think Sir Randolph was referring to Poland?"

"Who knows? But how many European countries share borders

with potentially belligerent neighbours? And, if this is such a deep secret that Sir Randolph won't name names at Bank of Canada executive meetings, there is a drastic security lapse somewhere. Shouldn't the governor be notified?"

"Probably. Go tell him."

"I can't go tell him!" said Frances. "I'm not on the Executive Committee. I was only at the meeting in the capacity of a substitute minute-taker. I'm not supposed to know what goes on there, really."

"Nonsense!"

"It wouldn't be nonsense to Sir Randolph. Could you tell the governor?"

"That the security of the gold movement might be compromised?"

"Yes. By now he must know the country and the time frame. If you mention Poland and September 15, he'd know if the pieces fit."

"And then what would he do?"

"Well, I don't know! I'm an office clerk, for pity's sake! But in spite of Sir Randolph's cryptic references, this gold movement is not much of a secret around bridge tables here."

"And what the salons of Ottawa know, the governments of certain belligerent powers might know as well?"

"Exactly."

"Okay, McFadden. I'll go see the old boy."

An hour later, Sandy walked into Frances's office and closed the door.

"The governor, that foxy fellow, did not confirm or deny details about Poland or September 15, even to his trusted Director of Research. He felt I was overreacting and that any action to counter the gossip may give it the sound of truth. Which, by the by, suggests to me that it *is* the truth. Anyway, he's the governor, and he thought it best to let sleeping dogs lie."

"That's all?"

"He's quite preoccupied these days. Marriner Eccles from the U.S. Federal Reserve is coming up to Ottawa on the weekend. I've been working on several background papers for their meeting. The governor always looks confident, but I think he feels a little edgy playing host to the big boys."

On Sunday morning, Frances's phone rang at 8:50 a.m. "I'm running a little late, Frances, dear," said Anna Deloitte. "Can you keep the coffee hot until 9:15, and I'll be up then?"

With an extra twenty minutes, Frances had time to race around to Hawley's corner store and get fresh coffee cream. On the way back, she picked up her Saturday mail in the lobby and was looking through the advertising flyers as she waited for the elevator. The elevator door opened and a one-armed man stepped out. He was handsome, and he lifted his fedora to Frances with a slight bow as he passed. Frances watched dumbfounded as he took a coin out of his pocket and wordlessly handed it to Miles, who held the door for him.

Upstairs, Anna Deloitte looked both tired and radiant. "I need my Pride of Arabia strong this morning," she said, sagging into a living room chair.

"A little weary?" commented Frances, whose hand was shaking as she poured the coffee.

"I just heard that a good friend is leaving Ottawa, and I shall miss him."

"Someone from the church?"

"No. It's Max Kessler. He's been in and out of Ottawa since June." There was a smile in Anna Deloitte's eye. "He's spent a good deal of time visiting rural areas trying to drum up interest in Krupp farm machinery.

"Last year, he placed a large order of Krupp products with the Department of Agriculture to try out at their experimental farms across Canada. Tractors and harvesters, and the like. Max says everything has all worked out beyond expectations, but he hasn't been able to generate more orders from local farmers. The equipment is expensive, and the times are still tight. He did get a large order for spare parts with the Department of Agriculture."

"And now he's moving on?"

"Yes. Quite unexpectedly," Anna sighed. "He's been ordered to head west. He's taking the noon train to Toronto to set up a Krupp booth at the Canadian National Exhibition. Then he'll do the fall fairs in London and Windsor before going on to the prairies."

Frances gulped. *There is no noon train to Toronto.*

"Max doesn't have the personality to be a salesman. He isn't pushy enough. He claims Krupp products are the best in the world, and quality should sell itself."

"And then will he return to Germany?"

"And then," said Anna Deloitte with a delightful smile, "watch for a nuptial announcement in the social column in the Ottawa papers! But that is absolutely confidential. Max is quite close to his parents and his sister and worries about them with the uncertainties in Europe these days. I told him that bridge club gossip about the Polish gold reserves being shipped to England mid-September."

Frances's heart, already pounding loudly, almost seized up. "What did he say?"

"He just laughed."

"He laughed? At the Polish concern?"

Mrs. Deloitte reflected as she nibbled a slice of banana nut loaf. "Actually, I think he was laughing at the fact that England would offer to assist the Poles at this point. Max did prep school and university in England. He thinks the British suffer from delusions of grandeur. Nostalgia from their days of Empire. What he said, actually, was, 'Now isn't that just like the British—a dollar short and a day late.' "

A dollar short and a day late.

Frances put a hand to her mouth to stifle a cry.

Anna kept up an amiable chatter as they walked to church. Frances barely heard a word.

The Sunday school children and teachers assembled down in front of the chancel for a blessing, then a processional hymn marched them off to their classes.

"All blessing, thanks, and praise to thee, Lord Jesus Christ be given:
Thou hast our brother deigned to be, our foes in sunder riven."

As they paraded away, Frances rose from her back pew seat and slipped silently out of church by the rear door.

46

OPEN SECRETS

Frances called God's judgment down on shoe manufacturers as she awkwardly raced home in her dress pumps. Perspiring freely, she stumbled through the front door of the Balmoral Arms, into the startled gaze of the doorman.

"Are you all right, Miss McFadden?" Miles asked.

Frances leaned on the elevator button while panting deeply. "Just some nausea, Miles. I didn't want to risk being sick in church. A glass of water and I'll be fine."

Her mind whirred in concert with the elevator motor as she rode up to the seventh floor. *Is Max Kessler a spy? Is Anna Deloitte a spy or an unwitting accomplice? Does it matter that Max Kessler knows about the Polish gold shipment? If he is a spy, why doesn't he care that the gold is being shipped? She had no answers. She only knew one thing for certain from four years of booking travel itineraries for Bank of Canada executives. There was no Sunday noon train to Toronto.*

Frances phoned the desk of the head redcap at Union Station just to make sure. Amos had been a big fan of Mrs. O'Brien's oatmeal and raisin cookies. Frances could hear his wide grin when he answered the phone.

"Miz McFadden! How you doin'? Thing's just fine at the station. Pretty quiet Sunday mornin'."

Herr Kessler from Krupp for the noon train to Toronto?

"No noon passenger train, Miz, but there is a freight. Lemme check." The clock ticked. "Big bunch of wooden crates with Krupp Company stamped all over 'em loaded on the Toronto freight. To be delivered right to the Canadian National Exhibition site. But no Mr. Kessler. Wha' he look like? Tall? Moustache? One-arm fella? Wait a minute." She could hear him call out, "Leon, who dat one-arm fella come by ten minutes ago? Yeah? Yeah?

"Hello, Miz McFadden? One-arm fella just checked in for the New York express. Moustache. Dark hair. Name o' Wagner, though. Yeah. Two big steamer trunks. Booked a sleeper for New York City. Bags checked right through to a liner name o' *Prince Ludwig*, berthed at pier numba five in the New York harbour. Sailin' for Germany tomorrow night. Yeah. Leon see'd the suite confirmation for the ship. Name o' Wagner. Otto Wagner. Ain't many one-arm fellas, Miz McFadden. Maybe you got the name wrong. Yeah. The New York Express pulls out at 12:30. Stops at Montreal and Sherbrooke on the way. Not at all, Miz McFadden. Y'all take care."

Anna Deloitte's fiancé had changed his name and was skipping the country. Either Anna was a marvellous actress, or she was being stood up.

Who was it that said, "Sudden changes in routine would cause concern"?

Frances phoned Inspector Hollingsworth's home number. "Good morning, Inspector. It's Frances McFadden. Just fine, and you? Listen, I'm on my way out, and I have a big soup bone for Beauregard. If you two are walking past the corner of Metcalfe and Somerset in ten minutes I'd be happy to pass it along. Good! See you then."

Now what?

She called Dr. Grace's home number. No answer. Sandy Skelton lived way out in the country past Navan, and she had no idea of his phone number. Frances had never telephoned Governor Towers at home. It seemed such an invasion of privacy. Mrs. Towers answered.

"Oh, yes, Frances. Graham told me you were doing a wonderful job while Miss Briscoe is indisposed. No, he's not here. He was working very late at the Bank last night getting ready for Mr. Eccles's visit and just stayed there."

Frances called the governor's office. No answer. If his bedroom had a separate phone number, she didn't know it. Surely he could hear the phone ringing in his office right next door? She called Murray at Red Line and told him to pick her up at the corner of Metcalfe and Somerset in twenty minutes. Her meeting there with Inspector Hollingsworth and Beauregard was brief.

I hope he doesn't mind my finding him in his pyjamas! thought Frances, as the elevator shot up to the fifth floor. She intentionally banged closed the governor's office door to warn him.

"Governor Towers?" she called, as she approached the open door of the bedroom adjoining his office. He wasn't there. The bed had not been slept in.

Okay . . . not here, not at home . . . Frances went over to his appointment book on his desk. There were several meetings listed for Saturday afternoon; then 7:00 p.m., Château Grill—M.P.

M.P.? Member of Parliament?

It was almost eleven forty-five a.m. She phoned Raymond, the maî-tre d' at the Château, who would be seating early arrivals for lunch.

"Good morning, Raymond; it's Frances McFadden. I'm trying to track down Governor Towers. Is he there? Was he there last night, then? And who was in his party? Oh. And how late did they stay? Was he? Did he? Well, he is very careful about not driving under the influence. Can you connect me to the front desk?

"Hello, Gib. It's Frances McFadden. Some petty bureaucratic thing has come up, and Governor Towers needs to be informed. Do you know if he stayed at the Château last night? Raymond told me he left the dining room quite late in no state to drive, and may have bedded down there. No?"

A desperate thought occurred. "We have booked the King George Suite for the Chairman of the U.S. Federal Reserve, Marriner Eccles and his wife. Didn't know if they were coming in last night or today. Did they register? No? Well, might the governor have used the suite? Oh. It must be the governor. He has a very messy hand." *Even when sober.* "Can you put me through to the suite? Well, it's kind of an emergency. Yes, I understand . . . no, Gib, I don't want you to get fired. Let me think. Okay. Can you connect me with room service?

"Hi, Emile! It's Frances McFadden. I *so* miss those Eggs Benedict you used to bring up to me every morning when I lived at the Château. Listen, have you received a room service request from the King George Suite yet? Oh good! Could I ask you to put a two-word note in with the poached eggs? Thank you, Emile! You're a saint!"

Frances left the door to the governor's office open so she could hear his phone. She picked up Miss Briscoe's phone and called Detective Hollingsworth's office, but he was not in. She gave the governor's office number to the receptionist. Frances paced, then sat down at Miss Briscoe's desk and began to type. In ten minutes, the governor's phone rang.

"Good morning Governor Towers, it's Frances McFadden. I apologize for the intrusion. Something has come up that needs your immediate attention." She listened.

"It's not really a topic for the telephone, sir. Could you come to your office at your earliest convenience? I fully appreciate that, Governor. I have typed out my resignation and placed it on your desk. If I've made a judgment error, then I accept the consequences. Thank you, sir."

At exactly 12:30 p.m., Graham Towers marched briskly into his office. The governor never raised his voice, even when provoked, but his eyes flashed with lightning.

"How did you find me?"

"I phoned your home from my apartment. Your wife said that you had worked late and slept at your office. I phoned your office. No answer, so I came right down." Frances looked through the adjoining door at the unused bed. "Then, I checked your appointment book, which led me to the Château Laurier. The front desk told me that the Eccleses had not checked in yet, but the King George Suite had been signed for, although they couldn't make out the signature. The front desk would not override the 'do not disturb' directive to put a call through."

"Did you tell my wife where I was?"

"What business would that be of mine?"

The governor sat down and lit a cigarette. "So, Miss McFadden, what makes 'Culloden File' a side dish for my poached eggs?"

"It's the Polish gold," she answered, and related the details. Ever the orderly man, Graham Towers pulled out a pad and began making notes.

When she finished, he said, "Do I have this correct?

"One. The RCMP are interested in a Krupp tractor salesman named Kessler.

"Two. Kessler is the same one-armed chap that Scotland Yard alerted Sir Randolph Buckley about.

"Three. Kessler is a camera enthusiast and has a great deal of film developed locally, as well as sending film regularly to a processing lab in Düsseldorf.

"Four. Kessler tells his fiancée that he is travelling to western Canada on business, but instead, assumes the name of Otto Wagner and takes a train to New York, to connect tomorrow with an ocean liner to Hamburg.

"Five. Kessler has heard of the Polish gold export to England planned for mid-September.

"Six. He finds this rumour amusing.

"Seven. Your Inspector Hollingsworth will try to have a look at Herr Kessler/Wagner's luggage before it leaves Canada."

Graham Towers leaned back and blew a series of perfect smoke rings. "Very circumstantial. Could be just a series of coincidences." He drummed on his desk with his fingers for a moment, then added, "But I think we should get a round table set up just in case. Would you mind calling up all the members of the Contingency Coordinating Committee? Get them down here for, say," he looked at his watch, "three this afternoon? I have a cracking headache and need a shower. Can you order in lots of coffee? Thank you, Miss McFadden, for all of this." He ripped her resignation in two and dropped it in the wastepaper basket.

Major Stenson from the Department of Defence was out taking target practice at the Connaught Ranges, and Alex Binkley from the Department of Trade was in Chicago, but the other four all assembled in the boardroom at 3:00 p.m. Frances related, again, the series of events.

"So it's not so much that a suspected German agent learns that the Poles are trying to covertly move their gold out next month," said Edward Jackson from External Affairs. "It's that he's so dismissive of the news."

"Exactly," commented the governor. "Now *why* don't the Germans care?"

"They've got lots of gold, and don't need any more?" suggested Sandy Skelton.

"*A dollar short and a day late,*" echoed Sydney Turk. "Sounds to me that by September fifteenth, the fate of the Polish gold reserves will already be sealed."

"You think the German army will be in Warsaw by then?" asked Jackson.

"That's my guess."

"So what can we do? Send them a telegram to watch out and hurry up?" asked Sydney.

"Didn't your Inspector Hollingsworth say that any public form of communication—telephone, telegraph, even the mail—may be compromised?" asked Sandy.

Frances nodded.

"Governor," said Dr. Grace, "did Montague Norman at the Bank of England specifically name Poland and the September 15 date to you?"

"He did."

"And you told no one?"

"No one. Until this very minute."

"Then," added Dr. Grace, "this rumour has come from somewhere outside the Bank. How about Sir Randolph Buckley?"

"Are you suggesting that the British High Commissioner is a German agent?" exclaimed Edward Jackson.

"I think that unlikely," replied the governor. "But somewhere in his information chain from his own government, or the Bank of England, or the Polish National Bank, there's been a leak."

"Therefore," concluded Sandy, "whatever our plan is, it shouldn't use any of those channels."

"What is our plan?" asked Sydney.

"The logical man to deal with this is Scotty Meldrum," said the governor. "He's in Switzerland, as close to being on the scene as we've got."

"And he'd certainly know what's-his-name, the Governor of the Bank of Poland?"

"Byrka. Vladyslaw Byrka," said the governor.

"Who would be right there at the same Bank of International Settlements meetings in Basel," said Sydney.

"So we tell Scotty to put the word in the ear of Governor Byrka? And that's it?"

"Scotty is very resourceful," smiled Graham Towers. "He thrives on logistical challenges. This is right up his alley. I feel perfectly comfortable leaving everything to him and Byrka."

"Scotty may need an operating budget," said Dr. Grace.

"True, we can send him a cashier's cheque. Are there any other Canadians in the area for logistical support?"

"Frances, can you call around to the Momsies and see if they know who we might have on the ground in Europe?"

By four-thirty, Frances had only one lead. The Department of Agriculture had a small team visiting Poland and the Ukraine.

At 4:45, Inspector Hollingsworth of the RCMP phoned in. Twenty minutes later, he was ushered into the Bank's boardroom. After introductions, he made his report. "My men found forty-six black canisters of unexposed film secreted away beneath a false bottom of Herr Kessler's steamer trunk. They only had time to develop about a dozen rolls. His tastes seem to run to factories, steel mills, harbours, train stations, and power plants all over Eastern Canada. Very meticulous. A photo collection that would be very handy for saboteurs. Curiously, there were also a dozen red canisters of film. My fellows developed half of these. They appeared to show German factories and munitions plants."

"Well, Inspector?" asked the governor.

"Forty-six rolls of film of sabotage targets are not circumstantial. Kessler could only be conducting espionage reconnaissance. Throw in his false trail heading west, his name change and his quick departure for Germany, and the case against him is pretty solid."

"Did you arrest him?"

"No. We didn't want to tip our hand."

"Won't he figure out something when he discovers the film gone?"

"We left the film where we found it."

"You left the film!"

"My men exposed all the undeveloped film to the light. It's ruined. They also carefully replaced the rolls they developed with lengths of spoiled film."

Sydney Turk returned them to the question at hand. "So how do we get to the deputy governor in Basel if we can't telegraph? Does Scotty have the new code books? "

"They haven't passed Exec yet," said the governor, "so he wouldn't have taken a set."

"We could telegraph him to expect 'the Culloden File' by courier," said Frances. "That should clue him in to at least stay put in Basel."

"You know," said Jackson, "Pan American Airways has just started a new trans-Atlantic air service from New York to Marseilles. We could fly someone over and get the jump on Herr Kessler."

"But who?" asked the governor. "Eccles and his people from the Federal Reserve will be pulling into Union Station any minute now. I can't bow out, and I need Sandy, Sydney, and Dr. Grace here for the next three days of meetings."

"Well, don't look at me," said Jackson. "We're trying to hash out emergency evacuation procedures for all our European embassies."

Frances was scribbling furiously to keep up with the minutes. It was thirty seconds into the silence before she looked up to see the four men staring at her.

"You must be joking!" she exclaimed. "I get motion sickness on the Ferris wheel at the Ex. I can't fly to France! I'd die!"

47

TRANSATLANTIC

"Sydney," said the governor, "book a sleeper for Miss McFadden on the next express train to New York. Then call Pan American Airways for the first possible clipper connection to Marseilles."

"Now," he said, returning to Frances, "you'll need two cover stories."

"Two?" Frances felt weightless, like Alice falling down the rabbit hole.

"Yes. You'll need a back-story to explain to people in Ottawa why you're not around, and a front-story to explain why a young woman is travelling to Europe alone."

Sydney snapped his fingers. "Our district offices are having difficulties with the new Bank operating procedures manual. Frances could be travelling across the country sorting out the problems."

"Yes!" exclaimed the governor. "We could say that you're running training sessions from Toronto to Vancouver. That should cover your absence for at least three weeks."

"I don't lie to people," stated Frances flatly. A favourite homily of her mother's had been *Oh what a tangled web we weave when first we practise to deceive.*

"What if you said: 'There are problems understanding the new procedures manual. I've got to leave town for two to three weeks on Bank business.' Both sentences are true. If people think they're somehow related, well . . ."

"We need a good front-story, too," said Dr. Grace. "Bank clerks don't fly to Europe these days. Airfare is exorbitant. You're bound to raise eyebrows."

"Well, if it's too expensive," said Frances desperately, "perhaps I shouldn't—"

"Let's remember," cut in Sandy, "the prize here is forty million dollars. The airfare is peanuts."

Frances felt herself slipping toward capitulation. "We could build on this parts purchase by the Department of Agriculture," she said. "They bought all those new tractors and combines from Krupp last year. Now the new D.M. at Agriculture wants to lay in a five years' supply of spare parts. He has a team in Europe trying to close the deal, and get the parts on a freighter. However, the Krupp factory now wants cash up front due to the uncertain times."

"This could work," agreed the governor. "You can be taking over the certified bank draft to expedite the sale."

Sydney hung up the phone. "F. McFadden has a sleeper booked to New York Tuesday. She arrives Wednesday, and catches Thursday's Pan Am Dixie Clipper for Marseilles."

"How long does the flight take?" asked Frances.

"Couple of days. You're scheduled to arrive in Marseilles at seven Saturday evening."

Forty-eight hours of motion sickness?

"It's still five days faster than sailing," added Sandy. "By the way, do you have a will?"

"A will! I don't own anything willable."

Eyebrows shot up.

"Come, Miss McFadden. Your fashionable wardrobe? Your furnished penthouse at the Balmoral Arms?" said Sandy.

"Well, I don't have a will, and I'm busy right now trying to flee the country."

"Draft it right here. It just has to say something like 'I, Frances McFadden, being of sound mind and body, do hereby bequeath all my worldly assets to . . . whomever.' Perfectly legal, as long as it's dated and witnessed, and in your own hand."

In five minutes, the will was written, witnessed, and sealed in a stamped envelope addressed to Mr. Morningstar, naming him executor, and instructing him to divide her estate into four equal shares with Mary Bedford, the Deavy sisters, and the Presbyterian Church Missions as beneficiaries.

"Okay, now, operating funds. You should carry American dollars, Swiss francs, and British pounds. They are all easily convertible into other currencies as the need arises. Say, three thousand Canadian of each for expenses and contingencies."

"Nine thousand dollars in cash!" exclaimed Frances.

"I'll find out what Agriculture requires to close their deal on the tractor parts," added the governor, "and we'll give you a bank draft to cover it."

"And I'm just going to put all this money in my handbag?"

"When I travel on business," said the governor, "I wear a moneybelt under my shirt."

"Can't go," said Frances. "Don't have a moneybelt."

"Borrow mine," said the governor, searching through the bottom drawer of his desk. "Here it is."

"I don't own any travel luggage," said Frances. "I'll look like a hobo using my mother's hand-me-down suitcase."

"You can borrow my wife's luggage. We won't be going anywhere in the next month," said the governor.

Sandbagged.

On Monday, Frances cleared her desk and spread the back-cover story around the office, with nary a raised eyebrow. Mary would tell the Deavys. That night, Frances asked Gladys Gilhooly to inform the Balmoral crowd.

At ten Tuesday morning, Miles called up to say that Murray from Red Line had arrived. He kept the cab running on Sparks Street while Frances went in to pick up her travelling money and the bank draft. The governor gave her a reassuring smile. "This is a courageous thing you're doing. Don't let it frighten you."

"I feel much more secure now that I have my will updated, and I'm carrying over a hundred thousand dollars lashed to my stomach."

He chuckled. "Oh, I almost forgot." He extracted a small bottle from his suit coat pocket. "My wife also suffers from motion sickness. She recommended that you eat lightly, drink lots of water, and take one of these pills every four hours in transit."

The scenery from the train was beautiful, and Frances relaxed for the first time in two days. The Mohican rolled into Grand Central Station right on time Wednesday morning. She telephoned Pan American Airways from her hotel room, and the next morning, a burgundy limousine called for her. The liveried driver deposited her two bags in a cavernous trunk and politely declined the tip. At the St. Regis, they picked up a young couple who introduced themselves as Dorothy and Clarence Marshall. They had just married, and were so moon-eyed that they sought no information from Frances beyond her name.

At the marine air terminal, a smiling attendant checked them in, and directed them up a spiral ramp to a lounge overlooking Long Island Sound. A dozen passengers were seated comfortably around the spacious room. A snappily dressed cocktail waitress came over with a plate of hors d'oeuvres and a tray of champagne glasses. The Marshalls giggled, and took a glass in each hand. Frances asked for ice water. She walked over and looked out the window. A huge airplane, like a whale with wings, sat there, tethered to the dock. Men were moving luggage and supplies down a gangway.

At eleven o'clock, a handsome man in uniform introduced himself as Lionel, the flight's head steward. "Let me give you a brief orientation to our home for the next two days," he smiled.

"The Pan American Airways Dixie Clipper is one of six Boeing B-314s currently in passenger service. This is the largest airplane ever to fly. We offer every service you would find on a luxury ocean liner, and get you to Marseilles five days quicker. The plane is powered by four Wright "Double Cyclone" fourteen-cylinder air-cooled engines. We normally cruise at 120 miles per hour."

"How high do we fly?" someone asked.

"The Clipper can reach 19,600 feet, but we would only go that high to get above thunderstorms. Normally we fly at about 500 feet above the waves."

"What if an engine quits on us?" a woman asked.

"Each engine is fully tested before every flight. However, should anything that unlikely happen, the plane is essentially a flying boat, and can always land on the water.

"We're refuelling every 2,800 miles, in Bermuda, the Azores, and Lisbon en route to Marseilles. You're welcome to get off and walk around when we dock. We're normally ready to take off again in about three hours.

"We're heading out today with seventeen passengers. A couple will be travelling in the honeymoon suite at the rear of the plane. They've asked that you kindly respect their privacy.

"The plane is set up in compartments, much like a train. The dining room is small, so there will be two sittings at each meal."

Frances shared a compartment with three businessmen. Mr. Eck was a railroad man from Alabama, Mr. Franklin was the vice-president of American Steamship Lines, and Mr. Leonard was an investment banker from New York. Mr. Leonard asked the other two men if flying boats would put them out of business.

"Trains been around a lot longer than planes, sir. Hard to move coal or sugar cane on this rig," drawled Mr. Eck.

"Yes," added Mr. Franklin. "If the Depression didn't kill the boat lines, I don't think this itty-bitty little flea will. Our flagship carries four hundred passengers. I don't know how Pan American covers expenses with seventeen paying customers."

"This your first flight, Miss?" asked Mr. Eck.

"Yes," said Frances. "I'm quite excited."

"I've flown ten times already," replied Mr. Eck. "It's my new hobby. This is my first flight over water."

Frances took her meals at the second sitting. Her tablemates were a Belgian diplomat and two New York sisters who were travelling without their husbands. Mrs. Getty was fortyish, and fatigued. Her sister, Mrs. Forbes, was younger and bouncy. Mrs. Forbes leaned forward and whispered, "Any rumours from your compartment about the occupants of the honeymoon suite?"

"Oh, Dolly, don't be a bore over dinner," said her sister.

"Well," continued Dolly, "one of the Frenchmen in our compartment swears the man is a Hollywood actor! Saw him boarding the plane and recognized the face, but couldn't remember the name. Not a lead actor. He described him as 'the guy who always gets killed in the gangster movies.' I'm dying to know who it is! The stewards are sworn to secrecy."

"Just like your own servants, Dolly," put in her sister.

"Well, it must be someone famous, or why the mystery? And that big man sitting by their cabin door must be their bodyguard."

"Dolly, you are unbearably dramatic."

Frances was amazed at what a divine meal could be served up from a galley kitchen in a flying machine. The entrée of their four-course meal was sautéed scallops of fresh duck foie gras with hearts of endive. This wasn't Rochester Street.

To circumvent the pre-bedding-down washroom rush, Frances headed to the rear of the plane early. A large man with a patient face was sitting outside the door to the honeymoon suite, reading a magazine. He looked up briefly when Frances turned in to the women's restroom. Teeth brushed and face washed, she was leaving the restroom when the door to the honeymoon suite opened. A striking young blonde stood in the doorway beside an older man. Seeing Frances, she grabbed the man's arm. Her eyes purred.

"Recognize him, sweetie?"

"Yes," replied Frances, and the coquette's face lit with a victory smile.

The man gazed quietly at Frances from deep-set eyes.

"Recognize me?" asked Frances.

The coquette pursed her lips and scrutinized her carefully, before saying, "Nope."

"My advantage then, I'd say. Sweetie," returned Frances.

The man burst into a deep, gravelly caw, which drew glances from the forward compartments.

"Touché, kid, touché," he said.

To cut short the coquette's sulk, the man said, "May I introduce Mrs. Smith?"

"And may I introduce *Mister* Smith," responded the coquette, eyes twinkling.

"And this is Joe Moss," added Mr. Smith, gesturing to the man with the magazine. "He's my assistant."

The coquette giggled. Joe Moss nodded silently to Frances.

"Pleased to meet you, Mr. and Mrs. Smith," Frances said. She turned to the seated man and returned the nod. "Mr. Moss."

"And you're . . . ?" asked the man.

Frances paused, then said, "Miss . . . Smith."

The man cackled again. "Checkmate!" he said. "Pleased to make your acquaintance, Miss Smith. Hope you're enjoying your flight."

Frances wasn't back in her seat thirty seconds before Dolly Forbes and her sister, pretending to be reluctant, plunked themselves down across from her.

"Well?" asked Dolly, "was that who I think it was? His hair is longer than it was in *The Petrified Forest*."

"He introduced himself as Mr. Smith," replied Frances.

"That's not his wife!" said Dolly. "I've seen their pictures in the movie mags lots of times. His wife is some belligerent woman named Mayo something. They're always getting into fights in restaurants." She looked at Frances with a new respect. "Are you intimately acquainted?"

Frances reflected. "Acquainted, but not intimate."

The flight to Bermuda was uneventful. Molly Towers's pills worked their magic. Frances stayed away from the windows, and other than being aware of the sound of the engines, had little sense of flying at all. Two hours into the flight to the Azores, Joe Moss stuck his head into the dining compartment. "Looking for a fourth for bridge. Interested, Miss?" he asked.

"Oh, I play bridge," exclaimed Dolly Forbes with a bright smile. "So do I," Mrs. Getty threw in.

Joe Moss eyed them both, then turned back to Frances. "Miss?" he asked again. Frances followed Joe Moss to the back of the plane under envious stares. The honeymoon suite was spacious and opulent. A large bed. A private bathroom. An ebony dining room table that sat four comfortably, where a deck of cards was splayed like a slash across the dark wood. They drew for partners, and Frances drew Joe Moss.

"Uh-uh," said Mr. Smith. "This ain't gonna work." He sat down across from Frances. "Mrs. Smith and I have enough to fight about, without being partners at bridge."

The blonde was good at cards. Slow to play, but made few mistakes. The man was a swashbuckler, and would bid on almost nothing. Lionel came in regularly to freshen drinks and replenish the bridge mixture. There was little small talk during play. Betsy Knowles would have approved. At six o'clock, Lionel whispered in the man's ear.

"Lionel is preparing dinner, and wants to know if you'd like to join us," the man asked Frances with a smile. His mahogany voice had a delicious cadence. The blonde shot him a sharp look through narrowed eyes.

"Thank you, no," said Frances. She rose to go.

"Would you like to play again tomorrow?"

Frances checked the blonde again, who gave a neutral sideways jerk of her chin.

"If you feel up to it," said Frances, and let herself out the stateroom door.

Her dinner companions were dying for information.

"What's the suite like?"

"Did you talk about the movies?"

"Who's the woman?"

"The suite is very well appointed. We played serious bridge, and there wasn't much small talk. They're all good card players."

The disappointed looks of chastised children stared back at her from around the table.

The next day, they refuelled in the Azores. Later, Joe Moss invited Frances down for another rubber. The blonde was moodier this time. Her hands were poor, and she lost interest after an hour. "This is no fun," she said, throwing her cards down on the table.

The man apologized with his eyes. "Care for a drink?" he asked.

"Maybe a ginger ale," replied Frances.

"Don't drink the hard stuff?"

"I have a delicate constitution. I was warned against indulgences during the flight."

"Never flown before?" he asked.

"No."

"You're not an American, are you?" the man said.

"No," said Frances.

"Howdja know that?" asked the blonde, examining Frances for some clue that she had missed.

"Just the way Miss Smith carries herself, and her careful enunciation."

"What are ya then?" asked the blonde. "You're not British."

"Canadian."

"Never been to Canada," said the man. "What's it like?"

"It's cold in the winter, but otherwise pleasant."

"Canadians don't seem very curious about the movie business," said the blonde, lighting a cigarette. "Ya got movie theatres up there?"

"We do."

"Seen anything he was in?" asked the blonde, jerking a thumb at the man.

"Yes. I've seen *San Quentin* and *Kid Galahad*."

"Whatcha think?" asked the blonde with an impish grin that was quite attractive.

"I'm not a very good judge of movies," replied Frances. "I like them all."

The blonde wrinkled her nose. "You must find some better than others."

"If it makes me forget how cold the winter is, I rate it good entertainment."

"We're getting off in Lisbon," said the man, changing the subject. "You?"

"No. I'm going on to Marseilles."

"Woo," said Joe Moss. "Rough town. Been there once too often."

The man and woman laughed at a private joke on Joe Moss.

"Business or pleasure?" asked the man.

"Business."

The man smiled. "You don't look like the business type," he said.

Frances smiled back. "Good. Maybe I'll catch them off guard."

"Business ever take you to California?" the man asked. "The winters are warm."

"No."

"So we'll probably never see each other again," said the man.

"She'll see lots of you, honey," smiled the blonde.

"Probably true," agreed Frances.

"And what will you remember?" asked the man.

"I'll remember that you never had the ace and king of the suit you bid," said Frances. "The same way my mother used to play bridge."

"I remind you of your mother?" the man asked.

"Yes," said Frances.

He slapped the table with his hand, his raw-throated guffaw as loud as the engines.

48

BASEL

In mid-morning, Lionel came around to announce that Portugal could be seen out the port-side windows, and even Frances felt compelled to risk a look. The relentless monotony of the rippling grey Atlantic had seemed endless. She had felt cocooned in a suspended space between continents, never anywhere, but always in between. It was a relief to see the jagged, wave-washed headlands of Cabo Raso.

The Boeing B–314 crossed the Lisbon harbour breakwater and dropped gull-like into the Rio Tejo estuary near the Doca Dos Bicos. Mr. and Mrs. Smith went public at last, nodding politely on the dock before a waiting car whisked them north on the coast road. Only the newlyweds, Mr. Eck, and Mr. Franklin were going on to Marseilles with Frances.

In the Pan American office, Mr. Eck asked the attendant to wire ahead to Marseilles for a reservation at the Metropole Hotel. As he turned to go, Frances asked, "Do you recommend the Metropole?"

"Well, li'l miss, it's no five-star joint, but it's right across the street from the train station, and I'm catchin' the Paris express first thing tomorrow morning."

"Good enough for me," said Frances. She also asked the Pan Am hostess to book her out Sunday morning on the first train to Basel. Mr. Eck had picked up a day-old copy of the *Paris Herald Tribune* in the waiting room. A bold headline announced the signing of the Russo-German non-aggression pact on August 22.

The newly minted Mrs. Marshall peeked over his shoulder to read it. "Oh, that's a relief," she said. "Momma and Poppa were worried we'd get mixed up in something over here that might ruin our honeymoon."

Mr. Eck snorted. "The only thing this guarantees," he said, thwacking the headline with his index finger, "is that the Reds and the Nazis gonna have Poland for lunch. Wouldn't head to Warsaw on your honeymoon trip if I were you."

"What about the French and the British?" asked Frances. "Didn't I read that they have treaties with Poland?"

"Good question, girlie," replied Mr. Eck. "This Mr. Hitler, he's been slicing off li'l bitty bits of countries for the last five years. The Saar, then Austria, then the Sudeten, and now he's lickin' his chops at that Polish corridor. Now, I'm a Quaker, and I don't believe in fightin', but if nobody stands up to this Mr. Hitler and says 'Whoa, boy,' well, he jus' goin'ta keep on eatin' countries up till there's nothin' left."

The sun was just setting when the Marseilles harbour appeared out the airplane windows. An off-shore breeze made for a very bumpy landing. Two small French tugs had trouble getting lines aboard the plane in the swell, and it was dark as they disembarked on the quay. Frances shared a cab to the Metropole with Mr. Eck.

"Wouldn't walk 'round these streets on your own, li'l miss."

"I'm exhausted," Frances said. "I just want a hot bath."

Frances's tickets to Basel were waiting at reception. The train departed at 10:00 a.m., via Lyon to Geneva and Berne, and wouldn't get in until late. She sent a warning cable to Scotty Meldrum:

Arriving Basel 9:00 p.m. Sunday with Culloden File. McFadden.

It would have been amusing to surprise him, but she felt circumstances wouldn't allow her the indulgence.

The next morning, a bellman carried her luggage across the street and guided her through the mammoth Marseilles train station to the first-class lounge. The train was slowed up crossing the border into Switzerland, and again outside Berne, where they were shunted to a siding while two long freights passed on the main line. The Basel train station was almost deserted when she disembarked shortly after ten-thirty p.m. An elderly redcap put her suitcases on a small dolly and led her to the taxi stand in front of the station.

The lobby of the Intercontinental Hotel had an old-world grandeur to it. Jazz music leaked through some frosted glass doors off the lobby. Frances was exhausted after six days of travel across six time zones. The fortune wrapped tightly around her waist in the sweaty moneybelt was an added burden. There was no answer when the front desk rang Scotty Meldrum's room. *Where could the man possibly be at eleven o'clock at night?* Then the concierge handed over her key, and a message. It said simply "*Cherchez le* Macallan."

Frances blinked. "Do you have a bar?" she asked.

"*Oui, mademoiselle,*" he replied, and pointed in the direction of the jazz music.

Frances swung the door open into an expansive lounge. It was almost empty, but a dozen people were clustered around two tables down front. Three couples were dancing. Scotty Meldrum, looking like a bear doing an absurd mockery of the tango, was dancing with a tall red-headed woman in a backless dress. Frances got to the table just as the music stopped with a crescendo and Scotty Meldrum had the laughing woman up off her feet, as though he was about to flip her over his shoulder.

"Frances McFadden!" he called out, dropping the woman back to earth with a jolt. "Let me introduce you to some marvellous people!" It was a bankers' crowd, but there was no one from the National Bank of Poland.

"Waiter! More champagne and a glass for the lady," Scott sang out, as the music started up again. "Come, Miss McFadden!" He dragged her out on the dance floor to "The Tennessee Waltz." "So good to see a Canadian!" he said, giving her a big hug.

"Mr. Meldrum, I am exhausted. And we have to talk. Privately."

"There is nothing quite as private as a public space," he replied as he whirled her around the empty dance floor. He was quite light on his feet for such a big man. "What's new?"

"Well, there's a back story, and a front story, and the real story. Where would you like me to begin?"

"How did you get here so fast? I just got the Culloden telegram from the governor a few days ago."

"I flew from New York."

"You flew! Across the Atlantic! That costs a fortune!"

"It was not cheap, but compared to some other fortunes, it was deemed a justified expense."

"Ah!" nodded Scotty. "The Polish gold."

"Very good, Deputy Governor. You figured it out. Maybe I didn't need to come all this way after all."

"Vlady Byrka was with us until about ten, then begged out," replied Scotty. "This Russo-German treaty has finished him, or finished the National Bank of Poland, he figures. He's heading to Warsaw tomorrow to see what can be salvaged. He's worried that September fifteenth is too late to move his gold reserves out."

"I'd say he's right about that," said Frances. "We need to talk to him tonight."

"Think so? What d'ya know?"

After two more dances, Scotty returned to the party. "Alas, dear friends, Miss McFadden has brought me homework and insists that I deal with it before I'm completely incapacitated." He laughed at the thought, and the others in his group sighed at losing the life of the party. "See you all at the final banquet tomorrow." Scotty waved cheerily. "Adieu, adieu!"

Vladyslaw Byrka was a distinguished-looking man with a large forehead. His unruly grey hair and deep-set eyes reminded Frances of Beethoven. He listened silently while Scotty retold Frances's story.

"Now, that's the bad news, Vlad," summarized Scotty. "The good news is that McFadden and I are here to help you out."

Governor Byrka smiled. "It's good to have friends," he said. "Ten German panzer divisions against Byrka, Meldrum, and McFadden. That should even the odds."

"This can't be that big a surprise, or you wouldn't have contacted the Bank of Canada in the first place," said Scotty. "What's the situation in Warsaw?"

Governor Byrka sat back with his eyes half-closed. He looked as tired as Frances felt. "The Polish government began to make contingency plans about a year ago. There are abandoned coal mines in the Carpathian Mountains down near the Romanian border. The government has built a series of bunkers there as a strategic retreat in the event of a German incursion. Two months ago, departments began to ship records and archives down there so they could carry on if we were forced to leave Warsaw.

"President Moscicki wanted me to move the gold reserves there. I never liked the idea. Boxed into the mountains with the Romanians between us and the sea? Dudek, the Finance Minister, was even more insistent on the move. He knew about our negotiations with the Bank of England, but didn't believe the British would last any longer than we would against a German offensive. Montague Norman told me that the Bank of England didn't have room for our gold. I used his good offices to inquire about moving our account right to Ottawa."

He paused for a moment. "With Dudek pestering me relentlessly, I feigned a move of the gold south to the Carpathians."

"You faked the move?" exclaimed Scotty.

"Yes. In early July, a convoy of ten trucks drove into the courtyard of the National Bank in Warsaw and left with a hundred crates under heavy guard. Today, a hundred crates of rock sit in a mine shaft, south of

Sanok, still under heavy guard. The gold is in the basement stockroom of the National Bank in unmarked boxes, under some tarpaulins next to the cleaning supplies. The vault is empty."

"You don't trust your own Finance Minister?"

Governor Byrka smiled again. "Mr. Meldrum, the Polish political situation has all the hues and substance of a rainbow—as colourful as it is ephemeral. The Polish nation has a long history as a culture, but limited experience as a country. For hundreds of years, our identity has been subjugated by Russians and Austrians and Germans. Polish self-government is less than twenty years old, a gift of the Versailles Treaty of 1919.

"Extracting ourselves clear of foreign imperialism to build a modern, Canadian-style democracy has been a challenge. Do I trust the Finance Minister? I trust that he thinks he is acting in the national interest. But what is the national interest? A Polish thesaurus would have to define 'patriot' twenty different ways to cover the breadth of parties, factions, movements, and associations that currently exist. My countrymen are not simple-minded people. Perhaps that is why they harbour such a wide range of strongly held opinions.

"Some say, 'The Germans are coming anyway; why not just accept it and plan a rapprochement?' Others hate the Germans and think the Russians are our best hope. Communism is so completely opposed to fascism that Poland would have a natural alliance there. But Polish capitalists, justifiably, do not want to be eliminated by Communist doctrine. And as for the large Jewish minority, well, many are successful businessmen, and Communism is anathema to them, but they are also Jews, and they know how they would fare with the Nazis.

"Then there are the Polish patriots who wrap themselves in the flag and are capable of any romantic folly. Within the Bank of Poland, within every government department, the army and the church, subsets of all these divergent opinions exist.

"That's just the people of principle. There are significant German and Ukrainian minorities in Poland. Where does their loyalty lie? Would they betray Poland for their own ethnic interest?

"And this is not to mention the criminal element. Street hooligans are taking advantage of unsettled times. Petty crime is rampant."

"So," asked Scotty, "who can you rely on?"

"Exactly the Polish predicament," smiled the governor. "Finally, next to all those political philosophies is the most basic of human desires—survival. Poland is a victim of its geography. If either the Germans or the Russians hold the hammer, who wants to be the nail?

"Beck, the Foreign Minister, has signed treaties with everybody—enough protocols to paper a house. Will it save us in the end?"

"But you have an army! Any Pole I've met has a great pride in his heritage. Surely they'll make a fight of it?"

"Pride does not stop tanks or fighter planes, Mr. Meldrum. My brother is an officer in the Polish cavalry. They have twenty thousand mounted hussars. The German cavalry is mounted in panzer tanks. My brother is brave and is very fond of brandishing his sword and saying, 'Let them come!' Should the weather be bad, and the tanks get mired in the mud, we might last six weeks. But if the Russians move in from the east while the Germans attack from the west, we will be crushed between the hammer and the anvil."

"A helluva mess, Vlad," commiserated Scotty, "but we can still help, if we move fast."

Vladyslaw Byrka looked bleak. "I have outsmarted myself by not moving the gold earlier. I built the National Bank as a fortress to protect the nation's treasure. The Vistula River forms a moat on two sides. The state police headquarters is across the street on the west, and the National Armoury faces our north wall. That sounds secure, but it brings the two main Polish political factions into play. 'The colonels,' comrades of the late president, Marshall Pilsudski, have their headquarters in that armoury. The 'Castle Group,' who support the current president, Moscicki, controls the state police. Neither group trusts the other. Nothing moves out of the bank without the army and the police knowing. The gold is trapped.

"Anyway, as soon as the first tank shows up at the gate of the National Bank, I'm a dead man. It doesn't matter if the gold is there, or in a coal mine, or at the bottom of the Atlantic."

Scotty Meldrum would not be daunted. "Vlad, having the gold safe to help rebuild Poland would be a wonderful legacy." He leaned forward and starting ticking things off with his fingers. "Okay," he said, "What do we know for sure? Dudek, your Finance Minister, thinks the gold is in a coal mine in the Carpathians. What does President Moscicki know?"

"He thinks we are shipping the gold out on September fifteenth via Paris, to the Bank of England."

"Does he know where the gold is?"

"He doesn't want to know."

"Who knows the gold is still in the basement of the Bank?"

"Besides me? Only the treasurer, Horowitz, and the four night watchmen."

"Are they reliable?"

"Absolutely. Horowitz is Jewish with a business background. He hates the Nazis and the Communists equally."

"And the watchmen?"

"They have all been with me since the Bank opened fifteen years ago. They are fiercely loyal. They think we should bring in small arms and defend the gold to the last man, then dynamite the place if the doors are broken down."

"Now," continued Scotty, "if bridge players in Ottawa are talking about moving your gold to England, there's a leak somewhere. And if the suspected spy Kessler, or Wagner, or whatever his name is, knows about it, we have to assume the Nazis know as well. Right?"

"Right."

"If the Germans know that September fifteenth is moving day, and aren't worried about it, they must plan to be in Warsaw by then."

"That's a safe guess."

"And it would probably take them at least two weeks to get there. Every farm and hedgerow will be fiercely defended. So," summarized Scotty, "we have two simple tasks. Sneak thirty tons of gold out of the National Bank basement, then get it out of Poland before September first."

"It's August twenty-eighth," said Frances. "We've got three days."

Scotty yawned and looked at his watch. It was almost three a.m. "I'm starting to fade a bit. Things always look brighter in the morning. Let's have a fresh kick at it then. Breakfast at seven-thirty?"

49

WARSAW

Frances staggered into the ornate dining room for breakfast after four hours' sleep. Scotty was holding forth with a group at the buffet table. He looked fresh as a daisy.

"Miss McFadden! Let me introduce you to my fellow bankers from Berlin."

The short, balding president of the Deutsche Reichbank, Walther Funk, was surrounded by a blond stockade of dark suits. All wore Nazi Party pins in their lapels; tall Nazis who bowed courteously as they shook her hand. Another shortcoming of Vera McFadden's parenting. She had neglected to teach her daughters how to make small talk with Nazis. It was a lot to face before the first coffee.

"Now, Walther, Miss McFadden has brought the news that some Canadians with our Department of Agriculture are stuck up in Warsaw at the Agricultural Exhibition, trying to close a deal on a Krupp purchase for our farmers back home. There is some bureaucratic mix-up, so we have to go up and sort things out. Bloody nuisance, but shouldn't take long. Then, could we stop in Berlin on our way home, and have you show us around the Reichbank?"

"Of course!" smiled the president.

Scotty leaned in and lowered his voice. "You know, they sent Holmes over from the Bank of England to help us start up. The man had *no* understanding of continental banking practices at all! We're in need of a lot of good ideas."

"We'll be happy to help in any way," continued the pudgy president. Eye flutterings amongst his entourage conveyed polite impatience to get on to breakfast.

Frances sat down and inhaled her first coffee of the day. "We're going to Berlin?"

"No, no, my dear girl. Just laying a little trail. The Germans need to know a reason why we're suddenly going to Warsaw. Now that they have one, and expect us back in Berlin, they won't need to worry about the merry little Canadians. Funk is as hard-line Nazi as I've ever met, and the rest of his blondie boys are certainly not bankers. They're in Basel doing pre-annexation reconnaissance. Our travel itinerary will be on the wire back to Nazi headquarters before you've finished your coffee. Fortunately, they see Canada as far away and far from significant. And," Scotty smiled a toothy grin, "they think I'm a buffoon! Me mother used to say, 'The easiest way to be smarter than ye look is to act dumber than ye are.'"

Scotty stopped to load his fork with sausage and egg. "Telegraph the Bank of Canada with our plans. Assume that every phone call and telegraph will be monitored by friend and foe alike. Now, who are these Canadians in Warsaw?"

Frances opened her notebook. "Three men from the Department of Agriculture. There's a barley specialist named Bailey, and a man named Doyle who is researching wheat seed that germinates quickly in cold climates. Then there's a mechanical engineer named Roderick, who's there to make sure this parts shipment is finalized. Agriculture did a big purchase of Krupp farm equipment last year, and have been testing it out all across the country. Works great. The deputy minister wants to lay in a generous supply of spare parts in case there's any trade disruption with Germany."

"Very prudent. How big is the deal?"

"A hundred thousand, Canadian. Misunderstanding about payment. Department of Agriculture assumed 'delivery' meant 'received in Canada,' as was the case with the equipment shipped last year. The Krupp people now insist that delivery means, 'we hand over the crates in Warsaw, you hand over the money.'" But the Aggies don't want to pay for goods that might be impounded for years in a belligerent country."

"Why in the world is this transaction between the Canadian Department of Agriculture and a German manufacturer taking place in Warsaw?"

"The paperwork dragged on and on in Ottawa. That's why Herr Kessler/Wagner was there for so long. Suddenly, there has been an inexplicable tightening of shipping traffic in and out of German ports. This Warsaw Agricultural Exhibition is a huge fair for the farming industry. Implement manufacturers come from all over the world. Krupp is the biggest European player, and they were going to be in Warsaw anyway, so they brought the tractor parts along with them. They can be transshipped more easily out of a Polish port."

Frances patted her stomach. "I've got the cashier's cheque for one hundred thousand Canadian right here to close the deal."

Vladyslaw Byrka sat down at their table with a plate of fruit and cheese. "Vlad," said Scotty, "where exactly is the Agricultural Exhibition site in Warsaw?"

"It's right next to the central train station."

"And where's the National Bank of Poland?"

"A stone's throw away. On Mostowa Street, in the Old Town."

"Good!" beamed Scotty. "Now, how do we get in touch with these Aggie lads?"

Frances referred to her notes. "They're staying at the Duke Casimir Hotel."

Governor Byrka wrinkled his nose. "A first-rate Pole of the twelfth century, a third-rate hotel of the nineteenth century. Caters to commercial travellers."

"Vlad, how long does it take to get to Warsaw from here?"

"There's no direct route from Basel. We must go through Munich and Prague. It can take eight hours or more by train."

"Okay, Frances, get us out of here as fast as you can this afternoon. Warn the Aggies we're coming. Take a walk around town. Oh, and Vlad, if we need to grease the skids a bit in Poland, what currency would be best?"

"Grease the skids?"

"If there are shipping agents and dockyard workers who need extra encouragement to be quick and careful, would Polish zloty do, or would they want pounds, or Reichsmarks?"

"I hate to think that you would need to bribe a Polish citizen to do his duty."

"Bribe? Heavens, no! Canadians are far too clean-cut for that. Offer encouragement."

"If 'encouragement' is necessary, zloty would do."

"Could I call upon the good offices of the National Bank of Poland to facilitate some currency exchanges if necessary?" asked Scotty.

"At your service," replied the governor.

The train north from Basel quickly fell behind schedule. Once they left Switzerland, military uniforms blossomed in the passenger cars and on every station platform. It was after midnight when they walked into the lobby of the Duke Casimir Hotel in Warsaw. It had seen better days.

"For the love o' God," Scotty grimaced, looking at the peeling walls.

"The city is completely booked up with this Agricultural Exhibition," said Frances. "I was lucky to get us in here."

"Let's grab some shut-eye. I'm meeting Vlady at the National Bank first thing tomorrow to case the joint. You get in touch with the Aggies and set up a meeting here for lunch. Sweet dreams."

After a watery coffee and a greasy sausage for breakfast, Frances took the short walk over to the Warsaw Agricultural Exhibition. It was in an ancient cavernous warehouse. Great rows of tractors and cultivators and harvesters and instruments that Frances couldn't even imagine the use of were parked in rows and blocks, with pedestrian streets in between. The Krupp display was the largest there, taking up a huge corner. All the Krupp equipment was painted imperial Prussian blue with a gold stripe.

Frances approached one of the nattily dressed sales representatives. "Hello. I'm trying to get in touch with some people from the Canadian Department of Agriculture who are here to finalize a purchase of Krupp equipment. Have you seen them by any chance?"

The sales representative went back to a man seated at desk, who stood up, put out a cigarette, and came forward to speak to her. "You're looking for Mr. Roderick and the biologists?" he asked in very good English. "They were just here. Try the restaurant in the corner under the clock."

The restaurant wasn't crowded, and there was only one male threesome. A youngish man in a wrinkled suit with an unkempt flop of brown hair. The two others were wearing checkered shirts open at sunburned throats. The taller sunburn was regaling the others with the contents of a Polish newspaper. They were all having beer and hard-boiled eggs for breakfast.

"Might you be Messieurs Roderick, Doyle, and Bailey? I'm Frances McFadden from the Bank of Canada."

Roderick jumped up and pumped her hand. "Are we glad to see *you*!" He introduced the biologists. "We have worked so flippin' hard getting this equipment deal set up, and then Krupp cross-checks us with this 'pay-before-shipping' policy."

"Well," said Frances, "I guess any business doing international transactions these days would have concerns about borders closing or accounts being frozen. I have your money." She showed them the Canadian government bank draft.

"Will that be good enough for these buggers from Krupp?" asked Bailey, the barley man.

"The National Bank of Poland will cash it in the currency of their choice." replied Frances.

"Let's drink to that, then!" said Doyle, the early germinator, who had been reading the Polish newspaper. He raised a huge beer stein, and they all clinked glasses. "A drink, Miss McFadden?"

At nine o'clock in the morning?

"No, thanks," said Frances. "Can you let your Krupp contacts know that you're ready to close this deal? My boss, Mr. Meldrum, would like to buy you all lunch back at the Duke Casimir."

The dining room was poorly lit and over-furnished with heavy tables and large side chairs. Scotty was slouching in an armchair when Frances arrived just before twelve. There was a large bottle of Gdanska Wódka and a small pepper mill on the table before him. He was not his usual chipper self.

"The Poleskis water the Scotch they import, so it's weak as weasel piss," he said. "However, they do have this delightful chilled vodka. It's served with a sprinkling of fresh pepper and packs a tremendous kick. Like some? Where are the Aggies?"

"I told them to meet us here at noon," replied Frances. "One of them can read Polish. That might come in handy. How do things look at the Bank of Poland?"

Scotty drained a tumbler of vodka and pepper, wincing as it went down. "Not good. Our man Byrka has built the best mousetrap I've ever seen. A twelve-foot wall surrounds the courtyard. The only entrance has a huge cast-iron gate that faces the police station. Then we've got the armoury just around the corner. There are so many uniforms swirling through the streets outside the Bank it looks like a parade. Stan showed me the gold in the corner of the basement storeroom. God! Thirty tons of gold take up a lot of space. And it's heavy! You can't put many bars in a box, or the crate would break."

"Do the army or the police know where the gold is?"

"Vlady doesn't think so. They both provided escorts for the fake transportation of the rocks south to the mines.

"Vlady's brother in the cavalry told him that German reconnaissance flights over Poland are increasing every day. Something is going to happen soon. Everybody's jumpy. I don't see how it's possible to sneak a postage stamp out of that Bank without the world knowing." Scotty shook his head. "Maybe we should just help the Aggies get their tractor parts on the next boat home and call it a day."

The door to the dining room swung open, and the three Canadians entered, engaged in a heated exchange. They hushed for the introductions, then Roderick, who was twenty years younger than the biologists, broke the news.

"Big fracas with this guy Stoiber, the Kraut in charge of the Krupp machinery display. I told him we had the money and were ready to go. Could change it into any currency he wanted at the National Bank. Then he smiles a little sheepishly and tells me he's no longer authorized to approve the sale."

"Did he say why?"

"Nope. Makes me think this was a surprise to him, too. Yesterday he was gung-ho. God, it's frustrating!" said Roderick, who sat down and poured himself a peppered vodka. "It took me ten months to get all the ducks in a row in Ottawa for this purchase. Then Krupp sidelines us with this nonsense about payment here. We want this stuff badly, but we do *not* want to take receipt of all these crates in the middle of Poland. The money arrives with Miss McFadden and I thought we could close. Boom! Stoiber backpedals."

"What's changed?" asked Scotty.

"Can't figure it out," said Roderick. "There is clearly something stuck in the pipeline. I don't even know if Stoiber knows the answer. Says that the head office is sending some high mucky-muck up to deal with us. He's supposed to get here tomorrow."

"And that's just part of the problem," added Bailey. "The captain of this Canadian freighter at Gdynia, a guy named Hyland, wants to vamoose. He has cargoes to pick up in Oslo and Greenock. Ships tied to a wharf don't bring in much income, and he's paying dockage fees every day he's there."

"Anyways," said Doyle, "Bailey and I are only in Warsaw to check out the seed agents at the Exhibition. We've been trying to give young Roderick some moral support, but we have to get on up to Vilnius and then into the Ukraine next week to finish our field research."

"When's this Krupp fellow supposed to get here?" asked Scotty.

"The Warsaw Express from Berlin gets in just before noon tomorrow," said Roderick.

"And tomorrow's the thirtieth already," sighed Scotty. "We'll be lucky to get out of Warsaw with our underwear." He began pouring tumblers of ice-cold vodka all round.

—— 50 ——

SHELL GAME

A light drizzle was falling in Warsaw when Frances woke on August 30. Ten days ago, she'd walked to Knox Presbyterian Church in Ottawa with Anna Deloitte. It seemed like another century.

Over breakfast, Scotty Meldrum conceded defeat. "I tossed and turned half the night trying to figure this mess out. The goddamn gold is a writeoff. It would be easier to get into Fort Knox than get anything out of the National Bank of Poland. So, let's move on to Plan B, and help the Aggies get their tractor parts out of here. The Exhibition wraps up today, and the place is a shambles of half-dismantled displays. I've bribed the station agent to get us a meeting room upstairs at the train station. Stoiber will meet the Berlin Express and bring the Krupp bigwig up.

"This *Mont Royal* that's waiting up at Gdynia is a Canadian Pacific Railway ship. I wired CPR headquarters in Montreal to get them to hold her sailing until tomorrow."

Frances raised her eyebrows. "And does CPR Headquarters jump to the call of the Bank of Canada Deputy Governor?"

"Tubby Shouldice is the vice-president of the CPR marine division. He's a member of the Five Lakes Fishing Club. I let him beat me at poker occasionally."

"So he's indebted to you?"

"I'd certainly say so," smiled Scotty. "If the *Mont Royal* is still tied to the dock when we get to Gdynia tomorrow, we'll know for sure."

Frances, Scotty, Roderick, and Bailey sat along one side of a long table in the room above the Warsaw train station. Pictures of trains and quaint country stations decorated the walls. Doyle was drifting around reading the captions. The assistant dispatcher, a morose Pole named Ludz, fidgeted at the end of the table.

"Where did you pick up your Polish?" Scotty asked Doyle.

"Mother's Polish Catholic. Father's Irish Baptist."

"Irish Baptist?"

"A small but zealous lot. Grew up on a wheat farm outside Brandon,

Manitoba. Not much to do when chores were done. Father drilled us on the Bible every night and twice on Sundays. Ask me anything about Deuteronomy. The only relief came when Mother taught us Polish and how to cook perogies."

Shortly after twelve, footsteps and German conversation filtered up the stairs. Herr Stoiber ushered in a tall, handsome man and introduced the Director of Overseas Sales for Krupp International, Herr Kessler. The empty sleeve of his suit coat was pinned up. If he remembered Frances from the lobby of the Balmoral Arms, he gave no indication. Scotty shot Frances a questioning glance, and she nodded.

"Five Canadians in the Warsaw train station!" he said jovially. "Including Deputy Governor Meldrum, no less. Who would have guessed that the Bank of Canada was interested in tractor parts?" Wheels turned behind Herr Kessler's sparkling blue eyes.

"Too bad we couldn't wrap this contract up in Ottawa. I felt there was a genuine desire to purchase the Krupp products, but bureaucratic difficulties kept delaying things. I never quite managed to be sitting at the table with the player who could clinch the deal. Have you read *Little Dorrit*? It quite reminded me of the Circumlocution Office."

"Well," said Scotty with a smile, "I'm your man. And are you the player from Krupp?"

"I am." Herr Kessler took out a monogrammed silver cigarette case and offered it around. The case had been cleverly designed to be used with one hand. A spring lever pushed a cigarette part way out a small portal. A lighter was built into the spine. "What a masterpiece of engineering," commented Roderick.

"It was custom-built by Schunk and Ebe at their precision tool works in Fulda," replied Herr Kessler. "A gift from my regiment at the end of the war. A one-armed smoker has trouble with matches.

"Now, to business. Clear and simple, in order to release the crates of Krupp machinery parts—how many are there, Herr Stoiber?"

Herr Stoiber flipped through a manifest list. "Eighty-four altogether, sir. Of various sizes."

"And where are they now?" continued Herr Kessler.

"They are packed in six Henschel three-ton trucks parked at the back of the Agriculture Exhibition Building, and they have to be moved out by six o'clock tonight."

"What's the hurry?"

"Another exhibition is setting up tomorrow. They need to clean the building first."

"And why is Krupp equipment on Henschel trucks?"

"I had very short notice to bring the parts to Warsaw. I couldn't put my hands on a freight car or a Krupp truck to carry them."

Herr Kessler grimaced. "You shipped eighty-four crates of precision tooled parts all this way over Polish roads? Was there any damage?"

"I asked that very question, Herr Kessler," said Paul Roderick. "Herr Stoiber allowed me to check. Everything was fine. Expertly wrapped and tightly packed in straw."

"Good," continued Herr Kessler. "We have your order, in good condition. Do you have the money?"

"I have a government cashier's cheque for one hundred thousand dollars Canadian, Herr Wagn . . . Kessler," stumbled Frances, waving the bank draft. *Shit!*

Herr Kessler paused. "Krupp would prefer Reichsmarks."

"Governor Byrka of the Polish National Bank has agreed to convert the Canadian bank draft into any currency," said Scotty.

"You know Governor Byrka?"

"We met at the Bank of International Settlements meeting in Basel last week. I made the acquaintance of Walther Funk there as well. Herr Funk has invited us to Berlin as soon as we get this business sorted out."

Herr Kessler gave a congratulatory smile. "You have friends in very high places, Mr. Meldrum."

"The Bank of Canada is very new and we have much to learn. Governor Byrka and President Funk have been generous."

Herr Kessler took a deep, reflective drag on his cigarette. "Now, Herr Stoiber tells me that you prefer not to finalize this transaction in Warsaw."

"No," put in Roderick.

"Where then?"

"Normally, a manufacturer ships to a purchaser, and payment is made on receipt of the merchandise," said Roderick. "That arrangement was satisfactory last year when we purchased a million dollars' worth of Krupp equipment."

"Quite right," agreed Kessler. "Operational procedures have changed. Not your fault or mine. What do you suggest?"

"A Canadian freighter, the *Mont Royal*, is in the harbour at Gdynia. We would be willing to take delivery on the Gdynia quay, and hand over a bank draft for the four hundred thousand Reichsmarks as the ship loads."

Herr Kessler shrugged. "Sounds fair. Can you get the crates to Gdynia?"

"Hold on," said Scotty, "we have accommodated Krupp by agreeing to pay you in Reichsmarks, by completing the transaction here in Poland, and by picking up delivery costs from Gdynia to Canada. Krupp could at least get the crates to the port."

Herr Kessler addressed Ludz for the first time. "Can you get freight cars to haul this gear to Gdynia?"

Ludz furrowed his brow, and Herr Kessler repeated the request in fluent Polish. Ludz snorted before replying.

"There are no boxcars to be had anywhere within a hundred miles of here," Doyle translated.

"Well, the parts are all on Henschel trucks," said Herr Kessler. "I suppose we could truck them up. When does this freighter sail?"

"It was scheduled to sail last week," said Scotty, "and has been waiting for this cargo, at no small expense to the ship owners. I telegraphed company headquarters in Montreal, and was able to extract one final delay until tomorrow afternoon. The *Mont Royal* sails at four p.m. Thursday, with or without the Krupp parts."

Herr Kessler sighed. "The road north to Gdynia is *not* the highway to Berlin. It's two hundred miles of winding dirt road." He looked out the window at the rain. "Or mud. Every farmer uses that road to move his cows from field to field and to carry hay on his donkey cart. We'd be lucky to make the trip in forty-eight hours if we drove straight through."

"Are there any rail flatbed carriers we could load the trucks on?" asked Roderick.

When Herr Kessler translated, Ludz shook his head.

"*Any* kind of rolling stock at all?" asked Scotty.

When Ludz heard the translation he shrugged before replying. "Every piece of rolling stock that isn't in the repair shop is in use," translated Doyle.

"What's in the repair shop?" pressed Scotty, and Doyle translated. "Just train cars that are being rebuilt."

"All we need is something with wheels and floorboards," said Herr Kessler.

Ludz pointed to a phone on the desk under the window. "He doubts there's anything, but he could phone if you like."

"How many flatcars would we need to move the trucks?" Scotty asked Herr Stoiber.

"Six Henschels? Three flatcars would do."

Scotty opened his wallet, and spoke to Doyle while he handed Ludz 600 zloty. "Please ask Mr. Ludz to accept this small token for his favourite charity. There will be 600 zloty more for each flatbed he locates for us."

The offer of a year's wages had a transforming effect on Mr. Ludz. He sprang to his feet, and jabbered animatedly into the phone, making several calls.

"Leaving the parts on the trucks is an excellent idea," nodded Herr Kessler, as he handed around his cigarette case a second time. "They can be damaged each time they're moved. This way, they only move once, from the truck to the ship."

"But what do we do with the trucks in the meantime?" asked Stoiber. "We need to get them out of the exhibition hall."

"Could we just park them on the street overnight?" asked Frances.

"Not safe," said Scotty. "Governor Byrka warned me there are unsavoury elements roaming the streets of Warsaw these nights."

Herr Kessler snapped his fingers. "Why don't you ask Governor Byrka, if we could park the trucks in the courtyard at the National Bank of Poland? Just for one night. The police station and armoury are both next door, so that should be as safe as it gets in Warsaw. The police chief and armoury commandant might even volunteer extra vigilance." He smiled. "In return for a donation to their favourite charities."

Ludz got off the phone and spoke excitedly to Doyle.

"Mr. Ludz has arranged to get three 'train platforms on wheels' moved to the end of track four in the marshalling yard tonight. Tomorrow morning we can drive the trucks straight onto them from the platform. A mixed freight leaves at seven a.m. for Gdynia, and the flatbeds can be hooked in."

"Mixed freight?" asked Scotty.

"Boxcars, flatcars, passenger cars," replied Ludz in a heavy accent.

"Can we book a compartment on a passenger car?" asked Scotty.

Doyle translated, and smiled at Ludz's response. "Possibly, if the conductor receives a donation to his favourite charity."

Scotty handed over another 600 zloty to Ludz. "For the conductor." He fanned 1800 zloty in his large hand. "For you, Mr. Ludz. Tomorrow, when the trucks are loaded on the flatcars."

"Track four. Five a.m." confirmed Ludz, his eyes glistening.

Scotty nodded. "Now, let me phone Governor Byrka to see if we can use his courtyard overnight."

The lengthy conversation suggested some reluctance on the governor's part. Scotty accelerated the use of his persuasive Scottish brogue, stressing extra security from the police or the armoury. He turned back to Stoiber. "Can your people drive the trucks around to the Bank at four this afternoon?"

Stoiber checked his watch and nodded.

"And pick them up at four-thirty tomorrow morning to drive them onto the flatcars?"

Stoiber nodded again.

Scotty hung up the phone. "Well, gentlemen, I think we've worked out all the kinks. You'll join us for the trip up to Gdynia tomorrow, Herr Kessler?"

"I'd be delighted."

Scotty asked Doyle, Bailey, and Roderick to ride over to the National Bank with the truck drivers. When he and Frances got to the street, he began to whistle merrily.

"You're thinking larcenous thoughts, aren't you?" said Frances.

"I can't believe this fell into our lap! These things usually only happen in the movies."

"Question," said Frances. "We have six three-ton trucks, and thirty tons of gold. Can a three-ton truck carry five tons?"

"They just have to carry it from the Bank to the train yard loading dock. That can't be four hundred yards. Downhill. I'm betting yes. I'm going directly to Vlad's office to see if he's game. There are a few details we couldn't discuss on the phone, but he knows this is his only chance at bat. You go back to the hotel and pack. Then book us a compartment to Berlin tomorrow night from Gdynia. Telegraph Walther Funk at the Deutsche Reichbank to expect us Friday, September first.

"Get the dining room to put together a big picnic hamper of sandwiches and things for a Canadian farewell-to-Warsaw feast tonight. Be back at the Bank before four."

The six stately Henschels rolled through a light rain into the courtyard of the National Bank of Poland just after four. Two state policemen stood on duty to the left of the gate, and two army privates stood on guard to the right of the gate. Herr Stoiber was a passenger in the lead truck, and Herr Kessler rode with the final driver. Rawicz, the gatekeeper, directed them to a large garage around the west side of the Bank. Four armoured cars and two black limousines had been moved out and were parked along the courtyard wall. It was a squeeze, but all the Henschels could be stored out of the rain.

"Wonderful," said Herr Kessler. "The canvas tops get saturated after a while, and I don't want water leaking down on those crates."

"Not until you're paid for them anyway," said Scotty with a smile. He held out his hand to Herr Kessler. "It's been a pleasure doing business with you. I like a man of action. Can you leave the keys in the trucks in case they need to be moved?"

"Certainly. Herr Stoiber and I will try to keep the drivers sober tonight, and get them back here at four-thirty a.m."

When the Germans left, Paul Roderick clapped his hands. "Fantastic! I thought we never were going to pull it off! Let me buy you a drink, Mr. Meldrum."

"Wonderful idea," said Scotty, pressing a buzzer by the loading dock door. "Let's just check in with Vlad first."

Several bolts were thrown, and an armed guard swung the steel door outward. Governor Byrka gave them a quick tour of the building, starting with the gold in the storeroom, and ended upstairs, dwarfed in an ornate, high-ceilinged boardroom.

The governor poured generous crystal glasses of chilled vodka all around while Scotty outlined the new plan. Roderick was devastated. "You've got to be kidding! All those hurdles and setbacks to come all this way. Today, finally, victory. And you want me to give it all up?"

"Well, son," said Scotty, "A hundred thousand dollars' worth of tractor parts versus forty million in gold. We get to choose one. And, we need everybody's help. There are just the five of us and the four night shift guards plus Vlad."

"Love to help you out, Mr. Meldrum," said Bailey, "but Doyle and I have train tickets to Vilnius tonight. We've got a dozen agriculture stations to check out between there and Minsk over the next two weeks."

Scotty refilled their glasses with chilled vodka, and delicately peppered the tops. "Mr. Doyle, Mr. Bailey, Canada needs you tonight in the basement of the National Bank of Poland, and tomorrow to ride shotgun on the train to Gdynia. Let's give one day to Poland, and change the life of a nation. It's something few men could ever brag to their grandchildren about. The wheat and the barley will wait one day for you. The gold needs you tonight." Scotty handed them the brimming tumblers of vodka. "Please?" he said as he lifted his own glass to salute them.

The biologists looked at each other. Bailey shrugged his shoulders, and Doyle said, "Oh, what the hell." The three drained glasses slammed down on the table to seal the deal.

Scotty checked his watch. "We've got eleven hours to unload the trucks, dump the parts out, load the crates with thirty tons of gold, and get it all back on the trucks before the drivers show up at four-thirty a.m. tomorrow."

Roderick threw up his hands. "It's impossible! Even with hydraulic forklifts and dollies. Think of it. Take a box off the truck, load it into the freight elevator. Take it down to the storage room. Open it, unpack it, re-pack it with gold. Nail it closed. Forklift it into the elevator and back into the truck. Eighty-four times? In eleven hours? That's *eight minutes a box*! You'd be hustlin' to get a box done in an hour."

"Well, there's ten of us," countered Scotty. "They have four forklifts and several hydraulic dollies. What if we worked in teams of two?"

The engineer in Roderick spoke again. "If nothing breaks down, and we don't stop to pee, *maybe* each team could do a box an hour. Fifty-five boxes. Just over half. Don't want to rain on your parade, Mr. Meldrum, but it ain't humanly possible."

"Is half the gold better than no gold?" Scotty asked Governor Byrka, who walked nervously up and down.

Bailey, the barley biologist, tapped his empty glass thoughtfully on the table. "How 'bout this. We take all the boxes down. We unload and re-pack a few of the Krupp parts boxes and bring them back up. We paint the Krupp markings on the rest of the gold boxes and load them on the trucks. A box is a box. Who's going to see what boxes are loaded on that freighter at Gdynia?"

"Kessler will be there to take payment," said Scotty. "He's the only one who might know the boxes have been switched."

"Has Kessler even seen these boxes?" asked Doyle. "He was asking Stoiber for all the details."

"Kessler just wants the four hundred thousand Reichsmarks," said Frances. "Getting the boxes loaded on the ship is our problem, not his. Hand him the money and take him to a bar."

Scotty looked around the table. "Any better ideas?" There was a long silence. "Well, let's go, then. If we can get it half done by ten p.m., we'll break for a picnic dinner; if not we'll work straight through. We go with whatever is on those six trucks when the drivers show up tomorrow."

Doyle copied the Krupp logo onto a piece of cardboard and cut out several templates. Rawicz, the night watchman, found paint that matched the Prussian blue of the signage. The other watchmen scrounged hammers and crowbars, and quickly taught the Canadians how to drive the forklifts and use the hydraulic dollies. Every two hours, Rawicz took picnic goodies to the guards outside the front gate.

Unloading, shunting, unpacking, hefting, re-packing, painting, re-loading. Exhausting. It was a game of sorts, and the clock was the referee.

51

GDYNIA TRAIN

As soon as the six Henschels were firmly strapped down on the platform cars, an ugly little switcher engine began shunting them to the rear of the Gdynia train. The Canadians scrambled across several rows of track in the marshalling yard to the passenger platform.

"Sorry! So sorry!" The conductor gesticulated wildly in support of his 600 zloty stipend. "Small train, many passengers. Three seats only left in first-class compartment. Others must ride in coach."

"Can you buy beer in the coach?" Doyle asked. The conductor nodded. "Good enough for me," he said, drawing Bailey with him. The others were ushered into a compartment where they found Herr Kessler bantering in German with a small, ominous man in a dark trench coat and a black fedora. Perched by the window across from him was a woman in a brightly coloured outfit with a red kerchief over her hair. She looked like a member of a peasant dance troupe. They both might have been extras in the movies.

Herr Kessler smiled disarmingly. "Oh! Herr Eckardt, these are some delightful Canadians whom I met in the train station. Miss McFadden, Mr. Meldrum, and Mr. Roderick."

In heavily accented English, the man said, "How do you do?" He smiled briefly, revealing discoloured teeth. The woman nodded, but didn't speak.

Frances sagged into the corner by the door. She had teamed with Paul Roderick to lift, remove, paint, pack, and load. Her arms throbbed from shuffling hundreds of gold bars. The exercise was strangely devoid of the awe that proximity to such wealth should bring. It had been heavy, frantic, sweaty work.

As the train picked up speed through the suburbs of Warsaw, Herr Kessler passed pleasantries with Herr Eckardt, whose replies became briefer until he eventually turned to look out the window. They passed countless stations with unpronounceable names. A vendor came by selling Polish sausages on buns, and beer. By ten o'clock, the track drew parallel to the Wisla River, and followed it toward the northwest.

Herr Kessler had pulled out a slim volume of Rainer Maria Rilke's *Sonnets to Orpheus* translated into English. He was chuckling and annotating the poems with notes in the margin. "What a terrible translation," he commented to Herr Eckardt. "Look at this." Herr Eckardt glanced briefly at the page before returning to the window.

"Interested in German poetry?" he said to Frances, and passed the book across to her. On the bookmark, underlined in block letters, was printed: *SD: GERMAN INTELLIGENCE OFFICER.*

Frances read the sonnet, then passed the book to Scotty. The sonnets travelled to Roderick, whose Adam's apple bobbed several times. The train rocked and swayed along the east bank of the wide river. Herr Kessler stretched and stood up. "I need some fresh air and a cigarette. Would you care to join me, Herr Meldrum?" he smiled.

"Certainly," replied Scotty, patting his breast pocket for his cigar case.

"And you, Miss McFadden?"

"I'd—" began Frances, when Scotty gave her a surreptitious elbow in the ribs, "—be delighted."

The train slowed as it negotiated the cliff edge above the twisting river. The breeze was quite fresh on the open platform between the cars. Herr Kessler pulled out his silver cigarette case, and offered one to Frances. They all laboured to get their tobacco lit in the wind, especially Frances, who had never had a cigarette in her life.

When Scotty's cigar was finally in full glow, he said, "If Eckardt is a Nazi agent, why the devil does he dress like a Nazi agent?"

Herr Kessler smiled. "Could be the perfect disguise. Didn't Churchill describe Clement Atlee as 'a sheep in sheep's clothing'? So Herr Eckardt is either incredibly clever, or incredibly stupid."

"What makes you think he's in the espionage game?" asked Scotty.

"I wondered why he was swathed in a trench coat in this heat unless he had something to hide. I clumsily bumped against him as I sat down, confirming a shoulder holster and a second handgun in his right pocket. Unusual accoutrements for a casual traveller.

"When I introduced myself, he spoke Polish with a heavy German accent. I switched to German and asked what brought him to Warsaw. He said he had been at the Agricultural Exhibition. A good cover story, actually, because the event attracts thousands."

"So it might have been true."

"It might have been, but when I inquired about his interest in agriculture, he told me he sold farm machinery for Krupp."

"Are all tractor salesmen multilingual?" asked Frances.

"My family had an estate in East Prussia where we summered when I was a boy. All the servants were Polish. The young acquire languages effortlessly, like a suntan. I had an English nanny. My mother's French maid taught me a great deal as well," he added wistfully.

"Do you still visit the estate?" asked Frances.

"Father lost everything in the inflation after the war. A few photographs is all they have left from East Prussia. My parents now live in their former hunting lodge with two servants. Genteel poverty."

Scotty checked his watch. "How long till we get to Gdynia?"

"In a few minutes we will enter the first of two tunnels in the Wisla valley cliffs before beginning our descent to the port. We will be on the quay at Gdynia in forty minutes. So we need to negotiate quickly."

Scotty and Frances exchanged glances.

"You act the colonial bumpkin very well, Mr. Meldrum. A regular thespian. Perhaps you missed your calling."

Scotty puffed on his cigar in innocent perplexity.

"I know the Polish gold reserves are loaded onto those six Henschel trucks."

"That's absurd!" exclaimed Scotty.

"Please, Mr. Meldrum, spare me further theatrics. I'm *glad* you have the gold. It took me a while to figure out why the Deputy Governor of the Bank of Canada was in Warsaw ostensibly purchasing tractor parts that Canadians don't need. Krupp machines are virtually indestructible. If they're kept clean and well oiled, they should last for twenty years."

"You sold the Department of Agriculture the spare parts, didn't you, Herr Kessler?"

"I advised against it. However, I am a commissioned agent, after all, and one can only protest against one's own self-interest for so long.

"Once it dawned on me what the real game was, I did my best for you by suggesting Governor Byrka harbour the trucks in the Bank courtyard overnight. I didn't know which side Stoiber or Ludz worked for, so I had to be circumspect."

Scotty and Frances remained silent.

"You thought I was playing into your hand? Well, I was *creating* a hand for you, Mr. Meldrum, so you could get the bullion out of the bank vault. In return for this not inconsiderable service, I need a small commission."

"I don't know what you're talking about," harrumphed Scotty.

They were plunged into darkness as they sped into the first tunnel. The sound of the train echoed deafeningly off the tunnel walls. In fifteen seconds they were back in the Polish sunshine.

"Thirty minutes to the Baltic Ocean, Mr. Meldrum. Now, I can deal with you, or I tell Herr Eckardt that you are smuggling one hundred and sixty million Reichsmarks' worth of Polish gold out of the country." He took a long drag on his cigarette. "Can you imagine the meteoric effect it would have on Herr Eckardt's career should he detect this skulduggery in progress? He'd probably be invited to the Berghof for a weekend with Hitler."

"What's it to me where the Polish gold is?" said Scotty. "That's the concern of the National Bank of Poland."

"Mr. Meldrum, the clock is ticking. Actually, many clocks are ticking all at once.

"You know where the gold is. I know where the gold is. Frances McFadden of the Balmoral Arms, knows where the gold is." He stared at Frances, causing her to accidentally inhale. She lost her balance in a fit of coughing and grabbed the handle next to the carriage door to steady herself.

"Think of your fate, and that of your Canadian colleagues, Mr. Meldrum. You would all be arrested in Gdynia. And these are uncertain times. Should there be any disruptions, the Polish government's responsibilities would be heavy and the fate of a few incarcerated Canadians would not top their list. And should there be hostilities, and international boundaries violated, well, a Polish jail might be a blessing compared to a German military tribunal, should you be afforded such a civility. So can we give up the charade and discuss terms?"

"What do you mean by terms?"

"Thank you," Herr Kessler smiled. "Here's my offer. The Canadian freighter that's waiting in Gdynia harbour loads the Polish gold and sails away into the sunset. Some thirty tons of twenty-five-pound bars. Forty million Canadian. One hundred and sixty million Reichsmarks. A lot of money. I ask only for a small commission. Three bars of gold. Forty-five thousand dollars Canadian. One-tenth of one percent. Quite a modest fee. Krupp pays me a much better commission on tractor sales."

Scotty glared at him. "Even if the gold were on this train, and I'm not saying it is, I have no authority to negotiate commissions on behalf of the Polish government."

"Mr. Meldrum," replied Herr Kessler in a patient tone, "you are the de facto governor of the gold. There are no Polish Bank officials on the train. *That* would look very suspicious to inquiring eyes." He laughed. "So once again, *you* are the player at the table."

Scotty chomped down on his cigar, bristling. "Blackmail doesn't cut it with me, Kessler."

"Mr. Meldrum, you are a man of business. Isn't give-and-take a regular part of any business transaction? Here are your options. We work together, and you get 99.9 percent of the gold delivered to the hold of the *Mont Royal*. I work with Herr Eckardt, and you get no gold, and are incarcerated by the Poles, or shot by the German army should it show up in these parts. Your choice. You need to act quickly, if not for your own sake, at least for Miss McFadden's."

Frances's temper flared. "Don't try to use me as a pawn in this sick game. I've read lots about your Nazi Germany, and if even 10 percent were true, it's disgusting. I wouldn't want one penny directed to that gang of thugs because of me."

Herr Kessler raised his eyebrows. "I am saddened that you use the words 'Nazi' and 'Germany' interchangeably, Miss McFadden, because they are not the same thing. However, I take no offence, as I agree completely with your assessment of current affairs. Bloodthirsty lemmings control Germany today and they will lead the nation off the cliff."

"If you are so disdainful of them, why were you spying for them?" shot Frances.

"Spying? Oh! The film! Was that *you* who ruined my film? That was very bad of you, Miss McFadden. I knew it couldn't have been my Henckel camera, and I am not so careless as to expose *every* canister to the light. The film was a bargaining chip that I was unable to play. So now I need the gold."

"As a German agent, isn't it your duty to turn the gold to your country's use? Why this pretense at negotiations?" scoffed Scotty.

"I wouldn't give a nickel to support the Nazi insanity, Mr. Meldrum. Germany has abandoned me, and so now it is time for me to abandon Germany."

"Oh! So you don't like the Nazis, but you gladly provide them with Canadian sabotage targets," accused Frances.

Herr Kessler smiled. "Did you actually look at the film before it was over-exposed?"

"No."

"It was all a mirage. A biscuit factory in London, Ontario, a steel mill in Hamilton, some pictures of Niagara Falls. The factories hand out free pamphlets with more information than my photographs show. You can buy picture postcards of Niagara Falls in any drugstore."

"But surely in seventy-two rolls of film—"

"The Sicherheitsdienst, like most foolish bureaucracies, values quantity over quality. It would have taken them two years of filing and cross-referencing to realize that my film was of no practical value at all. The Circumlocution Office works to my advantage in this case. And, even if any of the places I photographed might at some future date have some strategic significance, the Nazis are so inept that sabotage in North America is completely beyond their capability. The photographs I took of German targets would have been more helpful to the British, but alas, they were also destroyed."

"You're a double agent?"

"I never thought of myself as a Nazi agent when all I submitted were voluminous bogus reports."

"Why did you even pretend to help them if you despise them?"

"A long story, on a train trip that grows shorter by the minute. My father had been vitriolic in his denunciation of the Nazis from the beginning. He was an aristocrat and a retired general officer—too important to kill—but once the Nazis consolidated power, he and my mother have been essentially under house arrest. If I didn't want worse to happen to them, I was required to make some good-faith offerings. It has taken me a long time to gain the confidence of these—'thugs,' did you call them?—so that they would ease restrictions on my family. A year ago, my sister was finally allowed to go to Zurich to do graduate work in biology. My father is in poor health, and only last month was my mother permitted to take him to a clinic in Geneva. They were allowed one suitcase between them and two hundred Reichsmarks. I had to bribe the doctor to exaggerate Father's condition."

"How can you be a spy for the British if Scotland Yard thinks you're a German spy?"

"You are remarkably well informed for a bank clerk, Miss McFadden. Yes! What a stroke of luck that was. First of all that the story was leaked, and secondly that Scotland Yard and the British Secret Intelligence Service mistrust each other and don't share files. When it came to the attention of my superiors that the British were suspicious of my activities, it enhanced my credibility tremendously. The Nazis have a very inflated opinion of the British Secret Service. This gave me a perfect excuse to exit Canada quickly.

"The British SIS agent I met on the ocean liner was willing to pay handsomely for my photographs of German industrial and military sites, but not for blank film. A disappointment that I apparently owe to you, Miss McFadden. So now, you see, I need three bars of gold. My family is finally safe in Switzerland. The Nazis are on the brink of igniting Europe and immolating themselves. I gave one arm in war for the German Empire. I lost my wife and son to the Spanish 'Flu in 1919. That's enough for me. I have booked passage on a Panamanian freighter that sails tonight from Gdynia for Buenos Aires. I'm moving to Argentina to start a little horse farm."

"What about your fiancée, Anna Deloitte?" demanded Frances. "She thinks you're in Western Canada, selling tractors."

"Anna is my love. I will send for her as soon as I'm set up."

"Another of your lies?"

"You are harsh, Miss McFadden. I confess that I misrepresented my whereabouts to her, but that was for her own protection. I was clearly being watched in Ottawa. Anna is too gentle a soul to be put in jeopardy on my behalf."

A thought occurred to Scotty. "We're going to give you a cashier's cheque for four hundred thousand Reichsmarks on the dock at Gdynia. Couldn't you just stiff Krupp and skedaddle? Why do you need gold bars as well?"

"The four hundred thousand is my 'retirement pension' from Krupp for fifteen years of loyal service. It took quite some finagling to get them to insist on the cash payment. That money is earmarked to cover my parents' debts. Aristocrats, even the nobly intentioned, adjust to squalor with difficulty. And Father's clinic in Geneva is the best in the world, a fact that is reflected in their fees. My family is dependent on me for the foreseeable future. So the four hundred thousand is spoken for. I need three gold bars for myself."

"Why just three?"

"I am not a greedy person, Mr. Meldrum. I just want what I can carry. Three bars will go far in Argentina, where the economy has suffered much from inflation, and gold fights well above its weight.

"Another cigarette?" Herr Kessler let go of the railing in order to offer his monogrammed cigarette case.

Frances shook her head.

Herr Kessler was lighting his cigarette as they sped into the final tunnel of the journey. In the darkness, the train lurched sharply, sending Frances sprawling across the narrow platform. She screamed as she flailed wildly, crashing into something hard and something soft. A vice closed on her left arm and suspended her momentum.

In seconds, the train came out of the tunnel. Scotty Meldrum let go of her upper arm as she caught her breath and regained her footing. They were alone.

Frances looked wide-eyed at Scotty, then down. Her right hand clasped the silver cigarette case.

"Did I . . . ? Did you . . . ? Oh, my God!"

Scotty said nothing. He took the cigarette case from her stricken fingers and examined it carefully.

"Beautiful. Beautiful," he said. "A pity." The August sunlight glittered off the case as it arched end over end before falling into the whirling trees by the side of the track.

— 52 —

1600 HOURS

The quay at Gdynia swarmed with expectation. Stevedores, truck drivers, deckhands, soldiers, port officials, and crane operators created a riot of colour, noise, and motion. It reminded Frances of the midway at the Central Canada Exhibition.

The train chuffed to a stop at the station platform. As the passengers disembarked, trainmen began uncoupling the freight and flatcars to be shunted to the marshalling yard or down the spur line onto the quay, where many ships were tied up.

Scotty took Roderick and the biologists back to the soot-covered Henschels. "Guard these trucks like a virgin daughter. Don't let anybody close unless they're moving the flatcars onto the quay toward the *Mont Royal*. McFadden, let's go find the ship and whip this captain into line."

Scotty marched down the quay with giant strides. Frances stumbled to keep up, numb with exhaustion and horror. The CPR trademark red-and-white-checkered smokestack identified the *Mont Royal*. They followed a narrow gangway up to a portal in the ship's side, skirted a NO TRESPASSING sign, and continued up a steep metal staircase without seeing a soul. A calico cat sat beside an empty milk saucer by the door to the bridge. The cat gave Scotty's legs the rub-around, and he was bent over scratching its ears when a sharp voice startled them.

"What the hell are you doing here?" asked a bearded bantam cock in a woollen turtleneck and a battered peaked cap.

"We're looking for Captain Hyland—"

"You've found him. Now, out with your business and on your way. This is private property."

"I'm Meldrum from the Bank of Canada—"

"I hate bankers. They foreclosed on my father's home and threw us into the street."

"Bill Shouldice in Montreal was supposed to—"

"Oh, Christ!" said Captain Hyland, wrinkling his nose at a metaphysical stench. "You're lard-ass's buddy boy?"

"Shouldice did wire you to hold sailing today until four o'clock?"

"He did, and I told him he was an idiot, whereupon the president of the CPR himself sent me explicit orders, so we're not sailing until sixteen hundred hours. Have you ever worked for an idiot, Meldrum?"

Seeing no profit in this direction, Scotty opened his briefcase and pulled out a full bottle of the Macallan. "Could I impose upon you for three glasses, Captain? A dusty train ride generates a powerful thirst."

Captain Hyland blinked at the bottle. "Why, yes," he said in a much more congenial tone. "Step onto the bridge."

The bridge was compact. The wheel stood before a back wall holding instruments, dials, and a speaking tube. A narrow table strewn with nautical maps hung under the windows facing the bow. Captain Hyland took out three thick tumblers and placed them on a chart of the Baltic Sea. Scotty poured generously, and lifted a toast.

"To steady seas and fair winds," he said, and they all clinked. The men drained, and Frances sipped. Scotty set them up again.

"Now, Captain," he said, "I'm an occasional fishing companion of Tubby Shouldice's. Although he can drop a fly into a teacup from thirty yards, I would never want to work for the man. So I have some appreciation of your situation."

"Do you, Meldrum?" said the captain, lifting a pair of binoculars from a hook on the wall. He pointed skyward, toward a fly-like speck out over the harbour. "Have a look." He handed over the binoculars.

Scotty tracked the smudge. "A float plane?"

"Yes. A German Arado reconnaissance plane, not a mile away. It's been doing flybys eight times a day for a week."

"Why doesn't the Polish air force chase it away?"

"I'm sure it's irritating, but the Poles don't want to start a war over it. The local bars and brothels are a-quiver with apprehension these days. In spite of lard-ass's telegrams, I don't wish to be tied to this goddamn pier one second longer than necessary.

"The Poles have four destroyers and half a dozen submarines based here. Last week all shore leave was cancelled. The whores and barmaids wailed like banshees when the navy left on manoeuvres Monday. Yesterday, the destroyers vanished completely from the horizon. See those barges over there?" Scotty focused the binoculars. "Those two dredges have to work full time to keep the channel open. Four rivers drain into the bay of Gdansk and she silts up damn quick. You usually hear them chugging twenty-four hours a day, but they've been silent for a week.

See that ship over there?"

Scotty swung the binoculars to the right. "I see cranes on the back. Some sort of trawler?"

"It's the *Gryf*. A Polish minelayer. Yesterday it pulled up all the starboard marker buoys in the shipping channel. Guess what they put down in their place?"

Scotty's jaw dropped. "Son of a bitch!"

Captain Hyland smiled and poured a third tumbler of Macallan. "I've been sending screaming telegrams to lard-ass in Montreal for a week, and he keeps telling me to wait here for some goddamned tractor parts. I'm a sitting duck for German planes, and the local wharf rats will steal your anchor chain if you turn your back for a second. Give me the North Atlantic in a force four gale any day." He drained the third glass. "I've booked a channel pilot and two tugs for sixteen hundred hours. The *Mont Royal* casts off the dock at four o'clock, parts or no parts."

Scotty checked his watch. It was 12:15. "Okay! I've got six truck-loads of boxes to move aboard. I'll get the flatcars shunted right down here." He looked up at the silent crane beside the ship on the wharf's edge. "How much can these suckers lift? My boxes are heavy."

"Crane is rated for ten tons, but could probably lift twenty. The cargo ropes would snap long before the crane engine would balk. These dock scavengers like the occasional broken crate."

"Whoa!" said Scotty. "I can't have any broken boxes!"

"Well then, you best sweet talk the crane man, and his stevedore buddies. You might have to buy some local insurance, if you catch my drift."

"Look!" said Frances. The flatcars with their six trucks were being trundled down the quay toward them.

"Huzzah!" responded Scotty. "Captain, can you clear your hatches to receive cargo? We've got ninety boxes to get aboard. Oh! Did Tubby mention we need staterooms for three passengers back to Canada?"

"Staterooms, for the love o' Jesus! Do ya take us for the *Queen Mary*, Meldrum?"

"We have to get out of here with you. Any space to bunk down will do."

"Well, there's two jeezly little cabins that are supposed to be for paying customers. I use one instead of the cupboard that passes for a captain's cabin. The two mates use the other to get out of the fart stink of the crew quarters down below."

Scotty opened his briefcase and began counting Canadian bills into neat piles on the chart table. "We don't wish to be an inconvenience, Captain. However, McFadden, Roderick, and I need places to sleep and grub for the passage. Here's a hundred dollars apiece for hammocks if need be, and another four hundred zloty for your cook to lay in some extra supplies. You're stopping in Greenock?"

"Aye."

"Two cases of the Macallan will come aboard there as well. One to ease the passage, one for your personal stores."

Captain Hyland gave him a measured glance. "You're a smooth one, Meldrum, I'll give ya that, friendship with lard-ass aside. But Charlie, my engineer, will start to fire up the boilers any minute now. Come hell or high water, we cast off at sixteen hundred hours."

Scotty gave him a light-hearted salute. "Aye, aye, Cap'n."

The three flatbeds had halted beside the ship by the time Frances and Scotty got back down on the quay. The little switcher locomotive had disengaged and was backing away. Scotty climbed up twenty feet of steel ladder to the crane cabin. It was deserted, but when he pushed a button beside the controls, a loud klaxon horn sounded, and three men disengaged from a crowd of smokers by the next ship and came toward them. A lithe man scrambled up the ladder to the crane cabin where Scotty shook his hand enthusiastically, and Doyle translated the negotiations.

Bailey the barley man and Paul Roderick unfastened the tarpaulin roof covering the back of the lead Henschel truck. The three metal ribs that had held up the tarpaulin like big croquet hoops were taken down and piled under the truck. Stacks of boxes in bright Krupp markings sat on reinforced wooden skids on the truck bed.

The Polish stevedores began threading thick ropes through the skids under the first stack. The men worked with an easy grace, manoeuvring the thick ropes like string, and knotting them together with an open loop at the top. The engine of the crane roared and a gigantic steel hook on the end of a chain descended toward them. The taller stevedore moved the hook into the rope loop and gave a thumbs-up signal to the crane operator. They all moved back as the rope went taut. The crane engine whined with a high pitch as the rope stretched tighter and tighter, but the boxes did not budge. Suddenly, the rope began to shred, strands snapping and coiling back. When the last strands popped, the hook shot ten feet up in the air before falling back, swinging wildly.

The tall stevedore gestured helplessly up to the crane operator, who turned the motor off and opened the door. A heated shouting match in Polish rallied up and down from the truck to the crane cabin. Silence. Scotty climbed down the ladder with Doyle and came over to the stevedores, who were taking a smoking break. Doyle and Scotty shook hands with them. Doyle explained something quietly to them, then gave them each a folded pile of zloty, while holding an even thicker wad up for them to see. The Polish stevedores flipped their cigarettes into the water and walked quickly back up the quay.

Scotty checked his watch: 12:50. "I warned Mister crane operator we'd need chains for the lift, but he didn't believe me. I told him it was hospital equipment. Very delicate, but very heavy. So now his boys are going to rent, borrow, or steal some chains. I'm giving him fifty zloty per load safely stowed and a five hundred bonus if we're all done by sixteen hundred hours. That's a year's salary for him, and half a year apiece for his two buddies down here. We're bleeding money, but what choice do we have?"

In ten minutes, a truck honked its way down the bustling quay and halted beside them. The stevedores got out and unloaded a snake's nest of thick chains with hooks at each end. They extracted even more money from Doyle for the emergency service. They threaded two chains through a pallet and joined them up over the crane hook. They ran a third chain laterally, lacing the vertical chains together like a web with the crates inside.

The crane engine started up, and the chains cinched tight. This time the Krupp boxes lifted clear, twisting in the air as they floated up over the ship's railing and disappeared. The men began threading chains under the next pile of boxes and were ready when the crane hook descended.

A rhythm quickly developed. Roderick and Bailey moved down the line of Henschels, stripping the canvas tops and removing the roof support bars. Doyle stayed with the stevedores, helping, encouraging, translating. It took five minutes to chain a load snug over the crane hook, then have it swung up and disappear aboard the *Mont Royal* before the hook and empty chains descended to them again.

Frances had only known Doyle, the Polish-speaking Deuteronomy expert, and Bailey, the barley man, for two days, but she felt strangely close to them. Smuggling forty million in gold together builds a bond. She desperately wanted them safe on the *Mont Royal* for the trip home. They reminded her they had field studies in Latvia and the Ukraine to complete. Frances climbed up to the crane cabin to enlist Scotty, but he only shrugged. "They're free, white, and twenty-one, lass. We can't order them about like kids." Doyle wrote a simple note in Polish for Frances to take to the train station, where she purchased their tickets to Vilnius on the 6:00 train.

Frances's aching arms moved luggage on board the *Mont Royal* while the men worked. By two o'clock, dark clouds of diesel started to rise through the *Mont Royal*'s smoke stack as the ship's boilers began to warm up. Frances could feel the ship vibrate beneath her. She leaned on the rail and watched nervously as the crane methodically stripped the trucks and swung the heavy Krupp crates up over the ship's side and down into the cavernous hold. She saw the black cook and one of the mates head up the quay and come back soon after in a delivery truck full of bags and cartons.

By three o'clock, they had cleared the first three Henschels of forty-six boxes without incident. At 3:15, the port pilot, a dignified man in a blue uniform, came aboard. By 3:30, they were chaining up the second-last load of the fourth truck, when Scotty climbed quickly down from the crane cabin and scrambled aboard the *Mont Royal*, heading right up to the bridge. In two minutes, he and Captain Hyland climbed down and joined Frances at the rail.

"We're not going to make it," Scotty said.

"The pilot wants us to leave now," said the captain. "He's got to get two other boats out tonight before dark. I held him off until sixteen hundred hours, which was our contract, but that's all I can do. The tugs will be alongside in ten minutes to take on towlines."

"Did you tell the captain that we're not just concerned with tractor parts, here?" asked Frances.

Scotty nodded. "I told him we're going to leave fourteen million in gold on the quay for the wharf rats or the Germans. It's a goddamn shame. We've come so close, and now we're going to let poor old Byrka down." He kicked a capstan in disgust.

Frances turned to Captain Hyland. "How much did you say that crane could lift?"

"It's listed for ten ton, but I've seen them lift fifteen ton easy. Why?"

"Why don't we lift the whole truck in?" said Frances.

Scotty shot a glance at the yawning cargo hold. "Would it fit through the hatch opening?"

Captain Hyland squinted at the Henschel and looked over his

shoulder to gauge his cargo gate. "Might need a shoehorn, but I'd say so."

Scotty gave Frances a spontaneously jubilant squeeze. "McFadden, you ol' truck thief!" He half dragged her to the gangway. "I'll tell the crane man, you get the stevedores to chain a truck for the lift."

By linking every chain together, the stevedores crafted a wide double sling to run under the truck chassis. A doubled chain linked both slings like a handle above the back of the truck. The crane hook was set in the centre of the handle. The crane engine gave a mighty roar and the fifth truck lifted slowly off the ground, twisting slightly, but holding level. Up, up into the sky floated the Henschel, clearing the deck rail and moving slowly until it was square over the cargo hatch. A thumbs-up to the crane operator and the truck began its descent, sinking slowly into the lake-like hold. The wheels disappeared, then the fenders, then the body. It touched down, and the chains went slack. *Mont Royal* hands cleared the chains, gave a signal tug, then up came the big hook trailing a nest of chains that it lowered toward the final truck.

The last Henschel lifted into the air as the *Mont Royal*'s whistle blew the all clear, and the deck throbbed like a heartbeat with the full power of the ship's engine. Paul Roderick shook hands with the biologists and scrambled up the gangway as the sixth truck sank into the hold. Crewmen unhooked the great thick docking ropes fore and aft and capstans snaked the ropes up into the ship. The gangway came aboard seconds before the pull of the tugs drew the *Mont Royal* slowly away from the dock. A widening gulf of water appeared, churned white by backwash from the ship's propellers. The stevedores waved their hats. The crane man bowed. Deuteronomy Doyle and Bailey the barley man blew kisses before turning away and walking up the quay toward the train station.

——— 53 ———

MONT ROYAL

The *Mont Royal* throbbed as the engine picked up power. Frances had never been on a boat bigger than the Deavys' old cedar strip canoe at Kingsmere Lake. It was like being encompassed inside a living thing with a purpose all its own. In half an hour, they were just east of the Helisk Peninsula. The pilot saluted the captain, and said: "That's all I can do for you. The German light cruiser Königsberg is out there somewhere. Probably off Falsterbo, guarding the entrance to the Oresund. Be wary." The *Mont Royal* hove to in the lightly rolling Baltic as the pilot boat came alongside to pick up the pilot for his return journey to shore.

When he had gone, Frances asked, "What's a light cruiser? And what's the Oresund?"

"The Oresund is a very narrow channel between Sweden and Denmark that is the only exit to the North Sea," said Captain Hyland, pointing to the map. He took a dog-eared copy of *Jane's Fighting Ships* from a bookshelf and opened it flat on the chart table. In the section on the German Kriegsmarine was a diagram and photograph of the *Könisgberg*, along with details.

Displacement: 7700 tons

Speed: 32 knots

Armament: nine 6-inch guns, 22 anti-aircraft guns, torpedoes, and mines

"What if the *Königsberg* has heard that we're carrying all this gold?" asked Scotty. "Can we be stopped for inspection?"

"That would be in violation of international law, but guns often make their own law."

"Can we outrun him?"

"Full out, he can travel three times as fast as we can."

"How much harm can a six-inch gun do even if they do shoot at us?" asked Frances.

Scotty and the captain exchanged smiles.

"A six-inch gun isn't six inches long," explained the captain. "It fires a fifty-pound armour-piercing shell that is six inches wide. We have no armour. That shell would go right through our hull and come out the other side." He looked down at the *Jane's* descriptor. "Reloads in ten seconds. They could fire fifty-four shells at us per minute."

"How many hits would it take to sink us?"

"At the waterline? One."

"Can't we slip by in the dark?"

"The Oresund is deep, but narrow. If we meet the *Königsberg* in the channel, we'll be less than a thousand yards apart."

"Could they hit us in the dark at a thousand yards?"

"Those guns can hit a target fifteen miles away that they can't even see."

Their quarters were cosy staterooms with a shared bathroom. Twin beds, a small desk and chair. Everything bolted to the deck. Brand-new bedding with the fold creases still visible. Fluffy, fresh towels. Scotty offered Frances a room to herself, and bunked with Paul Roderick.

As the ship turned west and picked up speed, Captain Hyland held a lifeboat drill. The raucous alarm drew them up two flights of stairs to the boat deck. Frances struggled into a cumbersome life jacket far too large for her. She waddled like a penguin through the evacuation drill. One lifeboat was uncovered, and the davits were hand-cranked to lower the boat until it hung suspended just below the rail. Maurice, the first mate, hopped in and helped the three passengers struggle over the rail into the boat. Four more crew joined them. The boat was lowered halfway to the water to check all systems, then cranked up again to let them off.

"You hear that alarm ring, you throw on the warmest clothes you own and sprint up here," said Captain Hyland. "If the weather's foul or we're listing, these boats are a bitch to lower."

"Ever been in a shipwreck?" Scotty asked.

"Once. Lost six hands who thought lifeboat drill was a lark. The grim reaper got the last laugh." He changed the subject. "Supper's sharp at eighteen hundred hours in the mess. Latecomers eat leftovers, if there are any."

Frances showered and changed. Her business clothes looked ridiculously out of place. If the German cruiser didn't sink them, rendering fashion statements moot, she'd go shopping in Oslo.

The crew called the black cook "Cookie" and teased him. "Is this really roast beef or is it that drunk Polack who pulled the knife on you in Gdynia? Very tender for a Polack, don'tcha think?"

"Watch yer gutter talk," Cookie replied. "We got normal human beings for company. They chipped in a whacka cash for victuals, and we're dinin' high on their dime."

Frances went straight to bed after dinner. She took one of Molly Towers's pills as insurance against the roll of the ship. Her body yearned for sleep, but her brain played bedevilling tricks. Slipping from consciousness, she found herself falling across the narrow platform of the Gdynia train toward disaster and jerked frantically back awake. Repeatedly, she felt the soft contact and the hard metal case and the vice on her arm. "I killed him! I killed him!" echoed in her mind.

After an interminable restlessness, she dressed and went up for a walk on deck. It was dark, and they were out of sight of land. The lights of a small trawler moved up on their right.

"Can't sleep?" asked a swarthy man who had stopped beside her. "I'm Charlie, the engineer."

"I'm absolutely exhausted, but cannot get to sleep."

"My mother used to say that if you had a clean conscience, you could always fall asleep," teased Charlie. "How's your conscience these days?"

Frances bit her lip. Tears welled in her eyes.

"Sorry! Didn't mean to touch a nerve. You don't look like the misdemeanour type."

Frances laughed, choking off her tears. That was a CrazyDeavy expression—"the misdemeanour type." "Things have been crazy lately," was all she would say.

"I can lend you some knockout medicine, if you'd like. There's only Kenny and me that can keep the engines roaring, and we each work twelve hours straight. So I've *got* to sleep in the other twelve hours."

Frances sighed. "Thanks. I can barely stand up."

He left to fetch the pills, just as Scotty Meldrum came along lighting a cigar.

"McFadden! You up to see us do battle with this German cruiser? Roderick's down there sawing logs, but I was so excited I couldn't sleep."

"I am past excitement," responded Frances, "but I can't sleep. Herr Kessler haunts me."

"McFadden, don't give yourself airs. You are *not* Lady Macbeth."

"I am! I am!" she stammered through tears. "I killed the man!"

"Stop beating yourself up. You've killed no one."

"I did! I pushed him off the train!"

"With malice aforethought? After careful planning?"

"Of course not! But I caused his death."

"Did you, now? Maybe I pushed him. Ever think of that? I grab you with one hand, and give Kessler the heave-ho with the other?"

"You wouldn't!"

"Wouldn't I? What I wouldn't do, McFadden, is give any two-timing, double-dealing blackmailer forty-five thousand in gold that was in my trust. We don't even know that he's dead, for God's sake! He left the train, that's all we know."

"You don't believe he survived a fall in that tunnel?"

"Who knows? The fellow seemed to lead a charmed life. Anyway, it was an accident. The train lurched. You bumped into him. You might just as well have bumped into me." Scotty took a long draw on his cigar. "Now, that's an interesting proposition. What if it was just you and Kessler standing on the platform when the train got back to sunlight? What would you have done then? That's exactly why we can't afford the luxury of you wallowing in guilt. Remember, you're second in command here. Anything happens to me, you're in charge of that gold. The gods left you and me on the platform. Accept it. You didn't plan it. I didn't plan it."

"It was certainly a convenient accident for us, and the Polish gold."

"The accident wasn't anyone's fault. The convenience wasn't of our making. The end."

"But I liked him," said Frances, tears streaming down her face.

"Oh, did you? A spy? A double agent? A traitor to his own country? A deceiver of his betrothed? A thief? Which characteristic did you admire the most?"

"He was going to marry my friend Anna. What am I going to tell her?"

"There's no point in telling her anything."

"But she'll be waiting for him, and he'll never be coming back! I'll know, and she won't, and that's another betrayal."

"Would it be better to tell her that her lover was an enemy spy whom you last saw on a train in Poland attempting to steal forty-five thousand in gold and another hundred thousand from his employer? She'd be better off to know nothing."

"But I'll feel so deceitful!"

"Part of being an adult, Frances McFadden, is living with some things we don't like. About ourselves. About others. About life."

Afraid of the sleeping pills, Frances fretted fruitlessly for sleep before heading up for her second walk in the night air. There was a damp shivering mist. The first mate, Maurice, was on the bridge and offered her hot tea from his thermos. "That's Sweden, the Falsterbo light to starboard," he said, and handed her the binoculars. "We're making good time.

"Oh-oh," he added quickly. "Can I have those binos back?" He stared intently toward some distant lights off the port bow. He had a quick look at *Jane's* on the chart table. "And that," he said, pointing, "is the German light cruiser *Königsberg*. Take the wheel. I've got to get the captain."

Take the wheel?

The captain arrived in moments, just as a signal from the closing ship began to flash in Morse code. Captain Hyland translated. "Light Cruiser *Königsberg* on bearing south south-east at twenty-six knots. Identify."

"He didn't say 'please,' but I usually don't press points of decorum with warships. Signal back 'Greetings. Canadian freighter *Mont Royal* on bearing west north-west at twelve knots.'"

"What are our chances if he fires on us?" asked Scotty.

"With one salvo of direct hits, we'd have six minutes afloat, unless they hit the boilers, which would blow us to smithereens. Two salvos? Maybe three minutes. Don't forget your lifeboat drill."

"Can't run. Can't hide. Have we any defence?"

"The 'Canadian defence.' Be very polite."

Polite worked. The *Königsberg* churned by in the night.

Finally, Frances took a sleeping pill. The medicine, or Scotty's absolution, or the passing of the Königsberg, released her into a troubled jumble of dream fragments.

A smiling Herr Kessler lighting a cigarette. Vera McFadden laying out a cross of cards on the kitchen table. The rank smell of Sloan pressing her against the vault door. Mary O'Brien tiptoeing into the board meeting to announce the police. Lady Margaret sprawled on the floor of her Rockcliffe den. The Laframboise brothers, drunk on the dock at Kingsmere Lake. R.B. Bennett clawing through the files at the CFRA office. Sandy Skelton opening the door to his Château Laurier suite in a turban. Mackenzie King handing her the umbrella at the cornerstone ceremonies.

Frances woke with a start. Her watch said four-thirty, but it was sunny outside her porthole. Could she have slept for twelve hours? She scuttled up to the bridge, where Captain Hyland was scanning the horizon with the binoculars.

"Well, if it isn't Sleeping Beauty," he said.

"Was I tired! Will we be docking in Oslo soon?"

"Not going to Norway anymore."

"Why not?"

"The Germans invaded Poland at four hundred and thirty hours this morning. Right after our friendly chat with the *Königsberg*. Full-scale attack. Tanks. Planes. Battalions. Everything. England and France have sent ultimatums, and are preparing for war."

"I slept through all that?"

"Also, Lard-ass wired us from Montreal to forget about picking up the twenty tons of sardines in Oslo. Too easy to be trapped if the Germans blockade the fjord. Wants us to head straight for Greenock to take on fuel and Harris tweed, then beat it home. Exactly what I want to do. It's certainly a sad day."

"That Poland's been invaded?"

"No. That I find myself in complete agreement with an idiot."

By the time they tied up in Greenock, at noon on September 3, Neville Chamberlain had put England at war. "If England's at war, aren't we at war as well?" Frances asked Scotty.

"That was true in 1914, but Canada is a sovereign nation now, don't you know? Mackenzie King will fuss about it for a few days, and walk his dog while he mulls over the situation, then declare war. The closer we are to home when that happens, the better. German submarines will probably honour our flag until war is actually declared."

"Everything is confusion and chaos and way behind schedule," said Captain Hyland, getting off the phone with the Greenock harbourmaster. "We can't load until this evening. The tugs can't take us out until first light tomorrow. You all might as well go ashore and stretch your legs. Last chance at solid ground for ten days."

"The toffs used to live in the west end, above the esplanade," said Scotty to Frances and Paul. "Why don't you two walk up there and check out the real estate? I've got to telegraph the governor and buy gifts for the family. Here's five pounds. I'll treat you two to dinner at the Dundee Hotel. You're on sea rations for the next ten days, so you might as well indulge."

It was a lovely sunny day for a war to begin. Paul and Frances drifted west up into the hills, viewing palatial Victorian villas above the estuary. "I might as well enjoy myself," Paul Roderick said. "I'll be unemployed five minutes after I return to Ottawa."

"Why?"

"Mr. Richardson will be most unhappy that he spent all that money sending me to Europe for tractor parts, and I'm coming home without even a washer. If he doesn't fire me outright, he'll banish me to the research station in Moose Jaw."

"Don't be silly! You did your best. You can't believe those tractor parts were more valuable than the Polish gold reserves?"

"It's not what I believe that counts. I was sent on a mission, and I failed in that mission. That's how Richardson will see it."

"Herr Kessler told us that those spare parts were completely unnecessary. He said if you keep the machines cleaned and oiled, they would last for twenty years. Tell *that* to Mr. Richardson. You saved the Department a hundred thousand dollars! You'll be the golden boy."

"You're a hopeless romantic, Frances McFadden," he said. "Will you write me in Moose Jaw?"

"And another thing. Scotty Meldrum pulled rank on you. You may be a hotshot engineer in the Department of Agriculture, but you're small potatoes in a turf war with the Deputy Governor of the Bank of Canada. Everyone in Ottawa knows exactly where they fit in the hierarchy. Take it from me, peasant bank clerk."

"Peasant clerks fly first-class to Europe, do they? There's more to you than meets the eye, Miss McFadden, for all your false modesty."

In the shops on the High Street, Frances purchased casual slacks, a windbreaker, a thick woollen sweater, and some deck shoes. Paul bought nothing for himself, but picked out Argyll sweaters in soft mauves and greens for his mother and sister.

After a second glass of wine in the Dundee Hotel dining room, Paul asked, "How come a clever, good-looking woman like you isn't married?"

Frances smirked. "You're three years older than I am. Why aren't *you* married, Mr. Roderick?"

"I asked first."

"For starters," replied Frances, "no one's asked me. I'm a high school dropout. Who'd want me? Secondly, I'm as good as married to the Bank of Canada. I work twelve-hour days. I have no room for domestic bliss. Take this little Polish excursion, for example. I'll have been away from home for over three weeks. I couldn't do this if I were baking casseroles and darning socks for a husband. There are trade-offs in life. This trip has been frightening and exhausting and exhilarating and intriguing all rolled together. Pretty heady stuff for a girl from Rochester Street. Married women don't get a chance like this."

"Married to the Bank of Canada, eh? Sounds like being a nun. Aren't they wedded to God?"

"Don't know any nuns, but it's probably about the same. I love the Bank. The people are fascinating and dedicated."

"But you don't have any actual authority, do you? Do you even get compensated for overtime?"

"Why should life compensate you for the things you love? It's like being a parent. You don't have children for the power or the money. You just want the joy of sharing and the gratification of a job well done.

"But enough about me. Why isn't Paul Roderick, mechanical engineer, married? You're a hot property. Steady job. Government pension. Kinda cute. And, a man doesn't need to wait to be asked."

Paul laughed. "Just 'kinda cute'? I was serious with a girl at university. She was intelligent, genteel, cultured. Went to plays and concerts and read the classics. I'd grown up on a farm in Southern Ontario. The girls I knew around Ilderton pretty well married farmers, or the social climbers married the garage mechanic in town. I'd never met an educated woman before."

"Where did you meet her? There wouldn't be many women in engineering."

"None. We met at a United Church Young People's group. We went to movies and things. She invited me down to Toronto over the Christmas holidays to meet her family. Lovely old house in Rosedale. Father a successful surgeon. Mother charming. Two younger brothers at Upper Canada College. Lots of dinners and dances. It was way out of my league."

"Come on! Are you telling me an engineer from Ilderton can't cut it in Rosedale?"

"You ever been to Rosedale, smarty-pants?"

"Once. Lovely people, but once was enough."

"Exactly. The night before I was to leave, the distinguished surgeon invited me into his study for port and cigars."

"To ask if your intentions were honourable?"

"I think my cash flow was more important than my character. He told me that Elizabeth was a modern woman and quite independent. He sent her a hundred a month for spending money at school. He thought she could probably get by on an allowance of two hundred a month once she married.

"Engineers don't gross that kind of dough until they've logged ten years of successful practice. When we returned to university in January, I had a heart-to-heart with Elizabeth. She understood better than I had anticipated. She gave me a parting kiss and was engaged to an intern by spring."

"Nobody in Ottawa interests you?"

"The Department of Agriculture is a male preserve. I've been introduced to a few sisters and friends of wives, but no one's struck my fancy."

The *Mont Royal* was well southwest of Greenland when the ship's wireless crackled with the news that Canada was at war with Germany. Raging at the news, the wind drove mercilessly from the north and the waves crested white. Molly Towers's motion sickness pills saved Frances. Paul Roderick wasn't so lucky. He carried a farm boy's appetite. A second helping of Cookie's figgy duff in clotted cream did him in. When Frances went to their shared bathroom in the morning to brush her teeth, she found him on the floor beside the toilet. He looked ghastly. His forehead glistened with sweat, but his hands and feet were freezing.

"What happened?"

"After my sixth emergency trip in here last night," he gasped, "I just decided to stay. Didn't want to keep disturbing the good Scot."

"Why don't you sleep in the second bed in my room? It's quiet, and I'm up for the day."

"No, no, I couldn't."

"Yes, yes, you must."

"What if I'm sick again?"

"If you've been in here six times overnight, there's nothing left to worry about. Don't be stubborn." She helped him stand and guided him into her room. His teeth were chattering. "I'm going to get you a hot water bottle. Do you want anything else?"

"My mouth's foul. I'd be grateful for something to drink, if I can keep it down."

Cookie didn't have a hot water bottle, but heated up a metal tray in the oven, and wrapped it in a towel. He peppered a mug of weak tea with honey. "This'll warm his tootsies. The sweet tea will give him some energy but not make him puke."

Warmed and comforted, Paul slept all day. Frances checked on him regularly. At 1500 hours she brought him two soft-boiled eggs, buttered toast soldiers, and more sweet tea. Paul relished each mouthful. He tried to stand up, but was still unsteady on his feet. He sat down on the end of the bed panting. "I've got to visit the washroom."

"Emergency?"

"No, but a certain urgency."

She helped him across the hall to the washroom.

"I can stay, if you need the help," she offered.

"No thank you, Miss McFadden. You've seen quite enough of me with my defences down. You don't need to see anything more."

He was soon asleep again, looking youthful and relaxed, his carved features softened by the sleep. At 2000 hours when she checked, Paul smiled weakly. She sat on the edge of the bed and cleared his long hair from his eyes. His warm hand came out from under the sheets and found hers. "Thank you, Florence Nightingale," he said.

"Glad to help."

"Can I ask you something personal?"

"I hate that question! I'm too curious to say no, even though I probably should. It plays to my greatest weakness."

"If a German sub doesn't sink us, and we get back to Ottawa alive, would you go to a movie with me?"

Frances squeezed his hand.

"If I bought popcorn?" he continued.

"Next to curiosity, popcorn is my greatest weakness."

ACKNOWLEDGEMENTS

It takes a village to write a novel. Heartfelt thanks to fellow villagers:

Amelia Kreitzer Hope
Alex Hope
Jay Hope

Bridget Hall
Herb Batt
Ann Hyland
Janet Shorten
Betty Eligh
Magda Seydegart
Bronwen Pritchard
Terry West
Peter Carver
Sylvia Warsh
Charles Marriott
Jim Allen

Don Hall
Don Ray
Dan Way
Dudleigh Coyle
Murray Young

Jane Boyko
Paul Jenkins
George Pike
Rob Edge

Charis Wahl
Frank Koller
Ted Jackson

Carla Hall
Warren Sheffer

Tim Gordon
Jane Karchmar
Magdalene Carson
Alison Roesler

Martha Hall
Daphne Strange
Bob Neilson
Richard Wiklo
Holly Massie

ABOUT THE AUTHOR

Ian McKercher grew up in London, Ontario. He attended Queen's University and moved to Ottawa to teach English at Glebe Collegiate. Ian lives in the Glebe with his wife, Amelia. *The Underling* is his first novel.

TO ORDER MORE COPIES:

GENERAL STORE PUBLISHING HOUSE
499 O'Brien Road, Renfrew, Ontario, Canada K7V 3Z3
Tel 1.800.465.6072 • Fax 1.613.432.7184
www.gsph.com